Praise for the bestselling

‘Captures the intensity of a brutal and unforgiving war, successfully weaving love, loss, desperation and, finally, hope into a gripping journey of self-discovery.’
The Courier Mail

‘An epic tale, grand in scope. An intimate, emotional portrayal of one woman's struggle to survive in a world where the old rules no longer apply . . . Packs an emotional punch that will reverberate far and wide.’
The Weekly Times

‘Stellar debut Aussie fiction combining historical tragedy, romance, and true stories . . . Superb and enriching.’
Better Reading

‘An intriguing look at when devotion to a political leader turns to disillusion and dismay . . . A tumultuous journey across the country, from order to bedlam, and from naive acceptance of the status quo to the gradual getting of political wisdom.’
Sunday Age

‘A hauntingly romantic and gripping read.’
Style

‘You'll fly through these pages of love, duty and survival and join me in awaiting a sequel.’
Weekend Herald

THE
GIRL
FROM
MUNICH

THE GIRL FROM MUNICH

TANIA BLANCHARD

**SIMON &
SCHUSTER**

London · New York · Sydney · Toronto · New Delhi

A CBS COMPANY

THE GIRL FROM MUNICH
First published in Australia in 2017 by
Simon & Schuster (Australia) Pty Limited
Suite 19A, Level 1, Building C, 450 Miller Street, Cammeray, NSW 2062
This edition published in 2018

10 9 8 7 6 5 4

A CBS Company
Sydney New York London Toronto New Delhi
Visit our website at www.simonandschuster.com.au

 A catalogue record for this
book is available from the
National Library of Australia

Cover design: Christabella Designs
Cover images: Mark Owen/Trevillion Images; Roy Bishop/Arcangel;
Ivan Cholakov/Shutterstock
Typeset by Midland Typesetters, Australia
Printed and bound in Australia by Griffin Press

 The paper this book is printed on is certified
against the Forest Stewardship Council®
Standards. Griffin Press holds FSC chain
of custody certification SGS-COC-005088.
FSC promotes environmentally responsible,
socially beneficial and economically viable
management of the world's forests.

For Oma, my grandmother – my inspiration
and who always believed in me

*'I have possessed that heart, that noble soul, in whose presence
I seemed to be more than I really was, because I was all
that I could be.'*
The Sorrows of Young Werther, Goethe

1

'Times have changed, Mutti. The war has made sure of that. Look at all the women who work to help the war effort – Heidi von Schmitt and Catherina Dollmann are both working for the Wehrmacht and their parents haven't died of embarrassment. I want to make a contribution.'

My mother stared at me with frosty blue eyes. She was beautiful, her wavy blonde hair glinting with auburn highlights in the sunlight, even though she sat there unmoved, sipping her coffee. I jumped up from my seat and went to the window, wishing I had her poise, her elegance and her tight control. I always thought better when I was moving.

I gazed out at the tree-lined street. It was hard to believe that war raged in affluent, cosmopolitan Schwabing. It wasn't far from the centre of München, where now the ravages of war could not be missed. A couple strolled past, holding hands, oblivious to anything but each other as a woman dressed in a tailored skirt and jacket moved briskly towards them, no doubt on her way to useful employment of some kind. I shook my head and turned back to face my mother. Why couldn't I have what I wanted? Time for a more forceful approach.

'I've heard the Ministry of Labour wants to change the conscription laws again. Unless I take action and choose what I want to do, I'll probably be drafted into cleaning the toilets at an army office somewhere like Poland. Is that what you want for your daughter after all her hard work to qualify as a photographer?'

'Charlotte Elisabeth, stop!' My mother put her cup down and the sharp clink it made told me her patience had reached its limit. 'When your father comes back from Berlin, I will discuss the matter with him and Heinrich's parents.'

'*Muttilein*,' I pleaded, sinking into the chair again. 'All I want to do is take photos and help the war effort. Karin Weiss graduated last year and got a job as a photographer with the army straightaway. I'll get a job easily.' I knew I sounded like a petulant child but I couldn't help it. The Bavarian State Institute for Photography had the best reputation in the country. Students came from all over Germany and from abroad to study there.

My mother's thunderous look stopped me in my tracks. It was no use continuing with her.

'Fine, we'll see what Vati says.'

I stomped up the stairs to my room and slammed the door. Already I was thinking how I would intercept my father before my mother could speak with him. I flopped on my bed, feeling deflated. After spending three years with artists, scholars and patriots and a year before that in Hamburg completing my land year helping on the local farms, I had learnt more about myself than I had in the previous fifteen years of privileged upbringing and stiff social conventions. I desperately wanted to be a photojournalist and follow in my beloved brothers' footsteps by joining the Luftwaffe taking photos for the military, recording the lives of the soldiers. When I was feeling especially patriotic and daring, I dreamed of going to the front as a photographic officer, taking photos of strategic importance, even getting involved in reconnaissance.

I reached for the photo on my nightstand of my two handsome brothers. It was taken the last holiday we all spent together – the last holiday before the war. We had been swimming in the lake and our bare limbs were browned from the days outdoors, our hair bleached white from the sun. My brothers were tall, strapping youths with easy dispositions, their lives in front of them. I missed them so much.

My oldest brother, Ludwig, was a pilot. He had died on the Eastern Front in Stalingrad, shot down by the Russians nine months earlier, only twenty-one. He was my idol. Tall, strong, handsome, with a winning smile that would melt any heart; he was the perfect pin-up boy, a soldier who embodied everything good that Germany stood for. I had thought he was invincible. It took days for my tears to come after we received the news. Even now I was unable to believe he was gone.

Willi was seventeen months older than me and I had always been closest to him. At nineteen, he was already a paratrooper, recently deployed to France with a new parachute

3

division. He had been home for a few weeks in April, the first time we'd been together since losing our brother. I couldn't get enough of being by his side, touching him to make sure he was really there, remembering Ludwig through him. It was almost unbearable to say goodbye to him again, the silent fear that he would be next gnawing inside me. After he left, my mother was inconsolable for days. Mutti clung to me, kept me near in any way she could. The loss of Ludwig had hit her so hard that Vati and I feared that the strain of another loss would kill her. I knew all the begging in the world wouldn't give me their permission to go anywhere. If I hadn't had my fiancé, Heinrich, during those terrible days, I don't know how I would have coped.

Heinrich understood. He had lost his older brother in the early days of the war and was all his parents had left. His elderly father kept him close on the pretext of helping him manage their vast estate. Sometimes Heinrich seemed like the only ally I had. We had known each other most of our lives and were best friends, kindred spirits. He was handsome and strong – and I was curious – but we had not dared to become intimate, despite being engaged. Naturally, we had fooled around a bit but the maiden's prized virtue of purity had been drummed into me since I was small, at school and through the BDM, the League of German Girls. I thought it was best to wait. Besides, the last thing I needed was to become pregnant before I was married. My parents would die of shame and if anything happened to Heinrich . . . heaven help me.

I rolled off my bed and sat at my writing desk to send a note to Heinrich. He was working a few long shifts at the hospital and I knew I wouldn't manage to talk to him in the next couple of days. At least with my note I could let him know of my mother's resistance to my plans and warn him about the upcoming conversation regarding our wedding. He would think of the best way to support me when the matter was raised with our families and explain why it was so important for me to get a job as a military photographer, even if I had to compromise by staying closer to home. '*Liebe* Heinrich,' I began, the heavy Sheaffer fountain pen, a gift from my father, balanced perfectly in my hand. I soon lost myself in the flow of words as I poured my heart out, sharing my frustration with my best friend. Still feeling anxious and strung out, I decided not to give my note to our servant to deliver. I would walk to the hospital myself. I knew Heinrich would receive it during his next break.

I made sure I was presentable, examining my image in the mirror and straightening my polka dotted dress, adjusting the belt at my cinched waist and smoothing my shoulder length blonde hair. Before the butler could object or my mother could call me, I ran down the stairs and out the door onto the street.

'Did you send a note to Heinrich asking him to help you find a way to get a job as a military photographer?' asked Vati in a low voice. My father had been away in Berlin for a week. If only I had got to him before Mutti did, I could have explained to him.

'*Ja*, Vati,' I said, looking down at the richly coloured Turkish rug set against the repetitive pattern of the parquetry floor. I didn't want to see the disappointment on his face. 'How did you find out?'

'Heinrich's mother found the letter in his shirt pocket when the new maid was organising his laundry,' said my mother. I could almost feel the waves of anger rolling off her. At least I could still trust Heinrich, although I wished he had been more careful with the letter. We had to stick together – our mothers could be so pushy. They were similar in age and had been close friends since childhood. Together, they were a force to be reckoned with.

'Sit,' my father ordered.

I obediently sat on the edge of the lounge chair, facing my parents. I could hear the ticking of the grandfather clock, steady and even, unlike my heartbeat.

'You want to postpone your wedding. Why?' Vati looked cool as a cucumber, impeccable as always in his army uniform, though his hazel eyes glared at me sternly.

Laying my palms flat on my lap, willing them to stay still, I decided to meet my father's eyes and tell the truth. Maybe he would understand after all. 'Heinrich and I agree we shouldn't get married yet. He wants to concentrate on finishing his studies. It looks like he might get a job at Schwabing Hospital when he's completed his training there . . . unless he's called away to another posting. Until we can be sure he has a good job, we want to wait, like you suggested.'

'I never suggested such a thing!' exploded my mother. 'The way this war's going, you'll either be the longest engaged couple known to man or you'll miss out altogether if Heinrich is killed – God forbid.'

'Mutti!' I said, horrified.

My mother put her hands up in apology. 'You have no excuse any more. You've finished your studies – why *not* marry now? It doesn't matter if Heinrich is still studying. You can live here with us if Heinrich's parents don't want you there, although I think they will jump at the chance to have a daughter around that empty house of theirs. If something did happen, you would be well taken care of by the Hoffmann family and Heinrich's estate.'

I shook my head, my blood boiling. 'I would never take advantage of his family like that.'

'These are strange times. You can prove your worth to his parents when the war is over. By all means, if Heinrich sees fit, go and work as a photographer after the war. If you're feeling really ambitious, maybe we can help you set up a studio. You know we have the right connections. It won't be hard to manage.'

I couldn't reason with my mother, I knew that. I sent a pleading look to my father. 'Please, Vati!'

My father put his large, powerful hand over my mother's small, shapely one and gave it a gentle squeeze. Her expression softened at once. He leant across, touching his dark hair to her fair, wavy locks, and whispered in her ear. The look that passed between them made me feel that I shouldn't be in the room. I watched them, suddenly wistful. I wondered if that look had always been there for them, or if it came with the bond of intimacy. Heinrich and I didn't look at each other like that.

'What's this all about, Lotte?' asked my father gently.

'I've spent all this time learning to be a photographer. Now that I have the skills, I want to use them. So many others I've trained with have good jobs with the Wehrmacht, making a real difference, some of them even on the front. I want to prove myself, make a contribution and help the war effort.'

'She wants to go to the front, Johann!'

'You wouldn't do that to your mother, would you?' Vati's tone was conversational but I knew that anything that upset my mother also upset him. 'Don't you think she's been through enough? How would she cope if something happened to you?'

I stared at my feet, ashamed. 'I know, Vati but I'm not a little girl any more. I'm a grown woman now. I want you to be proud of me,' I whispered, daring to look up at him again.

The frown of consternation on my father's face was reassuring. 'We are, *liebchen*. You're a fine photographer. But your mother is right. These are strange times and we only want what's best for you. You are the apple of our eye. Neither of us could bear to lose you. We only want to keep you safe.'

'We'll be proud of you when you marry that boy,' snapped my mother, her face as rigid as her attitude, but I could see the tears glistening in her eyes. 'Heinrich's mother and I have agreed to set a date sometime this summer.'

'I'm not so sure,' said my father. 'The talk in Berlin is that Goebbels wants to increase conscription to women, boys from the Hitler Youth as young as fourteen and men up to sixty-five years of age. Single and married women with no children will get no exemptions. Once called up, there will be no choice of where you're posted. I'm afraid that the chances are Heinrich will be called again, although God knows we need more doctors here, with all the bombings.'

'All the more reason for them to marry soon.' My mother sat straight and tall, as if she were made of glass and could shatter at any moment.

'*Nein, liebling.* She doesn't need that boy's money or security. I give my blessing for them to marry when Heinrich has finished his studies and has a good job.'

My mother nearly jumped out of her seat with alarm. I had to wipe the smirk off my face as she glared at us but she didn't bite back as I thought she would.

My father placed a hand on her shoulder. 'I know it's not what you wanted. But in light of this new information, I think it's wise for us to enquire about military work opportunities. It would be best if Lotte had a position before any enforced conscription begins. After that, we can't guarantee where she'll end up or what she'll be doing.' He glanced across to me. 'I don't know that we'll find a photography position. Most likely an office job, but this way she could be close to home, involved in the war effort like she wants.'

My mother looked slightly mollified, although I could tell my father still had some work to do to fully convince her.

'Close your mouth, Lotte,' said my mother brusquely, 'unless you want to swallow flies.'

I dutifully obeyed, swallowing nervously as I looked at my parents.

'I suppose it won't hurt to see what's available. A job will teach her some discipline – and the value of money, which will be useful when she has to manage her own household. A few conditions: I want you to promise that we both agree on the job and I want her to stay in München.' Mutti reached for Vati's hand and squeezed it tightly. I could see the tips of my father's fingers turning red.

'Of course, my dear. I wouldn't have it any other way.'

My mother smiled sweetly at him and released her grip. He had the good grace not to snatch his hand away to ease the circulation back into it.

I leant back in the lounge chair, watching my mother. She had done it again – manipulated the situation so that she got what she wanted. True, my father had vetoed a summer wedding and allowed me to work with the military but, sure as hell, my mother would make sure I stayed close by. I could almost guarantee she would ensure there was no photography position, just to spite me.

'What do you think, *liebling*?' my father asked, smiling. I could see that he thought he had negotiated a solution between his two girls quite successfully.

What could I say without hurting his feelings? 'Fine, Vati.' I leapt up to hug him. The smell of the smoke from his pipe clinging to his tunic met me like a familiar friend as he enfolded me in his strong, comforting arms. My mother caught my eye, her icy gaze accusing me of ruining all her plans and her family's impeccable reputation. I squeezed Vati tighter and was rewarded with a kiss on top of my head. I could not disappoint my father. He thought the world of me and I adored him.

Johann von Klein had only come into my life recently, not long after the war began, when he and my mother married following a two-year courtship. He was a family friend from Berlin, ten years Mutti's senior, but she hadn't seen him for many years. Mutti grew up near the Luxembourg border and had married my natural father after the Great War; he was already over thirty but she was only twenty. She never spoke about the war years but I knew that although my natural father was a decorated hero, he did not cope well with life after the war. I remember him as a moody man who exploded with fits of rage at my mother and who sank into periods of deep depression. All he gave me besides those bad memories were his looks. I was tall and fair like him, with his square face and broad forehead.

I was only ten years old when she divorced him, but I remember it was such a scandal to have a divorce in the family. Mutti couldn't bear to stay, so she moved from Düsseldorf to München, where her grandmother had left her an apartment. My mother couldn't afford to have us with her – she had no money because my father had spent all her inheritance as well as his own. My father kept my brothers but not me – I went to boarding school. Sometimes I wondered if Mutti sent me away because I reminded her of my father. My mother would come to see me at school one day every year, and what a day it always was. She lavished me with love, hugs and kisses, small gifts and her undivided attention for the whole day but then she would be gone again. Although I knew she had it tough, I was only a child. I thought that nobody wanted me.

I was fifteen and just finishing my land year when she married Johann. Mutti fetched me home. Her new husband was kind and generous. He paid for me to study photography and spoilt me like I was his own daughter, as he had no children of his own. He insisted on my introduction to high society, as he was from a long line of barons himself. My mother agreed that it was my birthright, joyfully arranging my 'coming out' ball. Nobody had ever bothered about me before and I was beside myself to finally become the centre of attention, in awe of being allowed to choose a magnificent gown for the occasion. I was crushed when it was cancelled. The war was escalating and many of our men were dying; it didn't seem right to observe the social niceties when so many families had lost their loved ones. Already we could feel the perpetual optimism that buoyed a city like München, making it sparkle and shine, begin to fade.

And then we lost Ludwig.

Vati didn't give up. On my eighteenth birthday, he presented me with adoption papers. He wanted me to be his daughter, to take his name. All the times I had been over-looked paled into insignificance. I was ecstatic.

I met Heinrich at one of our favourite places in the Englischer Garten. It was a good place to talk without our mothers lurking nearby. Entering the calm, cool green of München's beloved parkland, the creeping unease I had begun to sense on the streets – despite the Führer's assurances that Germany was winning the war – fell away, along with the chaos and noise of a functioning city, defiant in the face of war.

Heinrich was already waiting when I arrived, standing by the bank of the Schwabinger Bach, hands resting easily in his pockets, staring into space. He stood straight and tall, broad shoulders straining against the fabric of his suit jacket. I smiled to myself. I might just be able to surprise him this time. Approaching as silently as I could, I moved out of his line of sight, watching the close-cropped blond head that so reminded me of my brothers drop as though deep in thought. He was just about to start his exams and I was sure he was thinking through some medical procedure.

I was a few feet behind him and he still hadn't moved. I couldn't help but grin as I reached out with both arms and poked him in the ribs.

Heinrich whipped around faster than I thought possible, catching me off guard. I whooped, startled. He grasped my arms, pulling me towards him and as I glimpsed his sly smile, I realised he had been ready for me. Pulling back as he dug into my ribs with powerful fingers, I shrieked with uncontrollable laughter before we lost balance and fell among the grass and wildflowers of the meadow. I wheezed, winded by the fall, laughter still bubbling up from inside of me. I had landed on top of him. His smile of triumph faded as he looked up at me, his bright blue eyes clouding with concern.

'Are you all right?' he whispered.

I nodded, leaning on the elbow that had hit the ground. Worried I must be crushing him, I tried to straighten to take my weight off him, wincing at the stinging in my elbow.

'No,' he said softly, his eyes glittering. 'You don't get away that easily.' He pulled me close to him, his muscular frame taut against my softness, his cotton collar tickling my cheek. 'That's better,' he murmured, wriggling his hips under me.

'Heinrich, no! Not here where everybody can see.' I felt the blood rush to my face, mortified. It was a warm summer's afternoon and I could hear people milling about the park. 'What if my mother finds out?'

I watched the gleam of wicked humour in his eyes disappear before he sighed. 'Such a spoilsport,' he said. 'Give me a kiss.' He drew me into a deeper embrace. He tasted of cigarettes and strawberries. Smoking was a habit he'd picked up

13

on the front but now he only smoked at parties and when he was studying.

'Now,' he said, allowing me to slide onto the grass next to him. 'Let's have a look at that elbow. I think it requires some expert medical attention.'

'My mother is so angry,' I told him as he examined my elbow. I gazed at the ducks bobbing calmly on the stream, the sun filtering through the thick foliage of the trees near its bank, making the water glisten in the afternoon light. Part of me wished I had brought my camera. 'She wanted us married before the end of summer.'

'Is this what you want?' Heinrich let go of my elbow and sat very still, as if bracing himself.

My heart fluttered and skipped a beat. 'We agreed, didn't we? You want to finish your studies and we both want to be working and independent before we marry. We want our own place without our parents interfering with our lives. You don't want us to live at home, do you?'

'We wouldn't be very happy.'

I slowly released the breath I had been holding. 'Of course we wouldn't,' I agreed, my heart resuming its normal rhythm. 'Can you imagine either of our mothers telling us what to do all the time?' I grasped Heinrich's hand and gave it a squeeze. 'We'll be so happy in our own place. It doesn't have to be much because it will be you and me.'

'I know we will.' Heinrich kissed my hand. 'I want to get more work at the hospital and prove my worth before I graduate, so I have a better chance at a permanent position. After all, I'll be cheaper than a more experienced doctor. I'd rather be here and really make a difference than at a field hospital. There are too many who can't be saved on the front,' he said quietly. 'I don't think I can do that again. It destroys the soul.'

My skin prickled to hear him holding back tears. The familiar anguish I had seen him carry after two tours to field hospitals on the Eastern Front never truly faded and could resurface at any time; it was something he didn't like to speak about but I had seen his torment.

'It's a good plan,' I said, my voice strong for his sake. 'It will see us through this war. With good management, we'll both have jobs here in München. I'll promise Mutti that as soon as that happens, I'll begin planning this wedding. I need you here to do that – otherwise between my mother and yours, they'll drive me crazy. You have to keep me sane!'

'All right, all right.' He laughed, raising his hands in defeat. 'I promise to do my best not to go anywhere. Tell your mother that we'll begin planning the wedding but we'll set a date for after I've graduated, when I'm sure I'll have work. I want us to have every chance of a long and happy life together.'

'You haven't asked me how I feel about letting go of my dream.' A stab of pain pierced the pit of my stomach. I couldn't believe that he'd offered me no support in the one thing I really wanted, the one thing I had worked so hard towards. My dream defined me and I couldn't believe it had died before it had ever had a chance to live.

'I'm sorry they won't let you go,' he said softly. 'You know how it is for me with my parents, they hold me so tightly, so I understand your predicament ... but I think it's for the best. You know that your mother will never cope with you away. Ludwig's death took such a toll on her, as does always wondering if the same will happen to Willi. I don't know that she'd survive if something happened to you.'

I pulled my hand away, unable to look at him. He didn't need to remind me that I was being selfish. Vati had already made me see reason. Shaking my head in irritation, I picked a flower stalk and flicked it at him, trying to hide the deep hurt that made my gut twist and ache. 'It's not fair.'

'Come now, Lotte. It was never practical or achievable. How can we plan a wedding if you're working away from München? Besides, women from our kind of background don't need to work. If not for the war effort you would never have studied photography or considered a career.'

'But I want to work,' I interrupted, appalled that in these modern times, he would disregard a woman's career as unnecessary. A thrill of panic rushed through me. I thought Heinrich understood my need to contribute to the war effort, to make my brother's sacrifice mean something, but this was the first time he had ever told me that he didn't really support my efforts to become a photojournalist on the front – or anywhere outside of München for that matter. 'Did you show your mother my letter?' I held my breath as well as his gaze, waiting for his answer, not sure how I would react if he said he had.

His eyes widened with hurt at my accusation. 'No. I would never do that to you, I would never betray you. It was an accident.' He grasped my chin, his blue stare penetrating. 'You know that, don't you?'

I nodded, sighing, and Heinrich released me. Despite his protestations, I felt numb – desolate and betrayed.

'If anything happened to you . . .' Heinrich's voice caught. I jerked my head up in surprise, catching the glint of tears in his eyes as he turned to look at the stream. 'You don't know what it's like but I do. If I didn't lose you one way, it would be another. You would not cope with the things you'd see, with the terrible conditions, the human tragedy. It changes you, and I don't want you to change. I don't want you to go anywhere. I want you here, where you're safe, whole and happy. Then I can get through anything that might be ahead and come back to you, knowing you'll be waiting for me. I don't want to lose you.'

I stared at him stunned. 'I had no idea you felt that way,' I whispered. We had never really articulated how we felt about each other. But we had known each other so long, I had been sure we both felt we knew each other inside out.

'I can't wait to marry you. I want to keep you safe, make you happy and give you everything. I want us to be together always.' He kissed me passionately.

I couldn't help but forgive him. Heinrich was my future and my decision was already made. 'There'll be other dreams,' I said. 'You and I have many adventures ahead of us.'

Heinrich grinned, his forehead touching mine. 'With you, I can be sure of that! Life will always be an exciting ride with you by my side.' He stood, holding out an arm to help me up. 'Come, I have to get back to study.'

2

As I gazed at the imposing building of the regional command headquarters of the Luftwaffe, the bustle of the city faded away. Prinzregentenstrasse stood at the heart of München, where all its powerful players came together. It was an illustrious road – home to art, culture and the residences of the Bavarian Prime Minister and the Führer himself. Sculpted twin eagles sat above the main entry, nearly as tall as men, presiding regally over the work being done within those walls for the good of Germany. If anywhere could restore hope and confidence in Germany's victory, it was here. A burst of pride rushed through me. I hoped that my rusty secretarial skills would be enough to prove my worthiness for the job my father had found for me. As my mother had reminded me over breakfast, my behaviour – and success – would reflect on the whole family. I thought of my camera, sitting, almost abandoned, in my bedroom. It was a beautiful machine, a Contax IIIa, one of the best cameras on the market. My father had presented me with it on my first day of photography school and I had imagined a long and illustrious career as a top photographer. Instead, I was going to be a secretary. Nervously, I smoothed down my blouse and skirt and made my way across the street.

An efficient man in uniform ushered me down a hallway and into a sizable office. The door closed behind me.

'Come and sit down, fräulein,' said a deep voice.

Momentarily blinded by the bright light streaming in from one of the long windows I had seen from the street, I blinked and turned to the large desk. An older man with a bushy grey moustache sat behind it, age spots marking the hands he had folded on the oak desk, reminding me of the old-fashioned, no-nonsense, Prussian officers. He gestured for me to sit. Feeling foolish already, I murmured my thanks and slipped into the chair opposite him, my cheeks beginning to burn.

'My name is Colonel von Wissenbach and I run this section. We oversee the administrative, supply and maintenance requirements of all flying units at the airfields under our regional command. I know your father well. He's told me you're a hard worker, dutiful and obedient.'

I tried not to squirm at this assessment of my virtues and kept my mouth firmly closed.

'The secretary of one of my technical inspectors has left us recently for family reasons and you come at the perfect time. Your father assures me you are bright and will pick up any technical jargon quickly, that you have some secretarial skills and will manage the job competently.' He looked thoughtfully at me and his eyes became kinder, his official introduction complete. 'Now, is there anything you wish to ask me?'

My mind went blank. What could I ask? A million things and nothing of real consequence, I thought. 'No, colonel. I just want to thank you for this opportunity. I'll do my best and hope you will be pleased with my work.'

The colonel nodded. 'If there is any problem, make sure you come to me. It's the least I can do for your father.'

'Thank you, colonel. There won't be any problems, I know it.' I stood quickly, pleased the interview was over. '*Heil* Hitler!' I said, giving the Nazi salute.

'*Heil* Hitler,' responded the colonel. 'Fräulein Weiss will show you to Oberinspektor Drescher's office. Good luck, Charlotte.'

I found Fräulein Weiss waiting outside the colonel's office. She was a civilian auxiliary like me, dressed smartly in a navy skirt and white blouse, her red hair pulled into a tight French roll. I was glad I had dressed with care that morning: a blue blouse to match my eyes and black skirt that was modest but smart and my third-last pair of silk stockings.

Fräulein Weiss smiled brightly as she guided me to my new superior's office. 'Good to have another woman on the team,' she whispered conspiratorially. 'These men think they know everything but it's us women who keep it all together. If you have any trouble with the work, let me know. I've been here two years now. By the way, call me Bettina.'

I nodded, thankful for some support. She showed me into another office, much smaller than the colonel's, and less bright too, with only a small window allowing in the late summer light.

The man behind the desk rose gracefully to his feet, standing tall and lean. He was young, perhaps thirty, with a face that was smooth and unlined. His dark hair was slicked back and his green eyes watched me intently as I crossed the room. Even in his stillness, I felt the intensity of his presence, a charisma that pulled me inextricably towards him, like a moth to a flame. Not at all the middle-aged, overweight bureaucrat I was expecting. A hot flush crept up my throat and into my cheeks, setting them on fire.

'Fräulein,' Oberinspektor Drescher said, extending his hand.

Feeling already flustered and off balance, I was thrown that he didn't offer the standard Nazi greeting of *'Heil* Hitler'. Gingerly, I offered my hand across the desk. He grasped it in a thoroughly modern, firm handshake but his touch somehow left me feeling breathless.

'Oberinspektor Erich Drescher.' He gestured to the chair. 'Please sit.'

I sat, abruptly realising I was staring. I shifted my gaze. The Führer's picture hung on the wall behind the desk, looking down at us imperiously. A shiver ran through me. I was finally doing something to help my country – not what I had hoped, but this was a start and better than moping around at home. I glanced back to the Oberinspektor. He was beautiful in a classical way, with his aquiline nose, chiselled jaw and high cheekbones, reminding me of the statues I had admired of the ancient gods scattered around München. But those eyes; I could get lost in his eyes.

'Fräulein von Klein, thank you for coming in so quickly.'

Startled out of my thoughts, I nodded and smiled, unsure of what I had missed.

He must have seen the confusion on my face because he said, 'My secretary left rather suddenly and as you can see,

I desperately need the help of an organised and efficient assistant.'

The desk was covered in mountains of files. 'How long have you been without a secretary?' The nerves blossomed in my belly once again, like a hundred butterflies taking flight. I kept my gaze on the silver stitching on his tunic collar and the silver pips and oak leaf that distinguished him as one of the administration officers.

He sighed. 'Two weeks. Our department's requirements come far below those of other, more important divisions, and we've had to carry on as best we can until now. But I believe you come highly recommended.'

My pulse quickened. I had a lot to live up to but I discovered that all I wanted to do was to please this man, to make his job easier, to make him proud of my efforts.

'I will do my best, oberinspektor.' I sat straighter in my seat and looked directly at him, overcoming my nerves and daring him to tell me differently.

'Very good, fräulein. I should explain a little of what we do here. We ensure that all our assigned aircraft are maintained and fit for their operational purpose. You will organise my schedule and record the maintenance and supply data of each flying unit that we manage. I'll need your help to compile and review requests, orders and reports regarding maintenance procedures, required specifications, quality control regulations and supply requirements. Additionally, you will accompany me at times to various airfields in our command to supervise or conduct inspections.'

I swallowed hard. There was a lot to do and I wasn't sure I knew how to do any of it.

'I will guide you through your tasks today. I hope you're a quick learner because I have work coming out of my ears.' He smiled, lighting up an otherwise serious face.

I clenched my fists in my lap, silently berating myself for my silly schoolgirl fancy. I had to work with this man – I couldn't lose focus and show my incompetence on my first day.

I took a deep breath. 'Thank you, oberinspektor. I'm ready to learn.'

'Let's begin then, shall we?'

The first week was horrendous. I constantly felt awkward, not sure how to behave around someone I found so attractive. Despite my intense desire to please the oberinspektor, I felt that I did everything badly and far too slowly to be of any real help. My typing skills themselves weren't bad but I had trouble even getting up to the speed I needed and fell woefully behind. Thank God in Heaven I wasn't employed purely as a typist because I would have been asked to leave by the end of that first week. My shorthand was only a little better but I could manage the telephone calls and appointments well enough.

The oberinspektor was patient with me. He was a good teacher, explaining everything carefully, answering my questions no matter how stupid they must have seemed to him, overlooking my minor mistakes and calmly alerting me to the major ones and giving me time to fix them. I was trying my very best but I felt I was letting him down and it crushed me more than it should.

Bettina assured me that it was normal to feel inadequate and overwhelmed as she helped me through those first weeks, showing me shortcuts to the procedures, different ways of remembering the routines and the best ways to organise the schedules. 'You don't need to follow the way he has shown you,' she said to me more often than I could count. 'There's a much quicker and easier way to do that.'

'But this is the way he wants it done,' I whispered the first few times, horrified.

But Bettina always waved her hand. 'Bah! He won't care how you've done it, as long as it's done right. Let me show you.' I wished I could be that confident and in control.

Most evenings in those first weeks, Heinrich would meet me after work to walk me home. I moaned to him constantly about how terribly I was doing.

'I remember the first time I had to intubate a patient,' he told me one day after I rattled off a litany of mistakes I had made. We were strolling hand in hand through the Englischer Garten. 'Of course, I had learnt how to do it in my tutorials but this was a real patient needing this procedure in my first hospital term. The doctor in charge was called away to an emergency and the nurse thought I knew what to do.'

'What did you do?'

'Well, I pretended I knew what I was doing and I prayed to God that I looked confident and got it right. Luckily for me, I did. The patient suffered little discomfort and the nurse walked away satisfied.' Heinrich thrust out his arm in a gesture of victory.

I sighed. I wasn't sure I could pretend to know what I was doing; I wasn't as confident as him.

Heinrich bumped me gently as if the jolt would put me in a more positive mindset. 'Come on, Lotte. Where's your spirit? People have always looked up to those like us. The trick is to look like you know what you're doing, do the best with what you have until you've learnt enough to do better the next time. It will come together for you, I promise.'

'Are you sure?' I asked. 'You're so good at everything you do and you know how I am. Everything has to be done right the first time or I get so cross with myself.' I didn't tell him that I worried constantly that my father would walk into the apartment with a thunderous expression on his face after receiving a telephone call from Colonel von Wissenbach.

Heinrich slipped his arm out from mine and settled it across my shoulders, as if bringing me under his wing. 'Look, when I was posted to the field hospital for the first time, I had some hospital experience but not much. I had to learn everything by watching others when I could and by just doing it myself. Experience is the best teacher. Soon I was doing the basic procedures with my eyes closed. Trust me, you'll be an expert before long and your superior will think himself lucky to have the best secretary in the department.'

I nodded and put my arm around his waist, snuggling in closer to his side. A cool breeze had whipped up suddenly, a sure sign that summer would soon be over and we would begin the long haul through winter. I would have been a much better photographer, I thought bitterly.

Heinrich and Bettina were right. Over time, I began to relax and the work came more naturally to me. Work became less of a chore and I enjoyed the sense of accomplishment at the end of each day. I also noticed the oberinspektor's hunched shoulders gradually drop and his perpetual frown soften as the strain on him lessened. Constantly aware of his presence, my heart leapt as I realised that my hard work was making a difference to him. Much to my chagrin, I felt my eyes often slip across to him throughout the day, watching him surreptitiously, unable to stop myself. I was ashamed of my infatuation. I was engaged to Heinrich whom I would soon make a life with, but the oberinspektor had stirred something within me that I had never felt before. He captivated me in a way Heinrich never had. It left me feeling unsettled.

I felt foolish, too, as I tried and failed to set aside my crush to begin wedding preparations. Our mothers, however, were in their element, planning the society wedding of the year. Heinrich's mother, Tante Klara – as I had called her since childhood – had always wanted a daughter. I knew she was happy to have me as her daughter-in-law and she made the most of her involvement. Blonde heads bent over lists, magazines or in deep discussion about the benefits and disadvantages of each tiny detail. I noticed that the haunted, faraway look I often saw in my mother's eyes disappeared during her conversations with Tante Klara. Her constant worry about Willi faded into the background when she immersed herself in the wedding – this was something she could control, a way to obliterate, if only for a little while, the cruel reality of war. I was worried about Willi too. He was in France awaiting deployment and while he was safe for the moment we didn't know how long that would last.

Sometimes my patience was sorely tested when Mutti and Tante Klara forced their preferences on me. I was finding it harder and harder to care about the perfect wedding they were planning, unable to keep my mind from straying to the oberinspektor, struggling privately with the constraints I felt.

'What flowers do you like?' asked Heinrich's mother as we sat in our parlour one Sunday, flicking through catalogues.

'Something a little different . . .' I said casually. 'Perhaps peony . . . some delphiniums . . . cornflowers?' I heard the intakes of breath around me.

'They're not formal enough, dear, for the type of wedding you're having,' said Tante Klara quietly. 'How about some calla lilies or roses?'

I stared out to the potted geraniums on the wrought iron balustrade of the balcony off the parlour, the masses of red blooms cheering me up. Looking down at the catalogue once again, a particular picture caught my attention. 'Oh! I like that very much.' I looked closer at the arrangement and then glanced up quickly to the balcony, smiling. 'All right, roses it is.'

'Good,' said my mother.

Tante Klara was nodding next to her. 'Yes, dear, that will be very nice, white roses in a formal arrangement.'

'No,' I said quickly. 'Red roses, long stemmed, in a sheath, tied with a ribbon.' I raised the catalogue. 'See, like this.' I pointed to the picture. Both mothers craned their necks to study the photo. 'If Maria Anna is putting such an arrangement in her catalogue, it must be the next thing and soon everybody who's anybody will be doing their flowers like this.'

27

'Red roses are not appropriate for a wedding dear,' Tante Klara said, leafing through another booklet.

'White roses,' said my mother and the glare she gave me caused me to close my mouth with my objection unuttered.

'Here's one. Perhaps this could work for you, white roses in a cascading arrangement. Not what I'm used to but I think it could look lovely.' My future mother-in-law passed the booklet across to me. I had to admit, the arrangement was beautiful and at least she was willing to give me a little leeway but I had my heart set on the red roses now that I had seen them.

I shook my head. 'I don't think so.'

My mother stood, snatching the offending booklets from me and placing them on the side table. 'I think that will do for the flowers. We'll plan for white roses in a formal bouquet and work the other flowers for the wedding around that.'

It was pointless to fight what they both wanted, they would have their way and if I was honest, it was going to be spectacular. I wasn't sure I cared that much any more, though – the wedding was for our families, not for Heinrich and me. I reminded myself I only wanted to be with Heinrich, living our lives together, the details didn't matter. But the oberinspektor's sparkling green eyes were never far from my thoughts.

One night in October, just before the first anniversary of my brother Ludwig's death, I awakened to the sound of air-raid sirens, the high-pitched whine echoing in my bones. It was a sound we hadn't heard in over a year. My door was thrown open and my mother appeared in her silk dressing gown, her hair dishevelled and lines of terror etched across her face.

'Lotte, get up quickly. We have to go.' I could hear the strain in her voice even though it was still husky from sleep. I swung my legs over the side of my bed, a little disoriented and my chest tight with fear.

My father was right behind her, carrying her coat, pulling her away and extending his hand to me. 'Leave everything,' he said urgently. 'None of this matters if I lose one of you. Come.' I knew he felt the fear we did but he was steadfast and calm even in the middle of a crisis, always ready with a logical response or solution. It was one of the things I loved about him.

My heart pounding, I jumped out of bed, sliding on my dressing gown and slippers. I grabbed my suitcase with my treasures: my camera and photos. I couldn't leave them behind. Before I grasped my father's hand, I snatched Willi's most recent letter from my desk and jammed it into my pocket. Vati shoved my overcoat into my arms and dread coiled through my body like lead, weighing me down. The horror of the Hamburg bombings and subsequent firestorm in which thousands perished and hundreds of thousands were left homeless was fresh in my mind.

Huddled between my parents in the bomb shelter, neighbours and strangers pressed all around us like sardines in a can, I could only hear the muffled thud of a continuous stream of bombs pounding the city. I held my hand across my face, attempting to filter the air as I breathed through my mouth, trying not to inhale the overpowering smell of so many bodies in a confined space. Another explosion rent the air, and I jumped.

'It's all right, Lotte,' whispered my father, squeezing my hand. 'They're not close. I don't think we're the target tonight. Maybe one of the industrial plants on the edge of the city. Hopefully not mine.' Vati's factory had been consigned to the war effort and although his family still owned the business, he no longer had anything to do with its operation.

'What about Heinrich? What if he's still at the hospital?'

'He'll be all right. He'll be as safe as we are.'

I nodded, leaning against Vati in relief, wanting to believe him, drawing on his strength, wondering how my other friends and work colleagues were faring, Bettina and the oberinspektor included. Most lived close to the city and listening to the relentless whistle and thud of bombs, I couldn't imagine how München would survive such an attack.

Mutti clutched my other hand in terror, holding tight as though she would never let go. She was shuddering. I let go of Vati's hand, gesturing to Mutti. Vati stood and squeezed in on the other side of her, putting his arm around her.

'It's all right, Amelia. We're safe tonight,' he murmured into her ear.

'Just keep Lotte close. I don't know how much more of this noise I can take.'

Mutti's panic was feeding my own anxiety and I didn't need any more of that. I slipped my hand into my pocket and felt the coarse paper of Willi's letter. I hoped that, wherever he was, he too was safe. I closed my eyes to shut out the pale faces in shadow and silently recited Willi's letter to myself.

Liebe Lotte,

By the time you receive this letter, I will have become a cultured expert on the sights of Rome!

My division was dispatched to Italy a few weeks ago and we discovered that our aim was to disarm the Italian army and secure the city of Rome. You may or may not know, but the Italian Government was planning to abandon us and defect to the English. Despite a few small battles and skirmishes, we now hold Rome. Your brave and courageous brother, as part of the 2nd Parachute Division, played an important part in this victory for Germany! Make sure you tell all your friends!

I received your last letter telling me about your new job. Nice to see you've kept it in the family, working for the Luftwaffe. I'm sure by the time you receive this you will have whipped your section and superior into shape. I know your dream was to work as a photographer. I'm sorry that Mutti doesn't understand what makes you tick but I'm glad you're working in München.

Believe me, the front is not somewhere you want to be. It's a place of madness and insanity, a place that will haunt you for the rest of your life. North Africa was bad but they say the Eastern Front is the worst. That's not something I want for you. I want you to be happy, to always hear your laughter, to keep your great joy for life. When I think of you, I think of your very unladylike laughter, straight from the belly. There'll be plenty of time after the war to make your dreams reality and show Mutti what you're made of.

Anyway, how are you coping with Mutti and her planning for your wedding? Is she driving you mad yet? You must be a stronger person than me, because I quiver in my boots thinking of the day my future wife and I have to deal with her fastidious and controlling planning! I think I'll stay with the military a while longer . . .

Jokes aside, I know that it's her way to show how she cares. She only wants the best for you, so if you can, take a deep breath and grin and bear it. I know you've said that it will probably be a summer wedding next year but let me know when you've set a date. I will do everything I can to get there. You know Heinrich is like a brother to me and he's a fine man. Just be happy. Maybe after this war is over, I will be so lucky to find such a woman as you.

To be sure, just as we begin to relax, we will be sent to another hot spot to support the army. So I will make the most of my time here in Rome. When I can, I will enjoy the local cuisine (all the pasta I can eat), the fabulous ancient sites (I can't wait to see the Colosseum), architecture (any of it will do, there's so much to see), artwork (I hope to see the Sistine Chapel) and of course, the local girls (belle ragazze)! See, my Italian is coming along! I look forward to sharing this all with you (well, maybe not all of it) when I next write.

Your affectionate brother,
Willi.

I could just imagine my incorrigible brother in Rome, living it up in spite of the war, sweeping some voluptuous brunette off her feet. His letter reminded me of when we were younger, maybe eight or nine, at a time before our parents' divorce. Willi and I were walking through a meadow in the height of summer. Ludwig was helping our father as he was old enough to be of value and rarely had time to play with us any more.

'Come on,' urged Willi. He ran towards an abandoned shed on our father's property. He was always the risk taker, encouraging me to follow his lead.

'No, we're not allowed to go near the shed,' I said, stopping in the tall grass, the swaying tips tickling my arms.

'But I have to show you something. I can't show anyone else.' Willi grasped my hand, both of us hot and sticky with sweat. 'You're the only one who will understand.'

'All right,' I said tentatively. Hand in hand, we raced to the shed, my heart in my mouth, terrified someone would see us.

Willi opened the door of the shed carefully, its hinges complaining from lack of use. It was dark and cool inside, and something moved in the corner, a dark shadow, making me scream.

'No, don't scream,' hissed Willi. He placed his hand reassuringly on my arm. 'You'll scare him.'

'Scare who?' I took a step backwards.

'Prinz.' Willi dragged me towards the bench and retrieved a flashlight. He flicked the switch and shone the light into the corner.

A ball of dark fur cowered against the timber wall.

'What is it?' I said, intrigued but not moving any closer.

'It's a puppy.' Willi grinned from ear to ear. 'I found him a few days ago. He's too small to be on his own and I looked everywhere for his mother. I've been looking after him ever since. Isn't he cute?'

I nodded, not yet sure. 'You know we're not allowed to have a puppy. It will scare the chickens. If it kills them, Vati will have our hides.'

'Vati has his hunting dogs. Why can't we have our own dog?'

'I know. But if he finds out, we're in big trouble.'

'He doesn't have to know. Prinz can live here and we can visit him every day.' Willi crouched down near the puppy, its wide dark eyes watching his every movement warily. He pulled a paper bundle from his pocket. Unwrapping the package, he placed it in front of the trembling puppy. The tiny black nose twitched, sniffing the contents before it crawled towards the paper.

'What is it?'

'Scraps of meat from yesterday, cut up into tiny pieces,' Willi said, watching the puppy carefully.

The puppy devoured the meat, licking the paper when it was finished. It sat back on its haunches, pleading for more.

Willi scratched the puppy's head. Before we knew it, both of us were cross-legged on the dusty floor, the puppy wriggling between us, little grunts of ecstasy emitting from its mouth as we scratched it behind the ears and on the belly.

'We have to keep him but we can't let Vati find him,' I said, the soft fur smooth under my hand.

'I knew you'd understand.'

I helped Willi look after Prinz, slipping away to make sure he had ample food and water. Although we were already close, Prinz brought us even closer together. But as the days shortened into autumn and Willi prepared to begin classes at a new school, Prinz disappeared. Willi was distraught and I cried for days but nothing brought him back.

'Let's hope he's somewhere safe,' Willi whispered before he left for school.

'He will be,' I said, trying to be strong. 'One day, he'll come home to us. I'll watch out for him.'

'I know you will. I can rely on you.' Willi smiled and then he was gone.

The following summer my parents were divorced. Our childhood innocence was gone.

Tears rolled down my face. I missed Willi terribly.

'It will be over soon,' Vati whispered. 'Stay strong. Remember everything you have to live for.' My mother, tucked into his other side, stroked my face, her hand clammy with fear, but said nothing. 'We must lead by example. When we display strength and calm, others will follow and together we can get through this difficult time.'

He was right. My father knew how to get the best out of me. I kissed him on the cheek, the glow of that long ago summer still warming my blood. I knew how to be strong.

3

'**L**otte,' called Bettina, as I was shrugging out of my overcoat. 'Have you heard?'

'No, what?'

'Berlin was bombed again last night.'

I swung back to face her. The Allied campaign targeting Berlin had been raging for weeks. My father had been recalled to the army and sent to the capital. My eyes widened in alarm and I grabbed Bettina's arm. 'Where? How bad was it?'

'Bad. The western part of the city was hit – the Ministry of Munitions, several arms factories, some barracks and a few embassies. Fires have been blazing all night, destroying anything the bombings left.'

'The Führer?'

'Fine. But something else – pamphlets were dropped saying that Germany has lost the war, that the Führer won't concede defeat because it means his end. It's disgraceful, the worst kind of propaganda to shattered and broken people.'

Bettina shook her head in disgust. 'None of the government or Wehrmacht offices were hit. I'm sure your father's fine. We can find out from his office where he went. It's all right.'

I nodded, too choked up to respond otherwise. I had to telephone my mother, it was best that she heard it from me.

'Mutti.'

'Is everything all right?'

'I just wanted to let you know that Berlin was bombed quite badly last night.'

'Vati?' Her voice quivered with fear.

I took a deep breath, trying to stay strong for her. 'His offices weren't hit but we're trying to find out where he is.'

'All right.' I could hear the catch in her voice. 'Let me know the moment you hear anything.'

'We might not hear from him immediately, communication lines are down. But don't worry. I'm sure he's fine.'

'Just call me as soon as you know anything.'

'I will, Mutti. Goodbye.' If anything happened to Vati . . . it didn't bear thinking about.

Bettina used her connections to discover where Vati's meeting was in Berlin and where he was staying. She plonked herself at my desk later that day.

'He should be fine,' she said quietly, the monotonous tapping of typewriter keys continuing around us. 'He was nowhere near the bombings.' She patted my hand and I just stared at her, not sure whether I could let myself feel relieved yet.

With no word from my father, life at home was tense. My mother and I moved around the apartment like zombies, jumping every time the telephone rang or the door opened.

Heinrich joined us at home on the second evening. The bombings in Berlin had continued again through the night, and I had gone to work at my mother's insistence, but I'd been next to useless. Heinrich and I tried to make small talk with my mother but every attempt fell flat. She hadn't eaten all day and by the dark circles and bags under her eyes, I was certain she hadn't slept and had spent a good part of the day crying.

The shrill buzz of the doorbell punctuated the silence. The tap of heels across the marble foyer told us the butler, Herr Schmitt, was attending to the door. With a nod from me, Heinrich rose and went out. I glanced at my mother, her face frozen in fear mirroring the rush of despair I suddenly felt. I couldn't stand it another minute. I jumped up, determined to meet this news head on, when Heinrich called, 'He's home! He's all right.'

My mother sagged in her seat and I rushed to help her to her feet. Arm in arm, we crossed the parlour floor just as Heinrich entered the room with my father by his side.

'Johann,' my mother whispered with joy.

'Amelia, *liebchen*,' he murmured, as she smothered him in kisses. 'It's all right. I'm home now.' My father's hollow eyes rested on me and he smiled wearily. He held one arm out and I was in his embrace, solid as ever. 'My strong girl,' he murmured and kissed the top of my head. It was only then that I allowed myself to relax, the relief flooding my system making me giddy and sick to my stomach.

Heinrich took my arm as my father moved to the settee, still entwined with my mother. 'You look pale,' he said. 'You need some fresh air.'

I nodded, too overcome to speak.

He guided me onto the balcony, where the sharp bite of the evening air numbed my face but was a cooling balm to my clammy skin, settling my stomach and clearing my head. I looked up into the night, stars faintly visible as tiny pinpricks against the inky sky. It was still strange to look out over the dark street. Ever since blackout had become a way of life I missed the cheery circles of the streetlights.

'Better?'

I nodded, breathing in the frigid air. 'How much longer can this war go on? Too many people are dying, too many lives are shattered. I sometimes wonder if it's all worth it.'

Heinrich's arms encircled me from behind, the fine mist of his breath caressing my cheek. 'Sometimes I think about those who have resisted the course of this war, questioned the Führer's wisdom.'

'You mean the White Rose?' Heinrich had told me how members of the resistance group, fellow students of his, had been arrested earlier in the year. He had been shaken by the viciousness of the Gestapo and the harsh sentences inflicted on those he knew and worked with.

'They didn't deserve to be executed. They were peaceful, young and idealistic and had seen so much. I served with a few of them on the Eastern Front – it was enough to make anyone question their beliefs.'

'Shh, Heinrich. Don't talk like that. It will only lead to trouble. You can't mean it.'

Heinrich sighed as he shook his head. 'Of course not. I was just thinking that there's too much wasted life. We need to win this war, I agree, but it has to be soon. And you're right, too many have already been maimed or died most horrible deaths in the name of this war.'

I wondered about the Allied pamphlets Bettina had told me about. 'We will win, won't we? We've sacrificed too much not to.'

'There's talk we're not doing well on the Eastern Front, although the news reports suggest otherwise. The truth is I don't know.'

Cold fear blossomed in my blood, making me want to run away to a place that had never heard of war. Heinrich pulled me close and I leant back into him, his warmth seeping through my clothing, his desire pressing against me. I closed my eyes, giving in to primal emotions, aroused by his need for me. My breathing came in fast, shallow bursts as I imagined how this situation might develop if we were alone. I shuddered as the oberinspektor's face appeared behind my eyelids. I turned in Heinrich's arms, intent on reminding myself who I was promised to. I wondered how much longer he would suppress his passion before I either gave in or he looked elsewhere. I kissed him gently to rid myself of the image of the oberinspektor's intense eyes and Heinrich drew me closer, his hand on my back, sliding lower, his mouth insistent, his tongue exploring and searching. I moaned, suddenly weak in his arms, letting him push thoughts of the oberinspektor away. A knock on the glass door made us pull apart, a little breathless. Herr Schmitt coughed delicately before announcing that dinner was served.

'We're waiting for the designer I've managed to secure to custom-make your gown. She does all the big society weddings,' said my mother as we sat with Tante Klara on elegant Louis XVI settees upholstered in pastel shades of silk brocade in one of München's most fashionable bridal salons. Mutti had decided that the perfect thing to lift our mood after the fright of my father's visit to Berlin was to begin the search for a wedding gown. I was secretly excited about finding the right dress. What girl didn't dream of the perfect wedding gown to wow her groom on their wedding day?

'These are her latest designs.' Mutti passed me the drawings the designer had done for her. 'She wants you to try on some dresses in a similar style so we can see what suits your shape.'

I looked at the variations of design, some of them easy to imagine in fabric, some more difficult. There was a limited supply of silks, satins and lace, but those with money could still purchase such luxuries. Salons made it their business to source the best fabrics from around the world and guarantee a gown that befitted the social elite of München.

'Frau von Klein?' a tall, elegant woman said in a musical voice with a slight accent I couldn't quite place. My mother introduced her as our designer, Frau Andree.

'So you are the bride to be. Such a special time. Have you looked through the designs I sent across? Are there any you particularly like?'

'They're all beautiful,' I said nervously. I didn't want her to think I was inept with fashion choices and style. 'It's a bit hard to know which would look the best on me.'

'Yes, of course,' she said. 'That is very true. Now come over here, please, so I can have a look at you.' She guided me to the centre of the room and walked around me, taking in every detail of my appearance. It was very uncomfortable and I was worried she would find my body inadequate for her designs.

After the necessary measurements were taken and calculations made, gowns were finally brought out for me to try. It was a haze of white satin, silk, lace and organza – skirts that were full, straight, A line; bodices with high necks, V neck, round neck, collars turned up, down and Grecian style.

I paraded in front of our mothers.

'Not that one dear,' said Tante Klara to a dress with a full skirt and layers of silk ruffles and an unusual bustle. 'Not very elegant.'

I had to agree. It was awful and made my behind look huge.

The designer dismissed the dress with a wave of her hand. 'Too many ruffles for you,' she said.

One gown felt wonderful. It was satin, figure hugging, with leg-of-mutton sleeves and a skirt that flowed sensuously around my legs as it fell to the floor. I held my breath as I was led to the full-length mirror.

'Not bad,' said Frau Andree. 'Now we're getting somewhere.'

I stared at the vision of elegance in the mirror, hardly believing it could be me. I was reminded of glamorous movie stars. I let out my breath slowly. I could hear our mothers murmuring in the background but I ignored them. I twisted and turned to view the gown and my profile from all angles. It was not a gown just anyone could pull off. My height allowed it to flow as it should, sleek and slimming. The only thing on the gown I wasn't sure about was the plunging V neckline. Admittedly, I had the bosom to accommodate such a style and it was very daring and sophisticated, but it was not me.

I needed something with a higher neckline, possibly something that buttoned up at the throat. Suddenly the designer's hands were inside the gown and I drew in a sharp breath, startled as she deftly lifted each breast so that it settled into the fabric more advantageously.

'That's better,' she said. And it was. She placed a small halo of satin and silk with an attached veil on my head. It added to my height and I felt like a statuesque goddess. I felt like a bride. I imagined how Heinrich would view me in this gown and blushed deeply. Then I wondered what my father would think and my heart dropped. This was not the gown for me.

'Not very modest,' said my mother disapprovingly.

'But it is very elegant,' said Tante Klara.

'Turn, dear,' said Frau Andree. 'Let your mother see the full effect of the gown.'

I turned obediently, as the skirt swished across the floor behind me.

'What is your objection, Frau von Klein?'

'Too figure hugging. It doesn't leave much to the imagination and that neckline is too risqué.'

I blushed deeper, embarrassed now, feeling guilty that I had loved the dress at all.

'I don't think it's the gown, really,' said Heinrich's mother, leaning forward, warming to the task at hand. 'I like the way the satin falls on her, there's enough fabric in the skirt.'

'What if we change the neckline,' suggested the designer. 'It will change the whole look of the bodice.'

My mother stared at me without really seeing me. I felt like a mannequin with no thoughts and feelings of my own and squirmed with discomfort at the scrutiny.

'Maybe,' Mutti said after a time. 'Perhaps a round neckline, I liked the single ruffled neckline on that earlier gown.'

Although I wasn't asked, I agreed with their suggestions and knew that whatever the mothers and designer decided upon would be stylish. I could imagine myself as a bride now. I wanted to make Heinrich proud. Thoughts of the ober-inspektor came into my mind. I pushed them away. Heinrich was my groom and my future.

It was early December when I found my mother in the parlour, white as a sheet, clutching a paper to her chest.

'Mutti, what's the matter?' I asked, although my mouth had gone dry.

She began to tremble and looked at me with blank eyes. My body tingled with apprehension.

I rushed to sit by her side, fear weighing me down so I felt like I was moving in slow motion. I could feel her tiny frame wracked by waves of shaking. I put my hand on her shoulder. 'Mutti?' I said desperately. 'Is it a telegram?'

The physical touch must have got through to her. 'It's Willi.' She looked at me, her eyes wide with shock and filled with pain.

I knew then that Willi was dead.

Pushing my own horror aside, I wrapped my arms around her. She remained stiff and unyielding in my arms, fragile and still trembling violently.

Heinrich chose that moment to walk into the parlour. 'Lotte, what's wrong?'

I heard his voice as if from a distance. I pulled away from my mother long enough to look over to him. 'It's Willi. Mutti just received a telegram.'

44

Heinrich crouched in front of us, dressed immaculately for the concert he was supposed to be taking me to. My shocked mind focused on the shine of his black shoes. 'What's happened?'

'I don't know,' I whispered. 'I haven't read it yet.'

Heinrich gently pulled the paper from my mother's grasp. I watched his face carefully as he read. His wariness quickly turned to grief as his shoulders and face sagged. 'Bloody war,' he murmured, shaking his head.

'Tell me,' I demanded, looking into his blue eyes misty with sorrow. I held my breath.

'Willi was killed in action on the Eastern Front near Kiev a few days ago.'

I released my breath in a ragged sob. Heinrich placed a hand on my shoulder in sympathy. Distressed as I was, I still wondered why he didn't pull me into his arms to comfort me as Vati would have Mutti.

My poor mother moaned. Her second son had been taken by this cruel and relentless war. How much more sacrifice did the Führer expect us to make for the Fatherland? I pulled her closer, comforting myself as much as my mother.

'Are you sure?' It couldn't be. Willi had seemed safe in Rome in his last letter. Surely I would have known – we were so close.

Heinrich nodded, grief cracking his solemn expression. 'The telegram's from his commanding officer, General Lieutenant Wilke. The 2nd Parachute Division was deployed there from Italy a couple of weeks ago. There's no doubt.'

My heart felt like it had stopped and then exploded into a million shards of grief and pain. I couldn't breathe. 'No, not Willi too,' I gasped. 'Oh, Mutti.' Tears ran freely down my face, soaking her hair. It had barely been a year since we lost Ludwig. I was all that was left and by the way my mother clung to me, it felt like she would not let go.

'Never leave me,' she whispered. 'I need you.'

Numbness settled over me as I began gently rocking her, cradling her head against my chest like a child's. 'Of course, Mutti, I'm always here for you.' I knew I had to be strong for her and push my pain aside.

I was unaware that Herr Schmitt had called my father home until he was by our side.

'Amelia, Lotte.' Vati drew us to him, his strong, dependable shoulders a safe haven from the bewildering events that had occurred. I breathed in the pipe smoke that clung to his coat and immediately felt soothed. My mother broke down into convulsive sobs, and my father pulled away to devote his attentions to her with an apologetic kiss to the top of my head.

Heinrich finally held me as I drowned in my own grief and the grief of everyone else in the room. I was sure I would never be able to break to the surface and breathe again.

There was no body to bury, no funeral to prepare, no graveside to visit. There was no way to say goodbye and that weighed heavily on us. Over the next few weeks my mother took to her bed and would not get out. She would not eat and she refused to see even her closest friends. Vati and I were worried about her, looking after her until she was on her feet again, but we were in mourning too. I couldn't bear to think of Willi alone and so far away from us in a foreign land. He didn't deserve that. He didn't deserve to die. He had just turned twenty and his whole life was ahead of him.

Mutti kept photos of us on the sideboard of the sitting room, photos of both boys proud in their uniforms on their first day of service; the final photo of Willi taken the day he left us for the last time. I picked up the photo in its silver frame. The Luftwaffe side cap sat jauntily on his head and his mouth held the hint of a smile. I remembered taking that photo like it was yesterday.

'Stand still and stop fidgeting,' I'd said to Willi, taking my job as family photographer very seriously. I could see the mischief in his bright blue eyes.

'Come on,' he said. 'I'll die of hunger, standing here all day.' He shifted again.

'No, the light's all wrong now,' I said in exasperation. His grin widened. 'Behave, Willi. I want to get the perfect shot.' I turned his face to the best angle. 'Now don't move.'

'You're so annoying,' he said but did what he was told, trying to wipe the grin off his face.

It was a good shot. He exuded confidence in his woollen uniform, the tunic open at the neck, his medals worn over his left breast. The flying cap sat almost over one eyebrow, his blonde hair showing short and neat along the opposite curve of the cap. I clicked away, allowing for variations of light and position, until I was satisfied.

'Thank you,' I said. 'Mutti will be happy with these.'

'As long as you and Mutti are happy,' he replied, kissing me on the cheek. He swung his arm across my shoulder, propelling me along. 'I'm starving. Let's eat now, before it gets cold.'

The lines of Willi's face in the last photo were more defined. He was handsome and had grown into manhood. Then his image blurred as tears rolled down my face and my heart clenched in anguish. I kissed the glass and carefully returned the frame to its place of honour on Mutti's sideboard. He was still too young to die.

Grief over Willi's death affected Heinrich very differently from me. He knew what it was like on the Eastern Front. He could imagine how my brothers had died. He consoled me well enough, holding me tight as the tears came in private, whispering words of sympathy and strength and, when they didn't work, kisses and caresses to distract us both and remind us that life was still for living. But I felt Heinrich withdraw into himself. I was sure some of it was his fear of being called up once again. I knew he had no fear of death itself, the ultimate sacrifice for the good of the Fatherland, but he could see how my brothers' deaths had affected my mother and me, and he worried about what his death would do to me and his own family.

I had always been an optimist but now I, like Heinrich, questioned the point of this war. This was a war fought of necessity, I reminded myself. It was a war of self-preservation for the German nation. There were bound to be stiff sacrifices to give the next generation a stronger, independent, vital Germany. Heinrich began talking about the White Rose episodes of earlier in the year again. The arrests and executions of those young students had affected him deeply but it was treasonous talk. It frightened me to the very core, not just because I was scared that someone would overhear, but because it started to make sense to me, threatening to shake the deeply held teachings of my childhood, those learnt in the schoolroom and the League of German Girls. I had known Heinrich all my life, our grandparents were family friends, and I knew that he held these same beliefs as tightly as I did – it was only grief talking, for both of us.

It was hard to put one foot in front of the other but life had to go on. I forced myself to go to work each day. Where I had found satisfaction in getting my job done and providing efficient assistance to Oberinspektor Drescher, I now found it difficult to focus on the tasks in front of me. There were many occasions, triggered by the slightest association with Willi – and in my job that wasn't uncommon – when I rushed to the bathroom, overwhelmed and ready to burst into tears. My colleagues were kind. Most had experienced some kind of loss and understood what I was going through. Bettina was my greatest support, keeping me busy and trying to distract me with idle gossip and hilarious stories during our breaks.

I was most surprised, however, by the compassion shown by Oberinspektor Drescher. He asked after my family each day, thoughtfully allowing me to come in late some mornings while I tended to my mother and stay late in the evening to finish off my work, always ensuring I had somebody to either walk me home or if the hour was late, to drive me home. I almost wished he would keep his distance, as his kindness only further confused my feelings.

One evening, I made the oberinspektor some coffee. We were working late and going over some documents I needed to transcribe.

'Your brother fought on the Eastern Front?' he asked.

I froze, coffee cup to my lips. I didn't know if I could speak to him of Willi without my mask of calm and efficiency slipping. Placing my cup on the table, I looked into his eyes. I knew I would see compassion but did not expect the vulnerability I found there. I could trust him.

'Yes, both my brothers did. We lost Ludwig just over a year ago in Stalingrad and Willi near Kiev.' My eyes welled with tears, I couldn't help it. I dashed them away with the heel of my hand, angry that it took only this to show my weakness.

He nodded, briefly squeezing my hand across the desk in sympathy, his touch soft and warm from the coffee cup. Surprised by his touch, I glanced at his face, but only found kindness in his green eyes.

'Be proud of your brothers. The Eastern Front is a very hard place, with the most difficult conditions imaginable.'

The Führer's picture looked down on me as if disapproving of my mixed emotions – pride but also desperation. When would the Führer follow through on his promise of winning this war? My brothers' sacrifices had to mean something.

'So I've heard,' I whispered, looking into my cup. 'Have you been there?'

The oberinspektor sighed. 'Yes. I was based at the airpark in Lemberg in late forty-one, after I finished my diploma. I worked at various airfields in Silesia before that. It was close to the Eastern Front then, I saw too many horrific things and there were some terrible stories. We supported the boys in Stalingrad, ready to pull them out when the Red Army looked like they would overwhelm them. To this day, I can't understand the Führer's decision to leave them there at the mercy of the Red Army. We were all devastated by the losses, too many men died that needn't.' He stared into space with a far-away look.

I shuddered, unnerved that the oberinspektor had not only mirrored my disquiet with the Führer's promises but spoken it. The bitterness of this personal description of the battle that Ludwig died in stunned me. The Eastern Front had a brutal reputation and here was another example of how it touched and affected the men who saw action there.

A warm glow rose within me as I realised how much the oberinspektor trusted me if he was willing to make such a dangerous admission.

He leant forward again, fiddling with a clip on the desk. 'Not all Russians are bad, you know. I met many good Russian men, soldiers, fighting for their country just like me, except many were in our captivity. The Russian culture is very interesting and I developed a love for the Cossack music that some of the men would sing. It was deeply stirring and hauntingly beautiful.'

I was shocked that he would tell me such things. Cossack music was banned. And yet I saw a very different side to him, a softer side, and a man who would not be told what to think or how to live.

He sighed, not noticing my fear for him. 'I found it difficult to reconcile myself to the mass slaughtering of men on both sides. I can't say I was disappointed to be transferred to München last year.'

'Oh, I thought you'd been here much longer. Everyone seems to know you.' I was glad to move the conversation away from dangerous territory, talking about something other than my brothers and the wretched Eastern Front.

'Ours isn't a large section compared to some and we have a good team that works well together.' He smiled. For the first time, I noticed the crinkles around his eyes and the creases around his generous mouth, which only heightened his attractiveness. I blushed at the compliment and dropped my eyes back to the documents on the desk.

In my first weeks at work, Bettina had warned me that the oberinspektor was a 'ladies' man', who was known to flirt with the office girls, but he had only ever been professional and respectful with me. Not that that had stopped my infatuation. Until this moment, I had known nothing more about him personally, except what was suggested by the photo of his children on his desk and the absence of a photo of his wife. It didn't worry me that he kept his personal life to himself; that was as it should be. All I cared about was that he was a good superior, that I made his work more efficient, and that he was well respected by everyone, especially his peers and superiors, which of course reflected well on me.

But I was growing curious, fuelled by my inability to stop myself from thinking about him. What kind of relationship did he have with his wife and family? Where did he come from, when did he last see them and how had his war experience shaped his life? I had seen pain in his eyes when he spoke of his previous war posting and I found it hard to reconcile the considerate, thoughtful and professional man with the stories Bettina had told me. There was more to the oberinspektor and his situation than met the eye.

The war certainly made all manner of things more complicated. I almost looked forward to 1944 in the hope that it would bring an end to the war. Heinrich and I could be safely married and begin our life together. I dreamt of life going back to normal but a little voice in my head wondered how life could ever be normal again without the ones we loved and with the trauma this war had left with the living.

4

The social engagements of the Christmas and New Year season enforced some kind of normality for our family. Vati reminded me these were important connections that needed to be fostered, which were valuable not just during the war but in its aftermath. Mutti agreed and seemed to come back to life, forcing herself to dress up and smile prettily.

Christmas and Silvester were subdued affairs with immediate family. We still had the traditional Christmas tree, a live fir with silver tinsel, glass baubles and white candles blazing on its branches. It was a sight that never failed to bring a smile to my face and a renewed sense of optimism for the year ahead. There was still champagne in Mutti's good crystal goblets and a few traditional delicacies too. Nobody wanted to play fortune-telling games on Silvester but we drank to Willi's and Ludwig's memories. We were all aware that these times were precious and nobody knew what was ahead.

Often the München parties revolved around military schedules, since many of my parents' friends were members of the general staff or high-ranking Heer and Luftwaffe officers. It was inevitable that the older men would congregate, often in a separate room with their cigars and cognac, and talk about the state of Germany, the ongoing war, the various new policies and how they would affect the coming year. The older ladies would sit around with their champagne discussing their families, their latest projects and the most recent scandals. The young ones like myself and Heinrich mingled, some drinking heavily, some abstaining from alcohol altogether, many sneaking off to a quiet corner or the darkness of the gardens for late-night trysts, to satisfy a sudden urge, to remind us what living was about. Our generation had been traumatised by the atrocities of war before we had blossomed into adulthood. Everyone had been touched by loss through the fracturing and dislocation of families and the cruel reality of modern warfare.

It was a little uncomfortable to meet Colonel von Wissenbach at these social functions. I always felt a bit stiff, as if I should be on my best behaviour while mingling with my superiors from work, but he never failed to be courteous and engaging.

'How are you enjoying your job, Charlotte?' he asked one evening.

'Fine, thank you.'

The colonel nodded. 'Working well with Oberinspektor Drescher? He's been good to you, I hope.'

'Of course, colonel. He's patient and kind and I've learnt a lot from him.'

'I've heard good things about your work, you're efficient and conscientious. We could do with more like you.'

I blushed to think the oberinspektor had talked about me with the colonel, and looked at my toes. 'Thank you.'

'There you are, Georg. How is my daughter doing at work?'

I looked up and smiled at my father, noticing a striking man standing next to him.

'She's a credit to you and your wife,' said the colonel. 'It's hard workers like Charlotte who keep men like us moving forward with the war effort.'

I almost fainted with the praise and suddenly felt that maybe this was the work I was meant to do to best help our country – perhaps photography had only been the silly dream of a young girl.

'We are very proud of her,' agreed my father. 'Georg, you've met Claus von Stauffenberg before?' He gestured to the man by his side.

'Of course.' Colonel von Wissenbach nodded genially to the man.

'Claus, this is my daughter, Charlotte.'

The man smiled, an eye patch giving him a rakish charm but his gaze intense nevertheless, and I felt like he was focusing all his attention on me. He was most charismatic. He reached for my hand, his own missing a couple of fingers, and I felt a surge of pride in this soldier who had obviously sacrificed so much for our homeland. Then his soft lips brushed the skin on the back of my hand, making me shiver deliciously.

'Lotte, this is Lieutenant Colonel von Stauffenberg, the son of old family friends. I hadn't seen him for years until he began working with the Replacement Army a few months ago.'

'A pleasure to meet you.'

'The pleasure is all mine,' he said, bowing slightly.

'How are things with the Replacement Army?' asked Colonel von Wissenbach. 'Have the budget cuts affected you as they have the Luftwaffe?'

I drifted away to find Heinrich, feeling vaguely disconcerted.

Over the next few days, I found myself remembering that encounter, trying to analyse what had made me feel so strange. Was it the pride I felt in looking at the Lieutenant Colonel's war injuries that my father told me he'd suffered in North Africa? Was it the protectiveness I felt for him, a beautiful specimen of a man but maimed by war, especially after my two brothers, both handsome and full of life, had perished? These thoughts rolled around my head until they exhausted themselves and I finally had to face the truth: I had been physically drawn to him. That wasn't so much the problem – a man like that, a decorated hero, would make many a woman swoon over him – it was how it reminded me of my first meeting with the oberinspektor, how I was irresistibly drawn to him, how my initial attraction to him had not yet waned after working with him for nearly six months.

My face burned with shame and I turned my head to catch the lightly falling snow on my hot skin. I sighed. How could I feel this way about someone I had met only for an instant and who had barely touched me? The familiar yearning for a life of excitement rose within me, a life of my choosing, lived on my terms, outside the restraints and conventions of my social class and family. The war had opened doors to exciting possibilities never before available to a girl like me but my mother made sure I walked the rigid path of tradition. Those possibilities were so far out of reach for me, they may as well have been on the moon.

Part of the problem, I was beginning to see, was my engagement to Heinrich. I realised now that my life with him would probably remain as constrained and structured as he believed a wife of my station should be. We had been family friends since childhood and our mothers encouraged a relationship between us before we had a chance to discover if one would develop on its own. I had never felt that rush of meeting the person who would become my betrothed for the first time. Perhaps my attractions to the oberinspektor and von Stauffenberg were reactions to the idea that I had missed out on that rite of passage.

It wasn't as though I didn't have feelings for Heinrich, we had just discovered our love through friendship and familiarity. I knew I loved him with all my heart but part of me now consciously wondered how it would be different with someone you felt an instant attraction to.

I pushed those thoughts away as quickly as they surfaced, furious with myself for even thinking them. Thoughts of anyone or anything else were unacceptable and shameful. I was engaged to Heinrich. I was the luckiest girl to have a man with such a good profession, from a good family, who loved me as I loved him and who was my best friend.

Life slowly returned to normal for my family. Mutti was subdued and occasionally I would catch her lost in thought and knew she was thinking of Willi and Ludwig. She began to share memories of them with me, telling me stories of happier times when I was a small child. She seemed a little softer with me too, not quite so rigid and harsh, drawing me into spontaneous hugs, clasping my hand when I sat near her.

One Sunday, I finally persuaded her to leave the apartment and take a walk in the Englischer Garten. I knew the fresh air and exercise would do her good. Although the snows were now behind us it was still a brisk day and even in our long overcoats and gloves, we had to walk hard to warm up. Mutti kept up with the punishing pace until we stopped in the meadow, breathing heavily, our hands tingling pleasantly.

'That's better, isn't it?' I said, grinning at my mother. Her face now had a healthy glow, not the pasty, pinched look from weeks of being cooped up in the apartment. She smiled in return and nodded, pushing wisps of frizzy strawberry blonde locks from her face with a gloved hand.

'Should we walk to the stream?' I asked. I had brought my camera with me to photograph the change in seasons and brush up on my photography skills. You never knew when an opportunity to capture the perfect shot would present itself.

Mutti slid her arm through mine and we walked along the path, the sound of our shoes crunching on the dirt a rhythmical accompaniment to our thoughts.

'The smell of the pines always reminds me of a holiday we took when you were little,' said my mother suddenly. 'We were still living in Düsseldorf and came to München to visit my grandmother Katarina. It was one of the few times your father suggested a short holiday together, just the five of us in the Alps.'

I hardly dared to breathe. Although I knew they had corresponded after the death of Willi, any talk of my natural father and our life before the divorce was rare. The breeze through the pines seemed to settle as if the trees also wanted to hear this story.

'We motored down to Berchtesgaden from München. Already the scent of pine was noticeable as we travelled through the forests. We stayed in a comfortable guesthouse overlooking the town and the Watzmann. It was spectacular: the twin peaks of the mountain dusted with snow, the town nestled in the valley beneath it with the twin spires of the church, jutting out as if to mimic the mountain. Your father was well and happy there, breathing in the fresh mountain air, playing ball patiently with Ludwig and Willi – they weren't yet school age – and pushing you in your baby carriage as we looked around the town.

'We took a cruise on Königssee Lake and even the boys were fascinated by the majestic mountains that towered over us and the lone pine trees that sat precariously on the edges of the massive rocky cliffs. Of course, they soon tired of the view and your father took the boys to the edge of the boat to look for mermaids and pirate treasure. I can still see their little blond heads bent over the water, your father between them, holding them securely. I remember thinking how good it was to see him getting involved with the boys. I had seen that imaginative playfulness when we first met and it was something I loved about him. I was pleased that he was showing that side of himself to his boys, getting involved in their world.

'The boat stopped at St Bartoloma's chapel and while your father walked around the grounds with you, following the boys, I went inside. It was magnificent and, staring at the opulent gold-gilded altar, I felt moved to kneel and pray, thanking God for these happy days with my beautiful family and the return of my beloved husband.'

We continued walking in silence for a moment. I could see my mother struggling to contain her emotions – there was joy and grief etched across her face, her smooth skin marked recently by small lines around her mouth and eyes. I squeezed her hand in encouragement, shocked by the revelation that she had prayed to God to thank Him for her happiness – my mother had never struck me as being spiritual. If anything, I had come to believe that she had no regard for God. I could understand her bitterness. Her dreams of a happy marriage with my father disappeared and their divorce was difficult; she barely survived the scandal. Left penniless, wrenched from her children, now she had survived her two boys who were barely out of adolescence when they died in war.

My mother took a deep breath. 'The following day we were picnicking in a meadow with the most perfect view of the Hoher Göll peak before us. I was the happiest I had ever been. The boys were playing on the edge of the forest, the soft breeze was sighing through the pines as it is now, you were crawling on the grass next to us and your father promised me that this was the beginning of a better life for us all. Ludwig had made a lion from a pine cone, the branches and needles strapped together, and he was beaming with pride as he presented it to us. It was sticky with pine sap. Your father picked Ludwig up and twirled him, telling him how proud he was of him, and tickled him. As Ludwig shrieked with joy, your father laughed without a care in the world.

I really believed things would change for us then, that we had a chance to be happy. The scent of pine clung to my hands all the way home and reminded me of the joy we had rediscovered. Whenever I smell pine, it reminds me of that time.'

'Oh, Mutti,' I murmured, touched by her sharing of the memory with me. 'That sounds beautiful.' I leant my head against her shoulder.

'Not long after that your father had another turn and began to drink again. I was pregnant and, in one of his darker moments, he lashed out at me and I lost the baby. He didn't know what he had done. He often didn't remember the rages he found himself in or what he did during them. When he realised what had happened, he was distraught and pleaded with me to forgive him. I told him I did, but it was the beginning of the end for us.'

I stopped walking and stood in front of my mother, struggling not to cry. 'Mutti, I'm so sorry. I didn't bring you here to remember sad times. I never wanted to upset you. I thought the walk would make you feel better.'

'No,' my mother said, shaking her head, 'sometimes it's good to remember, just little moments, and I'm happy I can share them with you.' She placed a gloved hand on my cheek, the worn leather soft on my skin. 'Thank God in Heaven I still have you, Charlotte Elisabeth. You are a joy to me. I might not tell you often enough, but I love you.' Drawing me into an embrace, she kissed my forehead.

I couldn't believe what I had heard. I had waited so long to hear those words. I felt the tears well up inside of me but I didn't want to ruin the moment, so I swallowed them down.

'I love you too, Mutti,' I whispered and squeezed her tightly as I planted a kiss on her cheek.

'Oof,' said Mutti. 'Not so tight.'

I let go quickly and we started laughing.

'Look,' I said, pointing to a tree by the edge of the stream. 'The blossoms have started.' I pulled out my camera and adjusted the settings to take a photo of the clusters of delicate pink blooms against the bare, dark branches. Mutti waited patiently while I concentrated on finding the best position to take the perfect photograph.

When we continued walking, my mother pointed out potential landscapes for me. I humoured her and set about photographing them. We discovered the best spot while standing on the bridge that spanned the stream. Here the willow draped gently to skim the edge of the water, tiny green buds all the way along the length of its branches, showing the promise of the heavy curtain that would hang over the water in summer. I studied the angles, focusing on the lines and the direction of light, snapping away, lost in the creative work.

'We'd better get back,' said Mutti. 'We have an appointment with Frau Andree.'

'All right,' I said, lining up the last few shots. This had been a perfect afternoon with my mother and I didn't want it to end. 'I should have some good photos to show you and Vati.' A deep sadness settled over me, dampening my joy, as I realised it had taken the death of my brothers for Mutti to open up to me, for us to reconnect at last.

But I shrugged off my mantle of melancholy. There had been too much sorrow and I had so much to look forward to.

I was most excited to return to the bridal salon for a fitting of my wedding gown. It should be complete.

Herr Schmitt pulled up in front of the bridal salon and my mother prepared to get out of the car.

I stopped her, my hand on her arm. 'Something's wrong, Mutti. The door is closed and the lights are off.'

'Don't be silly. They're probably trying to do their bit for the city and reduce the electricity they're using.'

'I'll go and check,' I said. 'No point both of us getting out of the car if it's closed.'

'No, Fräulein Lotte,' said Herr Schmitt. 'Stay here and I'll find out what is happening with the salon.'

We watched as he tried the door, but it was locked. He rang the bell and knocked half-a-dozen times, but nothing.

'Whatever can have happened?' asked Mutti, craning her neck to see any movement within the salon. 'This is most unusual. Herr Schmitt confirmed our appointment yesterday and everything was fine then.'

'It's closed, Mutti. Maybe we can telephone them when we return home.'

Just as Herr Schmitt turned to leave, the door opened a crack. He whipped around, exchanging a few words with who-ever it was. He hurried back to the car and opened Mutti's door.

'The salon is closed but there's a woman who has your gown.'

'What's happened?' asked Mutti perplexed, her brows drawn together.

'She won't say, but I think it best if you hurry. I want us to leave as soon as practical. Whatever it is, I don't want you among it longer than necessary.'

Mutti shot me an astonished look, nodded and without further comment, we got out of the car.

The woman opened the door only far enough for us to slip inside, her eyes darting from side to side in fear. The salon looked the same as always but it was eerie. Something didn't feel right. Shadows fell across the room and I noticed the racks of display gowns were bare.

'What's happened here?' Mutti hissed. 'Where is Frau Andree?'

The woman began to shake in terror. 'I shouldn't have let you in. I'm only a seamstress.'

'Where is everyone and where are the gowns?' I asked, tendrils of apprehension coiling through my belly.

'I have your gown,' stuttered the woman. 'I was finishing the beading at home before your appointment today.'

'Where is Frau Andree?' Mutti repeated. The woman looked blankly at her. Out of patience, Mutti grasped the woman's shoulders and shook her. 'Tell me what's happened here.'

She slumped to the settee when Mutti released her. 'They took her. The Gestapo took her away.'

'Why?' asked Mutti more gently.

'She's been lying to us all. She's a Jew.' Tears were streaming down the woman's face.

I gaped at her in bewilderment.

'No, that's ridiculous. There's some mistake. She's München's top designer. Somebody would have known,' Mutti said.

'This is the Gestapo. There are no mistakes,' whispered the woman. 'They closed down the salon, took all her designs and any of the dresses they found.'

'What will happen to her?' I whispered. Dread spread through my body like an insidious fever, making me rigid with fear.

Mutti shook her head. 'We can't do anything for her now.' She turned her gaze to the seamstress. 'Do you have the gown?'

The woman nodded and hurried to collect the paper parcel. 'It's finished. Try it on at home. If you need any alterations, I can do them for you.'

'Thank you,' said Mutti, taking the parcel from her. 'It was brave of you to return to give us the gown. Make sure you give your address to my man and we will be in touch.'

The woman nodded. 'You'd best leave now. It's not safe to be here.' She opened the door to let us out. Mutti couldn't leave quickly enough, pushing me out in front of her.

On the drive home, I saw nothing but Frau Andree's face gazing intently at my dress, searching for a design solution to satisfy our requirements. It was a face filled with passion and a desire to please. She had done nothing wrong. I didn't think I'd known anyone who was Jewish. The anti-Semitic Nürnberg Laws had come into effect when I was only ten years old, the year my parents divorced and I was sent away to boarding school. Although we had grown up being taught that Jews were the root of all evil, I couldn't believe that of Frau Andree. She was a good woman, making people happy with her creative designs.

'How could they take her, Mutti? She never hurt anyone.'

Mutti clapped her hand over my mouth. 'Shh, Lotte. You mustn't say that.' Her eyes were filled with alarm. 'Promise me you'll never speak of it again.'

I nodded, silenced by my mother's fear. Something tugged at the back of my mind, an old memory. I frowned, trying to recall the detail. Something about when Willi was home for the first time after enlisting in the Luftwaffe, when he came to see Mutti and I. He had told me a story about visiting an uncle of ours that lived near Berlin. This was my real father's brother, a part of my family I knew nothing about, a timber merchant living on a large forested estate between a river and a lake. Willi told me his wife was Jewish and that our cousin was unlucky, not able to fight for his country because of his Jewish blood. I remember feeling shocked that we had Jewish relatives but Willi was worried about them because they were lovely people and part of our family. He worried what might become of them.

Now Willi was gone, I had no way of knowing what had happened to them. Mutti would never speak about my father and his family. After this, I knew she would never tell me anything about that branch of my family anyway, out of fear and to protect me. My cousin might have dodged death on the front line but had he escaped the Gestapo? Had they all suffered the same fate as Frau Andree? How could good people be treated this way?

I saw less of Heinrich as the weather warmed. He was studying for his final exams, working more than ever at the hospital – which was promising – so I was a little further down his list of priorities.

'What will we do if the hospital doesn't offer you a permanent job?' I asked Heinrich as we strolled down Leopoldstrasse, the huge poplars that lined the boulevard bright with their new green leaves. I had asked him to join me for a walk, promising to help him study and make it worth his while. Brightly coloured buildings reminiscent of the artistic feel of Schwabing sat side by side with those more classically designed. It was one of the reasons I loved living here, a melting pot for so many different influences. I prayed that the war would not touch this ancient enclave of creativity.

'I'm a junior doctor, I'm less expensive and I think I've proven I can do my job. I really don't think it will be a problem. And part-time or casual shifts will work to start,' Heinrich said with his usual pragmatism. I knew no permanent job was guaranteed but Heinrich was fast becoming part of the furniture at the hospital, available to cover any of the shifts needed. I prayed that would keep him safe and away from the front line and another field hospital.

'But what if?' I persisted.

Heinrich thought for a moment, his hands behind his back as he continued walking. 'There are other hospitals in München, not as convenient, but there is always plenty of work. Failing that, there are the military hospitals. They need doctors for surgery and rehabilitation more than ever. If I have to, I can use that as a stepping stone. The main thing is to have a job that shows I'm indispensable, that prevents me from being transferred to the front again.'

I grasped Heinrich's arm tightly and we stopped walking. 'I couldn't bear to lose you. I know we're supposed to sacrifice ourselves gladly for the Fatherland but you've done your duty on the front. Nobody can deny that you continue to support our country and the war by aiding civilians and soldiers here at home. Surely anyone can see that.'

Heinrich hugged me close and the street noise disappeared. 'It will be all right. You'll see.'

I realised there was nothing I could do but trust his judgement and hope he was right. Life was to be enjoyed and on a day like this, we had to make the most of it.

'Come on, give me your book and astound me with your knowledge,' I said. 'Time to test you!'

By the time we reached the Englischer Garten, I was quizzing him on diseases.

'Tell me about the diseases of the kidneys,' I said. Heinrich recited the list correctly and confidently, grinning like a Cheshire cat.

'Time for my reward,' he said, grabbing my hand and pulling me towards a copse of beeches.

'Wait,' I exclaimed, laughing. 'You haven't finished.'

'Oh, yes I have, and you know it. Come on, time to play.' He led me into the cool privacy of the small woodland.

'But you have so much more to do.'

'All work and no play makes a very dull boy.' He pushed me against a tree trunk, leaning against me and preventing my escape, the knobbly bark hard and scratchy against my back.

'You're my captive now,' he murmured, kissing me with gentle, whisper-like caresses, his soft lips on my mouth, my cheeks, my throat and shoulders. I had no reply for him, lost to the exquisite sensations he elicited in me, oblivious to my surroundings.

Seeing what it did to me, he pushed me further, his hand lightly skimming over my blouse and erect nipples, making me groan softly.

'That will do for now,' I whispered in his ear before pulling away into the bright sunlight. I was hot, bothered and more than a little disconcerted, but we had promised each other we would wait.

'Oh, come on, I know you want more.' His eyes glittered like a tiger watching its prey. Mesmerised, I stood mute and paralysed, unable to say no.

Suddenly he was crushing me against a tree. His lips, warm and supple, found mine, coaxing and demanding in turn. It made me feel heavy, light-headed and weak all at once – a rush of desire, the same I'd felt when I'd met the oberinspektor and von Stauffenberg. Finally it was Heinrich inspiring those feelings in me.

Only his weight against me stopped me from sliding down the tree. His roving hands cupped my buttocks to fit me to him like a puzzle piece and I felt his manhood hard against my belly. His hands continued up to gently graze my nipples until I felt a throbbing much lower down, deep within. He pressed the heel of his hand between my legs, intensifying the throbbing and making me gasp. I knew we had to stop. I didn't want to, but I broke from the kiss. Heinrich's smouldering eyes met mine and I could see the urgency there.

'This is just the beginning.' Heinrich's voice was low and throaty. 'You did say it would be worth my while but I want to make it worth your while too. Keep that in mind until our wedding day. I will wait, but expect no mercy then!' He kissed me with restraint before releasing me from the tree.

Trembling and flushed, I stumbled away, disoriented and slightly dishevelled. He watched me with hooded eyes, still dressed immaculately in suit and tie. Taking pity on me, he grasped my arm and held me steady while I straightened my clothes and composed myself enough to continue on the path once more. It serves you right, I thought, making promises you could never keep.

5

A change in the organisation of the high command of the military early in 1944 made no real difference to us in the office, although shortly after, there seemed to be a gearing up in activity at many of the airfields. By April, our main airfields at Riem, Neubiberg, Schleissheim and Bad Aibling had established airfield commands. The requests for plane parts, supplies and new aircraft grew each week and I struggled to keep on top of the collated lists and reports but I continued to work hard at my job, learning as much as I could to help the oberinspektor. He was happy to explain technical matters to me. How the different properties of each aircraft and its optimal uses for our zone transcribed into the performance statistics and requisitions lists I typed every few days.

About this time, I heard stirrings, filtered through the gossip channels of the office girls, that Germany was losing the war. We all knew how difficult it was on the Eastern Front but most of us still had confidence that the Führer had a plan and would turn the tide at the perfect time in spectacular fashion. All the reports over the wireless, at the cinema and in the local newspapers stated emphatically that Germany was winning the war. Slowly to be sure, but winning all the same, and I had no reason to doubt those reports. Our Führer knew what he was doing. At the end of this war, Germany would be transformed into the great nation it had been before the Treaty of Versailles. German pride would be restored.

'I'm not so sure,' whispered Bettina one lunch break. 'Magda's cousin has been seeing a high-ranking officer in the Heer. She wouldn't say who, but apparently he told her that things are not good for Germany right now. After our defeat at Kiev, we've continued to lose ground to the Russians and they've been slowly marching west.' She stopped as other office girls walked into the lunchroom. We were prohibited from speaking about military matters or mentioning anything contrary to the news reports the Reich distributed each week but it didn't stop the worried whispers continuing around the office.

'It doesn't add up,' I said, as I walked down the corridor with Bettina. 'It's totally different to what all the news reports have been saying.'

'Do you really think news like that would be released to the general public? Imagine the panic.'

I shook my head. She was right of course. Magda's cousin wasn't the first source of disturbing stories about Germany's losses and how the tide of the war had turned against us.

Bettina gestured towards the bathroom as she pushed open the door. I frowned, wondering what else she had to tell me, and followed her in. Bettina checked each stall to make sure they were empty. When she turned back to me, she looked worried.

'This is the thing that the Heer officer told Magda's cousin that really makes me wonder. He told her not to go to Paris for work. He told her to stay in Germany. When she pushed him for a reason, he finally told her that he had reason to believe the Americans were set to join the British to land forces on French soil and begin their attack against Germany.'

'No,' I said, aghast. 'That can't be right.' I knew the might of the Americans had already helped the British win decisive battles in North Africa and were now making a difference to the fight in Italy, causing our forces to retreat further north towards Rome. It did not bode well if they had joined forces with Britain to march across France towards Germany.

'That's what I said too, but Magda assured me that it's what he told her cousin and she has made some excuse not to go to Paris.'

I stared at Bettina, who was evidently relieved that she had been able to share the burden of this terrible piece of news. Our lives would be turned upside down. I took Bettina's hands, clammy with worry. 'Look at it logically. Surely we would have heard something here and we haven't.'

Bettina nodded. 'Yes, but that doesn't mean it's not true. Keep your ears open. We'll have to see if we hear anything.'

'All right,' I said. 'But I'm sure it's all just Chinese whispers.'

Only weeks later, rumours of the American and British landing on the beaches of Normandy were all over the office. At first they spread in hushed whispers away from the officers. Shock, consternation and astonishment were evident on the faces of most of the office girls but also on the faces of the officers and staff in our department. Soon, the whole building was abuzz and it was impossible to prevent or contain the news. We learnt that the Luftwaffe had been taken completely by surprise because there had been no reconnaissance of the area. The initial shock at the truth of the situation was quickly replaced with a flurry of activity, as all efforts were focused on defending our Western Front.

'This changes everything,' Bettina muttered, as I handed her a report for the colonel. 'I hope you like coffee and cigarettes, because if we thought we were working hard before, now we'll be lucky to see our beds. Welcome to your new home.'

'They may have landed on European shores but they won't get any further than that,' I said confidently.

'I hope you're right.' Bettina looked up from her typing, her brown eyes large with apprehension. 'Otherwise our world is about to change drastically and I don't think we're going to like it.'

The Allied landing soon became common knowledge, with speculation and trepidation simmering all over München. Fear blossomed silently on the streets. Nobody dared voice the worry that we were not winning the war, that we couldn't keep the Allies at bay, but the whispers made their way through the city nonetheless, like a deadly infection. Among my parents' friends, most of whom had seen Germany threatened before, there was deep anger, voiced only behind closed doors – anger that our country was threatened once again, anger about the inevitable loss of life that defending our homeland would produce.

Mutti felt the same way. Vati tried to calm her with his pragmatism, assuring her that much of our military resources were now thrust into the protection and defence of the Reich. Germany was strong and would prevail. I believed him too; I could see the evidence of that at work.

Only Herr Schmitt and Hilde the cook remained with us now. The other servants had been let go, returning to help their families. Vati refused to hire Polish workers at a fraction of the cost. 'We'll manage until after the war,' he told us.

Those warm summer days passed in a blur. I was up early in the mornings, my only joy the walk to work through the gardens that reminded me the world still continued outside of our frantic office building. Vati had arranged for Herr Schmitt to drive me home at night and I often dozed in the spacious backseat. Working so hard meant I rarely had to put up with Mutti's tirades, which fell squarely into Vati's lap. He and I worried about the toll the war was exacting on her.

The oberinspektor had always smoked but now his office was permanently blanketed in haze. His face was constantly drawn and pale, dark smudges beneath his eyes, and he slumped wearily in his chair.

'Oberinspektor, have you been getting enough sleep?' I asked one morning as I brought him a fresh cup of coffee.

'Ah, thank you,' he said, smiling weakly as he picked up the coffee and sipped. 'This keeps me going – and those,' he said, gesturing to the cigarettes on his desk. We still had real coffee in the office and cigarettes were in plentiful supply.

I wrinkled my nose with disgust as I picked up the ashtray filled with twisted butts and flakes of ash.

'I'll cut back soon,' he said apologetically. 'When things slow down and I have time to sleep.'

'I know.' I moved to the small window and opened it a little to allow the stench to escape and fill the room with the warm summer air. 'Keep the window open for a while. It'll help.'

'I realise you've been working long hours too. I couldn't manage without you.'

My eyes widened, not expecting his confession. I turned to face him, then shrugged and smiled, a little embarrassed. 'It's the least I can do. If I can ease your workload, then I know I'm doing something worthwhile.'

'It helps if we can all work together at times like this.' He ran his hand through his hair, pushing the dark strands that had fallen onto his furrowed forehead off his face. I had never seen him with a hair out of place before.

'What do you think will happen? Are we losing the war?'

His dark eyebrows shot up in surprise. Then he scrutinised me for a moment, before he leant back in his chair and sighed.

'I don't know. It's too early to tell for sure, but it's not looking good for us.'

I stared back at him, waiting for him to finish, wanting him to trust me as I did him.

'I don't know that the Führer's strategy has paid off. I've heard that generals who were against our troops remaining on the Eastern Front when it was clear that we were losing and would incur terrible losses, were removed from their postings. Maybe he should have listened to men with military experience. Perhaps now we would have more men on our Western Front to repel the Allied push.'

'Don't say such things,' I whispered in a rush. Fear bloomed through my body like drops of blood staining water. 'What you say might be true but if anyone hears you ... You know Bettina's cousin's husband was hauled away by the Gestapo for speaking out against the Führer to one of his best friends.'

'I know.' His mouth was set into a grim line. 'I wouldn't be so foolish to repeat this to anyone else but I wanted you to have my honest opinion.' His green eyes dared me to tell him he was wrong to believe in me. A warm glow filled me, despite my fear for him. He trusted me with his life.

'Thank you,' I said softly. 'I value your opinion a great deal.' My eyes filled with tears and I turned abruptly and left the room, so he would not see how much his trust meant to me.

As I emptied the stinking ashtray, I pushed my joy to one side as I mulled over the oberinspektor's appraisal. It was more realistic than what Vati had told Mutti, although the consequences were more frightening. For the first time, I entertained the possibility of Germany losing the war. I shivered, a vague sense of unease coalescing into a hard ball of fear in my stomach.

Lying in bed, thinking of Heinrich, too tired to sleep, I fiddled with the locket around my neck; one side held a tiny photo of Mutti and Vati, the other with one of Heinrich. He had finished his final exam that day. I hadn't had a chance to speak to him and hoped he was relieved and happy. All he needed now was his piece of paper to say he had graduated, and to be offered that permanent position at the hospital. We were getting married in a little over a month and were on the brink of making our dreams come true. My wedding dress hung in my closet, ready to wear.

Suddenly the air-raid sirens screeched into the still night. I sighed, my joyful musings dissipating into thin air. This was all I needed, a night with no sleep. I slid out of bed, dragged on my coat and picked up the small suitcase with my essentials by my door.

'Mutti,' I yelled down the hallway. 'Come on, we have to go.' I stood at the top of the stairs waiting for her. 'Mutti!' I shouted again.

Dropping the suitcase, I strode impatiently to my mother's bedroom and opened her door. She was still in bed, an eye pillow over her eyes, and hadn't stirred. I rushed over and shook her. 'Mutti,' I called gruffly, removing the blindfold. 'Come on, there's an air-raid.'

My mother opened her eyes a crack. 'What's wrong? Why have you woken me?'

'Can't you hear the sirens?'

She just stared blankly at me and began to close her eyes.

'Mutti, no, come on!' I shook her roughly and her eyelids fluttered open.

'Here, sit up,' I said, helping her upright, her body like a rag doll's. 'Did you take something before bed?' I glanced at her nightstand and saw a bottle of sleeping tablets. 'Oh no.' I swung her legs over the side of the bed and got her sitting. 'We have to go now.'

'I can't sleep when your father's away,' she muttered, her blue eyes dull. Mutti's temper had frayed almost to breaking point when Vati was called to Berlin with his superior.

'I'll help you.' I grabbed her under the arms and helped steady her as I pulled her up.

'I'm so tired,' said Mutti, as she shuffled into her slippers.

'You have to walk now. Can you hear the sirens? We have to go,' I said urgently, panic beginning to blossom in my belly. I grabbed her coat, draping it over her shoulders and tying it at the waist before helping her to the door. 'All right now?'

Mutti nodded and grasped the banister to walk down the stairs a little unsteadily while I held her other arm and brought the suitcase.

We were among the last to make it to the air-raid shelter. It was already packed with people and the sour scent hit me like a physical blow. The warden nodded as we made our way past him.

'Ah, there you are,' called a neighbour. She patted a spot next to her on the wooden bench. 'I was beginning to worry what had happened to you.'

Mutti and I sat down next to her. 'Thank you, Elli,' said Mutti.

The ominous drone of planes overhead began and a deep thrumming seemed to vibrate in my bones, even here underground. It was silent in the shelter, bodies shuffling as if trying to shrink from the threat in the sky, seeking protection with those next to them, as we waited for what came next. I looked at my mother, her eyes wide, mirroring my concern. The planes were very close. She reached for my hand and I held hers tightly.

I remember looking up at the ceiling, feeling so helpless, wishing I could see through it to what was happening outside. The bare light bulbs above us shone weakly, giving us some security in the darkness, before the whistling of the falling bombs reached our ears. The blast of the detonation followed quickly, and the ground shook around us. The howl of wind that rushed in their wake was enough to conjure up images of hell. We were battered relentlessly, only short periods of sanity between each bombing run when we became aware of the crying, the nervous coughing, the hysterical outbursts. Children were pressed tightly against their mothers, their little faces pale and streaked with tears. Some people rocked where they sat, eyes blank with terror, while others comforted the stricken with arms around shoulders and softly spoken words. The air-raid warden and his committee cast worried looks at the walls and ceiling but they were holding so far.

Time became meaningless. Our existence shrank to a pinpoint of surviving that moment. No other thoughts mattered – that basement became our world. Mutti and I clung to each other. I felt her shudder with each new explosion and, glimpsing the wildness in her eyes, I knew she was close to breaking point. I closed my eyes briefly during a lull to strengthen my resolve and keep my own terror at bay. I was all Mutti had and it wouldn't do her any good if I fell apart now. I squeezed her hand, glancing across, and she smiled weakly at me. 'It will be over soon, Mutti,' I whispered. A new explosion rocked the earth and the lights went out. Screams rent the air before the air warden's voice called through the commotion, 'It's all right. Everyone calm down. We have candles and we will have light in a moment.'

Sure enough, flickering light moved between the rows of seats as the warden's men handed out candles. As I took a thick candle from gnarled fingers, we heard a whoosh and roaring outside the shelter.

'Firebombing,' the old man muttered in disgust before walking rapidly back to the warden.

Mutti was trembling and whimpering softly. The shadows from the flickering flame made her face seem sunken, the odd angles garish and enhancing the nightmarish atmosphere that surrounded us.

'Be strong, Mutti,' I whispered in her ear. 'Be strong for Vati and me.'

She nodded and the whimpering stopped. I kissed the top of her frizzy head and we waited until the sound of bombs exploding disappeared, replaced with the distant crashing of what must have been buildings collapsing from the fire. Dread filled my heart as I wondered what we would find when we were allowed to leave.

Finally, after the all-clear was given, we plodded out of the shelter to find the city on fire. The night sky was blood red, the air filled with smoke. We stood rooted to the spot at the sight of fires raging only a few blocks away. Burning embers floating through the air fell on exposed skin, the cries and yelps breaking us from the spell. People began coughing as the smoke reached their lungs.

'Cover your mouth and nose and go to your homes,' ordered the warden. 'It will be safer there.'

Mutti and I, along with our neighbours, stumbled back to our apartments, relieved the building was still intact but apprehensive of facing the new day, which would show us the extent of the damage.

The air-raids continued for about a week. Heinrich and his family were unscathed, their home intact, and he came to visit every day to make sure Mutti and I were safe. Hilde didn't return to work – her daughter had been killed in the bombings and her grandchildren were orphans and needed her care. They left the city with the streams of evacuees to the relative safety of the countryside. Herr Schmitt also came back to us unscathed, much to our relief, and Heinrich's too. He didn't like us alone while Vati was away.

The city was in chaos. Every day, I heard more reports of traffic diversions, trams out of action, and electricity, gas and water being cut off in parts of the city. Walking to and from work, which had, thank God in Heaven, sustained no damage, I skirted around bomb craters and stepped over rubble on the footpaths next to once beautiful buildings in ruins, horrified by the blackened, twisted shells and the shards of broken glass crunching underfoot. There was dust everywhere. It was eerie and surreal.

Teams of workers, many in striped prison uniforms, moved from site to site clearing the debris, repairing essential services and shoring up buildings where they could. Bulldozers came in to demolish what was unsafe. I often found my cheeks wet with tears, and became weak at the knees at the sight of the dead, dug from the ruins and laid out for identification.

Volunteers from the National Socialist People's Welfare congregated in the worst affected districts, setting up soup kitchens and centres offering emergency first aid and accommodation. The vacant expression of shock on many faces as they wandered around lost and the hysterical tears of those who had endured more grief than they could bear clenched my heart with overwhelming sorrow. How could the dignified citizens of München be reduced to this? Why weren't we protecting our people better? Why weren't we fighting off these attacks?

I thought of the oberinspektor's words more often. Our hard work seemed to be having little impact on German life and yet we couldn't just give in to defeat and loss. We would find a way to continue, to live our lives and survive whatever the Allies threw at us. Maybe the tide of the war had turned against us but we would do everything in our power to turn it to our favour once again. We would fight for our survival.

We worked long hours to cover for those who were needed at home, and one day, the oberinspektor sent me home early to get some rest.

I found strangers in our parlour.

'What are you doing here?' asked an old woman, grey hair poking through her headscarf.

'I live here,' I retorted. 'What are you doing here?'

'I live here too,' replied the woman, scowling.

'What are you talking about?'

The woman thrust her chin in the air. 'My family has the right to be here. We were bombed out and my daughter was killed. The city officials have given us this place to live in. This is our home now.'

I stared at the woman as if I had been slapped across the face. 'Is my mother here?'

The woman shrugged and turned away.

In a daze, I moved from room to room, looking for my mother. Other families were squatting in the living areas, our furniture covered in their meagre belongings and pushed to one side to accommodate bedding. Even Herr Schmitt's room was occupied.

'Get out,' growled a heavily pregnant girl in a state of undress.

'You're trespassing,' hissed another shrunken figure.

Some just stared at me, as shocked as I was at their situation, their eyes blank and movements automatic. I stumbled away, bewildered and unable to believe that I was being made to feel like I didn't belong in my own home.

I found Mutti in her bedroom, her best furniture and Turkish rugs crammed into the room. She was lying on her bed, pale and quivering, her cheeks marked by tears.

'Mutti. What's going on? Why are all these people here?'

'The city has requisitioned our apartment,' she said. 'We now have the use of only two rooms and we were lucky to get that. The rest have been given to families who have lost their homes in the bombings.' She looked up at me then, anguish clouding her eyes. 'I don't mind helping those poor souls who have lost everything but I was given no choice in the matter.'

'Does Vati know?'

'I was handed an official order.' She gestured to the paper on her nightstand. 'They tell me that Vati approved this but he's not here, is he? Then these families arrived to take over my home.' Mutti sat on the edge of the bed and started to cry again, shaking her head. 'I couldn't do a thing about it. Herr Schmitt helped me move my best pieces of furniture in here, the artworks and my silver and crystal, but the rest will be ruined. There are already big scratches on the parquetry floors from where they've pushed furniture out of the way.'

A sudden spear of panic shot through me, making my throat close. 'The photos? The ones of the boys?'

'Yes, I got all the photos. They were the first things I thought of and the last portraits you took of Ludwig and Willi are still safe in the suitcase.'

I sighed with relief. 'Thank you, Mutti.' I squeezed her hand. 'Where's Herr Schmitt? What will he do?'

'He's gone to buy new locks for me. He said he'll move in with his sister, but he's promised to come whenever we need help. I can't go anywhere for peace except in here. Even the kitchen I have to share, and some of our rations have disappeared. We'll have to keep everything in here.'

'That's ridiculous,' I said, not able to believe how thoughtlessly this had been handled. If only Mutti had been given more time to make appropriate arrangements. I slumped to the bed next to her and picked up the order. 'I can't understand why Vati would agree to this. Why didn't he tell us?'

'I can't even contact him – the telephone lines are down. I'm not sure when he will be coming home.'

'Vati will be home in a few more days, but don't worry, I'll find out what's going on.' I wrapped my arms around her. My father had managed to contact me a few days earlier to make sure we were safe after the spate of bombings but hadn't said anything about the apartment.

Later, when Mutti had calmed down a little, I tried to get in touch with Vati. I couldn't get through to him but I managed to speak to his office, and was told that Wehrmacht officers were now expected to open their homes to the bombing victims – the emergency accommodation in and around the city was full and unable to cope with the number of evacuees. The Wehrmacht had to set a good example and each officer had to provide as many rooms as possible, at least until further housing had been built or could be made accessible. Those who were prepared to stay within München were now being directed by municipal officials to the homes where rooms were available.

I discovered that people were being pressured all over the city to give up their rooms to cope with the burden of homeless on the city. Heinrich called by and he was horrified by our situation. He couldn't understand why we didn't complain that we needed more space or use our connections to retain a more genteel living arrangement. His parents had 'voluntarily' offered a few rooms in their home. They were not happy about it, sharing their home with 'commoners', as he called them. At least they were able to choose what rooms to keep and how many – this time – and they were able to retain their privacy by sectioning off their area. I knew complaining would make no difference and these people deserved a roof over their heads. We would just have to manage until more housing became obtainable. Surely it wouldn't be for that long?

I made appointments to discuss our situation with the appropriate party and municipal officials in order to fully understand our obligations to our new tenants. I spent hours in a queue waiting to be informed that my parents would be compensated for the use of our home, with rent payable for each room in use, cooking facilities and heating costs. I was assured that, under the Evacuee Family Support program, each of the families was more than adequately subsidised to meet their needs and altered living circumstances without impinging on our family any further. I filled in the forms to register our claim.

Tania Blanchard

Mutti wasn't up to it, so I met with the new residents in the foyer, standing on the bottom step of the staircase. They stared at me warily, exhaustion lining their faces, ignoring children that pulled at their clothes. I would have to tread carefully if I was going to make this situation work. My neck and shoulders were coiled tight.

'My name is Fräulein von Klein. This is my apartment. I'm sorry for the loss that each of you has experienced and I welcome you into our home.' There was a murmur through the group but nobody stepped forward to speak; only expectant faces were raised to me, waiting to hear what I said next. I kept myself from wiping my sweaty palms on my skirt.

'I've spoken to the officials. The People's Welfare and the city will be sending beds, additional furniture and household goods to make you all more comfortable.'

Now there were relieved looks and nods. I continued while I was ahead, the strain of responsibility making my stomach roil with nausea.

'I will set up a roster for the use of the kitchen for each family, including my parents and myself, and designate areas for each family's kitchenware and food. The only way this will work is if we all stick to the schedule and respect each other's space and possessions.' A few dubious faces looked to interject but I kept speaking. 'I will be inspecting each of the rooms once a week for general cleanliness and damage. If I find any problems, I have been instructed to forward my complaints to the city. Depending on the ruling by the official in charge of disputes, the tenant may risk losing their room. I pray it never comes to that. Any problems or concerns you have about the apartment, please bring to the attention of myself or either of my parents and we will strive to resolve them as quickly as possible.'

Nobody said anything but I could feel the waves of anger and bitterness roll towards me. I felt faint but I smiled, wanting to appease my new neighbours.

'If there is anything I can help you with, please ask. I believe that if we all respect each other we can live harmoniously under one roof.' I tried to catch as many eyes as I could but it was too early for trust. Many turned abruptly away, returning to the sanctuary of their room, while others looked at me with indifference. Only one young girl smiled shyly at me before she was pulled away by an older woman. I was left standing on the bottom of the stairs. I took a deep breath. At least it was done. Time would tell if we could all get along.

Each day of these new living arrangements began with my guilt at leaving Mutti behind to manage on her own and keep a wide berth of the residents. With Hilde gone, she reluctantly resumed the responsibilities of shopping and cooking. Herr Schmitt and his sister accompanied her to the market the first couple of times, to show her the best places to go, where to find the freshest produce. But it was going to take some time for Mutti to brush up on her cooking skills and I was glad I had work to keep me busy and that I could eat at the office.

Vati arrived home, shocked to find what had happened in his absence. I was the first to greet him in the privacy of our two little rooms, away from the cold stares of the new residents.

'Lotte,' he said, gathering me into his arms. 'I'm sorry I had to leave you both for so long.'

It felt good to be in the protection of his embrace and I felt myself sag – now I didn't have to bear sole responsibility for my mother's safety and the new arrangements of our home.

Vati grasped my shoulders and looked into my face, his hazel eyes misty with emotion. 'I'm so proud of you.'

'What do you mean, Vati?'

'You've looked after Mutti and managed the household and all of its new changes on your own, even dealing with the city officials. I know many men who would have gone to pieces at the prospect of having to make arrangements for strangers to live in their home.'

'It had to be done, and Mutti wasn't up to it.'

'I know, my *liebchen*.' He kissed me on the forehead. 'Thank you.'

My mother entered the room. She dropped her string bags full of shopping with a small cry and flung herself into his arms. 'You were only supposed to be gone a few days.'

'We couldn't leave Berlin until the confusion about the Führer had been sorted out.'

'Do you know what happened exactly, Vati?' I remembered the day when, during the bombing campaign and our personal horror, Bettina called me over as I arrived at work.

'Have you heard?' she'd asked with a look of anticipation. 'The radio announcement last night?'

'We didn't have electricity last night.'

'There was a news flash announcing the attempted assassination of the Führer.'

'Is he all right?' I'd gasped, grabbing her arm. I couldn't imagine a world without him. What would we do if he was gone?

'He's fine.'

I had placed my hand over my heart in relief. 'Who would do such a thing?'

'Apparently some of the top Wehrmacht officers.' Bettina had shaken her head in wonder. 'There're no more details yet. We'll have to wait to learn more, I suppose. There'll be hell to pay.'

'Yes, there will.'

Later, I had listened to the Führer address the nation, beside myself with joy at the sound of the Führer's voice, as full of life and passionate as ever. A bomb had been detonated in the Wolf's Lair but he had sustained only minor injuries. He announced that a plot had been uncovered involving high-ranking members of the General Staff and promised revenge on the conspirators. I couldn't believe it. The Führer named names and I heard one I knew: Claus von Stauffenberg. I felt sick to the core. It couldn't be true. He was a patriot, a German hero, not a traitor and criminal. I still remembered the thrill I'd received from the touch of that gallant man who had addressed me at the party all those months ago. It couldn't be him.

'Was Colonel von Stauffenberg really involved?' I now asked my father.

'Yes, he was, and he died for his role in this plot.'

'He seemed so courageous and gracious that night I met him. He was a hero.'

'There were many high-ranking men there, good, decent men who have been executed. Killed like common criminals.' He looked sad.

'But they were, Vati,' I said, my BDM lessons taking over, galvanising me. I was steadfast in my conviction. 'It's treason to plot against the Führer.'

'Many didn't think so,' said Vati, lowering his voice.

'They had everything,' I said impatiently. 'Influence, power, the ear of the Führer. Why would they throw it all away and plot against the man who gave it all to them? The man who has single-handedly brought this country out of the shadows and reignited our national pride?'

'Have you quite finished?' snapped my mother, putting the empty shopping bags on the bed. 'Let your father talk.'

I looked at her, puzzled by her outburst. 'It's just such a waste of good men,' I whispered, dropping into a chair. 'We need good leaders and soldiers on Germany's side more than ever.' I thought of my brothers and ran my hand through my hair in frustration.

Vati sat next to me at the little table and grasped my hand. 'They believed they were working for Germany,' he said softly.

'What do you mean?'

'They blamed the Führer for all the bad decisions that have been made, particularly those that have caused such losses on the Eastern Front, decisions that have turned the course of this war.'

'But how can they blame him? Surely he only acts on the information he's given by his advisors? They're the ones who should be blamed. The Führer has only ever acted in Germany's best interest.' I looked from my father to my mother standing next to him and back again. Neither of them seemed convinced and that shocked me more than the confirmation of Stauffenberg's complicity. 'You can't agree with them.'

My mother shrugged. 'This war has gone on long enough. Something needs to change.'

'I don't think we'll ever know to what extent the Führer's been involved in the disastrous decisions that have been made on Germany's behalf.' Vati paled, aware of the danger inherent in his words, looking suddenly old. 'But with the Führer gone, there might have been an opportunity to end this war, save the lives of countless others and save what's left of Germany.' He sighed. 'That's all speculation now anyway.'

'Don't talk like that, even here. It's too risky ... You weren't involved were you?' I asked, my stomach clenching in terror.

Vati smiled wearily. 'No, I wasn't. I heard talk, of course, but I never believed it would amount to anything. Those men suffered the ultimate price for their actions but I don't believe they were acting against Germany. Many were good, upstanding men from military families, men I knew well and many I will grieve. Their loss is Germany's loss too.'

I nodded, remembering the oberinspektor's comments about Stalingrad and about the generals on the Eastern Front, and frowned. Both men were trying to tell me the same thing, but how could our beloved Führer be responsible for Germany's losses?

'I think we need to prepare ourselves for the inevitable,' Vati said. 'The Americans are now on European soil and march across France toward us. In the east, Lemberg has been taken by the Red Army and they march west across Poland. I don't see how we can win this war.'

'We have to win,' I whispered desperately. 'The Führer promised. Germany deserves to win. We've sacrificed so much.'

'Ah, Lotte,' murmured my father, smoothing the hair from my face. 'It's time for you to grow up and face the facts. I will do everything to keep you and your mother safe but we must be prepared.'

Discomfort swirled in my belly. I entertained the possibility that my father might be right although it went against everything I held true. I glanced at my mother, and she looked defeated too.

'Not again,' she said. Her face creased in consternation and I could tell that she was thinking back to the end of the last war and all the hardships it had brought.

I thought things couldn't get much worse, but I was wrong. Heinrich arrived at our door one evening not long before the wedding. He looked alarmingly pale and was breathing heavily, as though he'd been running.

'What's wrong?' I asked as I pulled him into our rooms. He almost collapsed onto the chair and held out an envelope, trembling. He looked at me with such despair that my throat closed.

'I received this today.'

I took the envelope and opened it carefully, afraid it would explode in my hands.

Heinrich watched warily as I slid out the letter but the strain became too much for him. 'I've been sent to the front,' he blurted. 'I leave tomorrow.'

The paper slipped from my hands. I made no move to pick it up as I stared into Heinrich's eyes and felt the blood drain from my face. 'No! You can't go. They need you here.'

He shook his head slowly. 'I'm sorry, but I can't do anything about it.'

I picked up the letter. It was hard to believe that something that looked so official could destroy our hopes so completely.

'The medical corps,' I read. 'Poland . . . you join the unit in Poland.' Tears stung my eyes, as I looked up to see Heinrich's beloved face tight with anguish. 'The Eastern Front,' I added unnecessarily, but it was something we both needed to hear. Heinrich nodded.

I sat on his lap, hugging him fiercely, as if I could protect him from this duty and the danger it posed for him. He held me tightly but could not stop the fine trembling of his body. He had only just been able to quiet his demons and now they would have full reign again.

'We were so close,' he muttered. 'All I want is to be married to you and to save lives.'

'We will have that life,' I whispered to him, my face pressed against his, the scratchy roughness of the day's stubble wet from my tears. 'It will be over before you know it. Just come home safe.'

'You'll wait for me?'

'You know I will. I love you. You're my other half. I can't do without you. Come home to me and we'll live the life we've dreamed of.'

Heinrich sighed and wrapped his arms around my waist, settling me more firmly on his lap. Even now, he couldn't hide his desire. 'The wedding. All the work you've put into it . . .'

'The plans will wait until you come home. This war will be over soon and we can marry without the worry of it hanging over our heads.' I nestled against him, determined to imprint the feel of him against my skin. I didn't want to talk any more. We'd been through this before and there was nothing else to say. Pressing my lips to his, I sought oblivion, wanting the memory of his love to be the thing I would remember, the thing that would sustain me through the long months until he returned.

Heinrich kissed me, a long, passionate, lingering kiss filled with promise.

'Let me stay,' he breathed. 'I want you close and more than kisses to remember you by.'

I pulled away. I was tempted to give in to desire but I had to be strong. I moved to put some distance between us before I succumbed, but saw a look of such longing in his eyes that I caught my breath. Then I shook my head.

'My parents.'

'They're not home. They need never know.' He reached for me, drawing me in.

'I can't disrespect my parents, especially under their roof.'

'We can go anywhere,' he said, clutching me frantically. 'We are promised to each other.'

'No, Heinrich.' I touched his cheek. 'I want us to do this properly. I don't want you to leave, having taken your pleasure in a few furious moments of desperation. What if I were to become pregnant?' I felt the flame of embarrassment rise up my cheeks but kissed him gently. 'We'll have something special to look forward to on our wedding day. I know it will be the most wonderful night.' I blushed even further. Heinrich's nearness and the thought of being with him were causing me not to think straight.

Heinrich stood, setting me on my feet without looking me in the eye. 'I have to go. I still have to pack. The train leaves in the morning.' His voice was suddenly cool.

'Heinrich!' I threw my arms around him and kissed him once more. He pulled away holding my hand as if he couldn't bear to break all contact just yet.

'Give your parents my best wishes. Tell them I will come home and become their son-in-law soon.' He let go of my hand.

'Come back safely to me.' I could barely get the words out.

'I will, I promise.' He stood at the door, staring at me for a moment, as if memorising every detail of my face, as I did with his. Then he was gone, the door clicking closed behind him.

6

I was inconsolable. The date of our wedding had come and gone. Crying in Mutti's arms did nothing to ease the gnawing ache that had taken up residence inside me. Vati's assurances that Heinrich would be home soon didn't fill the hollowness I felt. I knew they were worried about me. I don't know how Mutti did it; she not only had to put up with me but Tante Klara's fretful visits, beside herself with fear at losing her only child, all while cancelling our plans, their dream wedding now in mothballs.

Bettina consoled me in her way by telling all the office girls of Heinrich's posting and the postponement of my wedding. They lavished me with extra attention for a while but this was a commonplace occurrence in the war and their sympathies quickly moved on. The oberinspektor was kind and compassionate while remaining as courteous and professional as always. I moved listlessly from task to task, keeping busy, trying not to think. Nights were the worst, when images of Heinrich swam before my closed lids. Despite my fervent prayers to God, fears for his safety festered in my imagination until finally I'd manage to snatch a few hours of sleep as the dawn approached.

I missed Heinrich but at least he was still writing to me regularly. Once their company had regrouped in Poland, his unit had been sent to Latvia. That's all he could tell me, except that there were plenty of casualties and he had been busy performing surgery after surgery, often on his own. When his patients died, he never knew if it was his own inexperience or the futility of the surgery. I knew how hard his situation was but all I could do was try to distract him with news from home, encourage him to stay strong and hope that he would return soon. I asked God to keep Heinrich safe and bring him home alive and in one piece.

Then the oberinspektor informed me he was taking leave to visit his family.

'I'm worried about them,' he said one morning as I placed a fresh coffee on his desk. 'My daughter's sick, she's been vomiting for days. She's only nine years old and such a tiny thing anyway.'

'Has she seen the doctor?' I asked automatically, picking up the files from his desk.

'Of course, but he doesn't know what's wrong. She's been burning up with fever but hasn't responded to treatment. Who knows what I'll find when I get there?'

'I'm so sorry.'

'I've called a friend who's still in Sagan and has military connections to make sure everything has been done to help her, even if it means admitting her to hospital. There's nothing else I can do until I get there.' He ran his fingers through his hair, a sure sign of his frustration.

'Is she with her mother?' I asked tentatively, not sure I should be delving into his personal matters.

'Yes,' he said, sighing. 'Her mother wants me to fix this when the problem is that she leaves the children to their own devices too much. I know that she works but it seems that she's never in any hurry to get home to them.'

'Oh.' I wondered if I'd just opened a festering wound, surprised at the oberinspektor's frankness. 'I didn't mean to pry.'

The oberinspektor shook his head. 'No, it's just me. I'm worried for them. You may remember that I told you that I had been posted in Lemberg earlier in the war?'

I nodded. 'I heard that it was taken by the Red Army recently,' I said. 'I thought of you.'

His eyes glittered, perhaps with tears. 'There were men with families still there that I knew. I don't know if they got out.' He paused, his brow creased and his face drawn. 'I want to put a plan in place for my family if they need to leave in a hurry. My wife has relatives in Berlin. That should be safe enough but first I have to get my daughter well enough to travel.'

'Do you really think it will come to that?'

'I honestly don't know,' he said wearily. 'I want to be prepared if it does.'

I remembered the conversation I'd had with my father after the Führer's attempted assassination. He believed then that Germany was losing the war. I wanted them both to be wrong. Heinrich was out there now and more than ever I desperately prayed that we were winning. I held my tongue. It wasn't my place to argue. 'I'll make sure the office runs smoothly until you return,' was all I said, picking up another full ashtray.

'I know you will.' The oberinspektor smiled. 'At least I can leave with peace of mind that you will manage efficiently in my absence.'

'You can rely on me,' I said woodenly. I turned to leave.

'Thank you for looking after me, Lotte.'

My back still to him, I stopped and nodded before closing the door behind me. It was the first time he had used my first name.

How much I missed the oberinspektor caught me by surprise. I supposed it was the fact that we had worked together so closely six days a week for a year, but I felt a little uncomfortable anyway. With the oberinspektor away, I kept staring at his office. I realised that I missed our meetings, where he would explain the latest technical data to me, or the logistics of why we would recommend approving or amending the requisitions that came in from various airfields. He had kept my mind off Heinrich and made me feel that I was doing something valuable to bring about Germany's victory. I appreciated being taken seriously and having my natural curiosity and thirst for knowledge and learning valued by him. His enthusiasm for the new generation aircraft, the Me 262 fighter jets and the Ar 234 bombers that were in the final stages of testing before widespread distribution to each Luftflotte, was infectious. His deep understanding of how these machines worked and their superiority to the older aircraft gave him an expertise some other technical officers did not have. But the oberinspektor was still a complete mystery to me in many respects. I knew almost nothing about him except in a work capacity.

News of the Americans moving ever closer across France and the Red Army drawing further west began to change the way we thought. From office talk, I learnt that concern about how we were faring in the war was felt right across München. Gone was the jubilation of the early war years. Despite the positive weekly news reels at the cinema, most people were now sceptical about the stories of our successes. The ominous rumbles whispered from family to family, neighbourhood to neighbourhood, fanned the restlessness that pervaded the city. Many began to seriously entertain the idea that we could lose the war.

Perhaps the biggest shock came when we learnt that Paris had fallen, liberated by the Americans. What was worse was that the Luftwaffe counter-attack had failed once again. Morale was low among the office girls.

'What did I tell you?' said Bettina, waving her fork around while we ate a late lunch in the staff dining hall one day. The long benches were almost empty. 'Lucky Magda's cousin didn't go to Paris.'

'Where will they stop?' I whispered.

Bettina stared at me for a second and shook her head. 'They won't stop! They'll keep coming until Germany has fallen and we have no chance of getting up again. There's something I heard someone say the other day: "Enjoy the war because the peace will be dreadful." It will be too, when it finally comes, but what can we do about it? Whether we win or lose, Germany is kaput.'

I crossed my knife and fork on my plate. 'Don't talk like that,' I said, anger boiling in me. 'That's defeatist. There's still hope, we haven't been beaten yet.'

'Open your eyes, Lotte! Most of Germany's resources are now dedicated to the Defence of the Reich. We're no longer on the offensive and we continue to lose the ground we gained earlier in the war on all fronts. How much longer until Germany itself is threatened?'

I stared at her, my anger draining away. Fear for Heinrich was a tight band around my chest and I was finding it hard to breathe.

It wasn't much longer at all before Germany itself was in peril. The oberinspektor came back to München towards the end of August with the news that the Red Army had crossed into Eastern Prussia and was officially on German soil. He asked me not to tell the other girls. We both knew panic would result once the news got out. We had so much work to catch up on but I found it hard to focus. The advance of the Red Army was concerning enough but my primary thoughts were for the immediate danger to Heinrich. He was there somewhere with the German army probably in retreat, trying not to be surrounded by the Russians. I could do nothing but continue to write to him regularly and wait for his responses. It was the only way I knew he was still alive and well.

A few days after the oberinspektor's return, I brought dinner up to his office so we could continue working through the backlog that had accumulated in his absence.

'How did you go with your family?' I asked.

'Eva's got so big and Walter isn't a baby any more. He's nearly ready for school,' he said, pen poised over paper and sighing deeply. 'I hadn't seen them for over a year.'

'Your daughter, how is she now?'

'Thank God, she's fine now. She's nothing but skin and bone but that will improve as she begins to eat more. Inga, my wife, has extra rations for her, to build up her health. She gets tired very easily still so the doctor says it may be a month or two until she's strong enough to travel.'

'Couldn't you bring them back to München?' It was obvious that he missed his children. He should be able to be with them more. I wished I could tell him that they could stay with my parents and me but that was no longer possible.

'No,' he said, shaking his head. 'There's nowhere to stay here. I couldn't afford the rent even if there was anything available and I don't know if I'll be posted somewhere else. We've a plan for them to go to Inga's cousin in Berlin. She'll have support there and they should be safe.'

'I'm glad she's better. It sounds like you have it all worked out.'

'I'm sorry about Heinrich. I know you're worried about him. As long as you keep receiving letters from him—'

I grasped his hand, wanting him to stop. 'Yes, I know.' The words caught in my throat and my meal blurred in front of me as I willed tears away. I looked up at him as a tear escaped from my control, sliding slowly down my face, and I let go of his hand.

He didn't give me empty words of assurance, merely rubbed his thumb gently across my cheek, wiping away my tear.

'Eat up before it gets cold,' he said softly.

It was from my mother that I learnt of the Americans reaching the German border, just outside Trier. My grandmother had called her before pandemonium broke out. She and my grandfather planned to stay in Trier and weather the storm. There was nowhere they could go anyway, with rail services disrupted and roads closed. Mutti was upset but matter of fact about it. They had all been through this once before. I was angry. My grandparents were elderly and didn't deserve to go through a trauma like this. They lived peacefully in their home and had done nothing wrong.

The reality was that Germany could fall, invaded by the Allies and the Russians. All we could hope for was that the Americans reached us before the Russians; we had heard terrible stories of what the Russians were capable of. Perhaps our only hope was the release of the new aircraft we had been waiting for. Of course, the greatest problem was finding fuel, as we no longer had any access to the oil fields of the Crimea and our synthetic fuel plants were a major target of the American and British bombing raids.

My impotent rage made no difference to anyone. I decided to channel my fear for Heinrich and my grandparents and my deep anger into my work, working harder and longer than ever.

Everything now seemed to move at a rapid pace. Due to the changing structure within high command, all units were in flux, assuming new roles and moving locations. Our sphere of influence was shrinking. Many units were called back to Germany for the Defence of the Reich, but not Heinrich's. A new army of youth and the elderly was created, the Volkssturm, charged with defending our homeland. Herr Schmitt came to tell us he had been conscripted, as had his grandson. I stared at him in shock. How had we been reduced to seeking protection from such an inappropriate, untrained force? Tears welled in my eyes as I hugged Herr Schmitt goodbye, adding another good man and his grandson to my nightly prayers.

Many in the Luftwaffe now pinned their hopes on the new generation of aircraft that was rolling off the production lines, finally ready for mass release. We were very excited to have the lion's share of these aircraft in our district, along with the prestigious team of aces to pilot them. All aircraft were prepared for a large scale offensive against the West.

Our work was frantic and I accompanied the oberinspektor to the various airfields. With his expertise in aeronautic engineering and the new jet engines, he took a more hands-on role, liaising with local command to determine the needs of each airfield in relation to the new aircraft. We spent a lot of time at Neubiberg, just south of München, where a large contingent of the Me 262 fighter jets was to be based. We also travelled to Riem, Schleissheim and Erding, and the large airpark at Illesheim, west of Nürnberg, where much of the area's airfields' refitting, conversions and repairs took place. Sometimes it meant staying in the airfield barracks overnight, much to my mother's objections, although Vati assured her I was safe.

Moves were made to relocate our regional command office. We had to remain operational but it was risky to stay in the centre of München with the continuous bombing raids. So, when we weren't in the field, we were reorganising our office, getting ready for the move. With the restructuring of roles came a promotion for the oberinspektor. There was no time for ceremony, just an official letter stating his new rank of hauptinspektor along with the new duties he had already undertaken. Hauptinspektor Drescher was now directly answerable to Colonel von Wissenbach, and as I remained his secretary, Bettina and I often worked closely together.

'I can't believe he's not celebrating. Promotions like this don't come every day,' said Bettina when I told her the good news, walking to the Englischer Garten for a few minutes of fresh air.

I shrugged. 'I don't know. Work's too busy to celebrate.' As we stood waiting to cross Prinzregentenstrasse, a sleek black Mercedes-Benz drove past flying a swastika. It was a sight we saw most days, the to and fro of party and government officials becoming more frantic with the escalation of the war. An old man leered at us from inside the car. Bettina and I stepped back from the kerb in response, grimacing in distaste before darting across the busy boulevard and laughing.

'I think he's the quiet type anyway,' I said, finishing my thought as we entered the park.

Bettina laughed. 'Quiet? That's not what I heard. Although, he has settled considerably since you've arrived.' She looked at me speculatively, her eyes questioning.

'What?' I stopped under a maple tree, its leaves a golden yellow.

'Maybe he'll celebrate with you ... It could be you're a good influence on him.'

'Don't be silly. He's just professional. I wouldn't expect anything else from someone in his position.'

'I don't know,' Bettina persisted, taking the rare opportunity to tease me.

I started walking again. 'Look, I know what you heard, but I don't think he's really like that. From what I've gathered, he's hit a bad patch in his marriage. I don't think he was on good terms with his wife when he left for his job here in München.'

'Mmm, maybe. But I still think it's because of you.'

I could feel my face go red. 'It's just that I work hard and make his job easier. Besides, I've spent quite a lot of time with him out of the office now, travelling to the airfields, and he has never been anything but respectful, courteous and reserved.'

'All right,' said Bettina, holding up her hands. 'See if you can persuade him to celebrate this evening. I'm sure we can find something special from the staff kitchen, and I know where we can find some champagne. Otherwise, we'll celebrate the fact that you and I will be working a lot more with the girls anyway.'

'I'll try to persuade him but I don't like our chances.'

To my surprise, it didn't take too much to make the hauptinspektor stay. He was working anyway, so we just brought the party to him. When it became known that there was food and drink, many of our department staff joined us. Even Colonel von Wissenbach stopped by for a drink and to pass on his congratulations. Bettina didn't just find a bottle or two of champagne, but a whole case. I don't know how she did it, she wouldn't tell me. It was wonderful to laugh and relax for a change and to see the sociable side of those we worked with.

Once the food ran out, people began to drift away. Soon it was just Bettina, the hauptinspektor and I. Since we'd thrown the party, I felt we had to stay to clean up. I'd had more champagne than I should have but I didn't feel like going home yet.

'Time for bed,' said the hauptinspektor, yawning, lounging back in one of the office chairs.

'Yes, it is getting late,' I said, clearing away the last glasses.

'I'll walk you both home. I could do with the fresh air. That's the most I've had to drink in a long while.'

'Well, it was your celebration,' said Bettina, flashing a brilliant smile. 'I'd be upset if you didn't enjoy yourself. Lotte and I went to a lot of trouble, after all.'

'Thank you,' said the hauptinspektor quietly. 'I didn't expect anything like this. Nobody has thrown me a party since I was a boy.'

'What about your other promotions? Surely your family or work colleagues did something for you?' said Bettina, replacing the chairs to their original positions.

'A couple of drinks with the boys after work, but nothing like this.'

Bettina frowned at the revelation and shot a quick look at me, as if to say, 'Maybe you were right about him.' I could see that he looked wistful, almost sad, but he quickly shook off his reverie.

'Come on then, otherwise it will almost be time to come back.'

After dropping Bettina home in Altstadt, the hauptinspektor and I walked through Max-Joseph-Platz. I had been here many times before but now the majestic Königsbau, the royal residence that edged the square, and the Byzantine court church nestled alongside sat in the darkness, eerie reminders of the war and casualties of the recent bombings. The gutted façade of the National Theatre stood in front of me, destroyed in the bombings of the year before. As we passed the monument of King Maximilian Joseph, I wondered what he would think of the destruction of his glorious city.

Passing the silhouette of the main building of the university, desolate and damaged, made me think of Heinrich and all the times I met him under the beautiful domed glass ceiling that filled the atrium with light. Everything seemed simpler then. Now the world was turned on its head, the city a shadow of its former self. I missed those days and it made me ache for Heinrich. Feeling melancholy, I sighed.

'Something wrong?' asked the hauptinspektor, breaking the silence, a flicker of light glowing in the dark as he lit a cigarette.

'It's hard to see the city like this,' I said, glad we had something to talk about. 'How much more destruction before this is all over?'

'I don't know. I wish you could see where I come from in Silesia. Grottkau is a beautiful medieval town, perhaps as old as München but not as big, surrounded by the Silesian lowlands, river flats of the Oder River. I sometimes wonder if I will ever see it again as it was when I left it as a young man.'

'Do you still have family there?'

'My parents. My father has a furniture shop in the town.' He drew on his cigarette, the end illuminated in the night.

'Oh, does he make the furniture or just sell it?' I don't know why I was surprised that his father sold furniture. Perhaps I thought he had something to do with aircraft, like his son.

'Both, although before the war, he was so busy he didn't have much time to make furniture. I remember learning carpentry from him as a boy. He taught me how important

110

precision and determined execution of each task was in ensuring the final product was worthy of the showroom floor. Sometimes my hands itch for the chisel, plane and saw. To have an image in mind and then be able to build it, give it form and a practical application is one of life's great pleasures.'

I smiled, delighted to have an insight into what made this mysterious man tick. His creative flair, habit of thinking outside the conventional view and finding practical solutions was a gift. I saw it in his work. I understood that creative urge and only wished that I could bring my artistic desires into being. 'I know what you mean. I feel that way when I'm taking photographs.'

'I've heard from Bettina that you're a talented photographer. You must show me some of your work. I'd love to see it.'

'Really?'

'Really.' It was his turn to smile now, white teeth flashing in the darkness. 'What do you photograph?'

'Anything. People, landscapes, architecture, any object of beauty.' I thought for a moment, warming to my subject. 'It's not so much about the subject as my interpretation of what I find beautiful in that scene. It might be the way the light falls, the shadow, or the contrast of colours, shapes and textures.' Cars moved slowly beside us, headlights covered with slotted covers, dipped toward the ground, barely illuminating the dangers of the pockmarked road in front, piles of rubble spilling from the kerb. 'You would make a good subject,' I wanted to say to him, but didn't dare.

'Ah, you are an artist at heart,' said the hauptinspektor. 'Why didn't you make photography your career? From the way you're talking, I assume you studied.'

'Yes, for three years but my parents . . .' I shrugged. 'After losing Ludwig, they wanted me to stay in München and a position as a civilian auxiliary in one of the local military offices was the safest they could find for me.'

'I see.' There was compassion in his voice. 'Maybe you could show me how to take a good photo sometime. Although I enjoy it, my photos never turn out the way I want them.'

'Of course,' I said, flustered, as my heart started pounding in my chest. Perhaps he was really interested. Clasping my hands together tightly, I turned the conversation around, wanting to take the attention off myself. 'Did you work in your father's shop until the war then?'

'No. I worked there for a time after finishing business school in Neisse, managing the shop for my father, but my heart wasn't in it. I had always loved machinery, so I trained as a mechanic, learning to build motors at the technical school in Breslau. Planes were my passion and I had been gliding and flying small aircraft for years at the Gleiwitz Flight School. I found work there as an instructor and site manager, repairing aircraft as well, until I entered military service in 1938.'

'How did your family end up in Sagan?' I was feeling bold now, bolstered by the champagne. I heard the intake of breath as he stopped to stub out his cigarette and I immediately regretted my nosiness.

'My first posting was to the Sagan-Küpper airpark as an aircraft engineer. Inga and I were married and we had Eva. Things were already rocky between us but I thought that the move away from our families would do us good and for a time, it was. I rose to group leader and wanted to become a technical advisor but had to do my higher diploma in Berlin,

Jüterbog, actually, for a year. My family was settled in Sagan and Walter was only a baby. By the time I returned in late 1941, before moving to my new posting in Lemberg, I realised that our marriage could not be salvaged. I only saw them a few times before coming to München.'

I shivered and plunged my hands into my trench coat. He was a family man in a broken marriage and the sadness in his voice made me want to comfort him in some way.

'You're cold. Here have my coat.' The hauptinspektor stopped in his tracks.

'No,' I said, mortified. 'I'll be fine, maybe we could just walk a little faster.' The flush of warmth from the alcohol had passed and the brisk night air of late October had only now settled into my bones.

He wouldn't take no for an answer. 'Here,' he said, 'put this around you.' He draped the woollen coat across my shoulders and immediately the lingering warmth from his body surrounded me.

'Thank you,' I murmured. 'What about you? You must be cold.'

He shook his head. 'No, not one bit.'

'I feel bad taking your coat.'

'Well in that case, how about you take my arm? Walking close to you will warm me up.'

I blushed but it was reasonable request. 'Of course, we can't let you freeze to death,' I said lightheartedly, trying to cover my rising confusion, pleased he couldn't see my face in the darkness.

The hauptinspektor laughed, a deep throaty sound that made me smile, easing my anxiety. 'Not likely.'

113

I threaded my arm through his, feeling slightly self-conscious as we continued to walk.

'Thank you,' he said. 'I was very touched by the celebration this evening.'

'It was nothing,' I said automatically. 'Besides, Bettina organised most of it.'

'She's a great girl and an asset to our department. But you – you I can't do without.'

I felt a wave of delicious warmth bombard me and curl its way through my body, turning my muscles to liquid, until it came to rest in my belly, heavy and pulsating. I leant into him. He pulled me closer, his solid warmth reassuring, and I felt safe and protected by his side. The cool night air and the ugliness of a war-torn city disappeared, leaving only the hum of tension that ran through the hauptinspektor like a surge of electricity.

'I only do what I can.'

'You don't realise it, but you're a breath of fresh air, Lotte,' he said quickly, as if he had to get the words out before he lost his courage. 'Because of you, this posting isn't something I have to endure.'

I stopped walking, suddenly wary. I had never had that effect on anyone before. It left me with a feeling of power and a need to surrender all at the same time. I tried to peer into his face but all I could see was his silhouette in the dark. 'Hauptinspektor, I don't know what you mean. I haven't done anything but my work.'

'Yes, I know,' he said. 'You make sure I function each day, no matter what happens. Nobody has cared for me like that in a very long time.' I felt his body sag. 'The champagne has probably made me say things I shouldn't have said. I have no wish to make you feel uncomfortable. I just wanted you to know how valued you are . . .'

He was just grateful. I relaxed a little. I wondered if he would be embarrassed tomorrow.

'Thank you,' I said, forgiving him. I felt honoured that he had shared such vulnerability with me and sad that he carried so much pain.

We began to walk again, still arm in arm. To leave the awkwardness behind us, I began to tell him about my family and about my life in München. All the while I was very much aware of his presence by my side, the slight pressure of his arm against mine, the warmth that radiated from him. He was a good listener, with a quick wit and a dry sense of humour. I was enjoying myself.

'You laugh with such abandon, it's infectious,' he said, his own laughter fizzing away after one wisecrack. 'It's deep and heartfelt, just like your smile.'

His compliments made me weak at the knees and I was glad I was holding onto his arm. I didn't want this walk to end. 'I can't help it. I've always been like this. Mutti tells me it's not very ladylike but it's who I am. Anyway, I'm the eternal optimist and I believe in finding something good in every situation. Laughter is life and life's for living, isn't it?'

'Yes, it is.'

Then we were at the front of my building.

'Thank you for walking me home, hauptinspektor,' I said, removing my arm reluctantly from his and lifting the coat from my shoulders.

'It was the least I could do after such a lovely party.'

I smiled, handing him the coat. 'Maybe now you can stay warm.'

'Please call me Erich when we're not in the office,' he said. 'We've worked together so long now and we spend so much time together travelling . . . It's nice to hear my name sometimes.'

He stood close to me and, for a moment, I wondered what it would be like to kiss his wide, sensuous mouth. I looked up at him, confused, trying to discern his expression in the near darkness but could find nothing to fault in his courteous demeanour.

'All right.' After all I had learnt about him that night – alone without his family, without warmth and companionship – I supposed it would be fine. 'Goodnight, Erich,' I said tentatively, but I didn't want him to leave.

'Goodnight, Lotte. See you at work in the morning.' A car turning the corner briefly lit the inky blackness. Our eyes met and he smiled with such warmth that it caught my breath, before we were plunged into darkness once more and he was gone.

7

Requisitioned by the Luftwaffe, Kloster Scheyern was a grand old Benedictine monastery, built in the twelfth century, about fifty kilometres north of München. The main complex held an array of chapels and the basilica. The monks who were still there lived in the adjoining wing. Before the war, the furthest wing had housed a grammar school. Now this wing became our office building and the wing opposite the accommodation for all the staff.

It was hard to believe that a war existed as Bettina and I walked through the grounds to the new barracks. There was a sense of peace and tranquillity that lingered here. Order prevailed as I looked about the manicured gardens. I felt safe; this was a place of respite.

There wasn't much time to enjoy the beauty of the monastery or the surrounding countryside. I was kept busy setting up the new office and continuing with the regular work. Erich insisted that I no longer accompany him on his trips to the airfields, so that I could organise our office and get settled in the dormitory.

I was relieved, because I had so much to do but also because I was apprehensive about being alone with him outside of the office. Worried about how I might react to him. That night in München had done something to me, as if it had flicked a switch. I was aware of a subtle undercurrent. I loved Heinrich but Erich was like a magnet, drawing me to him. Despite my best intentions, I increasingly watched him throughout the day, often unconsciously. I sometimes found him watching me too. The intensity in his green eyes caused me to catch my breath and made my heart thump loudly in my ears. I'm sure I blushed more than once and had to quickly hide my face behind the stacked boxes or find a reason to leave the room.

But Erich was nothing but courteous and professional at work, as always. Nothing was mentioned about our evening walk and there was no hint of anything that had passed between us. I felt stupid, like I had created some silly little fantasy in my own head out of a few kind words. Erich had only told me he appreciated me but it had made me feel wanted, valued, even desired. Although I adored Heinrich, it didn't stop me wondering what it would be like to live in Erich's world. He had done so many things in his life already, experienced so much. I realised what a sheltered life Heinrich and I had had and probably would always have. I wanted to experience the world, discover what life had to offer, to be with someone like Erich, who might understand my creative passions and share my dreams. That night had changed everything for me. It was as if a tiny crack in my very ordered, planned world had appeared, allowing me to look at life around me, at the life I might want to take for myself. It was frightening to admit that a tiny part of me was willing to buck the social conventions that constrained me. Then I would think of Heinrich.

I had kept the last photo I had taken of him on my bedroom side table. I looked at it when I woke each morning and before I slept at night. I would sit in bed, photo on my lap, and tell him all that had happened in the day, imagining his responses, his reactions. It was a good photo, one of my best. Now it rested under my pillow in the dormitory and I barely had time at night to kiss his face and tell him I loved him before falling into a deep and dreamless sleep.

My mother was distraught at my moving to Kloster Scheyern. I could have stayed in München to look after her, as my father kept to a frantic schedule at work and could not take the time to spend with her, but I still felt that need for something more.

'Nobody would think badly of you if you decide to stay,' Vati had said not long before the move.

'I can't abandon my colleagues now,' I'd replied, exasperated. 'Besides, the hauptinspektor relies on me.'

'I understand how you feel but Hauptinspektor Drescher is a good man. He will understand your reasons. Besides, I don't think you'll be needed for much longer. The war will end soon and everything will be different.' He'd picked up his pipe, knocking the remnant of tobacco out, ready to refill.

'I don't know why you have to go,' my mother had said, banging the teapot on the table. 'I need you here. Isn't that more important than what your superior needs? Your father has no choice but to work, his job is very important.'

'My job is important too, Mutti! I do valuable work for the war effort and the Fatherland. My contribution is valued and appreciated, especially by the hauptinspektor. Colonel von Wissenbach will tell you what a good job I do, if you ask him.'

'You would be home, married by now, if you had listened to me. Then you would be out of harm's way and I wouldn't have to worry about you too.' My mother had rushed to her bedroom.

I could hear her sobbing and I stared at my father in despair. 'I didn't mean to upset her.'

'If you want to stay, we'll find a way to make that happen.'

'You know I have to go. Besides, Mutti has you and Tante Klara and her other friends to keep her distracted when you're not home. She can't wrap me in cotton wool.'

Vati had kissed the top of my head. 'I know. At least promise her that you'll come home every second Sunday and that you'll be home for Christmas.'

'I can do that.'

The first moment that I got to myself after we arrived at the kloster was a Sunday afternoon. I needed an escape from the constant noise and activity but I was glad I hadn't agreed to go home every week; I was bone tired and I wouldn't have got any rest in Mutti's company. Pulling up the collar on my coat, I shoved my gloved hands deep into my pockets. A bit of November cold wasn't going to deter me. I walked through the wood that surrounded part of the kloster for about an hour. I only wished I had brought my camera. Most of the trees were almost bare, naked branches like skeletons, twisting sinuously, clutching onto clumps of darkening leaves here and there. However, there were still brilliant patches of yellow, red and orange that never ceased to take my breath away. My thoughts wandered to how I would photograph Erich: brown hair swept back from his smooth, wide brow, high cheekbones under bronzed skin and large green eyes. My fingers itched to trace those lines and discover how the play of light and shadow could best enhance his portrait.

But after a time the walk and the gentle noises of the forest did their job, soothing my soul and clearing my head, giving me a sense of balance that I hadn't felt in weeks.

'Lotte!'

I jumped and looked across the garden to see who was calling me. My eyes fell on a figure rapidly approaching, waving its arm. Erich. I froze. I couldn't turn back into the woods because he had already seen me. I stood there under the branches of a moulting beech tree and waited, trying to force a polite smile onto my face while I burnt up with both joy and shame.

'Lotte, there you are. Bettina's been looking for you. Helga told her you'd gone for a walk but when you didn't return, she got worried. Why did you go off on your own like that?'

'I just needed some peace and quiet. I wanted some time to clear my head. It's been crazy in there.'

'I can see that. I'm sorry I wasn't here to help.'

I saw that his concern was genuine. 'That's all right,' I said, smiling. 'I'm sure it hasn't been easy for you either.'

Erich stepped closer to me and I could smell the cigarettes on his skin. He stopped and glanced around the garden and woods.

'I don't know how much longer we'll keep going like this. It's madness everywhere. Except here. I can see why you came here. I wouldn't mind a few minutes of peace. Is there somewhere you can recommend where I can gather my thoughts before the onslaught of the next week begins?'

'Well, maybe in one of the churches,' I said, standing rigid, forcing myself to stop thinking what it would be like if I just melted into his arms then and there. I couldn't deny my attraction to him. 'It's probably warmer there.'

'Yes, you're right of course. That's the sensible place to go, especially at this time of day. Perhaps next time I need some solitude, you could show me where you found your peace and quiet in the woods. I've always found nature to be very soothing, relaxing – a place where you can be yourself. Don't you think so?'

I stared at him for just a second, mouth agape, trying to work out if he was implying anything else, but my reflexes seemed dull and I was slow to come up with a retort.

'Come on then, before Bettina thinks you've disappeared for good.'

He placed his hand on my back to guide me forward as any gentleman would do but I felt the burn of his touch for hours afterwards.

I arrived home the following weekend to the smell of roasted meat wafting down the hallway.

'Your mother's been planning this meal for days,' said Vati. 'You know how she is. It's been a while since she's gone to this much trouble, especially now it's so hard to get what you want from the market, no matter what ration cards you have.'

Mutti cooking was impressive enough but for her to make so much effort told me that she had resigned herself to my situation and we were back on good terms. Although she had found it difficult to let me go, this was her way to show me how much she loved me and had missed me.

Vati followed me to my room, where the meal was laid out. Mutti still refused to eat in our dining room with the stares of our neighbours on her back. There was fresh table linen and even a small vase with flowers she had found somewhere. My eyes welled with tears as Vati flipped back the protective tea towel to show the brown crust of a well-done roast. The gravy boat stood alongside it, shimmering drops of fat glistening on the surface of the thick brown sauce.

'I haven't had Mutti's apple cake since my birthday,' I groaned in delight, spying the cake on my bed. 'It must have been near impossible to get all the ingredients.'

'She's been saving her rations to get extra butter and kept the flour she already had. She queued up for hours to get this meat and was so excited when she showed it to me. It's not so easy to find meat any more. Mutti took it on as a great challenge, as she does.'

I smiled. Mutti was managing quite well without the servants; it was as if she had become stronger.

'Luckily Tante Susie visited during the week and brought apples she'd picked up in the country on her trip from Windsheim.' Tante Susie was Mutti's sister who lived in one of the large towns near Nürnberg where her husband had worked as a doctor before the war.

'How did Mutti manage to do it with all the tenants?' I asked in hushed tones. Despite the cramped living conditions and Vati's enquiries, none of the tenants had yet been offered alternative accommodation.

'Your mother stood guard in the kitchen with a knife in her hand while it cooked. She stared down anyone game enough to even look into the kitchen with that determined gaze of hers. Nobody was going to steal her hard-earned feast!'

I roared with laughter, wiping the tears from my face just as Mutti entered the room, her face beaming with pleasure to see I had finally arrived.

After the meal, it was time to put together the Christmas parcel for Heinrich. Mutti had kept some of Tante Susie's apples and she had set aside enough butter, eggs and flour for us to make gingerbread biscuits for him. They weren't the same as usual because we didn't have all the right ingredients but they were still good: homemade and baked with love. It was a special time, Mutti and I baking together. The steady rhythm of mixing, kneading, rolling, cutting and decorating was soothing while we shared snippets of our weeks apart. Vati prowled the hallway near the kitchen, keeping away most of the curious neighbours, even when the smell of cooking biscuits drifted to the front of the apartment. He even helped us put together the advent wreath and find the pack of red candles we still had somewhere. It was a tradition of ours and I looked at the wreath decorated with holly and the four red candles on our little table with satisfaction.

I managed to find a few chocolate bars and plenty of cigarettes with the rations I had kept and Vati had acquired a small amount of real coffee and a little bottle of whiskey. I packed the box with photos, poems and a long letter I had begun in Scheyern, telling Heinrich about my work, our move to the kloster and the beautiful churches, grounds and countryside that I had only really glimpsed but intended to explore. But it was only after reading the letter Heinrich had sent me more carefully in the privacy of my mother's room that I was able to finish my own letter.

> *I'm coping. Each day is busier than the last with the new casualties, the back-to-back surgeries and the care and management of the men's wounds and injuries. This is what keeps me going while we constantly move backwards in retreat, disturbing the men, packing up when we have to. Sadly, we lose more men than we need to this way but we're all trying to stay ahead of the Red Army and stay alive.*

I could only imagine the nightmare Heinrich was living. My stomach clutched in fear and concern for him but also because of my ridiculous schoolgirl crush on my superior and the terrible guilt and shame it brought, especially when I knew how much Heinrich was sacrificing.

I read again the part I had been most looking forward to.

> *In my few moments of quiet before sleep, thoughts of our life together sustain me. I look forward to celebrating our wedding with our family and friends, finding a job at one of the München hospitals and settling into our own apartment to begin married life. In all truth, I would be happy to have a quiet life where nothing unexpected or very exciting ever happened again. I have seen enough action and upheaval to last a lifetime.*

I miss you most of all – our conversations, your unerring support and your smiling face. I can't wait to see you and hold you in my arms once again.

All my love,

Heinrich.

Something nagged at me and I frowned, trying to work it out. Heinrich expressed everything about the life we wanted to build together. Then it hit me. Where were the words telling me how much I meant to him, how his life was nothing without me? Even on paper he couldn't express his feelings for me. Girls at work had shared the erotic letters their husbands and loved ones had sent them, making us all breathless. I was quite envious and wondered if it was maturity and experience that made a man able to write those kinds of things. My thoughts wandered to the kind of letters Erich would send me if he were my lover.

I shook my head. I wasn't being fair. Heinrich was in the middle of a war zone, doing all he could to stay alive, and here I was, safe, well and feeling sorry for myself. I just wanted this war over, so he could come home. If he couldn't express it in words, he could show me what he felt for me on our wedding night. I wanted to get on with our life together, a life that had been planned out for so long.

'My darling Heinrich,' I read, then scanned what I had written before ending the letter:

I miss you so much it hurts. So many times a day I think about all the things I want to share with you but of course I can't. I count down the days until you come home safely to me and I

*once again feel your strong, loving arms around me. I look
forward to our wedding day and the joy of knowing you will
always be by my side. We will have a wonderful life together.
You mean everything to me. Stay safe.*

All my love,

your Lotte.

Perhaps a little overdone, but at least I had conveyed how much
Heinrich meant to me, maybe even shown him how I wanted
to be written to. I prayed that my letter would give him some
measure of joy and hope as well as updating him on life at
home. Mutti promised to post the box the following day and
already I was imagining Heinrich's reaction and pleasure at
opening the box and the letter he would write back. I couldn't
bear to think that he would not be home for Christmas.

December came as operations moved into overdrive. Hitler
launched a major offensive on the Western Front through the
Ardennes to prevent the Americans and British from invading
Germany. There was hope in the office, as the new aircraft
were finally ready to be useful in the battles to come.

The office staff exchanged small Christmas gifts before
those of us who were able to returned home for a day or two.
München had been bombed again and Bettina's family had
left the city and she was unable to join them. She and Erich
had nobody, so at my father's insistence, they joined me to
celebrate Christmas with my parents. I couldn't let Erich
spend Christmas alone despite my inner conflict, knowing

how much he missed his family. I was only offering a kind gesture to colleagues at a time of difficulty. Colonel von Wissenbach gave us a lift in his private car, as he was travelling to München for the night.

We brought lots of Christmas cheer home with us and Colonel von Wissenbach sent an expensive bottle of Hennessey cognac to my father. My mother's tight expression softened into one of wide-eyed delight when we arrived with coffee, nougat, beer made by the monks at Scheyern, ham, real gingerbread, Belgian chocolate, winter apples, fresh vegetables, pine branches to give the room that Christmassy smell and other assorted delights.

Although it was a bit cosy as we gathered around the Christmas tree in my old bedroom, I was glad to be home, the flickering light of the candles shimmering in the glass baubles and silver tinsel, the scent of pine around us. Mutti proudly announced that we would have roasted goose for dinner, which Vati had managed to acquire for her, from one of his many contacts, I suspected.

As I helped bring in the food, I noticed Mutti had even managed to make stollen, quite a feat considering the high demand the ingredients would have been in. She told me that she and her friends had gathered the ingredients and split them. I cut thin slices and placed them on the platter to make sure there was enough to last. The bread was just like I remembered, sweet and yeasty with a good dash of lemon, almonds, vanilla and rum.

It was a wonderful evening, fuelled by good food and wine. Truthfully, I couldn't imagine spending Christmas Eve with anyone else – it was perfect. Except that there had been no news of Heinrich. I told myself I hadn't accounted for delays in the post with the disruptions that would inevitably occur with the approaching Red Army. But the ache in the pit of my stomach was a constant.

'I'm sure you must be missing your wife and children,' said Mutti to Erich.

He nodded, his eyes clouding over. 'They're still in Silesia. I had hoped they would be in Berlin for Christmas but my daughter has been unwell and not fit to travel.'

'How old are your children again?' Mutti asked, sipping her wine, relaxed now that the table had been cleared.

Erich's face lit up. 'Eva is nine and Walter has just turned five.'

'A perfect age to enjoy Christmas,' said Mutti wistfully. 'I still remember when mine were all that little. They were so excited waiting for "der Weihnachtsmann", and when he finally came and they discovered the presents under the tree, well, they were beside themselves. I never had any trouble keeping them awake on Christmas Eve. It was the highlight of their year.' My mother smiled indulgently at me.

'Were your family planning to just visit Berlin for the Christmas period?' asked Vati, draining his glass of cognac.

'No. I want to get them away from Silesia. I don't think it will be safe there for much longer. The Red Army is getting closer each day and I don't want my family anywhere near an invading force.'

'We've heard some terrible stories about the Russians,' said Mutti. 'I can see why you want to get your family to leave.'

I touched the pocket of my dress where Heinrich's photo sat, a stab of fear striking at my heart.

'Why Berlin?' asked Bettina. 'Why not come to München?'

I didn't miss the swift glance she cast at me but I kept my face politely interested, although I already knew the answer.

'My wife has relatives in Berlin she can stay with. There's nowhere to stay here in München and who knows where our department will end up?' said Erich.

'When do you think they'll be ready to travel?' asked my father. 'It gets harder with each passing day.'

'Yes, I know.' Erich sighed. 'I would have liked them to leave weeks ago. But my daughter is getting stronger and young Walter is growing and able to help his mother more too. I'm hopeful that they will be ready in a couple of weeks or so.'

'The sooner the better,' muttered my father.

'What about your parents?' I asked.

Erich looked at me gratefully and smiled. 'My father was conscripted into the Volkssturm about a month ago. At present, he is based in Breslau, training the young boys to be defenders of the Reich. When he wrote to me, he told me he suspects they will probably defend the towns along the Oder River. He said he could live with that, if it protected Grottkau, which is on the western side.'

'I'm so sorry,' I said, my face turning red, horrified I had brought up such a difficult situation for him.

'It's all right. It can't be helped.'

'What about your mother?' enquired Mutti, picking at the stollen on her plate.

'She's stubborn and won't come with Inga and the children as long as my father is nearby. She said she'll stay and look after the shop, convinced that nobody would bother an old woman. I'm not so sure, but without my father there, she won't listen to me and I can't force her to come.'

Mutti nodded. 'She might be right, you know. My parents are in Trier and they have been left alone by the Americans. It's not easy for them, of course, but they are safe and well. Hopefully it will be the same with your mother.'

'Hopefully,' echoed Erich, but his eyes clouded with pain.

'What about some of that chocolate we brought?' said Bettina brightly.

Later that evening, Erich found me in the hallway between the two rooms. *'Frohe Weihnachten,'* he said softly, pushing a small parcel into my hands. 'Just a little something to thank you for everything you do.' His hands touched mine briefly and a spark of electricity passed between us.

I stared at him a moment, searching his eyes, but found only guarded politeness. 'You didn't have to,' I said. 'I was only doing my job.' He looked hurt by this, his forehead crinkling into a frown, his shoulders hunching just a little. I couldn't hurt him, no matter how confused I was, so I smiled brightly. 'I'm pleased you're wearing the tie I gave you.'

'Of course.' He touched the knot in his tie. 'It's lovely, you have such good taste. I had to wear it. Open yours, please.' The look of tortured anticipation on his face, just like a child, nearly made me laugh. It was so sweet that he was worried whether I would like his gift.

I fumbled with the string and wrapping until I saw a corner of blue silk. I began to tear open the package as Erich stepped closer to inspect the contents with me.

I pulled out a soft scarf, patterned in two shades of blue. 'It's beautiful,' I whispered, 'and it's silk.'

'It's French. I knew someone coming back from Paris and I asked them to find me a blue scarf. I wanted it to match the colour of your eyes.' He held up the edge of the scarf next to my face. 'I think it comes close,' he said. 'Here, let me help you tie it around your neck.'

Erich moved so close to me I could feel the warmth of his breath on my neck. I shivered as he fastened the knot at my throat, his face barely a whisper from mine.

'You're cold,' he said, stepping away abruptly. 'Come on. Let's get back to the warmth.'

As I turned to go back to where the others were still gathered around our small table, Erich touched me on the arm.

'I'm sorry Heinrich isn't here to spend Christmas with you. This should have been your first as a married couple. I'm sure you have many Christmases together ahead of you. Take it from me, make the most of those early married days when he returns. Learn to know each other well and share your lives honestly with each other.' He looked down at the floor. 'I wish that Inga and I had done that. Maybe things would have been very different between us.'

I stood rooted to the spot, shocked by his revelation and confused by his well-intentioned advice about marriage. Erich smiled sadly and opened the door to return to the festivities. Courteous as always, he allowed me in first. Bettina noticed my new scarf and I saw the look of speculation cross her face.

8

The start of 1945 didn't bring us the news we had hoped for. The great offensive against the Western Front had ultimately failed and the Americans and British were pushing forward once again. Many of our new aircraft were lost before they even reached their destinations as factories and freight trains were bombed. It seemed like the dire predictions of Vati, Erich and Bettina had been accurate. Mutti had had every right to worry about our future. Unless the Führer could perform a miracle.

Then München was bombed once again.

I came home after the bombing to find our home still intact but much of the city in ruins. I was numb, too shocked to cry, and I stared in disbelief as I picked my way down once familiar streets that were surrounded by the charred, twisted remains of buildings. The gangs of workers couldn't keep up with the enormity of their task. Rubble and debris were scattered across the streets, which were almost impossible to navigate. There was no electricity or running water and sooty faces stared at me with eyes sunken from exhaustion and despair. Talking to neighbours, I learnt that many had decided it was time to leave the city before their luck ran out, before the city was decimated. They decided to take their chances in the country along with the streams of refugees we had heard about fleeing before the Red Army in the east. The exodus out of the city made me think of the panicked action of jumping from a sinking ship into the unknown; the general feeling was of self-preservation. As far as these people were concerned, Germany had lost the war and they had done their duty for the Fatherland but now it was time for survival.

There were many others who decided to stay, those who would not abandon their homes or the city they loved. The hope was that the Americans would reach München before the Russians. Vati, however, had decided it was time for my mother to leave and now I could see why.

'Come with me,' pleaded Mutti. 'Tante Susie can have both of us. She has plenty of room.'

'*Muttilein*, you know I can't come with you,' I said, smoothing out the piece of worn sheeting I was wrapping my wedding gown in. There was no delicate paper to softly cocoon my precious garment but it was time to box and store it so it wouldn't be ruined. Nobody knew when I would need it. My heart felt leaden. I couldn't shake the feeling that I was saying goodbye to München and my old life forever, leaving for the kloster and an unknown future. I knew now that nothing could be the same after the war. There was still no letter from Heinrich. His mother hadn't heard anything either. That we had received no telegram to tell us he was killed or missing in action was a relief beyond words but it was the not knowing that was the hardest.

I thought suddenly of Frau Andree. Where was she now? I held no illusions that we were ever likely to see her again. I couldn't forget stories whispered among the girls in the office, stories that told of Jewish round-ups, herded like cattle onto trains and then interned indefinitely in various camps across the country. Then there were the reports of gas chambers broadcast on BBC radio that trickled down to us. We were prohibited from listening to foreign radio but many did despite the risk, especially those with links outside Germany. I listened with horror, but part of me finally believed it was true. Nobody deserved to be treated like an animal. How could our Führer let this happen? This wasn't Germany, the virtuous and cultured shining star of Europe. This was barbaric.

The fabric of our society was torn. To me, it was inconceivable that there were so many missing, so many dead, so many families scattered and torn asunder. Germany as we had known it was falling apart. How would we ever recover?

I laid the gown gently in the box, closing the lid. Dread suddenly coiled through my belly, sharp and heavy, as if I was closing the lid on this part of my life, a life of privilege.

I kissed Mutti on the forehead. 'I can't abandon my work or my colleagues now. Besides, I'm just as safe if not safer at headquarters. The kloster is possibly the best place to be. Isn't that so, Vati?'

'Mmm?' My father lifted his head from the letter he was examining and removed his reading glasses. 'Yes, of course you're quite safe for now.'

Mutti hugged her arms around her and sat on the lounge chair, defeated.

Vati put his letter down. 'Now, once your mother leaves for Bad Windsheim, I'll spend most of my time at headquarters. It will be easier to eat and sleep there. Berlin is virtually shut down, so there's no need for me to leave München. I'll lock our rooms up and check on them every few days. Herr Mueller downstairs has promised to keep an eye on the apartment.'

I nodded, expecting as much, lifting the box up into the wardrobe.

'Do not come back to München after today, Lotte.'

I swung around. 'What are you talking about?'

'With all the bombings, it's not safe. When the war ends or safety becomes an issue, do not come back. Promise me. When the Americans or Russians reach München, I don't want you here. I've seen victorious armies before. They take whatever they want. It won't be safe in the city. Go to your mother in Windsheim. I will get a message to her when it's safe to return home or, God willing, I will come and collect the two of you myself. Until then, stay with Susie.' He grasped my hand firmly. 'Do you hear me, Lotte?'

'Yes, Vati,' I whispered. I couldn't believe it had come to this. I had come home to farewell my mother and celebrate an early birthday. I was turning twenty but I felt like I was one hundred.

'Stay close to Erich or Colonel von Wissenbach. They will try to keep you safe.'

Mutti glowered at Vati and me. 'This is a mistake. Lotte should be with me, safe at Susie's. It's bad enough that you have to stay. I don't want to hear any more about your plans. I have packing to do.' Mutti stood with a huff and left the room, slamming the door behind her.

I looked from the door to my father's pinched face.

He sighed. 'She'll be all right. She understands and will come round when she calms down. She can't wrap you up like a delicate ornament forever.'

'I know, Vati, but I worry about her.'

'She won't have time to fall apart. She'll be busy with Susie's boys. She's stronger than you think.'

I nodded. The country would be good for Mutti and Tante Susie was a pillar of strength.

'Vati.' I touched him tentatively on the arm. 'Have you heard any more about Heinrich?'

'No, I'm sorry, nothing. It's chaotic and I haven't been able to locate his unit yet. You know that it's mayhem on the Eastern Front. The Russians have taken Warsaw and at this rate, it won't be long before they reach the Oder. I hope Erich has managed to get his family away.' He stared at the table like he was debating what to say next. 'Many of the battalions have been decimated and our troops have been in constant retreat. I've heard stories of whole units surrendering or even deserting and making their way back home.'

He held my hand and looked into my eyes, then lowered his voice so Mutti wouldn't hear in the next room. 'You have to prepare yourself. If Heinrich's alive, it's possible he may be taken as a prisoner of war by the Russians.'

My heart began to thump wildly and my face crumpled in despair. Vati squeezed my hand in reassurance.

'I'll keep looking for him . . . it may be that he's in no position to write or as simple as the fact that the post is no longer getting through.'

'Thank you, Vati. I know he's alive. He has to be.' I hugged my father tightly, breathing in the comforting smells of tobacco and aftershave.

'You'll have that wonderful wedding before you know it,' he said, smoothing my hair from my face. 'Nothing's going to stop me walking you down that aisle to meet your husband.'

'I wouldn't have it any other way.' I felt a moment of desolation, wondering how long it would be before I saw Heinrich or my father again.

Vati reached into his jacket pocket. 'Here, I have something for you, for your birthday. It's something for you to record your memories and special moments while we're apart.' His voice caught as he pulled out a small package. 'I'm sorry I couldn't wrap it properly.'

'It doesn't matter.' I turned it over, breaking through the packaging. Three precious canisters of film lay nestled in the paper. 'Wherever did you find them?'

'It was difficult to get my hands on them but I still have contacts.' He smiled wryly.

'It's perfect Vati. I couldn't have asked for a better gift.' My eyes welled with tears. He knew me so well.

'I don't want you to forget your craft. You have talent. Perhaps one day you'll become a professional photographer. In the meantime, keep your camera with you wherever you go and use the film wisely. It will become impossible to find soon and even worse after the war. I don't know when I will see you next but one day I want to see the photos and share with you the things I have missed. Just promise me that.'

'I will, Vati and I'll think of you every time I use it.' My heart clenched in fear, suddenly apprehensive for him. Nobody knew what was ahead. There was a chance that this was the last time I would ever see him. My father's eyes were moist as he pulled me into a tight embrace. 'I'm so proud of you. You're a wonderful daughter. Stay safe.'

'You too, Vati. I love you,' I said. I didn't want to let him go.

Any tranquillity I felt at Kloster Scheyern was all but destroyed when we learnt that the Russians had reached the Oder River. It was Germany's last defence: once it had been crossed, nothing stood in their way to Berlin. We were under no illusions now.

Germany would fall.

I found Erich sitting at his desk one morning in late January, distracted and drawn.

'What is it Erich? Are you feeling unwell?'

Erich shook his head and handed me a postcard. 'I just received this. Inga has taken the children and they've left Sagan.'

I took the postcard and quickly read the scribbled message. 'At least they've got away. I can't believe how quickly the Russians have moved west. They were in Warsaw only a week or so ago.'

'Yes, I know. From all reports, the Red Army has spread out across Silesia, heading westward.' He gestured to the postcard in my hand. 'By the look of the handwriting, they left very quickly, perhaps when they heard word of the Russians reaching Poznan. I just hope they remained ahead of the Russians while on the road.'

'How were they going to travel with Eva not being well? The trains are out everywhere, especially into Berlin.'

'One of my old colleagues promised to give them a lift to Berlin but I haven't heard from him, so I don't know what's happened.' He shook his head in frustration. 'I think the whole town would have evacuated. It must have been crazy. At least Inga had some help from friends and my colleagues. My hope is that they were driven at least some of the way.'

'Surely they got out early enough to find transport to Berlin . . .' I checked the writing on the back of the postcard again. 'What's in Elend? Why would your wife go there?'

'I don't know but it will most likely be a safe place for her and the children if, God forbid, Berlin falls to the Russians,' said Erich, rubbing his temple. 'When we last discussed this plan, Berlin seemed like a perfectly safe option. I would have thought they'd come to München but with the trains so unpredictable, she probably thinks it's too far and not safe to travel here from Berlin now.'

'Let's hope the Americans reach Berlin first if it comes to that.'

'There's not much I can do now until Inga contacts me.'

'Isn't there any way you can find out where they are?'

Erich shook his head. 'No, I just have to wait.'

'What about your parents?'

'I don't know. The last I heard, my father was stationed around Oppeln but the town was evacuated last week and captured a few days ago. I don't know if he got back to my mother and as far as I know, she hasn't left Grottkau. I'm worried about her too.' He paused, his green eyes dull. 'The Russians have reached Breslau and Grottkau is only about fifty kilometres from there. I can't imagine any of these towns destroyed by war and occupied by the Red Army.' He stared at me despairingly. I knew he had desperately tried to convince his mother to come west and had arranged his family's evacuation weeks ago.

I rested my hand on his shoulder. 'You're not alone. If there's anything I can do . . .'

'Thank you.' Erich smiled weakly, patting my hand, his fingers cold. 'Now, Colonel Von Wissenbach is expecting this report and it won't write itself.'

'I'll leave you to it then,' I said, picking up the ashtray and leaving the room.

I couldn't imagine how Erich was feeling, how he managed to focus on his work. My stomach churned every time I thought about those children fleeing their home, too young to really understand what was happening but old enough to remember the trauma of being ripped away from everything they knew. I remembered that feeling well. I prayed they would find comfort before too long when they reached their relative in Berlin and felt the security of their father's loving arms around them.

Every morning after the post arrived, I entered Erich's office on the pretext of bringing in or picking up files or reports, fresh coffee or emptying the forever full ashtray. 'Anything?' I would ask.

Each day, Erich would shake his head, his brow furrowed. 'Nothing yet.'

I could see the tension in the set of his shoulders and the mound of cigarette butts in his ashtray but there was nothing more I could do for him. 'You'll hear something soon,' I told him. There was still nothing from Heinrich either.

One icy February morning I took an official telephone call from the police in Berlin. The call was for Erich. I transferred it through to him, then stared blankly at the report I was typing, trying not to breathe so I could hear through the closed door of Erich's office. But of course with the noise of the other office girls around me, I heard nothing.

'Fräulein von Klein.' The gently spoken words held a hint of urgency. My head snapped up to find Erich standing at the door. Once he had my attention, he turned back to the office before I could catch his expression. I jumped out of my seat, the skin on the back of my neck prickling with unease and I hurriedly followed him in, closing the door behind me. He was standing at his desk, swaying.

'What is it?'

He stared at me, eyes glazed, his face white as a sheet.

'Here, sit before you fall down.' I guided Erich into his chair. 'Was that telephone call about your family?'

Erich nodded.

'Drink this,' I said, placing his coffee cup in his hand. He dutifully did as I asked and I noticed his hand shake violently.

'I have to go to Berlin,' he said woodenly.

'Is everything okay?' I took the cup from him.

He looked up at me then, his eyes blank. 'Inga and the children made it to Berlin but have been killed in an air-raid.'

'No!' I dropped to my knees next to him, appalled that his wife and children had survived the perilous journey from

142

Silesia only to perish in one of the continuous stream of air-raids on the capital. 'What happened?'

'An envelope addressed to my wife . . . it had my details on the back.' He looked at me, desperation in his eyes.

'Go on.'

'It was found next to the bodies of those who died in the public bunker at Anhalter Bahnhof yesterday . . .'

'Are they sure? Were they travelling by train to the suburbs, to your wife's relative?'

'I don't know. I have to go to Berlin to identify the bodies . . . there's a salvage operation.' He could barely get the words out. 'I have to find out what happened.'

'I'm so sorry, Erich. I'll organise your leave with Colonel von Wissenbach and let him know what's happened.'

'I have to go,' he said leadenly.

I stood. I wished I could accompany him, to give him the support he needed but it wouldn't have been right and with him gone, I would be needed here. 'Go. I have everything under control. I'll find out if anyone is travelling up to Berlin.'

'No, I'll be all right.' I could see the effort he made to remove the emotion from his face. His eyes became steely and he took a deep breath. 'I'll be back as soon as I can.'

On impulse, I leant in and kissed him gently on the cheek. 'Good luck. I'll be thinking of you.'

Bettina was my solace. We both cried at the end of that day, releasing the grief that we could not show in front of others. The pent-up fear I had for Heinrich, held for months, gushed out uncontrollably like a raging river. I finally faced the possibility that Heinrich too was dead. Neither of us was religious but I felt compelled to pray and Bettina stayed with me as I slipped away each night to one of the small chapels in the kloster complex.

At first, I prayed desperately for Heinrich's life, like a mantra. I sat quietly on one of the hard wooden pews, soothed by the gentle lamp light, the flickering candles that glowed by the altar and Bettina's warmth next to me, and sought the words I needed to speak to God. Beyond my hope for Heinrich and a fervent wish to spare Erich his pain, I didn't know what to pray for. Nobody should have to bury their children and lose their whole family in one fell swoop . . .

Finally, I prayed for an end to the war. I prayed for life beyond the war and what it might offer despite the destruction of the country I loved and the losses we had all endured.

Only a few of days after Erich left, we heard that Grottkau had been taken by the Red Army. I wondered if he had heard and how he would take this further blow.

When Erich returned, he was gaunt, eyes bloodshot and sunken, and the hollows beneath them were black. Bettina and I approached him in his office.

'How are you?' Bettina asked quietly. 'Do you need anything?'

Erich sighed, rubbing his eyes. 'It was hopeless. I couldn't find them. I couldn't find anything about them or where they've been.'

'I'm so sorry, hauptinspektor,' said Bettina, glancing at me helplessly. 'Maybe they escaped the air raid.'

'I don't think so,' he whispered, staring out the window, 'maybe I'll never really know what happened to them.'

'I'll let the colonel know,' said Bettina. 'If there's anything you need, please ask.' Before she left the room, she cast another meaningful look at me, as if I should try to get more out of him.

'Are you all right?' I asked Erich.

'No, but I can't talk about it. If I start . . . There's so much to do. I have to focus on my work.' His face had a haunted look. Perhaps he was replaying the scenes he had witnessed over the last few days in his mind.

My anxiety grew as I watched Erich withdraw into himself, working hard but speaking only when necessary. He was often distracted and I'm sure he didn't eat – anything I brought him I took away again untouched. He seemed to live on coffee and cigarettes.

'You need to talk to him,' Bettina said one evening, as we walked towards the dormitory.

'I've tried.'

'He trusts you and I know you'll deny it but there's a bond between the two of you. If anyone can draw him out, it's you.'

'I don't know what you're talking about,' I said, unable to do anything about the flush of embarrassment that crept up my cheeks.

'I've seen the way he looks at you and I know you care about him,' Bettina said softly. I remained silent. 'You know, it's different to what he had with those girls when he first arrived. None were in our department. He kept work and pleasure separate. I only knew because one of the girls was my friend, but she's no longer in München.'

White hot jealousy seared through me.

She placed a hand on my shoulder, stopping me in my tracks. 'These are not ordinary circumstances for any of us.

145

We have to take comfort wherever we can get it because who knows what tomorrow will bring.'

I couldn't articulate my feelings for Erich; once out in the world, there was no recalling them and I wasn't ready to accept the consequences of making them reality. Smiling, I turned the tables on Bettina.

'So, how are you and Kurt going?'

Bettina shrugged, beginning to walk again. 'He's good fun, he makes me laugh and he's a good lover. What else do I need right now?'

'You're sleeping with him already? He's only been in the office a couple of weeks.'

'Why wait? The sparks flew between us the moment we met. The chemistry is there but I have to say I was surprised to discover that we also have a lot in common. I actually really like him.' I could see the joy sparkle in her eyes.

'I'm so happy for you.' But I wondered if this relationship would have happened in normal times and if it had a chance after the war ended – if any of us survived at all.

Later that evening as I left the dining hall alone, I was startled to feel a tap on my shoulder.

'Lotte.'

'Hauptinspektor, good to see you've made it down to dinner. Have you eaten?'

'A little,' he said. He looked desperate, fidgeting with the sleeve of his coat. 'Do you have a few minutes?'

'Of course. What's the matter?'

'I can't get the images out of my head. I wondered if I could talk to you about it ...' He hung his head in embarrassment.

My heart went out to him. 'Come on, I know a good place we can talk in private.'

Erich nodded and followed me in silence until we arrived at the door of the small chapel where I had prayed.

'Is this all right for you?' I whispered, turning to him. 'Bettina and I came here to pray while you were in Berlin.' I stopped, feeling a little embarrassed myself. His eyebrows rose but the nod of acknowledgement that followed encouraged me to continue. 'We won't be disturbed and it's peaceful.'

'Thank you,' he said as I pushed the heavy timber door open. The tranquillity of that sacred place told me it was the right space to voice the horrors he had seen.

We sat in a pew near a stand of burning candles. The flickering light glinted against the gold frames of images of the Catholic saints and cast strange shadows across Erich's pale face, already creased in pain.

'This brings back memories,' he said. 'I haven't been in a Catholic church since I was a child. My mother's Catholic, you know? I suppose I am too.'

'I didn't,' I murmured, distracted by his nearness. 'My mother's father's Catholic too.' Then I was suddenly worried I had done the wrong thing in bringing him here. 'Was this the right place?'

'I couldn't think of a better one. You're right, it is very peaceful here.'

'How are you feeling? Bettina and I are worried about you.'

'I don't know how to feel,' Erich whispered.

I waited while he stared at the burning candles.

'For four days I was accompanied by the men involved in the salvage operation. We rifled through that basement

147

looking for anything that could identity Inga and the children; looking for any clue that might give me some idea of their fate. There was nothing.' His voice caught. 'All I saw were mutilated corpses, crushed and damaged beyond recognition, but there was nothing there I could hold onto, that I could say, "This might be them."' He was shaking now.

'Oh Erich, I'm so sorry.' I didn't dare touch him. He needed to get this out.

Erich continued describing the four days of hell he had endured. I sat very still, but shuddering from time to time as I learnt what it was like to search for loved ones after a bombing. I sent a swift prayer to God, thanking Him for keeping my own family and home safe.

'The only reason I came back was that the salvage operation was cancelled when the basement filled with water,' whispered Erich. 'There's nothing else I can do . . . I don't know what the next step is.' He sighed. 'I can't say for sure that they perished in that air-raid shelter but I have no reason to believe they somehow survived it. I'm torn between a faint hope that they still live and the overwhelming and crushing reality that they are dead . . . something I'll have to accept and come to terms with.' He stared at the steady flames of the candles; candles that the Catholics lit for the souls of their dead.

'Tell me about them,' I said, touching his arm gently. I had seen the children's photo on his desk, they were beautiful – Eva smiling happily and Walter with the large, innocent eyes of a toddler.

It was enough to break Erich from his brooding despair. He told me about his life with his wife and children. He told me that maybe under other circumstances they would not have married, but Inga had fallen pregnant with Eva and he'd felt obliged to marry and take care of her and his child. They discovered that they were not well suited to each other but they tried to make the best of their situation and give Eva a good home and then Walter too, when he came along. Inga was a good woman but an unhappy one. Erich could not give her what she wanted in their marriage but despite the tension between them, he always returned home to his two wonderful children and their mother – he could do nothing else. I believed him when he told me he thought about them and what they might be doing every day.

'Now they're gone. I'm numb. I can't feel anything. Life passes me by while I just exist.'

I shivered, imagining his pain. As the tears began to flow down Erich cheeks, I was tempted to wipe them away but hesitated, not sure he would appreciate it. Tears rolled down my cheeks too, warm on my face. Grief for Erich and his family mingled with my own grief for Willi and Ludwig and my fear for Heinrich. Wanting to comfort him, I leant forward to grasp his hand.

Before I knew it, I held him in a firm embrace. It seemed to be the trigger for Erich to release his pain in a soft sobbing. I smoothed his hair, his head resting on my chest. How could I protect him from the agony? How could I help him bear his pain?

Finally, silence surrounded us like a cocoon. Erich lifted his head, the candlelight illuminating his face. I couldn't move, mesmerised by the deep, desperate and raw yearning in his eyes. My body tingled and my breath came quick and fast. His face was a hair's breadth from mine, filled with vulnerability.

Then Erich kissed me lightly, his lips soft and warm. I did not pull away. I had imagined this moment in my daydreams, but never like this. The reality was better. The connection between us felt right. We both needed comfort. We both needed healing from our pain.

The kiss deepened as Erich's arm slid up my back to cup my head gently with his hand, more insistent as the pressure intensified. Heat rushed through me, making the pit of my belly clench with pleasure. There was no doubt he was experienced, his sensuality evoking a passion in me so different from the one Heinrich inspired, a passion I wasn't aware I was capable of. I could imagine sliding into a world where there was just the two of us, falling deeper and deeper into one another. At this moment, I wanted nothing else. As I became aware of that thought, I pulled back, startled.

Puffs of white vapour stained the frigid air from my heavy breaths, as I stared at Erich, not sure what to think. 'I'm so sorry,' I spluttered. 'I never meant to take advantage of you . . . I just wanted to comfort you.'

'No, you did nothing wrong. I'm sorry.' He leant away and shook his head, looking dumbfounded, as if he couldn't believe he had done such a thing. 'I'm the one who kissed you, I shouldn't have done that. It was wrong of me. I wasn't thinking straight. Please forgive me.'

'Of course,' I said, smoothing my coat with trembling hands. I was relieved and crushed at the same time. 'You've been through so much – there's nothing to forgive.'

'If you're sure,' he said hesitantly. 'Thank you for listening to me. I didn't mean to tell you so much . . . I hope I haven't upset you?'

I shook my head. 'No, I'm honoured that you trusted me enough to share what you've been through.'.

'I would trust you with my life.' Erich grasped my arm as if to emphasise what he was saying. His eyes were shining. 'You've really helped . . . I can bear my burden now.'

'I haven't done anything special,' I murmured, feeling the warmth welling up inside of me. I stared at him, unable to convey my depth of feeling for him. I couldn't tell him that I trusted him with my life too. 'I told you we make a good team. As long as I'm by your side, I'll look out for you. You'll get through this difficult time.'

Erich kissed my forehead. 'I couldn't ask for anything more.' He rose to his feet and gave me his hand. 'Thank you for bringing me here.' He paused. 'But it's cold and I'd better get you back before you're missed at the dormitory.'

We walked in silence back to the dining hall where we went our separate ways.

'Goodnight, Lotte, and thank you,' Erich whispered as he walked away.

9

There was no time for me to feel awkward around Erich. In fact, I wasn't sure how I felt after what had passed between us. Certainly, I felt guilty for allowing Erich to kiss me and for responding to him. I knew that should never happen again. The problem was that every time I looked at him and our eyes met, I felt that connection to him. Something had definitely changed between us. I couldn't pretend otherwise.

Our personal dramas were quickly overshadowed by the news of the bombing of Dresden, one of the most beautiful medieval cities of Europe. It was obliterated by the firestorm that raged for over a week. Most of us knew someone who had lived there. So many died and we could only imagine what horrific deaths they were. Whole families wiped off the face of the earth – all traces of lives lived, gone. This could happen to any city in Germany, should the Allies choose. A sense of helplessness began to take root in those who had previously hoped for some sort of miraculous victory or amicable peace with the Allies.

One morning not long after receiving his heart-wrenching news, I heard Erich whoop with joy. I hurried into the office, wondering if he'd gone mad, not sure what I'd find.

'They're alive,' Erich whispered, incredulous. Standing behind his desk, he stared at me, his eyes large and wide, a telegram in his hands. I stood there stunned, trying to comprehend his words. Breaking out into a huge grin, he strode towards me, picked me up and spun me around. I shrieked and he put me down, kissing me on the cheek.

'Look,' he said, shoving the paper into my face, like an eager school boy. 'Inga and the children are in Elend. I don't know how, but they are.'

I read the telegram, my eyebrows rising in amazement. 'That's wonderful news. Thank God in Heaven they made it and they're safe.'

'I can't believe it.' Erich shook his head and dropped into his chair as the news sank in. 'I have to write to them and make sure everything's all right.' He opened his drawer, pulled out writing paper and then stopped, looking over to me. 'Could you please let the colonel know?'

'Of course.'

'I won't be long,' he said, setting pen to paper, his hand shaking violently.

Everyone was happy for Erich. We needed a joyful story among all the misery.

Bettina came to my desk on the pretext of discussing one of the reports I had typed. 'Everything fine?' she murmured, her head close to mine.

I shot her a perplexed look. 'Why wouldn't it be?'

'I've seen how things are between you and the hauptinspektor. I don't know what's happened, but you're closer than ever.'

'I don't know what you're talking about.'

'This news has to affect you. There's no doubt that after something like this, he'll go back to his wife and family.'

I glared at her, furious. 'I'm nothing but ecstatic that his wife and children have been found alive and safe. He's overjoyed and I'm very happy for him, as is everybody here.'

Bettina sighed. 'Oh Lotte, I know this is hard for you. Don't forget, I'm here if you want to talk.' She squeezed my shoulder before turning away.

My cheeks were burning with anger and shame. She was right, of course. Joy, desire, guilt and jealousy all warred within me. Erich was married and had an obligation to his family. I had promised myself there would be nothing further between us but it didn't stop my feelings for him. On the other hand, I felt the loss of Heinrich acutely. He was still missing; Vati couldn't find him and nobody had heard anything from him. Why couldn't a miracle happen to me?

The edges of Heinrich's photo were beginning to fray with wear. Gazing at it was the only way to remind myself of his familiar lines, imprint his expression in my mind. What I would do if he didn't return from the front? Feeling trapped, I took to wandering the woods, my thoughts going around and around. The cold and snow didn't bother me. In fact, it gave me peace and quiet – nobody wanted to be out unless they had to.

But often the walk to the woods wasn't enough to clear my head and on one afternoon off, I continued to the village of Scheyern. I found a quaint little inn that served Klosterbier. I wasn't normally a beer drinker but after the brisk walk, it seemed just the thing. Slightly bitter and earthy, the straw-coloured lager was refreshing and melted away the remaining tension I felt, uncoiling my muscles, relaxing the churning in my mind.

On my walk back to the dormitory, I was my cheerful, optimistic self once again. Heinrich would come back to me. I wouldn't entertain any thought of a future without him unless I knew for sure he was gone.

Bettina was waiting for me. She was agitated, almost jumping out of her skin. 'Lotte, where have you been?'

'What's wrong? You look upset.' I peeled off my coat, flushed and sweaty from my walk, determined to stay calm.

'It's the hauptinspektor,' she stammered. We were alone in the room and Bettina held out her shaking hands to me, clutching at my arms.

'What is it?' The back of my neck began to prickle.

'Let's sit down,' she said, guiding me to the tightly made bed. Bettina hung her head in shame. 'It's all my fault.'

'What is?' I repeated, confused and impatient.

'You know the hauptinspektor has applied for leave to see his family in Elend? Well, the colonel gave me the telegram from the hauptinspektor to attach to his leave form, proper protocol, you know. As I was putting all the paperwork together, I noticed that the date on the telegram was January, not February. There was a postmark from Berlin, although the telegram came from Elend and arrived here a month later.'

'How can that be?'

'I don't know, but from the date of the postmark, the telegram must have been ready to send from Berlin before the air-raid. Maybe it wasn't sent before the bombings and only sometime after was discovered and sent mistakenly to Elend.' She shrugged. 'Perhaps the telegram had been worded incorrectly and the message should have said that his wife and family had arrived safe and well and were leaving for Elend.'

'Maybe.' I shook my head, trying to work it all out. 'It doesn't matter anyway. They're safe.'

Bettina grasped my hand. 'I'm not so sure. I showed the colonel. He called in the hauptinspektor, who confirmed that he hadn't heard from his wife, even after the letter he sent telling her he was coming to get them.' Tears filled Bettina's eyes. 'We don't know if his family arrived in Elend at all.'

'No!' I clapped my hand over my mouth, aghast. My heart sank, the sunny optimism I had worked so hard to cultivate now grey and bleak like the afternoon sky. How much could one man endure? Erich didn't deserve this. 'How did he take it?' I whispered.

'He kept a brave face in front of the colonel, but he was shocked. The colonel agreed to help him investigate the whereabouts of his family and has already sent for information from people who can help.'

'Surely they're there.' Maybe if I said it out loud, it would be so. 'Everything's in such disarray that even telegrams are easy to misplace.'

Erich was a mess. He wrote more letters to Sagan, Berlin, Elend and even Grottkau, but heard nothing. The few friends and acquaintances he could contact to find out if his family had left Sagan knew nothing. There was no news of his mother in Grottkau either, no way of knowing whether she and his father were safe and well. He continued with his work but the strain on him showed in little ways: forgetting meetings; confusing reports on different airfields. These were things I could cover seamlessly but I couldn't help with the internal turmoil I knew he was experiencing. As he withdrew into himself, refusing to speak about it to anyone – including me – I could only watch and pray that he received an answer soon, one way or the other. It was the not knowing that was killing him.

After what seemed like an eternity but was only a couple of weeks, Colonel von Wissenbach's sources returned the information we had been dreading. Erich's wife and children were nowhere to be found in Berlin, Elend or Sagan. In fact, there was no trace of them anywhere. Inga's relative in Berlin had also disappeared. It was possible that she was carrying the envelope with Erich's details and she may have perished in the air-raid. Perhaps she had sent the telegram – nobody could tell for sure. The colonel's sources had advised him that the likelihood was that Erich's family had perished while on the run. It was tantamount to an official certification of death.

Erich refused to believe it and I could understand why. There were so many reasons why his family couldn't be found, all he wanted was time to find them or for Inga to contact him.

It was mid-March when I received Mutti's letter wishing me a happy birthday. After a long siege, the Americans had finally captured Trier, where my grandparents still lived.

Despite the chaos, they were in good health and were well treated by the Americans. That in itself was a good birthday present. Perhaps the Americans would treat us all well, provided they reached us before the Russians.

On the morning of my birthday, wanting to feel close to my family, I reread the letter, placing Heinrich's photo beside it. It was Sunday but there was so much work to do that any thought of a small birthday celebration with Bettina and a few of the girls was pushed out of my mind. Erich wished me a happy birthday but his eyes were dull, his skin was sallow and he seemed lifeless. He slumped over his desk, so alone and fragile, continuing to work through the pile of files stacked up next to him. There was nothing I could do to help him.

Bettina surprised me by announcing to the office that it was my birthday. Somehow, she had even managed to find a small cake that she cut into tiny slivers, giving each of us a soft, delicious mouthful. I savoured the sweetness and texture of the crumb in my mouth as long as possible, allowing it to take me back to the carefree days when my family was intact. Before the war, when laughter and joy accompanied the cutting of the birthday cake. After lunch in the dining hall, I decided to take Erich something to eat. At my insistence, Bettina was off to spend a few precious hours with Kurt. Our department was virtually deserted. I knocked on Erich's door before walking in with the plate of food.

'I brought you some lunch,' I said. 'You should eat it while it's still warm.'

Erich dropped his pen, leant back in his chair and sighed. 'Thank you,' he said absently. 'I never seem to get to the bottom of these files, no matter how long I sit here.'

Clearing a place on the other side of the desk, I put the plate down. 'Come and eat. You need your strength if you're going to continue, although you look like you could do with some fresh air.'

'I'm fine,' said Erich in a flat voice.

'You're pale and pasty. A bit of fresh air and exercise will get the blood flowing again, brighten you up. Then you should be able to concentrate.'

'All right,' he said automatically.

I watched Erich push the food around his plate unenthusiastically and finally stare out of the window.

'Finish your meal,' I said firmly. 'You'll get sick if you don't eat properly.' I picked up the perpetually full ashtray. 'When I come back in, I want your plate empty and then you're going for a walk.' I pretended not to notice the look of shock on his face as I left the room.

Sure enough, when I returned, Erich's plate was almost empty.

'I'm sorry. I can't eat any more.'

'Fine,' I said, taking his plate. 'Your stomach's shrunk after not eating much these last few weeks. Now get your coat, because we're going for a walk into the village. It'll do you the world of good.'

Erich didn't argue.

We walked briskly towards the village in silence while I tried to work out how to make conversation. He was a fit man and his long, athletic limbs moved with a gracefulness I found fascinating.

'You're doing this walk so comfortably,' I said, panting a little. 'I'm curious. Do you hike regularly?'

Erich laughed despite his sombre mood. 'I wish I had the time. I spent much time hiking and hunting in the days of my youth. You learn how to walk with the minimum of effort, relaxed but still keeping your wits about you.'

I nodded, remembering he had told me a little of his childhood in Silesia.

'You on the other hand,' he said, watching me carefully from under the visor of his officer's cap, a smile spreading across his face. 'You walk quickly and I can see you're fit but you're stiff and tight when you walk. You use much more effort than you need.'

'It's how I was taught,' I said, offended, my footsteps crunching solidly along the icy path. 'We learnt the right way to walk and hike when I was in the BDM. We spent many hours hiking through the countryside.'

'March, you mean,' he said, knowing exactly how to bait me. 'I bet you all made so much noise that the animals in the vicinity disappeared well before you got there.'

'I beg your pardon! Our group was always one of the best on the weekend hikes.' I whirled around, almost crashing into him. Erich grabbed me as I slipped – the leather soles of my shoes losing traction on an icy patch. I pulled away from his grasp, glimpsing the grin plastered across his face. 'I can manage just fine.' I strode away, nursing a bruised ego and furious, not only because he had teased me but also because I had reacted.

It was with some satisfaction that I heard Erich panting as he caught up to me.

'What are we doing in the village, anyway?' he asked, as if nothing had happened.

I refused to look at him. 'Well if you must know, the walk clears my mind and I found a little inn that serves Klosterbier. Good for body and mind.'

'Very good.' He was walking next to me once more. 'I didn't take you for a beer drinker but I'll buy you for a drink for your birthday. I'm sorry that with everything that's been going on, I haven't got you anything . . . '

My annoyance at his snap judgements disappeared in an instant. 'That's all right. Your company is more than enough.' Feeling my face redden, I pulled my scarf up over my cheeks. 'I don't usually drink beer but the Klosterbier is very good . . . I couldn't ask for a better way to spend my birthday.'

We sat at a little table at the inn. It was intimate and cosy with the fire crackling merrily, only heightening the anticipation of spending a few precious hours in Erich's company. My fingers and toes tingled pleasantly as tendrils of warmth thawed the frozen parts of my body.

One beer turned into two and then three as we relaxed and opened up about our lives. I told him about my early life back in Düsseldorf and about my parents' divorce and boarding school; how I had felt so alone and unwanted. I told him about Vati and how supportive he had been of me since he married my mother. I cried when I spoke about my long friendship with Heinrich. I couldn't believe that he might be gone. Erich wiped the tears from my eyes and somehow it felt right when he held my hand across the table, comforting and solid, immediate and real.

He told me more about his young life too, as an only child growing up in Grottkau, sharing his love of the outdoors and of flying and helping in his father's furniture shop, until the time he had met Inga.

'We should head back,' Erich said finally.

I looked out the window to see the shadows lengthening. 'Time passes quickly, doesn't it?' I said trying to distract him, sure that the mention of Inga had brought his pain to mind once more. 'Thank you for my birthday drinks.' Rising too quickly from my seat, a rush of vertigo came over me and I grabbed the table to steady myself. 'I think I had a bit too much.'

Erich was at my elbow immediately, standing so close that a small tremor passed through me and I broke out into a fine sweat.

I let go of the table and stood tall, taking control of my errant body. 'I'm fine. Nothing the walk back won't fix.'

He helped me shrug into my coat, his movements slow and deliberate, draping my scarf around my neck, his touch lingering on my skin.

'Here, take my arm until you feel better.' I looked into Erich's face and saw the concern in his furrowed brow. Still woozy, I nodded and took his arm gratefully as we stepped out into the pale, cold afternoon.

We were still arm in arm as we strolled by the woods near the kloster. The conversation had finally turned to Erich's family. He was having difficulty accepting that they were gone. We were both feeling emotionally raw. His anguish had brought my own grief for my brothers back to the surface, as if their deaths had only just occurred. The depth of my pain took me by surprise and the possibility that I had lost Heinrich made my sense of loss almost overwhelming.

'How about we walk back through the woods?' I asked, seeking a distraction. 'It's where I go when I want to find some peace, especially when things are going around and around in my head.'

'Is this the place you were telling me about?'

'Yes. I often take photographs there ... anything that catches my eye. Surrounded by nature, I find a sense of balance somehow.' I looked up into his face, hoping he understood what I meant.

He nodded, looking thoughtful. 'That sounds like just what we both need. Lead the way.'

I let go of Erich's arm, missing the warmth of him immediately. Trying to keep away from the flurries of snow, I found the little trail and followed it through the woods. He offered me his hand as I stepped across rocks and jumped over fallen logs. More than once, I found myself unsteady on my feet, leaning against his broad, firm chest, his arms around me keeping me safe. Neither of us said a word. We didn't have to.

We reached the small stream where I often sat, waiting for photographic inspiration to hit me as I mulled over my problems. It had stopped flowing now and was covered in ice, transformed into its winter glory as it glistened in the afternoon sunlight.

'You're right about this place,' he said, still holding my hand. 'It's special, I can feel it.' His eyes were alight with joy at the beauty at our feet. It made my heart clench – he understood what this place meant. He was just like me. 'Listen, you can hear the forest sounds. I know we've made enough noise but still the creatures of the forest are here.'

'What do you mean?'

'Close your eyes and see what you can hear,' he whispered. His breath brushed the hair curled in front of my ear, tickling my face. I closed my eyes, languid from the beer, the walk, the nearness of him and his breath in my ear. All my awareness was focused on him. 'Can you hear them now?'

I nodded. The tweet of birds and rustle of small creatures rooting through the undergrowth and the deep sighing of the bare trees that surrounded us registered dimly in my consciousness but I could have drawn every detail of Erich standing behind me. I leant back against him and he wrapped his arms around me.

I turned to reach for him instinctively – I couldn't help myself. He pressed his cold, soft lips against mine, and I welcomed the moist warmth of his mouth. My body was pushed hard against him, yet it didn't feel close enough. I drew his head towards me, and he clasped me to him, holding me like he'd never let go.

'Is this what you want?' he murmured between kisses.

'Yes,' I breathed, not wanting him to stop.

He slid one hand down my back to rest on my behind. I felt his manhood hard and rigid as he pulled me against him. A deep throbbing began low in my belly and my legs quivered so violently, I was sure I was about to fall. Swiftly, he lifted me so I straddled his waist. I should have been shocked but I just wanted him closer.

'I want you,' Erich said, his voice rough with need. 'Are you sure this is what you want too? Because once we start this, I can't promise I'll be able to stop.'

'Yes,' I groaned. His words and voice inflamed my desire. I knew there was no going back now. A force greater than myself compelled me to throw away rational thought and sensible decisions. There was no choice. I must follow this path.

'Let's find somewhere a little more protected,' he murmured in my ear.

'There's an old wood shed, through that stand of trees.' I pointed, amazed I was still capable of speaking, let alone lucid thought.

Moving with surprising speed, Erich carried me to the abandoned wood shed, still sure footed. I felt safe in his arms. He put me down gently and I could only stare, mesmerised, as he removed his coat, placing it on the dirt floor. He kissed me once more and lay me back on the coat.

We stared into each other's eyes, a little shy with the break in momentum.

'You mean a great deal to me, I want you to know that,' he whispered, brushing a lock of hair behind my ear. I reached for him and kissed him again, falling further into our private world, the cold, hard floor barely registering. He unbuttoned my coat and reached into my dress, his cold hands a shock at first. Our eyes locked as he kneaded my breasts and encircled my nipples until they were erect and exquisitely tender. I saw the desire grow in his sparkling eyes as he watched my response to him. I desperately wanted him to touch my nipples. When he did, it was so feather soft it was excruciating. I gasped as bolts of pleasure shot towards my belly. His power over me, his ability to arouse me like this, only whet my need for him further.

'I want you more than I've wanted anything in my life,' he said. His eyes were pools of endless green. I felt strong and powerful and I pulled him to me. He was heavy but not unbearable as he supported himself on his elbows. I lifted my hips towards him in greeting before he leant in to kiss me with such an intensity I thought I was going to burst. Then he was gone, the cold air rushing in where his warmth had been and I felt momentarily bereft.

'Don't go,' I cried. 'Come back.'

He was kneeling between my legs. 'I want you ready for me and I don't want it to hurt more than it needs to.' He pressed the heel of one hand against the hard mound between my legs. My shock drained away as the pulsing began. He lay alongside me now to keep me warm, his hand never straying from its work. As he massaged my softness with deft, gentle fingertips, I could think of nothing else. His touch became firmer and more insistent. It was almost unbearable and I moaned softly until I was unaware of the world around me.

Then he was lying over me, his voice low and hypnotic, telling me how beautiful and desirable I was. I felt the cold blow over my nether parts and then warmth, soft and firm against my dampness and a sudden sharp and searing pain as he forced past my barrier and slid into me. My eyes were wide with shock and Erich lay very still as I adjusted to the new sensations.

'The worst is over now,' he said, softly kissing my cheeks, my neck and my ears.

Carefully, he began to move and my pain was forgotten as I felt him deep within me. The pulsating continued, now in time with Erich's slowly increasing thrusting. I clung to him, our bodies joined as one, as we sought our pleasure and oblivion in each other. The rest of the world was forgotten. At the moment of his release, I watched his face move from joy to surrender and total vulnerability. I understood, then, the true meaning of this precious act – and the meaning of passion.

'I love you,' he said and I knew he meant it.

Our lovemaking left my emotions raw. There was no rest for me that night, tossing and turning, burning hot as with fever, images of Erich tumbling over themselves in my mind, making me want to reach for him again. Heinrich was my other constant, my memories of our carefree days, and in my fevered state, fantasies of making love to him colliding with those of Erich. Two men who loved me, opposites, like light and shade. Despite my duty and love for Heinrich, I couldn't deny that I wanted Erich in a very different way. To me, they were still boy and man. I was left exhausted at dawn, guttered like a candle burning at both ends, weak and helpless.

There was no time to consider what had happened in the cold light of day: the order came through to begin packing once again. The command headquarters was being evacuated to Markt Schwaben, east of München. The Rhein River, the final obstacle to Germany's full capitulation, had been breached by the Allies, who were marching rapidly east. From what we understood, many units were being called back towards south-eastern Germany, ready for a final retreat towards the Bavarian Alps.

While I was sorting through what had to be packed, Erich called me into his office. He was agitated, pacing the space between his desk and the window, swearing.

'What's wrong?' I asked, surprised at his ill temper and worried he was upset with me.

'I have to go the airpark at Illesheim. There's a problem with the new aircraft that nobody seems able to sort out. I can't afford the time to go but the problem needs to be dealt with.' He raked his fingers through his hair with frustration. These new aircraft were all we had left to pin our hopes on. They were to be our saviours in Germany's final assault, our last chance to defeat our enemies.

'How long will you be gone?' I asked, already distraught at the thought of him going.

'Only a day, maybe two.' He stopped pacing and met my eyes, fiddling with the contents of his pocket. 'But I wondered if you wanted to come. I thought you might like to see your mother in Bad Windsheim on the way back. I know you have lots to do here but it might be the last chance you get to see her before the Americans arrive.'

I wanted nothing more than to see my mother, feel her familiar embrace and know I was in a safe, uncomplicated place for even a short while, but it meant being alone with Erich. As much as that idea made me breathless, I wanted time away from him to consider how I felt. I was an engaged woman and Heinrich could still be alive somewhere; I had a duty to wait for him. Although I knew making love with Erich had been a mistake, it had opened up a new world for me. I was excited. I wanted to delve further into this forbidden world, explore new experiences beyond the boundaries of my chaste and restricted life.

Erich stood still, watching me with hooded eyes but not without compassion. Perhaps he understood my predicament.

'All right,' I said, desire outweighing prudence.

He nodded. 'We leave in an hour,' he said, turning his back on me, pulling open the filing cabinet.

I left the room, confused and my face burning with embarrassment. Suddenly I wasn't sure if he wanted me to come or not. Not sure if he still wanted me, now he'd had his pleasure from me.

The journey to Illesheim was tense. Chewing industriously on my fingernail, brooding over our last exchange, it took me longer than it should have to realise that nothing had changed between us. We were alone and the closeness of him made me want him so badly. His smouldering gaze told me that it was the same for him but he was a perfect gentleman, polite and attentive. It nearly drove me crazy.

Avoiding the potholes and crumbling edges of the dilapidated road took most of Erich's attention. I was happy to travel in silence, thinking I had got away without talking about anything consequential, but I was wrong.

'Thank you for pulling me out of the dark hole I've been in,' Erich said finally, glancing at me as the car hummed along a stretch of straight, undamaged road.

'I'm glad you're feeling better,' I said a little tightly, folding my hands in my lap.

'I'm sorry if I've been a burden on you. I didn't mean to drag you into my problems.'

I shut my eyes for a second. What Erich had been through would destroy many people. He was a good man and he had been through enough.

'No, I'm glad I could help. It's just that . . .' I couldn't finish the thought and I turned to look out the window, blushing furiously, barely noticing the barren fields.

'You didn't expect what happened between us in the woods.'

'Yes,' I whispered.

'I didn't mean for that to happen ... I'm sorry I lost control, but I'm not sorry for loving you. I've wanted you ever since the day you walked into my office, gorgeous and so full of life.'

My head jerked around in surprise but Erich's eyes were on the road.

'But not now.' I paused, turning to look back out the window, my fist over my mouth. Afraid that once I said the words, I couldn't deny them. 'Not now that you've had me.' I glanced back at him.

Erich's eyes were wide with surprise, his hands gripping the steering wheel tightly. His face flushed red.

'How can you say that? I told you I love you and I have done ever since the day you told me about your brother. I knew you were special the moment I first laid eyes on you. I would never disrespect you like that.'

He loves me, I thought, ecstatic. I wasn't being cast aside or discarded like a used thing. Relief flooded my body like air to a suffocating person. Then I remembered that this wasn't possible.

'How could you love me? You were married and I was planning a wedding,' I snapped.

'You know my marriage was in trouble long before I met you. Besides, you can't choose who you fall in love with.'

A white hot spear of jealousy arose from nowhere. 'What about the women you had when you first came to München? I know all about them. Bettina told me.'

'They meant nothing to me!' Erich slammed the steering wheel in frustration. He looked ahead for a long moment before he spoke again. 'After I left Inga for my posting in München, I knew that my marriage was over. In my self-pity, full of guilt, despair and loneliness, I sought comfort and oblivion wherever I could . . . but it made no difference. Only when I met you did I understand that my only redemption could be love.'

I sighed and shook my head. All this talk about love didn't help me at all. 'The war will be over soon and you know that I'll be marrying Heinrich when he returns home. It's all been organised.' Erich had to understand that I was committed regardless of how I might feel. It was right to put a stop to wherever our relationship was headed and right to remind Erich of my situation. But staring out the window at nothing, all I could feel was a deep disappointment that we wouldn't continue our affair. Despite my introduction to an irresistible new world, I couldn't accept the part of me that wanted to ignore my commitment and explore that path with Erich.

'I know, Lotte,' he said finally. 'I would never keep you from the life you've planned. You have a good future with Heinrich.' His eyes did not waver from the road.

I felt the blood drain from my face, surprised he had given in so easily. 'I wanted you too. We both lost control . . .'

Erich smiled, his eyes meeting mine, the naked need in them burning a hole through to my soul. 'Your desire does crazy things to me . . .' His smile faded. 'I should have known better though.'

I fought to find the words to justify my feelings for him, clenching my fists in my anxiety. 'You make me feel special,

171

valued, and you always treat me as your equal – with respect. It's the first time anyone has ever made me feel like that. All my life, I've been told what I must do and my thoughts and opinions are of secondary importance, if they're noticed at all.' I looked through the windshield at the tiny village we drove through. It seemed deserted.

Erich shook his head and sighed. 'I don't understand why anybody would treat you any other way. You're intelligent, curious and deep thinking. I know I couldn't have got through these last months without your kindness.' His shoulders slumped. 'I hope Heinrich realises what a lucky man he is.'

An unspoken question hung between us like a dark storm cloud: What would I do if Heinrich were dead?

10

The Illesheim Airpark was chaotic when we arrived. The Americans had reached Heidelberg, only one hundred and fifty kilometres away. The Wehrmacht was in full retreat and the airpark was being evacuated.

We didn't stay long. There wasn't much Erich could do there. While he was discussing matters with airbase command, I chatted with one of the office girls. I learnt that the various units were taking what they could with them, destroying what they had to leave behind or distributing items among the locals. It was sobering to watch the impending exodus first hand. It hit me hard that Germans doing their job for their country were being forced to leave their workplaces and homes for fear of being treated like criminals in the eyes of the invading forces.

Erich called me over as he strode purposefully back towards the car. 'I've spoken to Colonel von Wissenbach. Many of the aircraft are being redirected to München-Riem for now. He wants us to go there to manage the incoming aircraft and then meet them at the new headquarters in a couple of weeks or so.'

'Me too?' I asked, surprised.

'Yes. It'll be crazy and I could use your efficiency. There's no time to go back to the kloster – some of the aircraft are already arriving at Riem.'

'What about the packing?'

'I'm sure Bettina and the girls will handle it.' He touched my arm lightly. 'We won't be able to stop in Windsheim to see your mother. I'm so sorry. Colonel von Wissenbach wants us in Riem now.'

I stopped walking and stared at him accusingly.

'I didn't plan this,' he said. 'Truly. In fact, I thought before we came that perhaps you might have been able to stay in Windsheim with your mother. The Americans are closing in and soon it will be bedlam.' He frowned, as if a new thought had come to him. 'Maybe someone can give you a lift, one of the locals who works here?'

'It's a possibility,' I said, my arms crossed and my face stony. I would have loved to go to Windsheim that very day and stay with my mother until the end of the war. I was so tired, my conflict over how I felt about Erich draining me, and some distance from him would surely be a good thing. His offer was tempting but I also knew how much he needed me. His grief had taken its toll on him. In the state he was in, he would hardly manage on his own. Also, I took my responsibility to my job seriously and I knew I could still make a difference if I continued to Riem with him.

Erich waited patiently, lighting a cigarette, as if he had all the time in the world.

'No, it's all right. I'll come to Riem with you. You wouldn't manage without me anyway,' I said glibly.

Erich stared at the ground in front of him, the cigarette between his fingers. 'No, I wouldn't.' I saw the pain in his expression.

My heart clutched in regret. There was no reason to be cruel. There wasn't a malicious bone in Erich's body. 'I'm sorry,' I mumbled.

He sighed and nodded. 'Come on then, we'd better get going.'

Our eyes met and I saw that he had forgiven me.

I'd been to München-Riem with Erich before but had never realised how large the facility was. I was constantly on the go, running errands around the huge airfield. Luckily, I had help in the form of Marissa, the secretary of the technical officer at Riem. Her knowledge of the base and its inner workings was gold to me.

The great excitement at Riem was the arrival of the elite fighter squadron, the Jagdverband 44. Even Erich was enraptured by the full squadron of new Me 262 fighter jets at his disposal. He was in heaven and whenever I delivered files to his desk or picked up a report, he would explain his findings to me in great detail. I found it very difficult to hide my amusement, grinning at his earnest expression. But I was happy to see how the aircraft lifted his mood and gave him such excitement. And I was pleased to be able to arrange for Erich to meet with one of the heroes of the Luftwaffe: the flying ace, Adolf Galland.

Afterwards, Erich came to find me. He dashed over to where I stood at the filing cabinet, sweeping me off my feet and twirling me around with a whoop of delight.

'That was amazing,' he said, putting me down again. 'However did you manage it?'

I shrugged. 'Just lucky,' I said. 'I bumped into him in the corridor and I knew you would get a thrill out of talking to him.'

'You did that for me?'

'Of course.' His shirt sleeves were rolled casually up his forearms, his collar unbuttoned, revealing the soft tuft of chest hair that sprang from the smooth skin beneath. I was finding it hard to think.

'You did it only as your duty to your superior, I suppose. You're a good secretary, Lotte. Thank you for thinking of me.'

The words cut me like a knife. Yet there was no cruelty in his face, only guarded curiosity.

'How can you say that? After everything that's been between us?' Tears pricked my eyes. 'I did it because I knew how much pleasure it would give you.'

Erich stepped back and looked hard at me. 'You care for me.' It was a statement rather than a question, as if this fact had just occurred to him. A flicker of vulnerability flashed in his eyes before wariness took over.

'Erich, you know I care for you.' I couldn't help moving towards him. I placed my palm gently on his cheek, the stubble prickling against my skin pleasantly. 'We've worked together for nearly two years now and we've been through so much.'

'Is it just that?'

I sighed and dropped my hand. 'No, it's not just that. I know there's something more between us.'

'Tell me how you feel about me,' Erich demanded. 'I want to hear you say it.'

I hung my head, my face flaming with embarrassment. 'I feel an undeniable attraction to you, but as for the rest . . .' I shrugged, unable to express my confusion. 'I don't know.'

'Look at me.'

Slowly I lifted my head and stared into his intense eyes. Electricity sparked between us. The state of undress, the five-o'clock shadow and the lock of hair that had strayed out of place, falling over one eye, made him irresistible to me. I couldn't hide my feelings for him and I knew he could see it all written clearly on my face.

Then he had me in his arms, kissing me deeply. I felt every muscle in my body give way, ready for total surrender. I didn't think I could hold back much longer and deny what we both wanted. He stepped away, breathing hard, trying to control his ardour. He grabbed my face with both hands, the gesture intimate and possessive.

'Lotte, make no mistake: I want you. I want all of you now and forever but I'll wait until you tell me that you want me the way I want you.'

I didn't know what to say. Part of me wanted to tell him I wanted him more than anything in the world, that I wanted to be by his side, but I couldn't.

He kissed me gently on the mouth. 'Thank you for today. Your actions speak louder than words.' Then he was gone, leaving me breathless and very unsettled.

I wondered if what I was feeling for Erich was love but it was hard to tell among the tangled complexities of our situations, like a skein of knotted wool.

I thought of how Heinrich went along with the will of our families. He didn't have to fight for me, express his unwavering need for me, stand up for me against those who may have decreed we shouldn't be together. I wondered if he had ever thought about what he truly wanted. If he came home to me, I hoped that his time away would change the way he viewed the world, because I had certainly changed. I wished I had Bettina with me. I wanted to talk and was desperate for her perspective, her cool objectivity. She was probably in Markt Schwaben by now, only about twenty kilometres further east, but a whole ocean could easily have stretched between us.

Riem was close to München and over the weeks, during the American bombing raids we endured and the recovery and repair work that followed, I often wondered how Vati was going or if there was any opportunity to see him. I had sent him a letter to tell him where I was, and had scribbled a note to Mutti, giving it to a young member of the maintenance crew who lived there. He was going home on furlong to recover from an illness instead of joining us at Riem.

I was surprised when he popped his head into the office one day. 'Hans,' I exclaimed, glad I had remembered his name. 'What are you doing here?'

'I'm better now, Fräulein von Klein,' he said. 'I couldn't stay away and, to be honest, I prefer to be here than Windsheim. The Americans are crawling all over the district. I left the day they took the airpark at Illesheim. They would have arrived in Bad Windsheim the next day. It's taken me a week to get here.' He grinned. 'But here I am safe and sound and I have a letter for you from your mother.' He reached into his jacket and pulled out a rumpled envelope with what I recognised as Mutti's handwriting.

'Thank you, Hans,' I said taking the letter. 'I can't tell you what this means to me.' I jumped out of my seat and reached up on tip-toes to kiss him on the cheek.

Hans blushed furiously. 'My pleasure,' he said. 'I'm glad I made you happy. I'd better go and see my captain.'

'I won't forget your kindness, Hans.'

It was only later that day that I was able to read the letter privately, lying on my bed. Any news from home was going to ground me, I decided. Eagerly, I opened the envelope and slid out the wad of paper.

My dearest Lotte,

I'm sorry you couldn't join us in Windsheim. I'm only happy that you are safe and well. Thank you for your note. I'm sure you're working very hard. Now that you're closer to Vati, maybe the two of you could manage to see each other? Perhaps he could come and see you? It would ease my mind to know that you have each other.

We are well here, as well as can be expected. Tante Susie and I are kept busy with the children and preparations for the arrival of the Americans. We hear the constant drone of their planes overhead and expect them very soon. Thank God it is them and not the Russians. There is some trepidation about what they will do. Tante Susie thinks we will be fine, thanks to a group of local women standing up to

*the burgomeister and the local Wehrmacht commander. We
have been declared a 'hospital city' but I'm not sure that will
be enough.*

*On Easter Sunday, the Americans bombed the machin-
ery factory of Hans Schmotzer, the biggest industrialist in
Windsheim. The Schmotzers are old friends of Tante Susie
and Onkel Werner. The rail yards nearby were destroyed and
a few days later, more rail yards and a local food warehouse
were hit, and two boys were killed. There have been plenty
of small attacks in the area over the last month, which has
done nothing to reassure the people of Windsheim. It has been
very tense here, a town of anxious women, worried for their
children and families, their homes, livelihoods and the town
they live in. I have to admit, I feel the same, although you
and Vati are not here and our home is hopefully still standing
in München.*

*I would never have thought that a town like Windsheim
would be a dangerous place to be. Of course, we had heard
stories of the brutality dished out to those who surrendered
to the Americans. The Hitler Youth and the Volkssturm are
usually the instruments of this disgraceful behaviour but
burgomeisters and even ordinary citizens have been known
to exact revenge on those who see the reality of our situation.
I don't know if you've heard of the notorious 'werewolves' but
they roam the countryside looking for trouble or anyone they
think contravenes Himmler's edicts and the consequences are
dire for those they target. I think we've become a society of
savages and brutes, killing innocent people indiscriminately,
those whose only crimes are self-preservation and protecting
their families and homes.*

Did you know that it's a crime punishable by death to even hang white sheets out the windows, allowing safe passage to a victorious army? I've seen defeat and German surrender before but never like this! It's insane to expect civilians to barricade their streets and fight the incoming army when there is no chance of victory. Their homes, their villages and their lives are destroyed for nothing! We've heard those villages and towns that have resisted the Americans have been bombed from the air until there is little left and the Americans can sweep in unmolested. The loss of life and the destruction of ancient villages, the irrevocable carnage, is horrendous and can never be repaired.

Not only are there barricades erected at all the entrances of the town but to everyone's horror, antitank units and machine gun nests are placed 'in strategic positions' among the homes of ordinary locals! Some of the older veterans have tried to dissuade the burgomeister. He's a good man Tante Susie and Onkel Werner have known for a long time. He told them he was threatened with execution if he ordered removal of the barricades. In turn, the veterans asked the local Wehrmacht commander, a Major Reinbrecht, to remove the barricades and put measures in place to keep the town safe. The commander told them his orders were to protect the town from the invading army and prevent their entry at all costs.

Yesterday, our situation here came to a head. A group of women and children assembled in the markplatz to persuade the commander and the local party leader to order the Wehrmacht out of town. Tante Susie and I joined the edge of the crowd, where we could still see the house. The children were told to stay indoors and prepare for bed. A delegation of women led by Thekla Fischer went into the Wehrmacht command post set up in the rathaus to speak to Major Reinbrecht. We didn't have to wait long. The delegation hurried out of the rathaus, clearly furious. Thekla's voice rang across the square as she told the crowd that Reinbrecht did not hear their plea but had threatened to shoot anyone who did not leave the room immediately. I thought she must be lying because I couldn't believe that a highly ranking officer would threaten harm to a group of unarmed women, but I was wrong. Reinbrecht came out of his hole shortly after and soldiers were placed around the town square as a means of intimidating or controlling us, it doesn't matter which. I was incensed but I wasn't the only one. Reinbrecht read out the edicts once again and explained that his troops could not leave without authorisation.

There was much restlessness in the crowd by this time and murmuring at his disregard for our safety and our town became shouts of anger, punctuated by the waving of arms and fists. One of the local soldiers mounted a wagon to try to calm the crowd and reassure them that everything would be all right. Men! They think that if they speak, we should listen, agree and obey! Well, he was wrong to get involved. The crowd was wound up now, hurling abuse at him, spitting and jeering, harassing his wife, who stood nearby. He pulled his gun, threatening to shoot if his wife was harmed and, as he was the only one they could get to, the women nearby pulled him off the wagon. One of the elderly businessmen wrestled the gun away from him. Reinbrecht threatened to execute this elderly leader of the community on the spot. Thank God, a veteran was able to persuade him not to.

At this point, I didn't know what was going to happen. The crowd was beyond reason and surging towards Reinbrecht. Tante Susie tried to pull me away to the safety of the house before things turned nasty. As we turned to leave, we heard Reinbrecht shout, 'Jabos!' Only with the thought that there were fighter bombers overhead did the crowd break up, running for cover, and the square was silent once more.

Shaken by what had happened and unable to sleep, Tante Susie and I stayed up late, keeping each other company. Sounds of explosions punctuated the night but it wasn't until today that we realised that our own Wehrmacht had shelled the edge of town in revenge for our actions. Luckily, there wasn't much damage, but I can't understand how we came to this. It was hard to believe that a simple request had escalated into madness. The women were justified in their response, trying to protect everything they held dear, when so much had already been taken away from them. We had thought that was the end of it all, but it was not.

One of the women, Anni Schunk, was taken from her home this morning by soldiers and questioned by Reinbrecht. Apparently, he wanted the names of the ringleaders of our demonstration. As if the plea to save the town was an organised measure of resistance against the Reich! Of course, she had no names to give, not that she would. She was placed in stocks in the town hall arcade and guarded by two soldiers, who were told to shoot her if she tried to escape. What disgraceful behaviour! He even wanted her head shaved but the barber refused. Anni was released after a couple of hours, distressed at her ordeal but triumphant that Reinbrecht had not got what he wanted or broken the spirit of the women of this town.

The stupid man then paraded a sixteen-year-old Hitler Youth around town as a hero after awarding him the Iron Cross. He had slipped behind American lines and reported on the position of their artillery. We shook our heads at the idiocy and most of us stayed or went indoors, rather than watch.

I never imagined in my wildest dreams what came next. I can scarcely believe it even now and every time I shut my eyes, I can see the scene burned into my mind. We were going about our business. Tante Susie had the children in bed and we were walking across to the Schmotzers' to help them in the canteen next to their house. We heard a roar coming down the street and an official car screeched to a stop in front of the Schmotzer house. Christine and Hans were on the sidewalk when an officer jumped out of the car asking for Frau Schmotzer. Christine admitted that she was Frau Schmotzer and a man dressed in the black leather coat of a Gestapo officer climbed out of the car. He accused her of organising the demonstration. She immediately said no, that she had not, and began backing away. He drew his revolver. Tante Susie and I were standing still down the street, rooted to the spot. I couldn't believe my eyes. He fired at her as she was turning to flee. She fell to the sidewalk. I'll never forget the screams of her family around her. The Gestapo officer walked up to her while she lay there and shot her twice more at close range. I only later learnt that the first shot had hit her in the neck, the next two shots in her mouth and left eye. Who, except a sadistic monster, would do that and to an innocent, unarmed woman? Tante Susie and I were sobbing in each other's arms, shaking with terror and horror. We watched as

he placed a placard with big, red lettering on her body. It said:
'A traitor has been executed.'

I don't understand why Christine was targeted. She was a
good woman, not a troublemaker, no more involved in organ-
ising the meeting in the square as Tante Susie and I, or of
confronting Major Reinbrecht. All I can say is that thank God
the Americans are coming. This nightmare has to end. We
can only hope that they will treat us well, as they did with my
parents in Trier and that they leave the town intact.

So, my darling, I end this letter so that young Hans can
bring it to you before the Americans arrive. I hope you are well.
Stay safe. I pray that I see you again soon, that we will be all
reunited. I cannot think that my time is up yet but if it is, look
after Vati and remember that I love you.

All my love,
Mutti.

I lay back on the bed, staring at the blank ceiling, tears
rolling down my face. Mutti was right. This war had degen-
erated into something we could never have imagined. We
had heard that Illesheim Airpark was now occupied by the
Americans and as far as I knew, Bad Windsheim had avoided
destruction. The efforts of those women had paid off. The
sacrifice of Frau Schmotzer and the grief of her family had
not been in vain. I felt ashamed to be associated with the
Wehrmacht. Then I remembered how most of the military
had worked towards the good of the Fatherland and its
people, often sacrificing a great deal themselves. There were
always those who took advantage and abused the power they
had been given; it seemed that the war had not only brought

out the best in people but also the worst. I wondered if the Führer was aware of the actions of men like these. Surely he couldn't countenance such things?

I had to hide the letter carefully. Thank God, Hans had brought it straight to me and hadn't been intercepted by the SS – my mother's letter would be considered treasonous. I shuddered, thinking of the consequences if it had been found. I longed for the comfort of Erich's arms around me but I didn't dare seek him out. Instead, I tucked the letter into my brassiere, rolled into a ball on my bed, and fell into an uneasy sleep. I dreamt of skulking Gestapo and SS men searching for me as I tried to escape them, men who turned into American soldiers with revolvers pointed at my head as I screamed my innocence, running for my life.

A few days after I had received Mutti's letter, Vati sent news with a visiting official. His letter explained that he was well among the chaos of his München office, organising the retreat of the Wehrmacht in southern Germany. They were preparing for the arrival of the American army and he emphasised once again that I was to stay out of München, even though I was so close, and make my way to Windsheim to my mother. As Colonel von Wissenbach was in Markt Schwaben, Vati advised me to stay close to Erich, that he would protect me and get me to safety. It was ironic that I was being forced to spend more time with Erich, but Vati was right, and there was nothing I could do about our situation except what he suggested.

I breathed a sigh of relief to know that Vati was safe and well for the time being. Then I noticed that there was an additional page to the letter. I frowned at the quickly scribbled note.

'Are you all right?' asked Marissa, sitting at the next desk.

Looking up from the letter, I stared at her a moment, confused.

'Are you all right?' she repeated.

'My fiancé is alive,' I whispered.

11

I read the hastily scrawled words again. Vati had found Heinrich.

'Heinrich is working as a military medic in one of the refugee camps in Denmark. From what I understand he is unhurt and well. He was evacuated by boat from East Prussia, along with a number of Wehrmacht units and many civilians. I will do whatever I can to hasten his return home.'

Tears welled in my eyes. Heinrich had survived the Eastern Front and was safe. I felt an enormous weight lift off me, and a rush of elation erupted within me, making me weak with joy. Heinrich was coming home to me!

'Excuse me,' I said, rising from my seat, the letter clutched to my chest. Marissa nodded sympathetically. I suppose she was thinking that I wanted some privacy to release my relief and joy in tears. It's true. I did want to cry for joy. In fact, I could hardly keep my bottom lip from wobbling and I was blinking the tears away furiously. I rushed to the bathroom and barely made it to a stall before I vomited the contents of my stomach most violently into the toilet.

Wiping my face, I looked at my reflection in the mirror. I was pale, my eyes wide with shock. My skin felt clammy, although the nausea had ebbed away. I watched the grin on my face grow wider. He was safe. It wouldn't be long before this war was over and we could return to the life we had put on hold.

Congratulations and smiles greeted me as I walked back to my desk. I felt light as a feather, as if I were walking on air. Stories of joy were far and few between by this time but I noticed a few envious and wistful faces with the announcement of my news.

I thought it was only fair to tell Erich the news. My feelings of joy dissipated like fragrant flowers on the wind. I stared at the work in front of me, shuffling papers about but getting little done, my guilt and anxiety climbing. My duty and commitment to Heinrich outweighed my feelings for Erich but I realised that I couldn't imagine life without Erich. Heinrich was my future. He had been through so much; I couldn't cause him more pain. I had to make a clean break from Erich. It was the only thing to do.

Nausea bloomed in my belly as I approached Erich at his desk. His head was bent over his work, a cigarette sitting on his ashtray. It was better done here, in full view of everyone.

He looked up at me and raised his eyebrows expectantly. 'You wanted something?'

My mouth felt dry and I fidgeted with the seam of my skirt. I stared at him, suddenly unsure that I wanted to do this. It would hurt him and crush any hopes he had of us being together.

'Are you all right?'

I nodded and swallowed, feeling the bile rise to my throat. 'I just received a letter from my father.'

Erich's expression changed to one of concern. He put down his pen. 'Has something happened?'

'No, my parents are fine,' I said quickly.

'That's good.'

I knew I had to say it now before I lost my nerve. I took a breath. 'My father's found Heinrich. He was evacuated from East Prussia and is in Denmark. He's fine, working as a medic in one of the refugee camps.'

There was a heavy stone in my stomach as I watched for his reaction.

Steepling his fingers together, Erich smiled but it did not reach his eyes. 'I'm very happy for you, Fräulein von Klein. Is there anything else you wanted?'

'No,' I said, my cheeks burning. 'I just thought you'd like to know. I'll get back to work.' I whirled around before he could say any more, before he could see the tears in my eyes.

I avoided Erich as much as possible after that, only speaking to him when strictly necessary. I didn't think I could feel more miserable. I had hurt him and he had only ever been good to me. A great knot had formed in my gut, twisting and turning, making me nauseous whenever I thought about it or saw him. I became light-headed and dizzy, my skin clammy and I began to ache all over. I had heard about people making themselves sick with worry but this was ridiculous. I took to sleeping as much as I could as a way to avoid my pain and get over whatever was ailing me.

As more staff evacuated the airfield, the tension rose among those who stayed. The Russians were fighting to occupy Berlin and the Americans were nearly in München. Adolf Galland announced that his unit would move to the Maxlan airfield near Salzburg. It was time for the remaining units and staff to leave.

Erich sought me out. I was sitting in the dining hall, staring at my soup, not sure that I wanted it. He slid into the seat next to me.

'We have to talk,' he said urgently.

'What about?' I asked, pushing my bowl away. I didn't want to talk about Heinrich or about us.

'We have to leave. I have to get you to safety.'

His face was lined with worry, and it looked like he hadn't slept much in days. Past the concern, within the depths of his luminous green eyes, I still saw fire burning brightly – his fire for me. My heart raced and I broke into a fine sweat. My response to him was automatic, primal and irresistible. I dragged my gaze from him, glaring at the thin broth in my bowl, making my stomach churn.

'I'll be fine,' I said stubbornly, not daring to look at him.

I could hear his sigh of exasperation. 'No, you won't. We can't get back to our department in Markt Schwaben now and your father told me he doesn't want you in München when the Allies arrive. We have two choices: we can leave with the other units and wait in Chiemsee for the Americans to arrive or I can take you to your mother in Bad Windsheim.'

'We can't just go. We'll need authorisation.'

'I have it.'

I glanced up, suddenly hopeful.

He patted his jacket pocket. 'There's no need for us now, especially since the Jagdverband 44 is leaving. I can't contact Colonel von Wissenbach, or anyone in Regional Command for that matter. Airfield Command is taking responsibility for all the units and personnel at Riem. We can make our way home from here. I have discharge papers for both of us.'

The tension in my shoulders dissipated. We could go home.

A thought dawned on me. 'What about you? What will you do?'

Erich shrugged. 'I don't know yet. Let's just get you to Bad Windsheim safely.'

'You don't have to do that for me. I'm sure I can make my own way there.' I didn't want him to feel obliged to me, especially with the way things stood between us.

'I promised your father I would keep you safe.' His expression was earnest and I knew he meant to keep his word despite the risk of capture if he came with me.

'What if we stayed with the units in Chiemsee? What happens when the Americans arrive?'

'Nothing will happen to you, Lotte. You're a civilian secretary. At worst, I guess they may question you about what you know and they'll soon discover that you know no great secrets.'

'And you?'

'I'll be taken as a prisoner of war, I suspect, but where they'll send me, I don't know.'

I stared at him in shock. Then I thought of my father.

'Vati?'

'Probably the same, if he's stayed in München. He'll most likely be detained for a time but I'm sure he'll be released when he shares what he knows. I doubt he holds any state secrets either.'

My throat tightened with fear. 'He planned to stay. What can we do?'

Erich placed his hand on mine, warm and reassuring. 'Nothing. Your father has made his choice. We can only hope he will be fine.'

My shoulders slumped. Vati was my rock. I sent a swift prayer to the heavens to keep him safe when the Americans arrived. He was a good, kind man and I didn't know how Mutti or I could go on without him.

Erich squeezed my hand in sympathy. 'All we can do now is get you to safety.'

He was right, travelling to Windsheim with me was a safer proposition for him.

'Let's go to Bad Windsheim,' I said, my mouth set in a line of determination.

Erich and I thought hard about the best way to get to Windsheim. There wasn't much to decide, really, as the car we arrived in was being requisitioned by Airfield Command. We weren't sure how far it would get them – once the fuel ran out there was no more. What we were sure about was that we should avoid being intercepted by either the Americans or the SS. We decided to walk. I had my small bag of belongings that I took everywhere. I hid my engagement ring on my necklace along with my locket, long enough to sit under my dress. Erich, however, had only his uniform and some underwear. I carried the discharge papers in my bag, hidden among my clothes.

At first, I thought it would be a great adventure, hiking across southern Germany. The walking didn't worry me and I truly didn't believe that we would be accosted on the road. At first the flat surfaces made travel easy, despite the wear and tear of the road. The toots of vehicle horns and cheery waves as we passed other units heading south towards the Alps, to Chiemsee, added an air of excitement.

But I wasn't dressed for the journey, wearing a coat over my cotton dress and leather shoes with a sensible heel, acceptable for a half-hour stroll to work but not a full day of strenuous trekking, and it didn't take long for the reality of our situation to hit. There were reports of American units nearby from people on the road. Often they were civilians travelling between villages and were friendly enough with us.

'Get rid of your uniform,' one woman urged. 'I met a soldier in one of the villages who told me that some of the Americans are trigger happy with small groups of soldiers on the road. They shoot men just for the suspicion of escaping from surrender with their unit . . . under suspicion of being Nazis or worse still, SS. Who knows what they'd think of a soldier travelling on his own with a beautiful woman?' Erich dismissed the threat as nothing more than gossip and idle talk. But cold fear blossomed within me. What had I got Erich into? Rather than keeping him safe, I may have put him in more danger.

It wasn't the only danger we had to watch for. We encountered refugees from Silesia. They had been travelling for weeks, on their way to relatives in Southern Bavaria.

'Stay away from the road,' they suggested. 'We've seen SS patrols and Hitler Youth gangs roaming the main roads between the villages and towns that haven't fallen to the Allies yet. You've heard what they do?'

Erich and I agreed that we had heard and were being cautious. I told him about Mutti's letter, about what had happened in Windsheim. His brow furrowed with worry and he shook his head with sorrow.

'Panic's a powder keg for disaster. When order and calm disintegrate, chaos rules and the smallest thing can turn into a dangerous situation. Stay by my side and do what I tell you. We have to be watchful and careful at all times. I want to get you to your mother safely.'

I nodded, grateful to have Erich by my side. I felt safe with him, even if his ferocity alarmed me. He was strong, capable, practical and good company.

The first three nights we were given dinner and lodgings at farms. Erich told our hosts that we were cousins and he was taking me back home to my parents. It wasn't far from the truth and allowed people to feel comfortable about a man and woman, not married to each other, travelling together. I was exhausted at the end of each day, barely able to keep my eyes open and my feet were a little sore from my shoes. I was thankful for the rigours of the road, too, enough to keep the immediacy of Erich and my attraction to him at bay. At times I would catch the gleam in his eye and feel my legs turn to jelly. With thoughts of Heinrich in my mind, I wondered if I would continue to have the strength to stay away from Erich.

Although I enjoyed the walking, the brisk activity keeping the chill away, I was happy to stare out at the cold mornings and nights from within warm walls and friendly company. The food was basic, soup and stew, but hot and filling. Ravenous, I unapologetically polished off every last mouthful, grateful to our hosts. The straw-filled mattresses were lumpy but warm and dry and I slept like a baby, with Erich often by my side.

The third night we sat around the table of an elderly farmer and his wife with their daughter-in-law and small grandson, the radio playing in the background. The farmer apologised for leaving the radio on, which played a selection of classical music. The presenter intermittently reported that an announcement would shortly be made by the German government to the German people. None of us had any idea what it would be about. We waited for the news and speculated that it may be the declaration of the end of the war.

The farmer's daughter-in-law put her little son to bed while I helped his wife tidy the table. The orchestral strains were finally cut short at about ten thirty and the announcer told us that the Führer was dead. Erich and I stared at each other in shock. The report announced that the Führer had fought until his last breath against Bolshevism. I jerked as I heard what sounded like shots being fired in the studio. I frowned at Erich, unable to make sense of what was going on in Berlin. All I knew was that Germany would now fall into the abyss of chaos. Nothing would ever be the same again. The Führer, whom so many had pinned their hopes and dreams on, was gone.

I blinked the tears away, numb. The farmer's daughter-in-law began to cry, his wife comforting her by gently stroking her back, while the farmer stared at the table. I was sure

I could see relief in his expression and posture but he didn't say a word. He rose abruptly and switched the radio off before sinking into his seat once more.

'We are lost,' sobbed the daughter-in-law. 'Without the Führer, we can't win this war. How will we manage without him?'

'At least he fell fighting for Germany,' consoled the wife. 'He remained at his post at the Reich Chancellery until the end.'

The girl burst into fresh hysterics, her face in her hands.

After a few minutes of staring at the table uncomfortably, listening to the girl's sobbing, the farmer had had enough. 'Take her to bed,' he said gruffly. His wife nodded and gently gathered up the girl, arms around her, and led her to the back of the house. The crying was muffled behind a closed door.

The farmer looked at us, wariness in his eyes. It was awkward to know what to say next, in the presence of strangers, people whose thoughts and feelings about the Führer and this war you didn't know. Erich was still in his military uniform but, sensing the tension, he decided to break the ice.

'Admiral Doenitz must surely work towards our surrender now,' he said. I drew in my breath sharply. This was dangerous talk. 'The Russians are in Berlin, we know that much, and it won't be long before the Allies have all of Germany at their feet.'

The farmer's heavy brows knitted together and he nodded slowly. 'Yes, I think you are right. There is no other way for Germany. He must stop the bloodshed and the destruction of our country. It is over for us.'

I cried in the privacy of my bed, tears of grief and sorrow for our Führer. He had been like a father to those of us who had been raised under his leadership. Now he was gone and so was all hope for Germany. I felt hollow and empty.

Erich was not so stricken. He didn't have to tell me how he felt – he'd been trying to tell me for months that he believed the Führer was to blame for Germany's losses both on the battlefield and of human life. But he said nothing to me, respecting my mourning.

I'd heard the rumours that terrible things had happened to those held in the prison camps – dissidents and communists but especially the Jews. Reminded of the White Rose and Frau Andree, horror seeped dark into my heart. The doubt that Vati, Heinrich and Erich had expressed in the Führer's decisions now made me think twice about all I had learnt about him in school. How could he have let these things happen? How could Germany have stooped so low? After all I had seen and heard, I had to accept that the Führer wasn't the perfect man I had believed him to be. Germany was no better off. It was destroyed, its citizens left destitute, scarred and bereft. The memory of Colonel von Stauffenberg, a decorated war hero, and the ultimate sacrifice he paid because he no longer believed in the Führer came to mind.

We left the next morning and, after a couple of hours of walking, I had found my stride and rhythm. I was deep in thought, considering what was ahead for Germany with the passing of our leader, when Erich suddenly stopped.

'What is it?' I asked.

'Can't you hear them? There are trucks and vehicles up ahead but I don't know if they're ours or the Americans'.

We have to get off the road.' He looked around at the meadows that surrounded us. There wasn't much shelter.

'There should be a rise in the road just there,' I said, pointing to the hilly pasture beyond. 'I'll take a look and see if there's somewhere we can hide.' Erich was still in his uniform and the woman's story about the Americans remained at the forefront of my mind.

I was worried about him. The discharge papers I carried clearly stated Erich's rank and position. Normally higher civil service officials were mandatory members of the Nazi Party, something the Americans could be aware of. Erich received his promotion as a 'war time official' due to his technical expertise. He could not apply for a similar position in peace-time without the necessary university qualifications, ones he did not possess. Although not a member of the Nazi Party, I was afraid that the Americans would not care about this small detail which would exonerate him.

'No, Lotte, I don't know if it's safe.'

'Don't be silly,' I said. 'Those trucks aren't that close yet and we have nowhere here to hide.' I strode purposefully around the bend in the road before he could object. The rise in the road was where I had predicted and I smiled smugly to myself. It felt good to take the lead and be right as well.

As I topped the rise, I noticed a tract of woodland to my right. With a little luck, we could hide there. If the people were Americans, we could sneak past them quite easily.

'Fräulein,' called a male voice.

I whirled around to find a soldier standing at the bottom of the rise. He wasn't German. He wore a green tunic and trousers with a helmet on his head, rifle resting comfortably in his hands. I turned to run.

'Please stay where you are,' he ordered firmly. He spoke English, with his hand up, gesturing me to stop.

I glanced back to where I had left Erich. I wasn't sure what to do. I didn't want this man finding Erich but I didn't want to stay either. Perhaps it would be better to walk towards him.

'I won't hurt you,' the soldier said soothingly. Although his manner meant business, there was no malice in his expression.

'Who are you? What do you want?' I asked haltingly. My English was rusty and basic but I was suddenly thankful for the English classes my father had insisted upon when I began my photography course.

'I'm American,' he said, slowly approaching me. 'US Army.'

I was rooted to the spot, not sure I could outrun this man. He was young, fit and his eyes narrowed slightly, as if he were watching for signs of flight. Where there was one, there were surely others.

'You speak English?'

I nodded, my throat dry. 'A little.' All my focus was on the soldier, my heart thumping. I was watching for any sudden movement he might make. I realised that not only could Erich be in serious danger but that I might be too. I tried to think of any stories of American atrocities on civilians but could only remember the grisly accounts on the Red Army looting, raping and killing their way towards Berlin.

'What are you doing here?' He gestured to the road.

'I'm on my way home,' I said, stepping back out of reach.

'Where have you come from? Where is your home?'

I stared at him a moment, trembling.

'It's all right. I won't harm you. Do you understand?' His large brown eyes were filled with concern. Now that he was up close, I noticed he was clean shaven and younger than I thought, perhaps around the same age as me. I nodded again.

'Where are you from?' he asked again more gently.

'I've been visiting my sick grandmother in the next village on this road,' I said, pointing to where I had come from, 'and home is the next village that way.' I gestured behind the soldier with my chin. My heart was in my throat now.

He looked dubiously at me, scanning the countryside. I didn't realise I had been holding my breath until he nodded, letting my explanation lie.

'Have you seen anyone else on this road?'

'No,' I said, shaking my head for emphasis, 'no one until now.'

'You'd better come with me.' Striding towards me quicker than I could react, he grasped my arm, preventing my escape. 'It's dangerous on the roads for a young girl like yourself. I hear there are gangs roaming the countryside. Who knows what they would do to you.'

'I'll be all right,' I spluttered, trying to pull away from him.

'I couldn't allow that,' he said. 'It's better if I escort you home. It's not far back to the village, especially by jeep.' He smiled kindly. I believed that he was genuine and meant me no harm. Besides, there was nothing I could do but agree. I would have to go with him to keep Erich safe. I didn't know if Erich had seen what was going on and I prayed he had the sense to stay hidden.

'Fine,' I said calmly, like I had all the time in the world. I allowed him to lead me away from Erich. His grip loosened a little as we walked down the road to where a jeep waited. Another young American soldier was leaning casually against it. Exhaustion was plain in his haggard features, making him look much older than he was. He glanced at me with curiosity but smiled. Neither looked anything like my brothers but for a moment I felt disoriented, remembering Ludwig and Willi as I last saw them, proud in their military uniforms. Young lives cut down in their prime, all the youth forever scarred by the ravages of war. I wondered when these soldiers would next see their loved ones.

'Now, I can't take you to the village just yet,' said the soldier. 'We have to wait for the convoy to arrive. Why don't you hop into the jeep and relax? They should be here in another few minutes.'

He helped me climb into the jeep and released me. I sat there, my mind going a million miles an hour. How was I going to get out of this? The longer they delayed me, the more worried I was about what Erich might do. The threat of his discovery and capture escalated with every minute I was in the Americans' company.

'How about a chocolate bar?' The soldier offered me a wrapped bar with 'Hershey' written across it. I took it with a shaky hand and murmured my thanks but my mouth was dry and my forehead was beaded with sweat. I could feel a knot developing in my stomach.

'Are you all right? You look a bit pale.'

'I don't feel so good,' I whispered. 'I think I'm going to be sick.'

The soldier looked at me in alarm and quickly helped me out of the jeep. I ran into the meadow, where I vomited my heart up.

'Are you all right?' he called from the side of the road.

'I'll be fine,' I said, halfway between feeling embarrassed and absolutely miserable. 'I think I might stay here. I don't think I'm done yet.' Sure enough another bout of retching began. In the background I could hear the sounds of rumbling as the American convoy approached.

When the retching subsided, I wiped my mouth with my hand, the foul taste lingering on my tongue. What I could do with now was water. I glanced up to the road. The soldiers were occupied with the arrival of the convoy. In a split-second decision, my legs trembling so violently I could hardly walk, I made my way across the meadow towards the stand of trees at the bottom of the slope. If they saw me, I could say I needed to relieve myself and wanted privacy. I didn't dare look back until I reached the relative safety of the trees. No shout came, nor running footsteps. I knew I had to get away now. I ran through the trees, making as little sound as possible. Thank God in Heaven I had seen where the pockets of woods extended from the rise in the road. If I stayed among the trees and bushes, I might have a chance of remaining hidden until I reached the larger woodland.

My breath harsh in my ears, I ran as fast as I could, weaving in and out of the trees, crouching low to keep to the thickest cover. My heart was beating so fast I thought it would burst and a small part of me wondered how I had become so unfit.

Finally, I made the woodland. I ran in a little way, looking for a spot to hide, pushing through the undergrowth, twigs catching at my skirt and scratching my arms and legs. When I couldn't run any longer, I collapsed at the base of a huge oak tree, my back against its rough but solid trunk. With still no sounds of pursuit, my fear slowly ebbed away. My shivering subsided, my breath came back under control and my wild heartbeat regulated itself.

I had to find Erich but had no idea where he was. Was he still safe? A sharp stab of anxiety made me nauseous once again but I refused to allow it to get the better of me. I tried to think straight. All I could do was walk back to where we had parted, either through the meadows or back up on the road once the convoy had moved on. I felt desperately tired. I frowned at the odd sensation. Closing my eyes for a moment, I tried to collect my thoughts and work out what was the best thing to do.

My eyes flew open as I heard a crunch and rustle in the undergrowth. I had fallen asleep. Judging by the light, it had only been minutes, not hours. I tried not to breathe as I concentrated on the noise. It was big, not a woodland animal. Maybe the American soldier had found me. Heart racing once again, I carefully rose from the ground, ready to flee.

'Lotte!' I heard a cautious but familiar whisper but wasn't sure if I had imagined it. I stayed perfectly still.

'Lotte!' called the voice a little more loudly and urgently, the rustling coming closer.

I thought for a second. No, I hadn't told the soldier my name.

'Erich?'

'Yes, it's me. Lotte, where are you?'

I stepped out from behind the tree. I could see Erich just ahead of me, walking in my direction.

'Erich, are you all right?' I whispered.

Within seconds, he had me in his arms, holding me tightly.

'I'm fine,' he murmured. 'Are you hurt?' He pulled back to appraise my condition. A breeze whispered through the woods and the dappled light fell on his face, illuminating his eyes, which were large and round with worry and pale green just like the new shoots on the trees around us. They were beautiful.

I reached for him, pulling him close. 'I'm fine. Just a little shaken.' The world around us disappeared, the warmth and strength of his embrace all that mattered. I felt a tremor pass through him as he held me as if I was the most important thing in the world.

'I could have lost you.' His voice was thick with emotion. 'I wish you had listened to me.'

'I'm sorry. I only wanted to show you that I could do something useful on the road.' I dropped my head, remorseful.

'I already know how resourceful you are – and courageous,' Erich said softly, 'but our journey is full of unexpected dangers. Please don't be foolhardy. I promised your father I would keep you safe . . . I would never forgive myself if anything happened to you. You are too dear to me.' All traces of anger were wiped from his face, replaced with a look of such tenderness that I felt tears prick my eyes.

My face reddened. Erich was right. With him by my side, I felt safe and protected. I hadn't taken the dangers on the road seriously enough. 'I promise to be more careful,' I murmured.

'It's over now.'

'How did you find me?'

'I followed you to the rise and saw you being led away by the American soldier.'

'I told him I was a local.'

'Yes, I heard you talking to him. It was quick thinking, but I don't know how you didn't see him.'

'I was looking for tree cover, not at the road,' I replied sheepishly.

'Well, it gave me a chance to follow the rise across the field without being seen. I could watch you to see what they would do. I thought that if they took you to the next village, I could catch up with you there but I couldn't be sure, so I started to walk across to the road. It was only because they were occupied with you that they didn't see me.'

'I didn't hear you.'

'Remember, I spent many years hunting through the forests of Silesia. I can move quietly when I need.'

'They would have captured you.'

'Yes, but I wasn't going to leave you on your own with them.' He cupped my face, tracing the line of my cheekbones with his thumbs.

Tears filled my eyes, threatening to overflow. He was going to risk his freedom to keep me safe and protect me however he could. His actions showed his commitment to me, his love for me, and I had never felt so wanted and aroused.

'Shh, it's all right now.' Erich wiped the tears gently from my face and pulled me into another embrace. 'You saved me anyway by running into the field and just in time too, with the convoy so close. What were you doing? Were you sick?'

I nodded. 'It must have been the shock. Then I took the opportunity to get away.'

'You did. That was brave and it meant that both of us got away safely.'

Crying in earnest now, I sobbed, 'I didn't know where you were or what you would do. I wanted to keep the soldiers away from you. I'm so sorry I didn't listen to you. I just wanted to prove myself to you.'

Squeezing me hard, Erich kissed the top of my head. 'You don't need to prove anything to me. I already know that you are one in a million. Shh, it's all right now, we're both safe.'

'They might be still looking for me.'

'No, I saw the convoy leave and the two soldiers in the jeep too.'

I sagged with relief, calming down considerably. Sniffling, I reached into my pocket for my handkerchief. 'I'm sorry. I'm not normally such a cry baby.'

'Truly, you have nothing to be embarrassed about. I was ready to cry too if I didn't find you when I did.'

I felt something odd in my pocket and smiled. 'The American soldier gave me this.'

'What is it? Are you sure they didn't hurt you?' Erich lifted my chin to look into my eyes and I saw the ferocious concern in his.

'I'm sure.' I smiled again and brought the Hershey bar out of my pocket. 'Look, chocolate.'

'Well, I think we can sit for just a minute to enjoy chocolate.' He kissed me lightly on the lips before releasing me.

Sitting at the base of the oak tree, I blew my nose and wiped my face before breaking up the chocolate bar and sharing it with Erich. It had been some time since either of us had eaten chocolate and I grinned to hear him groan as he savoured his first piece. I closed my eyes as the rich, creamy chocolate coated my mouth and I wondered if anything was ever as good as the simple pleasures in life.

12

We stayed off the roads as much as possible, using only small back lanes when absolutely necessary. My encounter with the Americans brought stark reality to the fear I held for Erich's safety. The risk he had taken to bring me to Windsheim now rarely left my thoughts. Although he waved off the threat to him and the soldiers I had met seemed friendly enough, the possibility of Erich being shot made my blood run cold. He stood out in his uniform and I knew we had to find civilian clothes for him.

Although I loved walking across the open fields and through small pockets of woods, I was always pleased to walk on a solid surface. And we encountered more people on the roads. They were like us, trying to get home. Some people had nothing but the clothes they stood in, while others had their possessions piled high in carts. Most people we met were filled with the hope of reaching their destination and reuniting with their loved ones. Others were travelling aimlessly after arriving home to find their houses destroyed and their families dead or missing.

My heart went out to Erich every time we encountered someone with that story. He didn't know what had become of his parents and he would probably never find out what had happened to his wife and children. I could see his pain by the set of his shoulders, the tension in his body, whenever we came across someone with a similar story to tell. It was like reopening a wound, even though to anyone else he seemed interested and empathetic. We kept to the story that we were cousins, occasionally sharing that Erich's family had perished, fleeing Silesia ahead of the Russians but never disclosing more than that. Most were content with what we told them.

Entering the villages to find food was still a necessity. There were only a few places that still waited for the Americans to occupy them, and it was strange to see the white sheets and tablecloths that hung from balconies and windows to advertise the village's surrender. The locals were generally friendly enough, wanting to help other Germans on their journey home. I will never forget the generosity of some of these kind people who shared what they had when it was plain that they had so little themselves.

Sadly, it was also here that I saw for the first time the cruelty and brutality of those I called countrymen. In one village, there were no sheets. The villagers were wary and tense with strangers, reticent to talk or to offer food and shelter. We soon discovered why.

'Lotte, stop. Turn around and don't look this way,' Erich called urgently, reaching the village square before me.

It was too late. The corpses of four men and one woman hung in the middle of the square. A small cry escaped from my mouth. Two were shot multiple times in the chest while the other three displayed a single gunshot to the head. All five wore signs around their necks declaring them traitors to the Fatherland.

I had seen dead bodies before in bombing raids but never like this. Erich pulled me away. I stumbled from the grisly sight, too horrified to cry, gagging as the powerful stench overpowered me. Clinging to the edge of a building, I vomited, just missing my shoes. Erich held my head and shoulders as I retched again until I sagged against him, exhausted.

'All right now?' he whispered, smoothing the hair from my sweat-beaded forehead. I nodded and smiled weakly at him. Erich helped me stand as an older woman waddled out from a doorway. She handed me a cool wet cloth.

'Thank you,' I said, still gasping. I wiped my face and neck with a shaky hand, the cloth a welcome balm to my clammy skin.

'Come and sit down,' said the woman. 'You must drink some water.' She grasped my arm and led me to the doorway. I glanced at Erich and he shrugged as we followed the woman inside the building.

We sat at a small table and the woman placed a plate of hard biscuits and glasses of water in front of us. I eyed the biscuits greedily, aware that they were probably all she had left.

'Sip slowly,' she ordered. I did as I was told. 'Then you must eat something.'

'What happened here?' asked Erich cautiously.

The woman fiddled about the room for a moment before answering. 'The SS.' She tucked a wisp of grey hair into her black kerchief and turned to us. 'A couple of days ago, our burgomeister ordered we hang white sheets to surrender to the Americans to protect our village from harm. Some of our Hitler Youth and Volkssturm are fanatical and can't see reality for what it is. They could not accept the fact of our surrender, although the Americans are already nearby.'

I glanced at Erich in alarm. Fanatical men might take offence at him taking me home rather than fighting the enemy, especially since he was still in uniform. It wasn't safe here for us. It seemed nowhere was safe for anyone in a German uniform. He placed a hand on my knee surreptitiously to keep me calm and still.

'After arguing with the burgomeister, who was supported by the village, someone alerted the SS. They came shortly after and dragged the burgomeister and his wife, along with the head of the Volkssturm, who supported him, into the square. Many stayed behind closed doors, too afraid to be seen by the SS men, but some were brave enough to show their support for the burgomeister. Others came out to enjoy the sport.'

She shook her head and hobbled over to join us at the table. 'When it became obvious what they were intending, two of the old men stepped forward, arguing that they had done nothing wrong. When the pistols were pointed in their direction, many people fled. The men backed away. They were shot anyway and, as you could see, not just once.'

'The others were shot after that, without a trial or explanation,' finished Erich softly.

The old woman nodded, her eyes filling with tears. 'She was my daughter,' she whispered. 'They will not let me take down her body or give her a decent funeral.'

'I'm so sorry.' I placed my hand over her gnarled fingers.

'The Americans should be here by tomorrow. Maybe then I can have my daughter and bury her.'

Erich nodded sympathetically. 'I'm sure you will.' He refused to look at me and I knew that he was probably thinking the same as me: perhaps there would be no village left if the unrealistic men refused to relinquish control. They were the ones destroying the lives of their neighbours.

'You should leave here. It's not safe for you,' she said looking at Erich, 'and I would get rid of your uniform if I were you. My husband was about your size. I should have something you can wear.' She stood slowly, leaning on the table, pain flitting briefly across her face. 'Come with me.'

Erich looked at me. 'Please go,' I whispered, as the weight lifted from my chest at the thought of him finally out of uniform.

'Thank you for your kindness,' he said as he followed the woman to another room.

While I waited, I finished my water and nibbled the hard biscuit. The woman was right. It did make me feel better and settled my stomach.

She shuffled back out and sat at the table with a satisfied look on her face. 'He's just changing,' she said reassuringly. 'Now you, my dear,' she said, fixing me with a speculative stare. 'Are you feeling better?'

'Yes, thank you,' I said, my cheeks beginning to redden although I wasn't sure why. She narrowed her eyes as she scrutinised me.

'On your way home, are you?'

'That's right. Erich's my cousin and he's taking me home.'

The woman nodded with a knowing expression. 'How long have you been ill, dear?'

I frowned as I tried to work it out. 'A couple of weeks, I think. I must have picked up something that I just can't seem to get rid of.'

She smiled again, the light of amusement in her eyes. 'Have you been tired? Have you felt faint, aching all over, and ravenously hungry?'

My eyebrows rose in surprise. 'Yes. How did you know?'

She leant toward me and whispered, 'Have your breasts been sore?'

Jerking back, I stared in shock at her. 'What are you trying to say?'

The chair creaked as she leant back into it again, her expression filled with knowing. 'You may soon have some explaining to do to your cousin.'

I was angry now. 'What are you talking about?'

'Don't be angry, child. You don't know, do you?'

I just stared back at her, dread beginning to coil in my belly, making me nauseous again.

'You're with child.'

I continued to stare stupidly at her.

'You're pregnant,' she repeated.

'I can't be,' I whispered, aghast at the thought.

'I've seen this many times before my dear. I'm quite sure you are.'

'It's not possible.' I felt the blood drain from my head.

'You do know how babies are made, don't you?'

'Of course,' I snapped. It was possible but highly unlikely. This illness was surely something I had picked up at the airbase and the stress and the travelling just hadn't allowed me to get over it.

She must have seen all this on my face. 'It only takes once,' she said gently.

'I'm engaged to be married.'

'Not to your cousin.'

'No,' I said. Shame blossomed in my chest. I couldn't look at her.

'These things happen, my dear,' she said, patting my hand. 'If I'm right, you should pace yourself on your journey home. Eat as well as you can especially at this time because not only does it affect you but the baby also. If you can get milk, drink as much as you can.'

A door closed as Erich returned. He looked different, more casual, in wool suit pants, cotton shirt and vest. A jacket hung over one arm and a soft cap sat on his head. He would blend in better among the travellers on the road now. In the other arm, he held his uniform.

'Ah,' said the woman standing, nodding in approval. 'They fit perfectly and suit you a lot better than they did my husband. I would dispose of that uniform at the first opportunity you have.'

'Thank you,' said Erich. 'They're wonderful.'

'Well, you had best be on your way.' She wrapped the biscuits in a cloth and handed them to me as I stood. 'Here, take these to nibble on.'

I hugged her tightly. 'I'll never forget your kindness,' I said, kissing her cheek.

'You take care of yourself,' she said, before opening the door. Casually checking the street, she nodded for us to go.

Continuing our trek north, we walked through the fields and countryside. The blisters on my feet and heels had stopped bleeding and hard calluses began to form where my shoes rubbed. Often we slept out in the open or sheltered under bushy undergrowth with only our coats and jackets and each other to keep warm. Although it seemed a shame to leave behind the good woollen cloth of Erich's uniform and coat, it was too dangerous to be found with them. There was a strange expression on Erich's face when we left them hidden under a rock in the woods, as if he was saying goodbye to almost a decade of proud service to his country, working in a job that he loved. I felt sad he had no memento left of those years, remembering the two War Merit Cross medals he had received for exceptional service, left at the kloster.

We had bread and an assortment of vegetables from farmers we met. Our diet was supplemented with small apples from orchards or growing wild and foraged leafy green herbs such as wild garlic. Occasionally we were given milk to drink and at those times, even though I had dismissed what she had told me, I thought of the woman back in the village. My nausea had stayed with me but I rarely vomited after the day I'd met the American soldiers.

I pushed myself hard each day but there were occasions I had to ask Erich to stop so I could rest. At times I fell into an immediate and deep sleep. He sometimes looked at me strangely but I refused to acknowledge the questions I knew he had. Whenever he asked, I told him I was fine, just tired from the rigors of the road.

Almost a week after leaving the village with the shot villagers, we were walking across a meadow of spring flowers and poppies. Admiring the delicate red petals and black centres, I was explaining to Erich how I would best photograph them when we heard shouting and screaming. They didn't sound like the screams of agony or despair. Crouching low, we followed the sounds to a tiny country lane. The sounds of laughter and joy floated up to us on the hillside.

'What do you think it is?' I whispered to Erich.

'It must be the end of the war. I'll go down and find out.'

'I'm coming with you,' I said.

We walked casually onto the lane, joining the group of people that walked along it. They were travellers like us, smiling or laughing, and most had a spring in their step.

'What's happened?' Erich asked one of the men at the head of the group. Although it wasn't even midday, he was holding up another man, who appeared to be drunk.

'Haven't you heard?' said the man.

Erich shook his head.

'They haven't heard,' repeated various members of the group like a raucous cacophony of birds.

'The war is over!' The man laughed. 'An announcement was made this morning over the radio.'

'Here, toast to the new Germany!' slurred his friend, lifting a bottle of champagne that was three-quarters full. The dark-haired man took the bottle and offered it to Erich and I. 'Come, live a little,' he said.

'Why not!' I grabbed the bottle from him and took a few long swallows with the group cheering me on. Erich took the bottle from me as fizz dribbled down my chin and I wiped my mouth with the back of my hand, laughing. 'What about you?' I dared him. His green eyes shone with a mischief I had hardly seen before and, lifting one eyebrow cheekily, he guzzled a long draught of champagne to the joyous shouts of the group. He handed the bottle back to the man.

'What date is it?' Erich asked.

'Seventh May, 1945,' said the man, saluting with the bottle. 'A day none of us will ever forget.'

'You're right.'

'Good luck to you and your beautiful wife. Don't forget to celebrate this memorable day,' he said with a wicked twinkle in his eye. I blushed but said nothing.

'And to you,' said Erich, smiling broadly. 'I'm sure we'll find a way to celebrate, my beautiful wife and I.' He held my hand once again and we stood on the embankment of the lane, watching the rag-tag group, mostly tipsy, file past.

'Goodbye and thank you,' I called after them and saw the man raise his hand in farewell.

'So, do you want to celebrate, wifey?' Erich asked impishly. I elbowed him in the ribs and watched his eyes widen with surprise as he emitted a soft grunt.

I smiled innocently. 'Something wrong?' The laughter that bubbled within tugged at the corners of my mouth, making them quiver.

'No, not at all.' Erich stood tall, pretending to survey his surroundings. I could see his mouth twitch as he tried to withhold his laughter. I couldn't hold it in any more, laughing loud and with abandon and Erich burst into fits of laughter himself. He pulled me back into the meadow where we collapsed among the flowers, giggling uncontrollably like children.

'I haven't laughed like that in so long,' I said stretching out and sunning myself like a cat.

'I don't remember the last time I laughed,' said Erich.

The breeze rippled through the meadow, causing the grass and flowers to gently bend and sway, ruffling his hair, the chestnut highlights glinting in the sunlight. He looked peaceful. I noticed his skin had darkened to a healthy glow despite the lines of his face becoming more angular than I remembered, even underneath the growth that had begun to resemble a beard.

This would make a wonderful photo, I thought. I remembered my promise to my father, to record the special moments. An apt commemoration of a day we would never forget. I sat up, reaching for my suitcase and pulled out my camera and the precious film Vati had given me.

'Can I photograph you? I want a reminder of this day.'

'If you like,' said Erich lazily. 'How do you want me?' He cracked open an eye.

'Don't move. You're perfect just as you are.' His eye closed, a slight smile playing on his lips.

I took my time, my attention fully focused on him. I didn't want to waste film and I wanted to capture the moment perfectly. Erich rested patiently, allowing me to get lost in my work. It felt wonderful to be behind the camera once again and I silently sent my thanks to Vati, hoping he was safe.

'Done,' I said, putting the camera carefully away.

Erich still didn't move. I lay back down beside him.

'I could stay here forever,' I murmured sleepily, warm and content. The lines of Erich's body were long, lean and elegant and the desire to trace his form with my hands made them twitch with the control I imposed upon them.

'Mmm, me too.' Erich lifted his face to the sun, in obvious pleasure.

I turned onto my side to look at him better. 'Let's not travel any further today. I can hear a stream from here and I could do with a good wash and to soak my feet, couldn't you?'

'Is that how you want to celebrate this auspicious day?'

'Why not? There's no hurry to get home.'

'You've convinced me then.' His head flopped back down, as if it was too much effort to hold it up.

'You look very relaxed.'

Erich nodded, smiling, but didn't open his eyes.

'I don't think I've ever seen you look this relaxed.'

'It's been a very long time.'

'When did you last feel like this?' Travelling together, we had shared many titbits of our lives, but there was still so much about him I didn't know.

He thought for a moment. 'Flying gliders. Coasting on the air currents is the closest thing to total peace and exhilaration all at the same time. It's as if you're at one with nature and the world. It's there that I always felt anything was possible, that as human beings we haven't yet touched our true potential.'

I looked up into the expanse of blue sky, trying to imagine the feeling of flying on air. Both my brothers had described the elation of flying to me but Willi was the one who spoke about this kind of oneness.

'How do you feel right now?'

'I feel at peace with the world. With you here by my side, I feel like the world has stopped just for a little while. This is our moment of paradise, a time between lives, where our old lives are over but our new lives have not yet begun. In this moment, anything is possible and there are no pressures, no constraints to limit its possibility.' He rolled onto his side to look at me, head in his hand, supported on his elbow. 'Do you understand what I'm saying?'

'I know what you mean.' It surprised me that I did but what he said resonated deeply with me. 'I feel that way when I capture beauty with my camera. I felt like that when I photographed you.'

He stared deep into my eyes. 'So I was making some sense.'

I nodded. 'Yes, and I believe that we are capable of so much. It's easy to get caught up in our everyday lives but I know we can do more.' I stopped in frustration, finding it difficult to articulate what I felt.

'You want to leave your mark on the world,' Erich finished softly.

'Exactly! Nobody else understands that about me.'

'It's because I feel the same way.'

I stared at him, realising that this was exactly what we had always had in common and what had attracted me to him

221

all along. He was a passionate man who, like me, wanted to make the world a better place by sharing the wonders around us with others.

He leant in and kissed me. I couldn't help but respond, as if the kiss sealed the new understanding and bond between us. I drew him towards me, so that I felt his length against me as the kiss deepened. Although acknowledging the attraction I had for him, I had never, until this time, wanted to consider that it might be anything more than mere chemistry. I had never experienced such a deep connection to anyone in my life. It felt right and yet . . .

Erich broke off the kiss. 'A kiss to new beginnings and a new life of possibility,' he said. He smoothed my hair from my face. 'It might be the right time to find that stream and cool off.'

I burst out laughing. 'All right then.' I extended my arm towards him. 'Help me up.'

We slept out in the open, unable to find shelter until about a week later when we came across a farmhouse destroyed by fire. Erich steered me away from the building. We both felt that something terrible had happened here and I had no wish to face the horrors that might be found among the burnt remains. I had been plagued by nightmares of the bodies hanging in the village square. But he was too late to shield me from the placard resting at the base of a twisted willow tree. It was the same as the one we had seen in the village.

Shivering, I turned away and into Erich's arms. 'Let's check the barn,' I whispered. My feet and legs were aching and all I wanted was a dry, sheltered place to rest.

The barn was just what we needed. Exhausted and determined to get some sleep, I adjusted the uncomfortable bust of my dress and tried not to think about the placard and the atrocities that must have happened in this place.

I woke to Erich walking across to me, the rays of the early morning sun pushing their way through the gaps in the barn's walls. 'Look what I've got.' He held out a pewter bowl, smiling.

'What is it?'

'Milk. I just met some soldiers who found a cow.' He handed me the bowl as I sat up. 'I've had some already. It's fresh and good.'

I tipped the lip of the bowl, draining the rich, warm liquid. I wondered if I had ever tasted anything so good.

The soldiers asked us to share their breakfast. They wouldn't say how they acquired the side of cured pork they cut thick slices from, which they set sizzling in a hot pan over a fire. I didn't really care, burning my fingers as I crammed the meat into my mouth. We were starving, so thin after weeks of travelling and too little food but we couldn't eat much. Our stomachs had shrunk.

They told us they were returning from the Italian Alps where they had been fighting when the war ended. Many of their friends had perished trying to make their way out of the mountains; starving, freezing and succumbing to the treacherous mountain snow and ice. I could only stare at my feet when they spoke bitterly at the way the Führer had left them stranded in the mountains, abandoned with little hope of rescue. More and more I was learning that he was not the leader we had been led to believe he was. All I hoped was that they now found their families safe and homes still intact after all they had been through.

13

Cocooned from the realities of the world, Erich and I walked hand in hand through the Köschinger Forest, shafts of sunlight falling between the densely growing pine trees creating an almost otherworldly atmosphere around us. I could imagine that we were in some ancient fairy tale, perhaps Red Riding Hood and her huntsman or Snow White and her prince. The rustling of the underbrush suggested that there were many small furry creatures living in this mainly untouched place. I felt the magic of this natural sanctuary begin to heal me, reconnecting me with my sense of wonder, a deeper self that I had denied since I was a child. We slept on soft beds of fragrant pine needles, Erich's arm flung across me, our legs intertwined under my coat, curled together as if the world couldn't touch us. I wanted him by my side like this forever.

It was early morning when I stirred. I wondered what had woken me. Peering into the forest that surrounded us, I saw dark shadows prowling between the trees. I squinted and the shapes took on forms, not of the wolves that I had feared, but humans. They came into view, men with a wild look in their sunken eyes, hair matted, beards overgrown and dirty rags hanging off their pathetically thin frames. They eyed us hungrily. With a speed I couldn't imagine they'd possess, they pinned us down. Waving knives in our faces, shrieking in triumph, they found our bag with only a meagre portion of food left. I was terrified, shivering uncontrollably.

Erich wrapped his arms around me, protecting me with his body. 'Stay still. They just want our food,' he whispered urgently in my ear. Rifling through my bag, they found nothing they wanted, discarding the items on the forest floor.

As they released us, melting back into the trees, all I saw was their eyes. The forest dropped away and I was back in the village square. The eyes became red and bulging. Eyes that dropped from their sockets, leaving gaping cavities, revealing the swollen, blood-encrusted corpses. Flies buzzed around the open gunshot wounds and crows pecked at the remaining eyes. I screamed in horror.

I woke with a start. My eyes adjusted to the soft light of the room, curtains closed to keep out the morning sun. It was quiet and peaceful. I was in a clean, soft feather bed. Another just like it was a few steps away, empty with the covers pulled back, revealing rumpled sheets. Where was Erich? I missed the feel of him against me when I woke in the morning. Then I remembered.

We were safe and had arrived in Windsheim the day before; I was sharing a room with my mother at Tante Susie's house. Erich had stayed the night in another room and we had not yet discussed what he would do next.

Sounds of the boys shouting and scuffling, their mother yelling at them, exasperated, drifted to me. I had to smile. We had returned to reality and it was good to be with family again, among the day-to-day activities that defined their life. I remembered my dream and glanced at the suitcase that held my possessions and our papers. They were safe. Despite being robbed of our food by starving vagrants, the forest had been a special time for Erich and me – we had grown closer than ever. I wondered what he was doing and decided that although I didn't want to leave the luxury of warmth and a soft bed, it was time to get up and see.

Tante Susie and my mother were folding washing at the dining table. To look at, Tante Susie was almost the opposite of my mother, small and round, with the dark hair of their Bavarian grandmother. Having said that, she still commanded authority and like my mother, would not put up with any nonsense.

'You're up, sleepyhead,' said my mother, folding a pair of pants, a smile tugging at the corners of her mouth. She had been overjoyed to see me when we arrived, hugging me tight, touching me and holding my hand to make sure I was really there and unwilling to let me out of her sight.

I nodded, still groggy. 'Thank you for the clothes, Mutti.' I smoothed down the blouse and skirt my mother had given me. She was always a bit smaller than me, but I could still fit into her clothes if I had to. The blouse gaped a little at the bust although it was hidden by the soft bow that fell from the collar. The skirt was fine, if anything a little looser than I would have thought.

'You're so thin,' whispered Mutti.

'How are you feeling today?' asked my aunt, passing my mother one end of a sheet to help her fold. 'I'm surprised you didn't sleep longer, you were exhausted yesterday.' Her eyes widened as if she'd thought of something. 'Did those boys wake you up with their noise?'

'No, they didn't,' I said. 'I was already awake. It was nice to hear them, to hear sounds of home. I've missed them.'

'All right then, dear. Get yourself some breakfast. It's on the stove. Your mother's kept it warm for you. Everybody else has eaten.'

'Thanks, Tante, thanks, Mutti.' A warm glow filled my chest at all the little things my mother was doing to spoil me. She had missed me and, now I was here, I realised how much I had missed her. 'Where's Erich?'

'He's in the garden, playing with the boys,' called my aunt.

Standing at the doorway, eating porridge, I watched Erich with the boys. I didn't mind the gluggy consistency that stuck to the roof of my mouth and came from not using enough milk; it was rich, sweet and filled my belly, settling the nausea I was becoming used to. I felt sure that it wasn't regular breakfast fare but that it was made especially for my arrival.

Tante Susie had four boys ranging in age from five to thirteen. Erich was chasing them around the garden. The older boys were laughing as they kept out of his way, while the younger two shrieked as he got close to them. I couldn't help but laugh myself as Erich caught the youngest, Hansi, and tickled him until he was writhing on the ground uncontrollably. The other boys ganged up on him, jumping on top of him, trying to hold his arms and tickle him too. Erich wrestled with them, grunting with the effort, until he somehow had all four boys on the ground. He whooped in triumph and grinned at me. The boys took that moment to exact revenge and were on top of him once more, this time wrestling him to the ground. The boys cheered so loudly, I was sure the whole of the town could hear them.

Their mother came out to investigate this latest noise. 'Enough, boys,' she said clapping her hands. 'Leave Herr Drescher in peace for a while. Come, I have chores for each of you.' The boys groaned and Erich pulled himself to his feet, still grinning broadly. They reluctantly left the garden, dragging their feet as they trudged past me back into the house.

Erich dusted himself down, chuckling.

'Well, you looked like you were having fun,' I said.

'It took me back to my childhood games with my cousins,' he said. puffing a little. 'I'd forgotten how strong and rough boys can be.'

'You're a natural.' I wanted to hug him close but I didn't dare. Our carefree days were over.

'Hansi reminds me of my son,' he said, his voice catching just a little. I touched him on the arm, his warmth creeping into my chilled hand. 'Sometimes I wonder what it might have been like to see him and his sister grow to adulthood.' He sighed. 'It was good to spend time with Susie's boys. They certainly let you know that you're alive.'

'They've always been bundles of energy.' I looked back to the house for a moment, and then asked the question I had been dreading the answer to. 'What will you do now?' Erich had refused to broach the subject while we were travelling. There were so many variables that couldn't be addressed until we had made it to Windsheim.

He shrugged. 'I honestly don't know. I have no home to go back to but I'll look for a job, I suppose. I don't know when I'll be able to go back to my profession but maybe I'll find work at an airfield somewhere. Maybe that's the way to start.'

My heart went out to him. It wasn't right that he was left like this, like a leaf tumbling aimlessly in the wind.

'What about your parents?'

'With Silesia under Russian control, it's not safe to go back to look for them just yet. When I'm settled, I'll try to find them. Hopefully by then it will be easier to get information.'

I nodded, taking in every line of his face, like I couldn't get enough of him. I didn't want him to leave.

'Has your mother had any news of your father?'

'Mutti's beside herself. The last letter she received from him was as the Americans arrived in München. He was waiting to surrender with his unit. He expected to be interned at a POW camp but she's heard nothing since. I only hope that he's all right.'

'He's probably fine. Your father is no threat to anyone. Most likely, he's held somewhere near München. I'm sure they'll release him soon and he'll be writing for you and your mother to return home to him.'

'I hope so.' I was worried about my father. He wasn't a young man anymore but there was nothing we could do among the chaos that came with the fall of Germany.

The dry, tickling cough I'd developed began again now I was out in the cool air.

'Come on, you need to go inside until it gets warmer.' His hand pressed lightly on my back, but I felt his touch like a smouldering ember through my clothes. I let him guide me into the house and back under the watchful eye of my mother.

Erich and I were pressed into helping the household by a grateful Tante Susie. She was happy to have a man around the house and she asked Erich to stay until we knew it was safe for him to leave and look for work. The Americans had a strong presence in the town, especially with their occupation of the Illesheim Airpark nearby, which, according to Tante Susie, now accommodated a POW camp.

We helped the boys in the vegetable patch in the backyard, weeding, watering, picking off snails and harvesting the few potatoes, carrots and beets. Thank God in Heaven, the house hadn't been damaged during the war but that didn't mean that there wasn't work to be done. Using Onkel Werner's tools, Erich started on a long list of maintenance jobs. This kept him busy as he patiently showed the boys what he was doing and explained the process to varying degrees of interest. He was good with the boys and they warmed easily to him.

The biggest job was cleaning up the town, removing rubble from streets and public areas. The main water pipes had been damaged and the Americans were already repairing the ruined sections of pipe but we didn't yet have running water. We used the water from the rainwater tank in the yard sparingly. We were lucky there had been rain and it was summer; in winter, the water would be frozen solid. There was no electricity when we arrived, and gas was unavailable too.

We soon discovered coal and wood supplies were low. Our kitchen stove at home in München was electric. It was modern and beautiful to use but would have been no use to us now. Tante Susie's was gas but thankfully, allowed for heating by coal or wood as well. Somehow she managed with what we could get, using the stove to cook and heat water only when necessary, to extend the supplies we had. I prayed things would improve by the winter, because otherwise it was going to be very tough.

The burgomeister had organised rosters but the work crews were mainly women. I joined Tante Susie and Mutti when it was our turn. It was dirty, back-breaking work but we were proud of what we achieved, trying to repair the homes and town.

'No matter how long we move rubble, it seems we are no closer to finishing,' said Mutti one day as she wiped the perspiration from her brow with a once white handkerchief.

'We'll get there,' said Tante Susie, not breaking her rhythm, picking up pieces of debris from a pile and throwing them into the waiting American truck.

Younger women like myself carried the larger pieces across to the truck and, with the help of an American soldier, dumped them into the tray. I stopped for a moment and stretched my aching back, waiting for another woman to help me with a large piece of stone.

The American soldier smiled at me. 'All right?' he asked in English.

'Yes, I'm all right.'

He looked at me in astonishment. 'You speak English?'

It was my turn to grin. 'A little.'

'That's wonderful,' he said. 'I've been looking for someone to translate for me. Can you help me direct these ladies so we can get the job done more efficiently?'

I nodded shyly. 'I'll do the best I can.'

'That's good enough for me.' He reached into his pocket and pulled out something covered in a paper wrapper. 'Gum?'

I frowned, not understanding.

'Chewing gum.' He unwrapped the tiny parcel with deft fingers and popped it in his mouth, chewing deliberately. I smiled at his demonstration.

'No, thank you.' Walking around chewing all the time didn't seem very nice to me, not very classy at all.

Chewing away, he gestured where we had to go. 'Come and I'll explain to you what I want done.'

It was a great relief to take a break from the heavy lifting. I tired a lot more quickly than I had expected to, probably from being so run down on our journey home. The American soldier had worked in his father's demolition business before he enlisted in the army. He had good experience and organised our work crew so that before long, we began to see the results of our labour.

Erich stayed at the house. Despite his protests, Tante Susie agreed with me that it was too dangerous for him, a man of military age, to be seen out in public yet. Who knew what the Americans would do when they discovered his civil service rank and potential affiliation with the Nazi Party. He continued working around the house and yard and began tutoring the boys, as there hadn't been any school for them for some time. He was a surprisingly versatile man who could turn his hand to many things.

It was easy to keep Erich with us. And while Tante Susie had a need for him, he was happy to help. However, I didn't miss the odd scowl sent his way from my mother, who didn't seem too happy to have him around.

'When's he leaving?' she muttered, after a few days of holding her tongue. We were in the kitchen, preparing a vegetable soup from whatever we had.

'Amelia! What's wrong with you?' Tante Susie stared at Mutti in amazement. 'He's wonderful. He's fixing everything. He's good with the boys and allows me to take my eyes off them for more than a second. It's good to have a man around the house for security purposes too. Not that I'd tell Ernst that, because he thinks he's well and truly old enough to be the man of the house.'

'It's not right having him here,' spat my mother, banging a spoon on the bench.

'Johann sent him,' retorted Susie. She handed me turnips and peeled onions. 'He brought your only child home safely to us. Surely that's enough to trust in him?' She turned to me, her knife waving in the air. 'Do you have a problem with him being here?'

'No. He's got nowhere else to go,' I said. 'His family is dead and I'm worried that if he leaves now, the Americans will find him and send him to a prison camp and if they believe he's a Nazi . . . '

My mother mumbled something under her breath but we ignored her.

'Yes, he's a good man and he doesn't deserve that.' Tante Susie picked up the discarded spoon and began frying the onions in a pan. 'He stays until he wants to go or until

Werner returns home and that's the end of it.' She stared at my mother. 'He's under my roof and I don't want to hear any more about it.'

As life settled back into some kind of normalcy, I realised I hadn't bled for nearly three months. At first I thought it was from the stress of having to leave München and Riem, then the arduous conditions while travelling. Then I thought back to the old woman. I didn't know too much about pregnancy and its symptoms but I had to face the truth. I was pregnant.

That realisation made me woozy and nauseous all at once. What was I going to do? I couldn't have this baby. It would be seen as a disgrace by my family, scandalous and unacceptable.

My mother had been onto me already about setting the plans for my wedding to Heinrich back in motion as soon as was practical. Her face lit up as she explained to Tante Susie yet again – and in front of Erich – that Heinrich was safe in Denmark. She hoped for a wedding sometime soon and what a wonderful event it would be. I was mortified that she would do that but how could she possibly know what was between Erich and I? All I could do was whisper my apologies to him when we were momentarily alone. Erich could see how my mother got under my skin but he didn't really understand my frustration. He thought I should be happy to be back at home and I was, but I had changed and sometimes I found it hard being under my mother's influence, putting up with her domineering ways and inflexible opinions.

Under any other circumstances, I would have welcomed Mutti's conversations. I loved Heinrich and was overjoyed that he was alive. I was promised to him. My duty was to him. It was what I had assured Erich I would do when the war was over and Heinrich came home to me. Besides, Heinrich could give me the secure future I was looking for. I could see already that life in Germany would be difficult for years to come – and would only be made harder with a husband who couldn't find work in his chosen profession. I owed it to any children I did have to give them a good home, a good education and a stable life. That meant financial security. But the way things stood, I didn't see how I could marry Heinrich. He would never accept me like this, accept what I had done. The reality of my situation made me wish I could curl up into a tiny ball and disappear. I couldn't lose everything our families had worked for, everything that Heinrich and I had been.

I felt trapped, like a bird in a cage. I had to find a way free.

Tears of frustration, longing, desperation and pain sobbed quietly into my pillow left me empty and hollow. It was an impossible choice. This was Erich's child, perhaps his only surviving family. He would be a good father. The thought of this child tying us together didn't upset me, it gave me joy. It was my link to him, my chance to be with him. I had often wondered what it might be like if we stayed together after the war. But how did I know that he would welcome the news? A love affair was one thing but a family to care for was entirely another. Did he really want another mouth to feed when he had no job?

We still hadn't heard from Heinrich. I didn't know when he was coming home or if he was coming home at all. I couldn't raise a baby on my own with food so short and an uncertain future.

I had heard stories from the girls at work. I knew what I had to do. Some discreet enquiries and probably a journey to Nürnberg. It was the only way I could marry Heinrich and live the life we had planned together. But although I knew there was no time to waste, I couldn't make that decision. It was too final, too devastating and I wasn't sure I could do it. I wasn't sure I wanted to.

It all came to a crashing end before I could make any decision – my mother walked in on me washing. Although the door was shut, the lock had broken. I was only wearing my underwear and my condition was clear to anybody who knew what to look for. My breasts, lined with thick blue veins, had overfilled my brassiere, and my waist was beginning to thicken and change its shape. Although my belly was still flat, it was bloated and beneath it, I had felt the hardness that grew bigger with each week. I tried to hide the evidence from her, draping my dress over me.

'My dear God,' whispered my mother. 'Are you pregnant?'

I stared at her, not sure what to say, my face flaming with shame.

My mother sagged against the closed door, her face ashen. 'What have you done?'

'Mutti,' I said desperately. 'It's nothing. I'll be fine.'

'You call this nothing?' she hissed, her eyes burning with anger. 'How far gone are you?'

My heart pounding in my chest, I gazed at the pattern the tiny blue bathroom tiles made, weighing up my options. I wanted to lie but it was hard to be believable when she clearly understood what she saw in front of her.

'When did you do this?'

I stared blankly at her.

'When did you lie with the man who did this to you?' She put her hand across her mouth in obvious distress. 'Were you raped?'

'*Nein*, Mutti!' I couldn't hurt her like that to protect Erich and hide my culpability. I sank to the edge of the bath next to her. My head was spinning. I couldn't believe this was happening.

'Put your dress back on, in case someone else comes in.'

Hastily, I shrugged my dress over my head, Mutti tugging it down over the offending parts.

'So, tell me.'

'It only happened the once . . . on my birthday. I'm so sorry, Mutti. I never imagined this would happen.' Tears slipped down my cheeks as I stared at my bare feet.

Mutti sighed. 'Not yet three months . . . well, that explains a lot . . . We'll have to get rid of it.'

I felt like I'd been punched in the stomach. I had been contemplating this solution but for my mother to raise it without emotion shocked me.

'Who's the father?'

I didn't want to tell her, afraid of what she might do. Erich had nowhere else to go. I remained silent.

My mother peered into my face. 'Is it Erich?' She must have seen the truth in my eyes. 'I'm going to kill that man with my bare hands.'

'Stop, Mutti!' I grasped her arm. 'I've been frantic with worry, trying to work out what to do.'

Her gaze softened a little. 'Does he know?'

I shook my head.

'That makes it easier, but I want him gone. Do you hear me?' Her eyes were like ice now, cold and unyielding.

'No, Mutti.' I was shaking with terror. 'This was a mistake, but don't send Erich away. He'll end up in a prisoner-of-war camp. I can't do that to him.'

'It's more than he deserves and less than what I'll do to him.'

'Please, Mutti.' I was pulling on her arm, begging her now, tears running down my face. 'I'll do anything you want. Please don't send him away. Who knows what the Americans will do to him?'

'You won't have this baby and he can't stay here.' She had me by the shoulders now, shaking me like a rag doll. 'You will marry Heinrich. Do I make myself clear?'

'Mutti! Don't do this.'

She dropped her arms and took a deep breath. 'Don't you understand, Lotte? The reason I always wanted you to marry Heinrich? He's a good man from a good family but more than that, I know he'll protect you and keep you safe. He's dependable, reliable and can give you a good life. He loves you. Why do you continually have to fight me? It's the only way I can ensure you are cared for. You are all I have left. I couldn't bear if anything ever happened to you.' She caressed my face, wiping the tears from my cheeks.

Understanding clicked into place. This was something I had known deep in my heart but now that Mutti had said it out loud, all her arguing and manipulating made sense. She loved me with a fierce intensity and would do anything to keep me safe. Just as I would do anything to keep Erich safe. I couldn't let my mother or Erich down.

'I promise to do as you say.'

Mutti's shoulders relaxed imperceptibly.

Shakily, I took a deep breath. I had to do this. It was the only way. 'I know my future is with Heinrich but Erich stays until it's safe for him to go.'

'This is too much. You will do as I say and he goes today. That's the end of it.'

'I'll marry Heinrich at the first opportunity we get and this will be like it never happened, but it you ask Erich to leave, I'll tell everyone that I'm pregnant.'

That stopped her in her tracks. She was shaking now. 'How dare you!'

I held her gaze, quivering on the inside but outwardly steadfast and calm. I had to stay strong. I had to keep going to get what I wanted.

'It's a deal. We both get what we want and Erich stays until it's safe for him to leave. I will never see him again after that but I will not be the one who sends him to prison and further misery. He was the one who protected me and brought me safely back to you despite the risk to himself. It's the least I can do for him.'

I could see Mutti had a quick and angry retort on her lips as her jaw clenched with the effort of restraint. 'Do you love him?' she said instead. I saw a flash of pity and pain in her brilliant blue eyes.

I hesitated, not sure what to say. 'I don't know . . . maybe.' My mouth was dry. 'What I feel for him is very different from what I feel for Heinrich.'

Mutti sighed, her face crumpling in sorrow briefly before setting into stiff resolution, her eyes steely once again.

'It doesn't matter anyway,' she said brusquely. 'I'll look into making the arrangements as quickly as possible. You keep your condition hidden and your mouth shut. You marry Heinrich as soon as he returns home and I will say nothing to Erich, but don't expect me to be pleasant to him.'

'All right, Mutti.' One part of me was quaking in terror that my secret was out, one part horrified at what I had agreed to do to this life growing inside me. Another part was relieved that my mother was going to help me through this. There was no going back now. My primary concern was to keep Erich safe, just as my mother was ensuring my safety. I would keep my promise to Heinrich and make my mother happy. It was nothing more or less than what Erich expected. Yet I couldn't shake the fierce protectiveness I felt for this child – Erich's child. It was the greatest sacrifice I had ever had to make. I didn't know if it would break my heart in two, part of me ripped away and forever missing, but it was something I was prepared to risk.

A week later, everything was organised. Despite my reservations, Mutti had enlisted the help of Tante Susie, who knew everybody in Windsheim and knew how to make discreet enquires. Mutti had told her that I refused to name the father, preferring that nobody knew about Erich. Susie was a little more sympathetic than my mother, but agreed that this was the right solution to the problem.

The plan was that I would convalesce at home, keeping to my bedroom for a day or two, using the excuse that I was unwell. My cough was not better, I barked like a hoarse dog in the mornings and the cool evenings and sometimes struggled to get my breath. It was a plausible enough excuse that would keep my cousins from annoying me, and keep Erich from asking questions. I was relieved that Mutti and Tante Susie could keep an eye on me, as I was nervous about the procedure and the potential risks of complications. But I was more worried that taking this irrevocable step would change me forever too.

14

Every morning and night until my appointment, lying in bed, listening to the peaceful rise and fall of Mutti's breath next to me, I wondered again what it would be like to be a mother. I felt the hardness above my pubic bone as I did, imagining the little child forming within me. Part of me wanted this child so badly. A child I would lavish all my love and attention on, unlike my own childhood and difficult relationship with my mother. I thought about what it would be like to be part of a loving family, what it might be like if I told Erich the truth. I would never force him into something, especially as that was what had happened with Inga. I would rather be on my own but how would I manage to raise a child? I doubted Mutti would help me if I made that choice. I doubted Heinrich, who was very proud and stubborn, would accept a child who was not his. A child born out of wedlock would break my father's heart. But I remembered what it was like after my parents divorced, and I decided I couldn't do this alone. I couldn't see an alternative solution.

Onkel Werner arrived home unexpectedly just before my appointment. After serving with a medical corp within the Heer, he had been released by the Americans. He was gaunt, thin and bedraggled but he greeted us with joy, lighting up the house with his larger-than-life personality. The boys were all over him and for once he didn't discipline them, laughing at their exuberance, while Tante Susie hugged him tight, tears of relief and happiness sliding down her face. He welcomed Erich into his home, thanking him for bringing me safely. I was relieved when he offered for him to stay as long as he needed, understanding what our journey had been like. I noticed Mutti's eyes narrow but she kept her promise and didn't say a word.

Early in the morning the day after he returned, a knock startled me out of the merry-go-round of my thoughts and woke Mutti, who shuffled restlessly in her bed. Tante Susie's dark head poked around the door.

'We need to talk.' Closing the door behind her with a gentle click, she came into the room and sat on the end of my bed.

Immediately I sat up. 'What's wrong?'

'What's this all about?' croaked Mutti.

To my horror, Tante Susie started to cry. Besides last night, I had never seen her cry before. 'I'm so sorry,' she whispered.

'What's happened, Susie?' demanded my mother.

'It's Werner. He's found out about Lotte's condition and he's furious.'

I stiffened, feeling the blood drain from my face, making me woozy. This was not supposed to happen.

'How?' Mutti leant back into her pillows, her eyes wide, mirroring the shock I was feeling.

'He saw the slip of paper I wrote the name and the address of the doctor on. It was in my bedroom.' Her large brown eyes pleaded forgiveness from Mutti and me. 'With all the excitement of him coming home, I forgot to hide it. The address made him suspicious and he wanted to know what it was for. You know how insistent he can be. I couldn't lie to him. I thought he'd understand.' She covered her face with her hands.

'What did he say?' My mother was deathly calm and that worried me.

'He wants to talk to Lotte as soon as she gets up.' She threw a look of despair and apology at me. 'I'll do what I can to smooth this over.'

I began to tremble with fury. It wasn't Onkel Werner's business.

'Well, she's not talking to him without me there. Our plans can't be changed now. He has to know that and the three of us have to be firm together,' hissed Mutti, glowering at Tanta Susie.

'It will be all right, Mutti.' My stomach was churning, nausea blossoming from the tiny kernel in my womb. All I could focus on was not being sick. 'We'd better get it over with. After I go to the bathroom.'

I got up without saying any more. I couldn't look at Tante Susie. I heard my mother speak as I closed the bedroom door behind me.

'I can't believe you betrayed us, Susie . . . I hope you haven't ruined her life. You'd better fix this or I'll never forgive you.'

I didn't hear my aunt's reply as another wave of nausea swept over me and I rushed to the bathroom.

Standing in front of Onkel Werner was mortifying. I felt like a small child in trouble. I waited, listening to the clock's methodical ticking. Sitting at the head of the dining table, he sipped the chamomile tea Tante Susie had made him in the hopes of calming him down. At least Erich was out the back, building something with the boys in the garden shed. Mutti stood by my side.

Finally, Onkel Werner put down his cup. 'Is it true, Lotte? Are you pregnant?' He held up his hand. 'Now, before you answer, I can tell if you are lying. If you lie to me, I will put you and your mother as well as Erich out on the street. Do you hear me?'

I started to shake, intimidated by his threat. 'Yes, Onkel.'

'Yes to what?'

'Yes, I won't lie . . .' I looked down at my feet for a moment but decided I'd had enough of being ashamed. I lifted my head defiantly. 'Yes, I am pregnant.'

He nodded, satisfied. 'Do you know who the father is?'

'No, Werner. That's not necessary,' interjected Tante Susie, hovering beside him, wringing her hands.

'It doesn't matter,' agreed my mother. 'It won't be a problem for much longer.'

'I'll be the judge of that. Have any of you thought about the danger? She could die and I would never forgive myself. Besides, what you women want to do is a crime. If she gets caught, it comes back to me, and I will not put my family in jeopardy.'

'What else can we do?' stammered my mother, her face creased in distress.

My uncle ignored her. 'Were you raped?'

'No, Onkel.' My face flooded with colour. I had never felt so humiliated. I wanted to run away but I knew that my uncle would never allow me back in the house and Erich would be thrown out too once he knew the truth.

'So I ask you again. Do you know who the father is?'

My mouth was dry. I nodded, not trusting myself to speak.

'Please don't make her do this,' pleaded my mother.

Onkel Werner's stony face relaxed momentarily, as realisation hit him. He leant forward as if to emphasise his next words. 'Remember, you promised me the truth. Now tell me, is Erich Drescher the father?'

'Yes,' I whispered.

Tante Susie sighed, shaking her head. We hadn't told her about Erich but she must have guessed. Truthfully, it wasn't hard to work out, especially when they knew we had travelled home together.

'This is the man to whom your father entrusted you. The man he asked to get you home safely. Is this right?' He looked at my mother.

'I never liked him, but Johann saw something in him. There was no other choice for Lotte's journey home and he has brought her safely to us.'

'Safe maybe, but soiled.'

I hid my face in my hands for a moment, dying of shame. I wanted to curl into a ball so small that I would become invisible.

My mother was red with outrage. 'Don't you dare, Werner,' she hissed.

'Come now, Werner,' said Tante Susie, placing her hand on her husband's shoulder. 'Is that necessary? Lotte is a good girl and has been through a lot to get here. These are extraordinary circumstances and she made an error of judgement. Surely you don't think she should be punished for that?'

'She's to marry Heinrich as soon as we can bring him home. She'll have a good life with him.' Mutti put her arm around me. 'You know the wedding was postponed because of his posting.'

Onkel Werner looked at all three of us, his brows drawn together. His fierce gaze met mine once more and I quailed, sure I would melt like an ice cream under his blazing stare.

'Does Erich know of your condition?'

'No,' I muttered. 'I haven't told him.'

'Go and get him,' he said to his wife.

Shaking her head at my mother helplessly, Tante Susie left the room. Mutti moaned, sinking to the chair next to Onkel Werner.

'Please, Werner, don't involve him.' She placed her hand on his arm. 'We can make this go away. We can do it somewhere else and not return here. It's all planned. Think about Lotte. She has her life in front of her, don't ruin it. Heinrich is waiting. They're perfect for each other and so happy together.'

'You know I can't do that.' He patted Mutti's hand in sympathy. 'I understand what you're trying to do but I know about it now and can't pretend that I don't. You and Lotte are under my roof and in my care. I have to do what I think is best for you both. Johann wouldn't expect any less of me.'

'Please, Onkel Werner,' I said, dropping to my knees in front of him. 'Please don't tell Erich. It will break his heart.' I took a deep breath. I had to tell him if I was going to make him understand. 'It was a mistake with him. We were both lonely and grieving. He had just lost his family and I thought Heinrich was gone.' I kissed his hand. 'Mutti's right. I love Heinrich and I want to marry him. Everything's organised for our wedding to go ahead as soon as he comes home.'

'Oh Lotte,' he said, stroking my head. 'You're almost like one of my own. I've watched you grow from a tiny child into a woman. I don't want to see you hurt but you have to be responsible for the decisions you've made. Erich deserves to know the truth. Now, I think you should sit down.'

It was a good idea because my legs had turned to jelly and I didn't know if I could even kneel any longer. Onkel Werner began coughing, a harsh bark that was worse than mine, his face turning red before he gasped for breath. I sat next to Mutti and a swift glance told me she was barely holding on to her temper. Her face was glowering with an expression that would make most people wither. She grasped my hand and held it tight. That tiny act of solidarity made me feel a little calmer.

Erich and Tante Susie entered the room. My stomach lurched. Tante Susie sat on the other side of Onkel Werner. Erich sat next to her, across the table from me. He smiled reassuringly at me, although his brow was creased in confusion or concern, I wasn't sure which.

'I have only this morning discovered some troubling news,' began Onkel Werner. 'I have learnt that my niece Lotte is with child.'

My heart thumped loudly in my ears, my head pounded and my vision swam. I felt dizzy and found it difficult to breathe. I gasped for air as the urge to violently expel my insides threatened to overpower me, blotting everything else out.

'Lotte!'

I heard my name called as if from a distance and realised that someone was shaking me. I tried to snap out of it and realised that my mother's anxious face was peering into mine.

'Lotte, it's all right. It will be all right,' she said, still holding my hand.

I looked across the table and Erich's face was pale, his green eyes wide with shock.

'I don't know if I can do it,' I whispered to my mother, still feeling faint.

'Stop this, Werner!' yelled Mutti. 'Can't you see she's not well?'

'Enough, Werner,' said Tante Susie. 'She can't do this now. It's been too much for her.'

'No, it's enough when I say it's enough,' growled Onkel Werner, slamming his fist on the table. He pointed at Erich accusingly. 'Did you know about this?'

'No, I didn't,' he said softly, his voice filled with wonder. I was worried that he'd be furious that I had hidden this from him but his face was alight with joy. He knew the child was his and he was happy. He glanced at me, a small smile tugging at the corners of his mouth. I could breathe again. Then his eyes clouded, as he must have thought of the implications.

'Are you an honourable man?' shouted Onkel Werner. I shrank away from his horrible words, leaning stiff and frozen against my mother. Erich was the epitome of honour.

'Of course! What kind of question is that?'

'Lotte claims that the child is yours. Is this true?'

'No!' wailed Mutti. She wrapped her arms around me as if she could shield me from what was to come. Her body heat seeped into me, lending me strength. 'Please don't do this. You'll destroy her life.'

Erich looked from me to my mother and back to me again. I didn't want him to deny it just for me. I knew that it would kill him to lie about this, to be a dishonourable man. He would own up to his responsibility, no matter what. I nodded imperceptibly to him.

'Yes, the child is mine.' Erich looked proudly into my eyes, silently telling me that we could get through this together.

'I should throw you out right now!' bellowed Onkel Werner, red in the face and grimacing in disgust. Erich was furious and I could tell by the way he held his arms that his fists were clenched under the table. The two men stared at each other like puffed up roosters and I was worried about who would throw the first punch.

Tante Susie leant forward to put herself between them. 'Werner, let him explain. We have to work this out for the best of everyone.' She touched his face briefly. 'Please.'

My uncle sighed, breaking the tension, and nodded to his wife. 'I will give you a choice, Erich. Marry Lotte as soon as possible and make this child legitimate, preserving her good name and her family's reputation.'

My mother's grasp on my hand released and she clutched Onkel Werner's sleeve. 'Don't do this, Werner. You'll regret it.'

He shook my mother's hand free and glared at her. 'Don't tell me what to do in my own home.'

'Werner, think about Lotte,' whispered his wife desperately.

My uncle stared at her impassively before returning his focus to Erich. 'Or you and she can leave this house today.'

Erich's face was thunderous. His jaw was clenched as he fought to keep his temper in check. I understood how he felt because I was shaking with fury but I knew that opening my mouth would incur the wrath of my uncle and make the situation worse. I swallowed the bile.

'Werner, no!' pleaded Mutti.

'I love her,' declared Erich. I felt a ray of warmth pierce the frozen core of my heart, melting the fear I had held on to so tightly all morning, and I smiled back at him. Mutti gasped but I saw Tante Susie's smile, which she quickly wiped from her face.

'You tell me that you want the best for Lotte. Do you think that casting her out, causing her so much distress, is best for her?' Erich asked, his voice rising. 'Look at her, she's a wreck!'

Onkel Werner flicked his hand as if my distress was of no concern. 'I need your answer. What do you intend to do?'

Mutti turned to Erich. 'Please don't ruin her life.'

Erich stared at her a moment, his eyes like the stormy ocean. 'This is Lotte's decision,' he said gently. 'I've wanted to marry her ever since we first worked together. It wasn't a possibility then ... but it is now. She's known how I feel about her for a long time.' He turned his attention back to Onkel Werner. 'But I know Lotte's committed to Heinrich. She's planned a life with him. I won't take that away from her.'

Mutti's sigh of relief was audible. It made my hackles rise.

Erich stood abruptly and sank down to one knee beside me. I realised what he was intending to do and felt a rush of blood to my face.

'Although I know you have a life already planned with Heinrich, if you have to make a choice, I want to do this properly,' he murmured as if we were the only two in the room. 'I want you regardless. Your uncle's ultimatum doesn't change the way I feel about you, nor does our situation.'

Listening to his words stirred something inside of me. He took my limp hand and placed his other hand over it, heat flowing from him to me. Staring into his steadfast green eyes, I felt a calmness descend on me.

'Charlotte Elisabeth von Klein, I ask for your hand in marriage. I promise to care for you, love and respect you and give you everything I have, although I realise that isn't much. You have my heart and soul and I will do everything in my power to make you happy.' His face was so earnest I knew he meant every word and it made my heart melt.

'The rest is up to you, Lotte,' he finished, kissing my hand. He smiled as he rose, holding himself straight and tall with pride but not before I had seen the fine sheen of sweat on his brow betraying his anxiety.

Mutti began to scream, ripping through the cocoon of warmth and belonging that had curled around me, leaving me cold.

'She's all I have left! Don't take her away from me. You'll ruin her life and I'll never forgive you.'

Tante Susie and Onkel Werner looked on, horrified, and Erich was taken aback, not sure how to react.

'Shh, Mutti,' I crooned, putting my arms around her violently trembling body, soothing her, as her screams turned to whimpers. 'It will be all right.'

'No, it won't,' she moaned. 'I've tried to protect you and keep you safe but I've failed. All I want is for you to have a good life.'

Tante Susie moved to Mutti's side. 'Amelia, you'll make yourself sick. Lotte will be fine.'

Mutti raised her tear-streaked face to Tante Susie, her eyes suddenly hard. 'How could you do this to me and to my daughter? You know we have nowhere else to go. Don't force her to do this. There is another way.' She glared at Onkel Werner. 'Don't make me beg.'

Onkel Werner looked at Mutti, cold and emotionless. 'I'm not forcing her to do anything. If she's grown up enough to get herself into this situation, then she's grown up enough to make her choice. She's brought this problem here, under my roof. It affects us all now.'

I could feel the tension mounting in my mother, wanting to leap across the table at him. I didn't know how to feel – outraged, ashamed, regretful or humiliated. I wanted to leap across the table myself. I could see Erich was very still and wary, body coiled in tension, ready to respond.

'It was a very romantic proposal, Lotte,' Onkel Werner said, 'but the decision is yours. Think carefully because once you've chosen your bed, you have to lie in it.'

'You can't turn Erich away. You know what will happen to him.' Although my blood was boiling with anger, it was essential I remain calm to have any chance of bargaining with my uncle. 'I have to marry Heinrich. I made a promise to him. I will leave as you have asked, so I no longer pose any problem to you and your family, but I beg that you allow Erich to remain here until it is safe for him to go.'

'I have made my decision and I will not waver,' said Onkel Werner. 'Now you must make your decision.'

I felt stripped to the bone, the vestiges of my old life torn from me. But there was only one decision. Heinrich would manage without me and even Mutti would cope with Vati by her side but Erich would not. If he was thrown out with nowhere to go and picked up by the Americans . . . especially if his child and I were lost to him after all the losses he had endured. He was the only one in danger now.

I squeezed my mother tight, taking in every detail of that hug, feeling the long elegant lines of her body, the French perfume that lingered on her clothes, her soft breath on my neck. This might be the last time I would hold her.

With the bonds of my social and family obligations now in shreds, desire welled within me for my own family, one nobody could take away from me. With Erich, I could make that family. Together we could lavish love on this baby, make decisions about our future, and I could be loved, cherished and respected. Perhaps this was right after all. This was my chance to live on my terms no matter how I had envisioned it before. A surge of joy rushed through me. I released my mother, kissing her gently on the cheek.

'I will marry you, Erich,' I said, turning to him and smiling.

He broke out into a huge grin, his eyes shining with elation.

Mutti slapped my face, leaving a burning streak on my cheek. 'You will not,' she hissed. Her eyes burned with wrath, her fury unleashed.

'Mutti, I love you, but I have to,' I said, holding my scalding face.

'If you marry him, I never want to speak to you again.'

'Please, Mutti,' I whispered desperately. 'Don't make me choose between the two of you. He's the father of my child. If he walks out that door, I may never see him again. I can't carry his imprisonment, his injury or his death on my conscience. He's a good man. He will be a good husband and a good father to your grandchild.'

She turned her face away from me. 'I hope you can live with your decision because the day you marry him, you'll never see me again.'

15

The fear of what I was about to do threatened to overwhelm me during the month leading up to my wedding to Erich. All I wanted to do was run away. More than once I entertained the notion of sneaking off to the address that Tante Susie had given me but the thought of what I would have had to do far outweighed any improvement to my circumstances. I would still have had to marry Erich – my uncle insisted upon it. I had placed our family in a scandalous position. I had been alone with a man for weeks while travelling to Windsheim. In Onkel Werner's eyes that was enough to cast aspersions on my character. Because of that, Erich had no sanctuary unless I married him.

My decision put me in an impossible position. I tossed and turned most nights, nausea my constant companion, trying to find a way out of my situation, but always coming back to the facts. I woke most mornings listening to Mutti's soft breathing as she slept in the bed next to me and to sounds of the boys and Tante Susie preparing for the day. It was a fleeting moment when I felt that life was as it should be. Then my tender breasts reminded me of my condition.

There wasn't much to organise, unlike the preparations for my wedding to Heinrich. The legalities required us to lodge our intention to marry with the civil registry office in Windsheim a month beforehand. Erich faced the heart-breaking task of signing an affidavit declaring the death of Inga and his children. Mutti had begged me time and time again to think about what I was doing but from the day we registered, she refused to speak to me. In fact, she barely acknowledged anyone except the boys. She moved silently about the house, speaking only when she had to, continuing to pull her weight in the household with an air of martyrdom and disdain etched across her features. I know she missed Vati and his support, wondering where he was and if he was safe, as did I. But Mutti and I were now worlds apart and we could not turn to each other for comfort.

I had nothing but the two dresses I had brought from the kloster, both worn and neither fitting well. I thought wist-fully of my wedding dress, wrapped lovingly and boxed in my wardrobe in München, waiting for Heinrich to come home.

One day, while I was helping prepare the lunchtime meal, I noticed Erich return from delivering some furniture that he had repaired. He had a parcel tucked under his arm and he looked smug and very pleased with himself. The younger two boys, waiting restlessly for him, descended on him as he came through the door. Hanging off one arm, they demanded to know what was in the parcel.

'Shh,' I heard him whisper, 'it's a surprise.'

'A surprise for who?' asked Wolfgang in a voice that wasn't very quiet at all.

'Is it for us?' said Hansi, breathless with excitement.

'I'm afraid not,' said Erich. The boys sighed with disappointment. 'But maybe you can help me with it. If you can promise to keep it a secret for now.'

The boys giggled and I guessed they agreed, because all I could hear were hushed murmurings until Erich said in a loud voice, 'Off you go now, boys, you know what to do.'

'What are those boys up to now?' asked Tante Susie, cutting the potatoes.

'Some mischief that Erich's concocted.' I kept the washed potato skins. I could fry them up in the evening for another meal.

'He keeps them amused, that's for sure. He's good with children . . . he'll make a good father.'

'I know.' I sighed. 'It just isn't the way I'd planned my life.'

Tante Susie put down her knife and turned to me. 'I know you and Heinrich have been friends for many years and that both families expected you to marry.'

'I promised him and both our families,' I said, tears in my eyes. 'I don't break my promises.'

'In normal times I would agree but these are not normal times. Heinrich's a lovely boy but you don't need a boy, you need a man, someone who can give you what you require. I never did think you were the right match.'

'I don't want to hurt him – he's my best friend. He'll never forgive me.'

'He's always done what his mother told him. Maybe this will allow him to do what he wants. Have you thought about that?'

259

I shook my head. 'He had our lives planned out already.'

Tante Susie squeezed my arm. 'That's what was expected of him. Maybe he never knew any better, but the war has changed all of us. Nothing is what it used to be.'

'But he loves me and I love him.'

'What do either of you know of love?' She stopped at the confusion on my face and nodded knowingly. 'Maybe you do now.'

'I don't,' I said miserably. 'All I know is that I feel different with Erich. He understands me, he makes me light up . . . he makes me feel special . . . but he's fifteen years older than me.'

'Yes,' she said a little impatiently. 'Erich is a man, older, wiser and, from watching him, I agree that he understands how you think and feel. He may not be your mother's choice of husband but look where marrying your father, someone from the right family, got her. Then she fell in love with Johann and was lucky that he's from a good family too. He adores her, like I can see Erich adores you. He respects your mother and allows her to be the person she is. He brings out the best in her. I think it might be the same for you and Erich.' She filled the pot with water and turned back to me, her brown eyes soft and sincere. 'I think you're marrying the right man.'

'Thank you, Tante Susie.' I threw my arms around her.

'It's all right, dear.' She patted me on the back. It was comforting and just what I needed. 'Don't worry about your mother, she'll come around.'

At lunch, the boys seemed fidgety and Erich had a half-smile on his face, like he knew something nobody else did.

When we had finished clearing the table they disappeared in a rush and Tante Susie raised her hands in a 'who knows what they're up to' expression but she let them go. Mutti remained sullen as ever.

When the dishes were done, Hansi and Wolfgang reappeared, grabbing me by the hands.

'You have to come with us,' they said, hopping from foot to foot.

'Where are we going?'

'Just come with us,' Wolfgang insisted, pulling my arm.

'You have to close your eyes,' said Hansi.

'Fine,' I said, laughing.

The boys led me carefully into the garden, my eyes cracking open a little to make sure I didn't run into anything. I shut them quickly whenever the boys looked up at me.

'You can open them now,' said Wolfgang, releasing my hand.

I opened my eyes to find myself at the oak tree at the bottom of the garden. Sitting on the bench under the canopy of new green leaves was Erich, grinning from ear to ear.

'Come and sit down,' said Hansi, guiding me to the seat. 'Sit here next to Onkel Erich.'

I smiled, feeling shy. We had barely spent a moment together since our decision to marry. We were both kept busy, and it felt strange to be sitting side by side in the afternoon sunshine.

'What's this all about?' I asked.

'We have something for you, Lotte,' said Wolfgang. He and Hansi rushed around the tree behind us.

'I got it first,' shouted Hansi.

'No, I did,' yelled his frustrated big brother.

'Gently, boys,' said Erich. 'Remember to bring it together.' The scuffling stopped and the boys reappeared as a united front looking angelic and carrying the parcel I had seen earlier.

'This is for you,' Wolfgang said triumphantly.

'What is it?' I asked, taking the parcel and feeling it carefully. It was firm but yielding under the paper.

'It's something special from Onkel Erich,' said Hansi, jumping on the spot. 'Come on, open it.'

I looked at Erich but he gave nothing away.

'You'd better open it before the boys burst,' he said, still grinning.

Slowly, I pulled at the string that held the paper together, winding it up to use again. I unwrapped the parcel, the paper crinkling as I straightened it out. Two little blond heads crowded in, trying to glimpse what was inside. Neatly folded black velvet lay in the paper. I ran my hand across it, the plush fabric soft against my skin.

'It's for your wedding dress,' blurted Wolfgang.

I gasped. A thrill of spine-tingling exhilaration fizzed through me, raising the hairs on my arms.

The boys laughed at my surprise. 'It's a good surprise, isn't it?'

'It's a fantastic surprise,' I murmured, tears in my eyes. 'Thank you, boys.' I pulled them towards me, kissing each of them on the cheek.

'All right, boys,' said Erich, ruffling their heads as they squirmed out of my embrace. 'Thank you for your help with the surprise. How about you let me talk to Lotte now?'

The boys were satisfied that they had executed the great surprise successfully and were happy to go.

'Thank you,' I said. Erich's nearness after so many weeks made me feel faint. His eyes were magnetic, drawing me into their depths.

He leant in and kissed me, lightly at first but then with an increasing intensity that made it abundantly clear what was on his mind. I broke off the kiss, fearful of Onkel Werner's ever vigilant eyes.

'The children might be watching,' I murmured.

'But we're engaged,' protested Erich, a teasing smile lighting his face. 'It's my right and duty to kiss you.'

'Not here,' I whispered. 'You know how tense things are already.'

Erich interlaced his fingers with mine, his hand warm and solid. 'Another couple of weeks then,' he said with a mock groan.

I squeezed his hand and nodded. My free hand brushed the velvet again. 'The fabric is superb,' I said softly. 'Where did you get it?'

'I knew you didn't have anything to wear for our wedding day. I remembered you telling Bettina about the dress you had chosen in München and how excited you were.'

'You heard that?'

'I heard a good many things about your wedding plans. Bettina wasn't exactly quiet, was she, especially when she was excited about something.' He smiled ruefully. I smiled too. He was right.

'And you remembered?' I touched his face briefly, moved by his thoughtfulness. His stubble was soft and springy under my fingers. Razors were in short supply and men couldn't shave every day. I quite liked Erich with the beginnings of a beard. It made him even more manly.

'I tried to find white fabric or lace for you but all I could get was this black velvet. One of my customers had it lying around – their blackout curtains – and they were happy to part with it in exchange for some furniture repairs.' He shrugged. 'I hope there's enough.'

I pulled the fabric out, allowing it to drape across my body. To me it was pure luxury. 'It's perfect and there's more than enough.' I grabbed his face and kissed him in my excitement. I laughed at his astonishment, his eyes wide with surprise.

'I was worried about the black . . .'

I shook my head vigorously. 'No! Black is wonderful.' I wouldn't think about the magnificent wedding gown I had chosen so long ago, wrapped lovingly and stored away, waiting patiently for me. 'I always wanted a black dress but Mutti wouldn't let me. She said it wasn't appropriate for a girl my age – too risqué!'

'Are you sure?' His eyes held the desperate hope that he had done the right thing.

I wondered what I had done to deserve such a man. 'Erich, the velvet is beautiful. It means I will have my own wedding dress. It's more than I imagined. I'll enjoy creating my own design and I will wear this dress with pride on our wedding day.' I leant against him and he put his arm around me. 'You're so good to me.'

'You deserve much more,' he murmured, holding me close and kissing the top of my head. 'I promise I'll make it up to you.'

I didn't know what to say, my head against his chest, and the steady beat of his heart lulling me into a sense of security. I wasn't sure I deserved him at all.

'I'm sorry I couldn't get you the dress you wanted,' he murmured into my hair. 'I didn't want it to be like this. Your wedding day should be filled with joy.' I pulled away and looked into his eyes, clouded with regret. He hung his head. 'I know this is difficult for you. It isn't want you wanted, but I want you to be happy.'

Grabbing his hands in my own, I brought them to my chest. 'Don't speak like that. This is something out of our control. We're both alive, whole and healthy. We have clothes on our back, a roof over our head and you even have a job. Let's make the most of what we do have. The rest doesn't really matter any more. We're both different from who we were a year ago. The world has changed and so have we.' I kissed each of his knuckles fervently. 'My family is what matters most.' I gently placed his hands over the swell of my belly. 'It's just the three of us now.'

Staring at my reflection in the mirror before we made our way to the registry office, I hardly recognised myself. The short, puffed sleeves and figure-hugging bodice of the dress I had made showed how thin I was. My body and face were all angles except for the soft thickening of my waistline and glowing skin. In another time, pregnancy would suit me.

I traced the line of the V neck that allowed room for the swell of my breasts. My finger left a trail of silver in its wake – light and dark, just like my emotions. My eyes travelled further over the slightly gathered waist, hiding any tell-tale swelling, and a tailored skirt that fell below my knees. The dress was simple and elegant, yet demure. I was pleased with the result. It wasn't the gown I had wanted a lifetime ago, but these were different times and I had become someone else. A pang of regret and sadness shuddered through me and then it was gone. I smoothed my hair, behaving itself today, and pinned one side away from my face. I had decided to wear it free, shoulder length again and still streaked with strands bleached from weeks in the sun.

I had my summer wedding. It wasn't what I had imagined this day would be like, but then again, I never imagined my marriage would have such immediate and life-changing consequences – keeping my husband safe from homelessness and internment, giving our child legitimacy and some kind of stability. However, I couldn't shake thoughts of Heinrich, as if he were standing silently behind me, observing my actions with an expression of reproach and deep sorrow. Wherever he was, I hoped he would understand, but I knew in my heart that he could never forgive me for what I was about to do.

Sunlight streamed through the registry office window, slowly warming the chill morning air.

'Are you ready?' Erich whispered. His hand rested on my shoulder, heavy and reassuring, as we waited for the proceedings to begin.

'Yes,' I said, trembling, and not just from the cold. Staring at the registry desk at the front of the room, my body clenched tight and anxiety spiked through me once again. This wasn't how it was supposed to be. My eyes widened with fear and my heart was racing. This was my last chance to back out, to run away like a spooked filly.

Erich put his arm around me, leaning in close to whisper into my ear, 'It will be all right.' His warmth soothed my rigid body and calmed my trembling. 'Whatever happens, we can do this together. We've been through so much already. I know we can do this too.'

'I know,' I said quietly. I did my best to smile but it spluttered and failed like a flame struggling to stay alight. Erich stepped back a little, his eyes wandering over me, glinting with appreciation, his face unguarded, showing me what he thought of my bridal attire.

'You are breathtaking. Black suits you and that velvet against your white skin . . . well I shouldn't tell you what I'd like to do.' He smiled at me, slow and deliberate.

The breath caught in my throat and the fire within me erupted into life, melting my taut muscles and sinews, the heat rising up my throat and blazing into my cheeks. He never failed to make me feel this way, this uncontrollable fire we shared.

'You look very handsome too,' I murmured, blushing further. Erich wore an ill-fitting suit borrowed from Onkel Werner but he still cut a dashing figure. I couldn't believe I was standing here, ready to marry him. Remembering back to the day I had first met him and how I was falling over myself in his presence and now, here we were. It didn't seem real.

'Thank you.' Green eyes gazed at me intently. 'It's time.'

I nodded. Erich squeezed my hand gently before threading his arm through mine.

To stop myself from shaking again, I focused on the bunch of wild flowers I held. The boys had picked them for me, deep blue cornflowers, a few of the last pastel poppies and white daisies with their bright yellow centres. I couldn't have asked for a better bouquet. It was vibrant, colourful and picked with love from the meadows outside the town, and the only splash of colour in the nondescript room. The boys, despite their protests and tears, had not been allowed to attend but they were with me in this way.

My mother was missing too. How could I be married without her? Tears pricked my eyes but I did not cry. If only she had capitulated. If only my father were here; his arm in mine, holding me steady, lending me his strength, but we had no way of knowing if or where he was interned.

As if in a dream, Erich and I approached the registry desk. The official waited behind it in his dark suit. Onkel Werner and Tante Susie stood nearby as our witnesses. Drab seats lay in neat rows behind us for the guests and spectators but they were empty.

Erich took my clammy hand in his. His grasp was firm and solid, anchoring me to the here and now. I stared into his eyes, endless pools of green, calming as the still sea on a summer's day. My heart beat wildly as I paid little attention to the official's words. It was as if there was no one else in the room, only the two of us, locked in private conversation. Slowly my heartbeat returned to normal, my quivering subsided and a sense of calm settled over me. We were in this together. Watching Erich's face as we repeated the official's words, promising binding oaths of marriage to each other, joy flared hot in my chest. We were proclaimed husband and wife. Elation lit up Erich's face. Maybe this was right after all.

'I love you, Frau Drescher,' he whispered before bending to kiss my mouth for the first time as my husband, tender and restrained with promised passion. How could I ask for more than that?

For the first time, I was expected to sleep in the same bed as Erich, which was a new experience, despite the time we had been travelling together. Although my thoughts had often run wild about what it might be like to share his bed, I wasn't sure what to expect or how I would feel.

To make my wedding night special, Tante Susie had gone to a lot of trouble to make Erich's room comfortable and pretty. She dressed the bed in her best linen, scattered a few candles about – an absolute extravagance – which she insisted on lighting before we went in, and had put my bouquet in an exquisite crystal vase on the dressing table. The effect was magical.

Erich waited until I had changed into a modest nightgown and climbed into bed before he came in. He smiled reassuringly as he closed the door behind him. Sitting rigid in the bed, the covers pulled up to my chest, I tried to smile back but my face felt waxen.

'It's been a long day,' he said conversationally, sitting on the end of the bed to remove his shoes.

'It certainly has,' I agreed. My heart began to thump.

'Susie, Werner and the boys went to a lot of trouble to make the day special. Even your mother . . . She cooked most of the wedding feast while we were away.'

I raised my eyebrows. Little escaped Erich's notice. My nerves began to dissipate.

'They did. I was surprised by how much effort they went to. My mother's just very stubborn. The boys were so sweet, don't you think?'

In the candlelight, I saw a smile flicker across Erich's face.

'They made the day,' he whispered. A shadow of grief crossed his face and I knew he was thinking about his own children. Forgetting my anxiety, I threw off the covers to sit beside him. I put my arms around him, as if I could protect him from his pain. He was warm, even through the cotton of his shirt.

'Oh Erich, I'm so sorry.'

'There's nothing any of us can do,' he murmured. 'Susie's boys are still so full of life and innocence. They make me hope for better times ahead.' He lifted his hand tentatively, hovering over my belly, watching me intently. I did not move or recoil. He placed his hand on the slope of my belly and let it rest there for a moment. The gentle pressure of his hand made me feel protected and safe. He would look after us. 'I know we've done this the wrong way around but this child will bring us joy. We have a lot to live for.'

I put my hand over his. The butterflies fluttered in my belly once again. 'I know, but I want us to be together for the right reasons. You told me once before that you married Inga because she was pregnant with Eva. I know you loved those children with every ounce of your being but you and Inga were both so unhappy.'

Erich pulled me tight to him, whispering vehemently in my ear, 'I wanted to marry you anyway. You know I've always wanted you. This baby just pushed things along and allowed me to become the happiest man. It was never like this with Inga. With her, I was younger, greener and I married her out of obligation.'

Trying to stay focused on what I needed to say and not on the immediacy of him against me, I pushed away. 'Please let me finish. I know you told me this before we married, that you wanted me in spite of the baby. But if you were ever to feel like we were wrong for each other, do you promise to let me know? I don't want you to feel trapped like you did with Inga.'

Erich sank to the floor, kneeling in front of me. 'I have been in love with you longer than I care to admit. I thank God that you came into my life – you were made for me and I was made for you. I might be selfish for being happy that you're pregnant.' He rested his hands over my belly once more, this time possessively. A jolt of arousal shot through me at his gesture. Lifting his head to me, I could see the fierce joy in his face. 'Our child has ensured we'll be together, given me the opportunity and excuse to marry you. I know I wasn't what you wanted in a husband but I promise you that I will do everything in my power to make you happy.' He grabbed my hands then, kissing my knuckles, the touch of his lips white hot against my skin. 'I will cherish you like no other man can and love you always for the woman you are and the woman you will become. You are my home and my sanctuary and I bless my good fortune to have found you and to have you in my life. Is that good enough for you?'

I nodded, mute at the intensity of that passionate declaration. Tears filled my eyes, making the flames around the room double and dance. 'Oh Erich! Whatever did I do to deserve you?'

I pulled him to me. The feel of him was glorious and made me realise just how much I had missed his touch. There was not one bit of shame or guilt as I furiously removed any impediment in the way of feeling his skin against mine, becoming unaware of anything but Erich and the deep joy and exquisite pleasure that we shared.

Lying naked among the rumpled bedclothes, the candles burning lower, I gazed at the long, athletic lines of Erich's body sprawled out beside me. He was beautifully made, lean and firm from the weeks of walking and hours of carpentry. His face was bronzed from the sun, the delicate lids closed, rimmed with long lashes, his hair askew, long strands framing one side of his face. He was at peace and obviously comfortable with me beside him, like it was the most natural thing in the world, as if we had been like this forever. I'd love to photograph him naked like this, I thought.

The green eyes winked open, catching me out. A slow smile spread across his face. 'What're you looking at?'

'Nothing,' I said, quickly averting my eyes.

'Nothing? Maybe I'd better look at nothing.' He turned on his side, appraising my figure. 'Mmm, Raphael should have painted you . . . perhaps you're a bit thin now for his liking but in a few months you'll be full and ripe.'

I gasped as he kissed my belly, not sure what to make of what he'd said, shocked that he had picked up on my thought.

'Such perfect skin, milky white, soft and smooth.' He drew his finger softly over my arm and breast. 'Silky, shiny, golden locks that tumble to your shoulders.' He raked his fingers through my hair and I closed my eyes, shocked at the effect it had on me – I was mesmerised, as if I was under his control. 'Eyes the colour of the summer sky and lips to die for . . .' His fingers trailed over my closed lids and traced the outline of my lips, all my senses focused on his touch. 'Ah yes, if I could paint, I would paint you and all the world would glory at your perfection.'

I sighed with pleasure, feeling like the most beautiful and precious woman in the world. I opened my eyes to find him staring at me for a long moment.

'Do you know what Colonel von Wissenbach informed us all when you started in the office?' I shook my head. 'He told us that you were off-limits, from a respected family of high social standing. A young woman you married, but did not fool around with.'

'What?' I clapped my hand to my mouth in horror and embarrassment.

Erich chuckled. 'Imagine my surprise when I discovered you were to be my assistant. I was nervous, not sure what to expect, but when I met you, I couldn't believe how gorgeous you were. I could see straight away that you were intelligent, classy and beautiful but it was your smile that got my attention.'

I shivered at his delectable words. There had been mutual attraction at our first meeting after all. Attraction like that wasn't something you could fake. I understood now that it was something extraordinary.

'Your smile lit up the room and I knew that he was right. I knew you were special.' He gently lifted a strand of hair from my face and smoothed it back behind my ear, raising goose bumps across my body. 'I don't know what I've done to deserve you but I'm so glad you agreed to marry me, because I can't imagine my life without you.'

His eyes met mine, fire with fire. Then he bent to kiss me.

16

It was still dark when I got out of bed, trying not to wake Erich. Something had woken me. I didn't know what, but I was uncomfortable. It was mild, so I threw on my dressing gown and quietly padded out to the garden, where I wouldn't disturb anyone. Bathed in moonlight, I sat on the bench by the oak tree, relishing the quiet that surrounded me.

In the six weeks since the wedding, Windsheim had finally come under the American zone. The Wehrmacht was gone, as were many of the Nazi officials. The town was under curfew; this was part of the occupying force's conditions of a defeated country, not a liberated one as many had hoped. The Americans had requisitioned Nazi property – homes, furniture, radios, supplies – but often this wasn't enough and ordinary citizens were called on to supply the Americans' needs. Numerous people were angry at the intrusion and disregard with which many were treated, the soldiers coming and going as they liked, taking what they wanted, at times without payment of any kind. Gardens were left empty when they could be used for vegetable growing. Damaged buildings were repaired and at times refurbished to suit the requirements of the American command in the town. Despite all the frantic activity, however, they had not yet managed to improve the lives of average German citizens like myself.

The American soldiers proved to be friendly enough. They would arrive by jeep at the end of the day to their claimed lodgings, where American flags often flew outside. Usually they would change out of their uniforms and come out to play ball with the local children, teaching them a game called baseball and handing out chocolate and sugar treats they called candy. However, the curfew restrictions were adhered to strictly. Nobody could be out between the hours of seven at night and six in the morning without a permit. Windsheim resembled a ghost town. It made me miss München, which had always been so lively, although I felt sure it was in a much worse state than Windsheim.

My thoughts wandered once again to my father, wondering if he was still there, living in our apartment safe and well, or if he had been interned in one of the prisoner-of-war camps. We still hadn't heard from him and I was worried. Mutti fretted over him until she was almost sick. We hadn't heard anything further about Heinrich either. I wasn't looking forward to the day I came face to face with him.

I was glad that Erich was safe. The POW camp at the Illesheim Airpark had closed in July. The American air force controlled the base now, using it as a supply and maintenance centre, destroying our aircraft and military vehicles. All German forces had been formally discharged in June. Those without discharge papers were required to present themselves to the Americans, and most were sent to internment for processing. I thanked God Erich had secured his before leaving Riem. He no longer had to fear reprisals due to the Nazi affiliations that his rank generally held. It meant that we could move on with our lives – create some kind of existence within our occupied land.

Erich had work now, as a driver for Dr Schrieber, who had remained in Windsheim during the war, too elderly for active service. He had recently decided to give up driving, as his sight was failing him. Onkel Werner had helped Erich secure the job. We were very grateful for his recommendation to Dr Schrieber, who was a colleague and old mentor of Onkel Werner's. Erich didn't mind the work. Besides, he was kept busy: refugees streaming into Windsheim brought with them sickness and infectious diseases, which increased Dr Schrieber's load. Erich told me that there were many new complaints that arose out of the poor nutrition that we all had suffered in the last months of the war. It was a problem that was going to take time to solve.

Little had changed so far, even with the Americans' presence. Food was still scarce, despite the new rations brought into effect in June, and availability of staple foods could change within minutes. We were used to queues from the war days and it looked like this would remain a way of life for who knew how long. Clothes and household items were virtually impossible to find. Even with Erich's small income providing for the household, there wasn't much to buy.

There was a long way to go to rebuild our devastated country. The Americans had set up a military government and its focus seemed to be on security and dismantling the Third Reich, as we witnessed with the unscheduled house checks and requests to hand over weapons, ammunition, binoculars and radio transmitters. Large meetings of German citizens were also prohibited. Sometimes my translation services were called upon to ensure clear communication and smooth over tension in the town. My heart lurched when one of the Americans told me that in some towns, cameras had also been seized. Thank God in Heaven, not in Windsheim. I didn't know what risk cameras posed as there was no film or chemicals to develop it but I hid my camera and film anyway.

A rooster began to crow in one of the adjoining yards. I shifted restlessly and glanced up. Stars still filled the sky, like diamonds encrusted on black silk. To the east, the black seemed lighter, the brilliance of the stars beginning to fade, and I knew it wouldn't be long before dawn. The ache in my back was more pronounced, and I could no longer ignore it. Sitting was uncomfortable, so I began to pace around the garden. I heard the click of the back door and turned to see Erich dressed in a suit and fedora. He walked towards me, cutting a powerful but elegant figure, even out of uniform.

'What are you doing out here?' he asked, frowning.

'I woke up and couldn't go back to sleep. I didn't want to wake anyone, so I came out here. It's quiet and peaceful, a nice change to the hectic days with those boys.'

Erich wrapped his arms around me, kissing me lightly. 'Why don't you go back to bed now that I'm up?'

'No, I'm all right out here. I'd rather walk around for a while. It's not cold and it's the best time of morning.

I'll watch the sunrise. I love the way the light plays on objects at this time, giving everything a different dimension.'

'You should go and get your camera. You have some of your father's film left, don't you?'

'Mmm, that's a good idea ... maybe.' I pulled away as I felt the urge to move again.

'Are you okay, Lotte?' asked Erich sharply. 'Is something wrong?'

I shook my head and sighed. 'No, I'm fine ... just a bit uncomfortable and a sore back. I'm sure it will settle soon.'

Erich grasped my hand. 'Come and I'll make you a cup of tea before I go. Go back to bed and rest until everyone else is up. I'll give your back a rub when I get home.'

'Don't be silly, I'm fine. I probably slept the wrong way. Hansi and Wolfgang will be up soon anyway. I'll have something when I make their breakfast. Don't worry.' I squeezed his hand and kissed it before letting go.

Erich looked sternly at me. 'Look after yourself. Your mother and Susie are quite capable of looking after those boys and the household. You still have that cough and you're thin as a stick. The baby's taking it out of you. I'll try to find some extra milk this afternoon and maybe some honey. Rest today and conserve your energy.'

'I'm fine,' I snapped, although I knew he was right.

Erich held me by the shoulders, his green eyes searching mine, unperturbed by my irritation. 'Promise me.'

'I promise,' I said to get him to stop. He pulled me into an embrace, hugging me tightly.

'I would hate for anything to happen to you or the baby. You have to take care of yourself ... It's different now, there are two of you to think of.' He kissed me again and released me, the frown of concern still on his face.

'Have a good day,' I murmured, although my focus was already inward, my attention fixed on the growing ache in my back.

The ache did not improve. I felt sapped of energy and dragged myself around while making the boys' breakfast and cleaning the kitchen. I was putting away the last of the dishes when I noticed a sticky wetness between my legs. My skin prickled in apprehension. Surely nothing was wrong? I tried not to rush to the privacy of my bedroom but my breath was shallow and my heart was pounding with fear. A sob caught in my throat at the patch of bright red blood that stained my underwear. I stared in disbelief, then reality hit. 'No,' I moaned. I didn't know what to do and I didn't know what was wrong. Light-headed and giddy with fear, I searched frantically for Tante Susie but remembered she had gone to the market, leaving Mutti at home with the boys. Mutti still wasn't speaking to me, but I needed her.

I found her in the parlour, sunlight streaming through the window, a pile of mending on the table next to her. I hesitated by the door, not sure how to begin.

'Mutti,' I said, my voice cracking with fear and panic.

Immediately her head shot up, concern in her sharp, blue eyes.

'Mutti, I'm bleeding.'

She was on her feet in an instant, the mending dropped to one side. Her arm was around me. 'Is there much? Is it bright red or dark?'

'It's only a little,' I whispered, 'but it's bright red.'

'Come then, let's get you to your room.' Her voice was low and soothing. She guided me to the bedroom, her arm still around me.

My shaking eased with her by my side. I didn't have to go through this on my own. Mutti would know what to do. She would help me.

'Up on the bed now,' she said.

'Is it bad?'

'I don't know.' Mutti sat on the bed beside me, patting my hand. Her touch was cool and comforting. 'Some women bleed through their pregnancy, some bleed just the once and have no problems.'

'Did you?' I grasped her hand tightly. I desperately needed for this to be okay.

'No, but that doesn't mean that you won't.' Her face was guarded and I didn't feel reassured.

'What else could it mean?' My chest was tight with anxiety. I had to know what I was dealing with.

'Have you been feeling out of sorts? Anything else out of the ordinary that you've noticed?'

'I woke with a backache this morning that I haven't been able to get rid of. If anything, it's got worse. Does that have anything to do with it?'

'It could.' Mutti squeezed my hand, covering it with her other hand, as if she was trying to give me strength. 'If the bleeding continues, it could mean that you will lose the baby,' she said quietly, blue eyes levelling with mine.

Stifling a sob, panic propelled me forward. I threw my arms around her, resting my head on her chest, my blood loud in my ears. My mother drew me to her, her embrace a balm to my spiralling terror.

'What can I do?'

'Shh, shh.' Mutti smoothed the hair from my face. 'There's nothing you can do but rest and pray that the bleeding stops.'

Slightly reassured, the thumping in my head started to fade. I wanted to stay in her arms like this forever. I couldn't remember the last time Mutti had held and comforted me.

'How long will it take?' I whispered, feeling stronger now. If I could keep the bleeding at bay long enough, maybe I would be all right.

Mutti shrugged helplessly. 'I don't know. We can ask Onkel Werner. He's a doctor after all . . .'

'No Mutti! Not Onkel Werner.'

'What about Dr Schrieber?'

I sat upright. 'It's okay. I'll just rest for a little while. Hopefully it's nothing.'

Mutti stared at me, her face creased in worry, then nodded. 'Maybe that's the best thing. You rest and I'll bring you some tea.' She stood and kissed me on the top of my head. 'I won't be long.'

Mutti brought me a cup of chamomile tea, propping me up on the pillows so that I was comfortable, and left me to rest quietly, promising to check on me. I sipped the tea absently, all the while willing the baby to be alright. Feeling better lying down, my backache barely noticeable and with no more bleeding, I was convinced that if I stayed still for a while, I would be fine. My panic had subsided. The trembling eased into jitteriness and then into a drowsy stupor. I was surprised to find my thoughts wandering on the edge of sleep, my eyes drooping and fluttering shut. I had been up early after all.

When I woke, I felt refreshed. Checking my watch, I was amazed to see that I had slept for about an hour. I never slept during the day but the rest seemed to have done me good. There was no backache and no wetness between my legs. I stretched and, feeling guilty about staying in bed any longer, I swung my legs over the edge.

I doubled over in agony as a sharp pain gripped my belly. Gasping, I sat gingerly back on the bed as the pain subsided, leaving behind a dull ache in my back. My thoughts still fuzzy from shock, all I could think was that I had got up too quickly. I stood again but carefully this time, holding my breath. The pain did not return. I blew out the breath I had been holding as I walked slowly to the door and turned the knob. I felt a gush of warmth down my legs. I reached between my thighs and when I removed my hand, it was sticky with blood.

'Mutti!' I screamed from the open doorway. I held onto the doorframe, too afraid to move.

'It's all right, we've got you.' Capable hands held me on both sides and helped me walk shakily back to bed.

Minutes later, Tante Susie had pillows behind me and towels layered beneath me, while Mutti hovered over me anxiously. The pains began in earnest, each time holding my belly in a vice so tight I could barely breathe.

'What's happening?' I asked between clenched teeth as another pain came on. My body was coiled tight with tension, muscles quivering. 'The baby? Is it okay?'

'Rest, conserve your energy,' said Tante Susie, helping me to change position onto my side but there was no comfortable place – not in lying, sitting, standing or walking. The pain came regardless. It was relentless.

'It will be all right,' crooned Mutti, holding my hand tightly, so that the bones were squeezed painfully together.

'Don't leave me, Mutti,' I pleaded. 'Stay with me.' Pain, confusion and bewilderment all collided within me. They hadn't answered my question.

'I'm here,' she whispered. Her face was white as a sheet and her eyes were misty with tears. 'I'm not going anywhere.'

Then everything was washed away by the waves of agony that battered my body. My only desire was to ride it out and reach the other side. Survival took over as my world shrank to me and that pain. I would not die now. I had my whole life ahead of me.

I gasped for air, sucking it in greedily at the end of each wave, like a drowning woman bursting above the water. My body, trembling with exhaustion, sank against Tante Susie's or Mutti's hands. In between the pains, I rested in a daze. I had to keep my baby safe. Cool cloths wiped my hot and sweaty brow and soothing hands rubbed my aching belly and back. I turned my head at one stage to find Onkel Werner's concerned gaze upon me but I had no time to be upset as another wave rose to greet me.

A middle-aged woman entered the room. Tante Susie greeted her and spoke to her in an undertone that I couldn't hear, their eyes slipping to me every now and then. Mutti helped me into a sitting position as I recovered from another wave of pain. A feeling of dread settled in my belly, dropping like a stone. I clutched my mother's arm, a bolt of fear giving me a moment of clarity.

'Who's that, Mutti? Why is she here?'

'It's only the midwife. She's here to keep an eye on you, to make you comfortable and make sure you stay safe.'

'I'm losing the baby, aren't I? It's too soon for it to be born. I'm only five months along.'

Mutti looked away, unable to keep my gaze. 'I don't know, Lotte. That's why she's here . . . To see what's happening with you.'

'I can't lose this baby.' My breath caught in my throat. 'I have to keep my baby safe. I won't let it happen.' I started to tremble and could feel myself becoming hysterical, the panic and heat rising within me like a volcano ready to explode.

Mutti shook me. 'Stop, Lotte. We don't know yet. If she can stop your contractions, if you're not too far, the baby might be all right, but my main concern is you.'

I stared at her stupidly, trying to make sense of her words.

Mutti shook me again. 'Do you hear me, Lotte? I won't lose you.' She gathered me in her arms and hugged me tight, her tiny body wracked with sobs.

After another pain had come and gone, the midwife was introduced to me. She was a capable-looking woman with greying hair pulled back tightly into a bun. I wasn't sure how to feel about her very personal questions as I shifted uncomfortably – embarrassed and irritated or relieved to have someone who could tell me what was wrong. But that was nothing compared to having my underwear removed and my nightdress hitched up around my hips to suffer the indignity of an examination between my pains. My cheeks flamed with mortification but I endured the poking and probing, every muscle strung tight. I had to know what was happening.

The midwife shook her head sadly.

'I'm sorry, my dear. Your contractions are too long and close together. You're too far into your labour now. Sometimes it happens very quickly like this and I can't stop it. We have to let nature take its course.' She patted me sympathetically on the hand.

'You can't do anything?' I whispered, incredulous. I could feel the blood draining from my face.

'Nothing for your baby. It's too small to survive and its heartbeat is beginning to weaken. Your child will be stillborn, I'm afraid.'

'That can't be.' I felt oddly detached. Frantically, I searched the eyes of Mutti, Tante Susie and then the midwife once again. They all told me the same thing. I felt sick to my stomach. This couldn't be real. I had given up so much for this child to come into the world. I had wanted nothing more than to have my own family. It was all for nothing. 'Why is this happening?'

'Nobody can tell,' said the midwife, shaking her head. 'I've seen a number of pregnancies lost like this lately. Perhaps it's the poor nutrition – there's not enough food to eat and the baby just can't thrive. I think much of your energy may have been used when you walked home after the war and the baby didn't get enough of what it needed to grow properly.'

I stared at her for a moment, letting her words sink in. I twisted the sheet around my hands in frustration. It could be true but it still wasn't fair. After everything we'd been through, this baby deserved to live. My heart dropped. How could I tell Erich? He'd already lost two children.

'All I can do is watch that you come through childbirth healthy and well.' The midwife's voice, full of compassion and practicality, sounded a long way away. 'We owe that to the ones you love, don't we?'

Another contraction swelled within me. This time I gave in to its pain, overwhelmed by grief and hopelessness.

My cheeks were wet with tears when finally the contraction subsided. 'No!' I screamed with rage, glaring at the midwife. 'I won't give in. This baby has to make it.' I pounded the bed in fury. 'I have to stop these pains.' I noticed the worried glances between the three women but I had no energy for those who didn't believe in me. I had to focus on saving my child.

Minutes seemed like hours. The contractions were getting longer and closer together. Deep breaths became gasps, which became groans and wails of agony. With each contraction my fear that I was fighting a losing battle rose. My body was slick with sweat – my nightdress adhered to my skin and my hair was plastered to my forehead. In between, all I could do was shudder with exhaustion and anguish, my face wet with tears of hopelessness, aware that Mutti was by my side, wiping my brow and whispering words of encouragement. I didn't know what was worse, the contractions or the moments of clarity when desolation overcame me. As time ticked by, hope ebbed away.

The three women made the bed ready for me to birth the baby. I couldn't watch them, and stared out at the early afternoon shadows made by the oak tree across the yard. A pall of sadness settled across me. It was too beautiful a day for this tragedy to happen. I had been so happy in the stillness of pre-dawn.

'We're ready for you, Lotte,' said Mutti, her voice quivering. I nodded. Despite my best efforts, we had reached this point. She reached for my hand, warm in my cold grip, and kissed my waxen cheek, leading me back to the bed.

'Don't fight it, dear,' said the midwife, her warm hand on my shoulder. 'This baby will be born today, no matter what you do. Try to relax and go with it. Fighting it will only make it harder on you, tire you and draw this process out.'

Fire deep within me flickered into life as I clambered back into bed, a scowl of fresh determination on my face. A rush of energy flowed through me, making my body tingle. I would fight to the very end. I wouldn't give up on this child. I owed it to the baby, to Erich and to myself. I would do everything I could.

The nightmare truly began. My belly contorted with increasing intensity and frequency, barely giving me a breath in between to recover. All that existed was my fight, my screams of agony and despair renting the air while my body tried to expel the baby with red hot pokers of pain. Mutti held my hand, urging me on.

'Don't let go, Mutti,' I rasped, my throat raw from my screams. 'I can't do this without you.'

'Stay with me, Lotte. You can do this. Don't you leave me,' she whispered desperately into my ear. She held my hand tighter. I knew that women died in childbirth. Everything else that had come between us didn't matter.

'I'm not going anywhere,' I whispered. Then the pain clouded my conscious thought once again.

My body throbbed, hot, swollen and ready to burst. My desperation grew. With each pain, I knew my baby was one step closer to certain death and there was nothing I could do. It was futile and, as the midwife predicted, only lengthened the

experience and made it more painful. I refused to let go, sure
that if I succumbed, part of me would shatter and never mend.

The midwife issued calm instructions to me now. My
mother was constantly by my side and Tante Susie swam in
and out of focus.

'Push,' commanded the midwife. I couldn't do it. Eyes
squeezed shut, I did everything to stop myself from pushing,
my arm across my belly trying to prevent my child from
being sent inexorably to its death.

'Lotte, you have to push now!' Mutti yelled in desperation. 'You can't stop this. I'm sorry, but you can't. Please, my
darling. I've lost my grandchild but I won't lose you too.'

Thought crystallised in my mind. My mother was fighting
the same battle I was.

I screamed, heartbroken, as finally, my body overrode
my will and a primal urge to push overcame me, splitting my
body in two.

My son was born against my will, slithering out silently
between my legs. He was limp. He did not cry. He was perfectly formed – the size of a baby doll. I was not allowed to
hold him, the midwife covering his tiny face with the blanket
he was wrapped in. I took no notice of the activity at my feet,
only vaguely aware of my mother holding my hand tightly,
as if she didn't want me to move. I felt numb, this wasn't
happening to me . . . it was all a bad dream that I would wake
up from very soon.

I later learnt that Erich had waited alone outside our room
during the birth. He demanded to see his son when the

midwife emerged with the baby clasped to her chest. She was reluctant to show him – it just wasn't done – but he wouldn't take no for an answer.

At least he held our son. I longed to hold my child, gaze into his sweet face, peaceful in death, but he was gone. Only in my imagination could I feel the weight of him, the warm, soft skin, the roundness of his head cradled in my hand, the wonder of his tiny hands and feet.

Erich organised a Catholic burial for the following day while I was convalescing. He was the only one in attendance. I mourned our son from the privacy of our bed. I wished I had been allowed to join him, to say goodbye and to give Erich support as he stood at the tiny grave. Instead I was confined to bed, my mother refusing for me to be seen outside the bedroom, urging me to rest while I could. All the while, my thoughts tumbled over and over, torturing my mind with what I could have done differently to save my precious child.

My breasts ached. They were enormous – swollen and hard as rocks. I longed for my baby to suckle from them, especially when my milk came in. I didn't have to imagine what it would have been like, my body instinctively knew the feel of that tiny mouth around my nipple, closing tight and sucking greedily and the blessed relief that would come. Mutti showed me how to ease the pressure with warm cloths. There were no cabbage leaves to soothe the pain. Thin, milky fluid leaked from my nipples, staining my clothes, leaving me teary and opening the wound of my loss each time.

At night, I tossed and turned with discomfort. After a few nights, Erich turned to me tentatively.

'Are you all right?'

I nodded. 'As good as can be expected, but I'm finding it hard to sleep. Every time I close my eyes, I replay what happened and wonder if I could have done anything to prevent it—' My voiced caught. 'I'm so sorry, you've been through enough.'

Erich shuffled in against me, kissing my shoulder. 'There was nothing you could do. Just get well again. We'll get on our feet and together we'll decide what to do and where to go. There'll be another child for us when the time is right.'

'I know ... I'm so glad you're here.' I held his hand and snuggled closer. 'I don't think I can get through this without you.'

'I'm here for you. We'll get through this together.' He encircled me in his arms and, safe in the knowledge that I was not alone, I soon drifted off into a dreamless sleep.

'There's no reason for you to stay now,' said Mutti casually as we folded sheets together a month or so after the loss of my son.

'What do you mean?'

'You could come home with me,' she said concentrating on the sheet, refusing to look at me.

'Mutti, Erich has a job here now. If we stay, we can help until Onkel Werner can get back to work.' I brought the two edges of the sheet together, pulling it taut.

'I didn't mean for Erich to join us.' She paused in her folding. 'Come home. We can arrange a divorce. You have no obligation to Erich now. He can find lodgings anywhere in town. You don't need to stay to keep him safe.'

'Stop, Mutti.' I took a deep breath, trying to calm myself but I could feel my blood boiling. 'I'm not leaving him. I've made my commitment. It doesn't matter what the original reason was or that the reason is gone. He has been my rock since . . . he has taken care of me. I am going to honour my commitment to him as he has kept his to me.' I had broken my promise to Heinrich but I wasn't going to break another.

'But Lotte, Heinrich will still have you, I'm sure of it.'

My mother's perplexed expression made me furious. She didn't understand. I couldn't leave Erich. I couldn't do that to him after all we'd been through, after everything he had helped me through. Truth be told, I couldn't imagine being torn apart from him now.

'No, Mutti. I want to be with Erich. Don't ask me again – I won't change my mind.'

'If Vati were here, none of this would have happened.' Mutti scowled but I saw the fleeting fear in her eyes.

She continued to mirror my folds of the sheet until she handed it to me to make the final fold. I knew her silence was strategic. This wasn't the last time I would hear her argument but I couldn't stay angry with her. I knew she was worried about me and pining for my father. We had been waiting anxiously for news of him but had heard nothing. She badly wanted to return home, unwilling to be a burden on her sister any longer, although I think it had more to do with her strained relationship with Onkel Werner. She hadn't forgiven him for what he had made me do.

Mutti would feel better if I was with her in München, back where I belonged, among the high-born families, the only world I had known until recently. But everything had changed. My child had seen to that. Because of him, I had turned my back on the privileged life I came from. Because of him, I now had the chance to live my life the way I wanted. I owed him that much.

In bed, Erich was gentle and patient with me, slowly allowing me to get used to him after the trauma to my body. He knew how far to go. His sensitivity and experience as a lover helped unlock the vulnerable part of me that I had pushed deep within me since our loss. This enabled me to feel safe to relinquish control once again and get back in touch with the passion that we shared. He surprised me with how easily he aroused me and with the strength of my response to him. Each time, my walls came down a little more. Each time, I lost myself further to him. Joy and anticipation returned to our nights together and in this way, I knew that I was healing not just in body and mind but in spirit too.

A letter from Vati finally arrived in early December. He had just been released from a POW camp outside München and was back home. He was well, he told Mutti and I, and looking forward to seeing us again soon and to spending Christmas together. Mutti shot me an accusing look as she read those words and tears filled my eyes at the realisation that I would not see my father this Christmas.

'Come home with me,' whispered Mutti urgently. We were alone in the parlour, darning socks. 'I don't want to leave you here.'

'I can't, Mutti,' I said, shaking my head with regret.

'Don't be stubborn! Your father deserves to see you. Come home and then you can work out what you want to do.' She must have seen the tears in my eyes because she softened, placing her hand on my arm. 'Please . . . if you can't do it for me, do it for Vati.'

A single tear spilled down my cheek. 'I can't leave him, Mutti. I'm pregnant.'

Mutti stared at me, shocked into silence, the letter falling from her hand. 'You stupid girl. Now you've destroyed any chance of a future.' She stood abruptly and whirled away, striding from the room in fury, leaving Vati's letter on the table.

I crumpled into the chair, distraught. This was not the way it was supposed to be. I hadn't told anyone, not even Erich. I was overjoyed at this pregnancy. It allowed me to push past the misery that had lingered after the loss of my son. I knew that Mutti wanted only the best for me but she had stomped on my happiness. She had to get past her fear and let me live my life or it would destroy the closeness we had developed through our difficult times. But the thought of not seeing Vati now he'd been released was hardest of all. I didn't dare travel with this pregnancy and truth be told, I wouldn't leave without Erich. I was too afraid of what Mutti might do if we were apart. I dreamt of telling Vati my news in person and seeing his face light up when he realised that I was happy and that he was going to be a grandfather. I knew he liked Erich and would not be unhappy to have him as a son-in-law. Maybe I could visit him after the baby was born.

Erich was ecstatic when I told him the news, spinning me around with joy.

'It's wonderful!'

'Are you sure?' I said breathless. 'It's not the best timing. Things are still very tight and we're not settled anywhere yet.'

'It's never the right time,' said Erich, hugging me. 'I have a job and we've promised to stay until Werner's well enough to work. When that changes, we'll work it out. Don't worry.' He kissed me on the mouth. 'Come on, let's tell the others.'

'No, not yet. It's too soon.'

'No, it's not! I want to tell the world.' He grinned with excitement, reminding me of Hansi. 'Besides, this time you have to rest. Everyone has to know so you don't overdo it.'

In fact, Onkel Werner and Tante Susie were pleased. The boys whooped with joy at the thought of a tiny new cousin to fuss over.

Mutti returned home a week later, still furious with me. She refused to say goodbye but agreed to carry my letter to Vati, telling him of my news. Erich wanted to write to him too but Mutti would not have it. He decided to post his letter and hoped that Vati would receive it. I was surprised by how difficult it was to see my mother go but I was glad that she was going to Vati. She had missed him so much and her face was alight with joy at the thought of reuniting with him. I was finally beginning to understand what that might feel like.

17

The knock at the door was unexpected. It was late afternoon and already growing dark. The clouds had been building all day, promising another dump of snow through the night. It was February and we were in the heart of a bitterly cold winter, made worse by the lack of fuel and warm clothing. We were now into February and the weather hadn't eased.

Onkel Werner sighed as he went to the door. He was probably relieved to have a break from supervising the boys' homework while Tante Susie and I prepared the evening meal. Erich was still out with Dr Schrieber.

'Can I help you?' I heard Onkel Werner enquire as he opened the door.

'Doctor Jüngst?'

'Yes,' said Onkel Werner.

'You have to come with us.'

Tante Susie stopped chopping the vegetables and looked at me, puzzled, gesturing for me to be quiet.

'Whatever for?' asked Onkel Werner sharply.

'You're under arrest.'

My heart leapt to my mouth and I watched Tante Susie's face blanch in fear.

'Go to the boys,' she whispered urgently before hurrying to her husband.

I rushed to where the boys were studying in the dining room as quietly as I could. Tante Susie would deal with whatever was happening at the front door. In the meantime, I would do all in my power to keep the boys calm and safe, out of harm's way. If only Erich were here, he would know what to do.

'I've done nothing wrong! What's the charge?' I heard Onkel Werner demand as I reached the dining table to see the shocked expressions on the pale faces of the boys. Hansi and Wolfgang were already standing, inquisitive little boys wanting to peek to see who was at the door. I pulled them to me, trying to protect them from the ugliness at the front of the house. I narrowed my eyes and pressed my lips tight. Shaking my head, I gave Peter and Ernst, the two older boys, my sternest expression. *Please don't move*, I prayed.

'You're charged with being a filthy Nazi,' spat one of the men. These men were German, I realised. Probably police appointed by the Americans to carry out their arrests. My skin crawled with dread. I held my breath so I could hear what was going on but Ernst's eyes blazed with fury. I shook my head again.

'He's no Nazi!' exclaimed Tante Susie. 'He's a well-respected local doctor.'

'Exactly,' said the first man. 'All doctors have Nazi membership and must be reviewed by the board to assess their Nazi status. Until then, he has to come with us.'

Peter sat rigid in his chair, his face ashen. I tried to smile to reassure him but the smile died on my lips. Onkel Werner was in serious trouble.

'But he only had the membership because it was the only way to get a job,' argued Tante Susie desperately.

'I was never an active member,' said Onkel Werner.

'The new regulations stipulate that anyone who stated in the Fragebogen that they had Nazi membership or affiliations must be arrested, pending assessment of their case. I'm afraid there is nothing you can do.'

That wretched survey. As part of the 'denazification' process, anyone wishing to do business in the American Zone had to answer one hundred and thirty-one questions that assessed political affiliations and levels of personal responsibility for war crimes. Onkel Werner had filled it out months ago, hoping to be allowed to return to work as a doctor.

Ernst jerked out of his chair. 'No,' I whispered, holding his arm. 'You will only make it worse.'

He pulled his arm away with a thunderous expression but didn't move further. Peter just looked petrified. A sharp burst of cold air rushed through the room.

'No, please don't take him,' shrieked Tante Susie. I held onto Hansi and Wolfgang even tighter. Hansi squirmed.

'It's all right, Susie,' said Onkel Werner. 'Look after the children. Erich and Lotte will help you. I'll be back home before you know it. Say goodnight to the boys for me.'

Trembling, I kissed the top of Hansi's head to stop the gasp of horror from escaping from my lips.

The door shut with a thud. 'No, no, no . . .' moaned Tante Susie. Ernst and Peter glanced to me, eyes wide with disbelief.

I nodded and the boys and I rushed out to the hallway. We found her sitting on the floor by the door in shock.

'Mutti!' Wolfgang stepped towards his mother, ready to hurl his little body into her arms.

'No, wait. Help me get your mother up,' I said softly. I had no time to go to pieces. I had to be strong. The two older boys and I hauled Tante Susie to her feet. 'All right, let's get her to the parlour.'

We sat her gently in a lounge chair. Peter fluffed a pillow behind her back and laid a blanket across her knees but she stared into space, as if unaware of what was happening around her.

'Is Vati going to be okay?' asked Peter, his voice shaking with fear. 'Where did the men take him?'

Wolfgang tugged at his mother's sleeve. 'What just happened, Mutti?'

Hansi began to cry. 'Where's Vati?' he sobbed.

Tante Susie just stared at them, dazed.

'Come on, boys,' I said. 'Let's leave your mother be. How about we make her a cup of tea? Then you have to finish your homework.'

I dragged Hansi and Wolfgang out with me. Peter trailed behind while Ernst kissed his mother on the forehead, his face drawn in worry.

'What will happen to Vati?' asked Peter again, coming into the kitchen.

I turned and crouched beside the three boys. 'Your father has to answer some questions about his time before the war. It's just the law. All the doctors have to do it. He'll be fine. Now let's make that tea.'

*

Life went on. I knew Tante Susie worried over Onkel Werner but typical of my family, she did this privately and presented a no-nonsense, practical attitude to the world. She told the boys that their father would be home soon and that they would manage until that time, as they had done during the war. Erich took over the tutoring of the boys.

Tante Susie and I continued to run the household, although more and more of our time was spent searching for food. We would queue for hours in the snow, bundled in layers of clothes to stay warm. Often we would arrive during the night, the curfew finally lifted, to be among the first to receive whatever was available that day. We tried the surrounding villages and countryside too. Occasionally we were able to return with fresh milk or cream, butter or eggs, and a few times even a duck or chicken. Meat was becoming a rare commodity. We seldom ate it and when we did, we relished and used every last bit of it. Fat, cartilage, bones, feet, head and innards, nothing was wasted.

We discovered that the black market was alive and thriving. The Reich Mark was fast becoming useless. The best currency was American cigarettes. Supply and demand drove the value of a pack. At times, it might buy one pound of butter, at other times two pounds. Cigarettes became the preferred payment for my translation services, thanks to Erich. Sometimes he would drive me to where I was needed. I had introduced him to the Americans I worked for. Often the soldiers were wary of German men who weren't imprisoned, and sometimes they were hostile. But perhaps because of his association with me, Erich soon developed a rapport with the Americans, learning English very quickly. Before long he was almost as proficient as me, much to my chagrin.

My pregnancy was progressing well. The morning sickness had been less severe this time, abating after the first few months. Although I was still unable to put on any weight, I was nowhere near as tired. Erich ensured I ate a little extra to help the baby grow well and to keep me going. I refused to rest and be pampered when there was so much to do. Still a little nervous leading up to the five-month mark when I had lost my boy, I noticed Erich watching me carefully for any tell-tale signs that there was something wrong. But there was nothing.

At night when the electricity was working, we listened to the radio. American music was all we heard now, big bands like Glenn Miller, boogie-woogie and jazz. Besides the music, there were announcements of rules and regulations and broadcasts naming missing people with their ages, the name of their home, military unit and the date they were last seen. I found those lists wore me down. They made me wonder how many would be found alive and well, how many would have everything they knew stripped from them – loved ones, family, home and livelihood. We still had no idea what had happened to Erich's parents, where they were or if they were even still alive. Erich reached out to the Red Cross, filling out files on his parents. There was nothing more he could do except wait to hear back. Communication was still haphazard and nearly impossible in the Russian zone where Silesia was. From one of Vati's letters, I knew that Heinrich was still detained in a refugee camp in Denmark but had no idea how he was.

By March, further changes were made to the Fragebogen. Now all Germans over the age of eighteen were required to fill it out. An air of resentment sprang up around the town. The removal of all traces of the Third Reich and Hitler was understandable to most but now ordinary Germans who had endured so much were made to feel guilty for what the leaders of our country had done.

'But not all people who belonged to the Nazi party were bad,' I tried to explain to an American soldier one day. We were standing outside one of the partially repaired school buildings. He and Erich were smoking a cigarette while we chatted. 'Many were members of the party because they had to be for their professions. They had nothing to do with the party's workings or politics.'

Erich stubbed the butt of his cigarette against a piece of old timber, watching me carefully under hooded lids.

'You don't understand how many of us feel,' said the soldier bitterly. 'We've seen what the Nazis are capable of, what Hitler gave his blessing to . . . I was there when Dachau was liberated. I thought I knew what to expect, but I was wrong.' He shook his head, pain flitting across his face.

Erich and I glanced at each other. We had heard stories, terrible stories of the brutality of the Nazi Party. Those seen as enemies of the Reich, especially the Jews, had been treated in an abominable fashion.

'Before we even arrived inside the camp, we found over thirty railway cars on the siding outside. The stench was terrible. I knew what I would see inside but it didn't prepare me for the sight. The wagons were full of dead bodies, the stripes of their prison uniforms lying chaotically, one over the other. I don't know how they died . . . probably from starvation and sickness. They were nothing but skin and bone.

Many had their eyes open, like they were staring at us, as if telling us to seek retribution for their murders.' The American took a long draw on his cigarette, blowing slowly out as he gathered his thoughts.

I shuddered, appalled, and reached for Erich's hand. He grasped it tightly, as if he could protect me from the images that had formed in our minds.

'That was nothing compared to what we saw inside the camp. Pitifully thin prisoners suffering severe malnutrition, some waving small scraps of cloth like flags, hysterical at their liberation. Others looked fearfully away at our approach, like mistreated dogs. They were walking skeletons and some were too weak to stand. I couldn't believe my eyes. The conditions in which they survived were horrendous. You wouldn't treat an animal like that.' He stared into the distance, his eyes haunted, the cigarette between his fingers forgotten.

I stood rooted to the spot, horrified by his words, by the images that tumbled readily in my mind. I squeezed Erich's hand tighter, his warmth and immediacy my only link to the present. His eyes were clouded with despair. We remained silent. What could we say?

'Worst of all were the mounds of corpses next to the crematorium, in varying states of decomposition.' The American's voice broke and he wiped a hand over his face. 'Typhus was rife in the camp. There were men, women and children – thousands, too many to count. Piled neatly nearby were sorted stacks of folded clothing: clothing of the dead prisoners.'

Erich pulled me to him and I buried my head in his chest, muffling the sob that burst from my throat, clinging onto him as if for dear life. What insanity had created such horror? I felt a fine tremor pass through Erich. I knew he was as disgusted as me. Images of Frau Andree and the unknown relatives Willi had told me about sprang to mind. What had happened to them? Had they survived or perished in one of the concentration camps? Had my uncle suffered for his Jewish affiliations? I felt faint, my fingers suddenly icy, not sure I could cope. Erich held me close, as if to take away my terror.

The American hadn't finished. I turned to look at him, still in the protective embrace of Erich's arms. His face was ashen.

'We were all enraged, incensed and profoundly disturbed at the brutal treatment these people had suffered at the hand of their Nazi captors. Many of our men had to be restrained from wanting to kill the guards who remained. It was as if the normal rules of human decency didn't apply. We wanted retribution so badly ... but this was not the way.' He sighed and shook his head again. 'I never in my life imagined I would see such a thing, humans degrading another human being in such a manner. I wake up from nightmares drenched in sweat from what I've seen.' His eyes hardened. 'But I tell you, I will do whatever is in my power to make sure this never happens again. If it means rounding up every person that had anything to do with the Nazi party and the monsters that did this, well, so be it.'

There was nothing we could say. It was hard to believe the stories, hard to believe that our fellow citizens, Germans like ourselves, could be capable of such cruelty. Everything I had believed about this war, which we had put our hearts and souls into, was not so. I began to understand the obsession with finding any ties to the Nazis. I felt ashamed to be German.

Tante Susie, Erich and I were made to fill out our forms. We debated as to whether Tante Susie should lie on her form about her Nazi Party membership, which was taken out so Onkel Werner had a better chance at promotion in the hospital before the war. We decided it was too risky. They already knew Onkel Werner had had a membership. Plastered all over the newspapers and the questionnaire itself, and also on the radio, were warnings of the stiff penalties for providing false information. Thank God, Erich had no connections to the party because his civil service positions in the Luftwaffe were wartime appointments, and I had never climbed the ranks of the BDM.

We were doing laundry when Wolfgang came running in. 'There are two men at the door who want to see you, Mutti,' he said.

'What are you doing answering the door?' asked Tante Susie crossly, wiping her hands on a towel.

Wolfgang's angelic face fell. 'You didn't come, Mutti. I'm a big boy now, so I answered the door.'

I tried to hide my smile as Tante Susie sighed.

'It's all right, Wolfie. Come on, then, and we'll see what they want.' She took his pudgy little hand and Wolfgang solemnly led her to the door while I continued to scrub the clothes.

'Lotte, can you come to the door please?' Tante Susie called a few moments later.

Dropping the washing, I wiped my hands on my apron and hurried to the front door.

'Wolfgang, could you please go and check on your brother and keep him occupied while I talk to these gentlemen for a moment?' Tante Susie hugged Wolfgang tightly, kissing him on his blond head. 'You're such a big boy.' His chest swelled with the responsibility as he nodded and went off to play with Hansi in their bedroom.

As Tante Susie stood, she met my eye and I knew there was trouble.

I glanced at the front door and saw the two policemen waiting patiently. It couldn't be! Reaching Tante Susie's side, I grasped her hand tightly, my heart beginning to race.

'They're here for me,' she whispered.

'They're not taking you.'

'We have no choice. Don't make a fuss. I don't want the boys upset.'

'Ready, Frau Jüngst?' asked one man.

'What about a bag?' I asked indignantly.

'You can bring a bag to her later today. Her case has to be processed here in Windsheim before she's sent to a women's camp.'

I looked at Tante Susie. She nodded. 'All right,' I said, 'but how long will you hold her and where will she be sent? I have to let her family and children know. She has small children who will be without their parents.'

'We'll inform you where she'll be detained and the possibility of visitors. The children can write to her. As to how long?' He shrugged. 'Who knows? There's a backlog of cases now that everybody has to fill out the Fragebogen. I can't count the number of arrests we've done this week.'

I felt the blood rise to my face and I clenched my fists in my skirt. This was ridiculous and totally unnecessary. 'Please be reasonable. She's just a wife and mother. No threat to anyone.'

'Her case will be assessed in due course and you will be notified of her whereabouts and the outcome if there is a further prison sentence,' said the second man brusquely. 'Come now, we have a busy schedule today and we can't afford to run behind.'

Tante Susie embraced me, kissing me on the cheek. 'Look after my boys like they're your own. Tell them I will be home soon.' Her voice caught and I hugged her tight. 'Make sure they do their homework. Don't forget to plant the summer vegetables.'

'You'll be back before then, I'm sure. You've done nothing wrong, after all. We'll stay in touch and let you know what's happening at home.' I didn't want to let her go.

Tante Susie was hauled away like a criminal. I could do nothing but stand there and watch her go. It was outrageous – she was a good woman who had no political inclinations, who cared for her husband and children in the best way she knew. She did not deserve to be treated this way. I hated that I was helpless to prevent it and turned the anger that burned in my belly into caring for the boys.

The boys played up for a time, arguing, fighting and wrestling more than they should have. I don't know what I was expecting. They had been through so much during the war, growing up without their father, not knowing if he would survive, watching his arrest and then their mother being taken away. They knew their parents would be back with them soon but it was hard for them to articulate how they felt and after the initial conversations, they said very little about it. I often got comments like, 'Mutti wouldn't do it like that,' 'Mutti would let me do that,' 'Mutti's is better,' or 'I wish Mutti was here.' I tried not to take it to heart but sometimes it was trying. It was difficult to know how much to discipline them and how much to lavish them with love.

We kept to their daily routine, trying to keep things as normal as possible, but it was very hectic. I wondered how Tante Susie managed it. Ernst was a good help with his younger brothers. I was worried at first that he would resent taking orders from Erich and me but I was surprised by his maturity and his perceptiveness, often knowing what to do before Erich and I had worked it out. His brothers riled against him a little until we explained that we needed to work together for the sake of their parents. We wanted to send letters filled with good reports and all the exciting and wonderful things they were doing. Erich soon had them all eating out of his hand, engaging them in activities they loved, basic car mechanics and driving lessons for Ernst, woodwork and football for all of them. I wondered how it would be to watch him with our child as it grew from a baby to adulthood.

My favourite time was reading stories to Hansi and Wolfgang at night. They cuddled up next to me in bed, their soft bodies yielding tiredly against mine. At moments, when I felt the baby kick, I let them put their little hands over my thin, stretched belly, to find tiny hands, feet and knees with amazement.

We discovered that Tante Susie was interned at Ludwigsburg. It was a female civilian internment camp about one hundred and fifty kilometres south-east of Windsheim, near Stuttgart.

We sent letters to her and had some in reply telling us she was in relatively good spirits and health. Visitors were not encouraged. Onkel Werner had been transferred from internment at Dachau to a camp near Ludwigsburg. There was still no news about his case.

One morning in June while I was washing the dishes and the boys were playing in the back yard, there was a knock at the door. I wiped my hands on a tea towel and went to answer it. I opened it just a crack and shrieked with surprise.

'What is it, Lotte?' said Ernst, coming up the hallway behind me.

'Look,' I said, throwing the door open.

'*Muttilein*!' Ernst pushed past me and grasped his mother around the middle, lifting her into the air. 'You're home!'

'Put me down before you hurt yourself,' said Tante Susie, laughing. 'Let me look at you. You've grown taller and stronger since I've gone.'

Ernst shrugged but I could see the pride as he squared his shoulders a little more and stood straighter.

'Come inside,' I said. 'The boys are in the backyard playing. They'll be beside themselves to see you.'

There was a lot of squealing, shrieking and screaming, the boys hugging their mother tightly and refusing to let her go. They pulled her around the yard and house, showing her their projects, explaining the things we had done while she was away. She listened intently to all they told her, nodding and asking questions, and it made my heart glad to see them reunited.

Tante Susie was clearly exhausted. I made sure she rested after dinner that night, while I continued with the bedtime routine, coming in to kiss each of the children good night. Her eyes narrowed when she saw the two youngest cuddled up to me as we finished reading our story. She said nothing but I felt a little uncomfortable. When I returned to the parlour where she and Erich sat listening to the radio, I could see that she had something to say.

'The children are thin,' she snapped.

'You know how difficult the food situation was when you left. It's only got worse, as you'll soon see,' I explained, sinking into a lounge chair, exhausted.

'What about the rations? There should have been enough for them with the rations.' I could see that she was agitated and I frowned. This was so unlike her.

'We haven't been able to get all the rations. Some weeks certain things aren't available but we've tried to make up what we need on the black market or out in the countryside.'

'It's been difficult on the black market too,' said Erich. 'The usual food staples aren't always possible to find no matter how many cigarettes are offered.'

'They're skin and bone. How are they going to grow like that?' Tante Susie raked a shaking hand through her dark hair, streaked with more silver than I remembered.

'You're exhausted, Susie,' said Erich. 'The boys are fine. They'll grow into healthy lads.'

'No, don't try to defend her. I know what's happened here,' she hissed. 'She's taken the boys' rations for herself, the sugar and butter, to make sure this baby survives.' Her voice rose.

'What about my boys? They're starving! You were supposed to take care of them like they were your own.'

I stood, shocked at what she had accused me of. I had never seen her nasty like this.

'I would never do something like that. I love your boys and I've done my very best to look after them,' I said indignantly.

'Then why are they so thin and you're not?' she asked. She glared at me with a belligerent expression, her arms crossed tightly across her chest.

'Enough, Susie! You'll wake the children.' Erich was by my side in an instant. 'Lotte has done her utmost to care for your boys and she has done a wonderful job. You should be thanking her, not blaming her for doing something you know in your heart she would never do.' He pulled my dress tight across my belly and hips. 'Look at her. She's skin and bones. I have to stop her from constantly giving some of her portion of the rations to your boys and force her to eat. She's mindful of the responsibility she has to your children and would never let you down.'

Tante Susie glowered at us, trembling with fury. 'I want you out of my house,' she whispered, her voice now cold, like a shard of ice piercing my heart. She rose without another word, went to her room and closed her door.

Erich and I looked at each other, our eyes wide with shock.

'I can't believe she would even think that,' I murmured.

'I know. It's ridiculous. Let's sleep now and tomorrow we can look at it with fresh eyes.'

After a night of tossing and turning, becoming more distressed at the venom Tante Susie had directed my way,

I woke feeling dull, unrefreshed and depressed. Erich and I had no choice but to confront her again after she sent the boys outside to play.

'I apologise for my words last night,' she said as she slumped at the dining table, dishevelled and her eyes rimmed with black, puffy rings. She obviously hadn't slept much either and my heart went out to her, wondering what kind of torment she was going through.

'It doesn't matter, Tante Susie,' I said. 'We were all tired.'

'It doesn't change the facts,' she said, 'but I overreacted. Being without the boys and Werner has been difficult.'

'You've had a difficult time,' agreed Erich, 'but we've done the best we can to care for your children and they're healthy and happy, considering the circumstances.'

'Well, you don't need to worry about them any more. I'll look after them and you can look after yourselves.'

'I think you're being unfair,' said Erich softly.

Tante Susie stared at him, her large, dark eyes sparkling with anger. 'Do you, now? Who took you and your wife in when you needed somewhere safe and you had nowhere else to go?'

'You don't want us here?' I blurted, bristling with fury. 'Fine, we'll go.'

'I didn't say that.' Tante Susie's gaze fell to the table and I realised where this was going. She needed us to stay.

'I think you've made yourself quite clear, Susie,' said Erich. 'I promised Werner to bring an income into this house until he was able to. I will not leave you and your children destitute. We will stay until Werner returns home and finds work. Then we'll leave. Until then, however, I expect you to treat my wife with respect. Your boys are fit, healthy and happy because of her. Don't forget it.'

Tante Susie stood abruptly, her chair hitting the timber floor with a thud. She gave us a look filled with anger and hatred before storming from the room.

The next month was a nightmare. Tante Susie was cold and distant. I continued to help her around the house, cooking, cleaning and standing in the queues for food. The bedtime stories I shared with Hansi and Wolfgang stopped, although they still begged me to come to them at bedtime. They couldn't understand why their mother refused this small pleasure but I did. She was jealous, resentful of the bond I had formed with the boys, of the relationship they shared with Erich, instead of their own father. The tension was terrible and some days I could barely stand it, retreating to my room in tears. I began to dream of Erich and me in our own home with our child. Although I wasn't sure how we were going to manage it.

Erich spent longer days away from me, searching for somewhere for us to live. Accommodation was hard to find. Everywhere was full in the town, particularly with the streams of refugees from the east that had begun to settle in and around Windsheim. He widened his search to the outlying villages in the hopes of finding something, although it worried me how he was going to manage to get to his job in Windsheim each day without a vehicle. I was afraid of my impending labour too, worried if this baby would survive and how I was going to care for it.

The baby arrived in the height of summer. I had been in labour from the night before and every pain reminded me of my experience a year earlier, causing me to tense with fear.

I longed for my mother's touch, her comforting hands. It was only when the midwife arrived, assuring me that everything seemed fine and was progressing normally, that I was able to relax a little. Under her expert hands and guidance, I was able to face the pains head on, determined to see my healthy, bawling child soon. I did it silently too. I didn't want to give Tante Susie the satisfaction of hearing me scream. I grunted with the effort and my beautiful girl pushed her way into the world.

We named her Greta, meaning pearl. She was a pearl to us, a magnificent jewel that we had made and a joy born of the tumultuous times in which we lived. She was a healthy baby, perhaps a little underweight, but she thrived nonetheless. Erich was a proud father, showing her off, wrapped in her blanket so only her little pink face showed. The boys crowded around, overjoyed to finally see their new baby cousin.

'It's a girl,' said Hansi in wonder.

'She is,' said Erich.

'Now we finally have a girl to play with,' said Wolfgang, gently touching her cheek with his finger. Greta screwed up her face, worked one little fist free, waved it in the air and began to cry. The boys all laughed.

'Maybe she's not too excited about that,' said Peter.

'All right, boys,' Erich said to them. 'It's time for her to go back to her mother for a feed. Off you go.'

A little while later, a knock at the door woke me from my dozing, Greta still asleep in my arms. 'Come in,' I said, making sure I was decent.

I started at Tante Susie, shocked that she would come to me after weeks of stony silence and cool disregard. She came into the room slowly. It felt awkward.

'Are you all right?' she asked hesitantly.

I nodded. 'Yes, I'm fine, thank you.' I tried my best to keep the tightness out of my voice.

'The baby is healthy? A girl, I hear.'

'Yes, she's fine too.' I smiled, looking at Greta in my arms. 'She's fast asleep.'

She came further towards the bed tentatively, gazing at the baby longingly.

'Would you like to hold her?'

'Of course,' she whispered, her gaze softening. She reached out to take the sleeping baby. She drew a finger across the delicate cheek and the wisps of dark hair that protruded from the blanket. 'She's beautiful. Maybe she'll take after my grandmother's side of the family, like me.'

'Maybe,' I said, tears pricking my eyes. She handed Greta back to me.

'You've done well, Lotte,' she said, leaning over me. 'I hope you and Erich are very happy.' She kissed my forehead and smoothed the hair back from my face. She smiled sadly and left the room quietly.

I allowed the tears to spill from my eyes. I was overjoyed that Tante Susie had reached out to me. I knew that she still loved me but I had the very strong sense that nothing was about to change between us. I wished my mother were here. I missed her more than anything.

The next couple of weeks were a blur. Greta took all of my time and energy. Between the painful and frustrating exercise of learning to breast feed, changing nappies, washing nappies, bathing her and putting her down for her sleep, there was little time for anything else. Poor Erich barely got a grunt out of me most days before I would pass out with exhaustion. He seemed happy enough though, cuddling his baby daughter whenever he got the chance, even when I argued with him that it was her bedtime.

Tante Susie hovered in the background. I'm sure she was checking that Greta and I were doing well. The boys were sweet, trying to help with Greta when they could. She was still a novelty to them but I wasn't sure for how much longer, when she continued to wake them through the night with her cries.

Onkel Werner arrived home to this chaos. The boys went crazy, laughing, shrieking with joy and hanging onto him for dear life. They had been through so much and, as I watched them welcome him home, I held Greta a little closer, praying that her life would be blessed. Tante Susie just shook in his arms, tears running down her face unashamedly.

We learnt that the majority of the civilians interned for holding Nazi Party membership and not involved in Nazi activities had been released. Onkel Werner's medical licence was to be returned to him and he was allowed to practice medicine once more. It was time for Erich and I to leave.

18

Erich found us a derelict little farmhouse to rent
in Ickleheim, a tiny village about five kilometres
from Windsheim. Dr Schrieber most apologetically
explained that Erich's job was no longer available; Onkel
Werner had returned to work as his new business partner and
he did not feel it was necessary to employ a driver when he
was able to drive himself. I was sure our strained relationship
with Tante Susie hadn't helped.

I was very angry and hurt at the way we had been treated,
discarded when they had no more need of our help. I was
their niece after all – family – with a brand new baby, and we
had done so much for them. But it was for the best, I decided.
We had to start on our own and it seemed the right time.

Erich restored the farmhouse as best he could, hanging
doors, fixing window latches, repairing the ceiling and roof.
It was basic but it would do. We had running water that
flowed in temperamental fits and starts due to the ancient

pipes and once we got the wood-fired stove back into working order, the kitchen was functional and we could heat water. In a tiny shed outside the house were a sink and toilet, our bathroom and laundry. Besides the kitchen and a tiny lounge/dining area, we had two small rooms.

We wouldn't have managed except for the help of Vati. We had nothing. Baby Greta was swaddled in a couple of Hansi's old shirts and her nappies were only rags. Vati was a godsend, bringing my things from München. I couldn't wait to see him but butterflies fluttered in my belly whenever I thought about how he'd react in person to Erich and our marriage.

'Vati!' I called, running to him as he pulled up next to the house, towing a trailer filled with household goods tied down with rope. In seconds I was in his arms. His smells were the same, tobacco still clinging to his jacket. The surrounding farmyard, the constant mud and the old farmhouse all faded away. I was safe, loved and protected.

'I've been waiting to see you for so long. Letters are not enough. I wanted to see you with my own eyes, make sure you're safe and well,' murmured Vati. 'It's so good to finally be here with you.' He had been ill in the months since he returned home and only recently strong enough to now visit us.

'I've missed you so much,' I whispered, hugging him tightly. He was thin and bony under my embrace. I looked at his face and realised that the last months of the war and his incarceration had taken their toll on him. He looked old now, frail even. His face was lined, his skin wrinkled and sagging. 'How are you, Vati?'

'Well enough,' he said. 'Mutti sent you some things she thought you might need. Something has come up and she

318

couldn't make it.' He looked uncomfortable and wouldn't meet my eye. 'She promises to visit soon.' My shoulders sagged with disappointment. I knew Mutti was still angry with me and wouldn't come but I had hoped she might want to meet her first grandchild. I shouldn't have expected anything else. In her eyes I couldn't have fallen further, dirt poor and living like a peasant in a dilapidated farmer's cottage surrounded by mud.

'I've missed you more than I can say. Don't worry about your mother. It will be all right, I promise you. I'll bring her to visit you very soon, when you've set up your home.' He kissed me on the head like he used to and I felt young and carefree again. 'Now where's that husband of yours? I want to meet my granddaughter.'

Erich met us by the front door, handing me Greta as he greeted Vati. I held my breath and looked on nervously.

'Congratulations, Erich,' said Vati, clapping him heartily on the back. 'You have two beautiful women now. You're a lucky man.'

'I know. Thank you,' said Erich, smiling broadly. 'It's so good of you to come.'

Vati nodded but his attention was drawn to Greta and he looked wistfully at her. 'Can I hold her?'

'Of course,' I said, placing her in his arms.

He held her carefully, like she was a delicate porcelain doll. 'She's just perfect,' he said. 'The most beautiful creature I've ever seen.' He traced the line of her tiny snub nose, across her cheek and her jaw, his hand resting over the shock of dark hair that sat in spikes on her head, despite my attempts to smooth it down. His face glowed with joy and he planted a kiss on her forehead, like a benediction and sign of protection. I knew he was besotted and would do anything for her. My heart burst with gratitude for this man who had become part of my life.

Erich squeezed my hand. 'At least she has one grandparent looking out for her. See, she has him wrapped around her little finger already,' he whispered into my ear.

I smiled in agreement and pulled him close, glad to have him by my side and happy that he and my father were on good terms. It meant a lot to me.

'Come,' said Vati. He handed Greta back to me reluctantly. 'We'd better get this unpacked before it gets too hot.' He was right. The sun was beating down on us already. It was going to be a warm day and we had a lot to do.

When we were done, the empty room filled with furniture and boxes, Vati pulled me aside.

'*Liebling*,' he said tenderly, 'I'm very proud of you. Your daughter is magnificent and you have a devoted husband and father in Erich. You've done well, my girl.'

I looked into his eyes. He seemed sincere. 'You're not upset with me?'

'Whatever for?'

'For marrying Erich instead of Heinrich.'

'Never,' he said, shaking his head for emphasis. 'I've always said Erich's a good man. I knew he'd look after you. Life doesn't always go the way we plan but I think he's good for you, and you both look happy.' He frowned for a moment. 'Are you happy?'

'Yes,' I said.

'Well then, the rest will work itself out.' He kissed me on the forehead, as he had done to Greta. 'Keep well and my granddaughter too. I'll be back before long with your mother.

Otherwise Greta will grow too fast.' He smiled broadly and jumped into the car, waving out the window until he drove out of sight.

There was no work anywhere. Erich hoped he might find a job with the Americans at the Illesheim airfield but there was nothing. However, his enquires gave him an idea.

'I know how we can make money until a vacancy becomes available with the Americans,' he told me, hardly able to sit still on the bed next to me while I fed Greta. 'They've told me that with my skills and qualifications, there will be work, just not at the moment.'

'That's a start,' I said. I was worried sick about how we would live, especially with me at home looking after a baby. 'What's your idea?'

'I could use my electrical and mechanical skills to repair motor vehicles,' he said triumphantly.

I stared at Erich, feeling my stomach turn. 'But nobody has the money or fuel to run their cars, let alone fix them.' I didn't want to burst his bubble but it was the truth.

'I know.' Erich leant in, rubbing Greta's foot as her little mouth worked away greedily. 'But what about the Americans with their private vehicles, and those with families living outside the airfield? They all have money. They need their vehicles to get around and can't use air force equipment for private use.'

He looked at me with such enthusiasm and excitement, I couldn't say no. It was a good idea but I wasn't sure he would get enough work to support us.

Erich set up his business in Ickleheim but the work was slow to come in. He took to walking Greta in her pram along the country lanes, often returning home with vegetables, apples, eggs or whatever else he could find, hidden under her blankets. At first I was mortified that he would do something like that. It was stealing. But slowly I realised that it was the only way.

'What do you think I did today?' I asked Erich one evening as we had supper.

'I don't know,' he said, breaking a piece of bread into small chunks.

'You'll never guess,' I said, grinning. I hadn't touched my food yet, too excited to tell him my tale.

Erich looked up from his food.

'I was coming home from a walk with Greta and I couldn't believe when I saw one of our neighbour's geese wandering about, away from the protection of the farmyard.' I raised my eyebrows, daring Erich to guess.

Erich's jaw dropped. 'No! You didn't.'

'I did,' I said proudly. 'I've become quite the opportunist, you know.'

'How did you do it?'

'Well, I made sure nobody was looking and moved Greta's pram as carefully as I could, to screen the goose from view. I didn't want to scare it away. I darted forward and caught it. It was thrashing about madly but I managed to hide it under my coat. Holding it as tightly as I could, I calmly pushed the pram away and walked home as quickly as I dared. Thank God in Heaven, Greta didn't start screaming.' I grinned again, very pleased with myself.

Erich started laughing and I threw a corner of bread at him.

'See what you've turned me into!'

'Where is it now?' asked Erich between snorts of laughter. 'Not running around our house somewhere I hope.'

'No, of course not. I killed it myself, plucked it, cleaned it and it's hanging in our pantry, ready for me to cook. I'll do it in the middle of the night so nobody smells it. We'll have meat for the week and those feathers will be useful in our pillows.'

Erich looked stunned for a second. He reached across, grasped my face in his hands and kissed me. 'I can taste that goose already. What a woman you are!'

It was how we survived in those early days, until word of mouth spread and work increased, along with repeat customers. Sometimes we were paid in goods that were otherwise difficult to find, even on the black market. Erich's easygoing nature but attention to detail made him popular and the Americans warmed to him. Very soon, I was regretting my doubt in his venture, marvelling at his foresight. The connections alone were valuable, I was sure they would help him in acquiring a more secure and lucrative job with the Americans.

The weeks and months flew by, hardly registering with me between looking after Greta, the house and sourcing food, which was even scarcer with the extremely poor autumn harvest. After the war, there was nothing to plant, there were virtually no farmers and the fields were often scarred, destroyed by the last months of war. At night, Erich and I sat by the tiny radio that Vati had given us. The Nürnberg trials were finally over and as the judgements were announced, fierce discussion continued about the war crimes committed by top members of the Nazi Party. It was the first time we learnt unequivocally about the horrendous sins ordered and perpetrated by men we had believed in, men we had taken orders from, men who had ruled our country – men implicated all the way to the top, to the Führer himself. It was the first time we learnt the extent of the Holocaust and the mind-numbing details of the heinous acts ordered and performed by these men.

'They're monsters,' I said, horrified. 'They deserve everything they get.' The images that the American soldier had conjured up with his stories of Dachau had never left me.

Erich nodded, a fierce expression in his eyes. 'There's finally some justice for what they've done.' He hesitated.

'What is it?'

'You do know that Hitler's to blame too, Lotte? Just because he's dead, doesn't mean he didn't orchestrate all this.' Erich knew my struggle in accepting what our Führer had really been but after listening to the broadcast, he was angry, furious.

'I can't imagine that he would have sanctioned such unspeakable acts,' I whispered, remembering my youth and what great pride and hope we'd had in the Führer, in Germany.

Erich slammed his hand on the arm of his chair, making me jump. 'Wake up, Lotte! You were brainwashed as children, at school and in the BDM. I understand that, but you've seen and heard enough to know differently now. You can't pretend to know otherwise. For all those people who died because of him, you have to own up to the truth. You're not a child any more.'

I stared at him in shock. He wasn't trying to hurt me, I knew – he loved me. He was right. I couldn't pretend any more. Too much had happened. 'I know . . . I know you're right but everything we believed in . . . it was all a lie.' Tears welled in my eyes. 'How can I come to terms with believing in a man who was responsible for such horrors, who betrayed Germany and its people? We loved him, cheered for him, while all of this was happening. So many, including my brothers, died for him.' I viciously dashed away the tears rolling down my cheeks with the back of my hands. 'How can I do that, Erich?' I looked up at him desperately. There was sympathy and understanding in his eyes. 'What was everything that we've sacrificed and lost for? How can we as Germans ever hold our heads up again?'

Erich reached across the little table. I placed my hand in his and he squeezed. His touch was warm and reassuring. 'I know. I feel the same way. We were all deceived, all betrayed.' He had served his country with such pride but these terrible acts had been done in the name of Germany. I knew this association left him feeling ashamed too. The more details that had been released about activities during the war, the more he wondered what he had really been fighting for.

I bent to kiss his hand in acknowledgement of his pain.

He smiled sadly. 'I don't know how we deal with that but I suppose the first step is to accept the truth.'

I nodded, thinking of Frau Andree. What had she really thought of people like me? I blushed with shame and embarrassment. I hadn't known any better. I prayed that she had survived, wherever she was. Maybe one day I would find her again . . . but what could I say to her?

The early months of 1947 flew past. Greta filled my days and nights, delighting Erich and myself with her antics. She was beginning to eat solid foods and was teething, often sucking and biting the locket I still wore. My parents' tiny photo remained inside but I had replaced Heinrich's photo with an old picture of Erich. I wished I had a photo of Greta to put inside, unable to have my film developed yet, but her memory was imprinted on the locket anyway – these days it was often covered in baby saliva, little tooth marks pitting its surface. It was dearer to me than ever.

I photographed those early baby days with care, choosing between those little moments that presented themselves – the delight when she could sit on her own; milk all over her mouth when she was first learning to drink from a cup; the triumph on her face when she realised she could get herself around by crawling. Film was near impossible to get and I wanted Vati's film to last as long as possible. Thanks to him, I could capture those precious times and keep the dream alive that maybe one day I could practice my craft professionally.

Finally, I was able to wean her and was grateful to have my body back to myself. Erich was pleased too when Greta began to sleep through the nights and I could devote some of my energies to him once again. I had forgotten what slow, deliberate lovemaking could be like and I delighted in Erich's attentions, feeling like a desirable woman in his arms, not just a mother, a milking cow.

By May, I was pregnant again. Of course, I was thrilled, but how we would manage to feed another child worried me a little. Erich had no such concerns.

'We'll be fine,' he said pulling me close and kissing me tenderly. 'Don't worry about anything except looking after yourself and this little one.' He placed his hand gently over my belly. 'You'll see. Things will look up soon.'

I nodded, amazed at his optimism in even the most difficult situations.

Then he landed a job as an assistant superintendent of the Industrial Police, aiding in the security and safety of the industrial sites at the American Ordinance Depot in Illesheim. The American air force had left Illesheim and the US army had taken over. All POW labour had ceased early in the year when most of the prisoners of war were released across Germany. Now Germans were actively sought for employment.

My parents came to visit. Mutti had visited a few times with my father already, including for Greta's first birthday in July. I had been terribly nervous, worried about what she would say about our living conditions and marriage. I was terribly surprised to discover that she adored Greta and I think she was too. Whenever she visited, she doted on her, rocking her to sleep, playing with her in her crib, taking her for walks in her pram with Vati. Although she continued to look at Erich with disapproval, we were talking again, almost back to normal.

Mutti arrived waving an envelope excitedly in my face. 'Look what we received,' she said gleefully.

'What is it?' I asked, too tired to play her games. Greta had been unsettled all night and I had little energy with this pregnancy.

'It's a letter of course.' Mutti frowned, unhappy that I didn't share her excitement. 'Don't you want to know who it's from?'

'Who's it from?' I asked, thumping the teapot onto the table harder than I needed to.

'Heinrich.'

The smug look on her face made my blood boil and I had to work hard to control the shaking of my hands as I poured the tea.

'He's finally left the camp in Denmark and he's back in Germany.'

I sat heavily on my chair. I had been dreading this for years. 'Is he all right? Is he home?'

'He's in good health, he says, and in Hamburg.' Mutti took a delicate sip from her cup. 'He comes home in a few days and he's looking forward to seeing you.'

All the old emotions surfaced once more, the guilt, shame, sadness at what might have been and the loss of my best friend. A wave of regret washed over me.

'I'm glad he's safe and well,' I said softly, not looking at my mother. 'He doesn't know, then?'

'He will when he gets home. His mother's furious with you still. She'll have him married off to the first eligible girl she can find if you don't claim him first.' Mutti put down her cup. 'He loves you and I think he will take on Greta as his own if you go to him. As for this other child, you could almost pass it off as his if you move quickly.'

I stood, shaking with rage. 'I've told you already, I won't leave Erich. He's the father of my children and we are a family. You don't have to like it but it's not about to change.'

'You'll break his heart. He doesn't deserve that.'

'I know,' I said, stricken by the pain I would cause him when he found out. All the anger flowed out of me and I stared at her, deflated. 'It's too late to change what's happened. I'll have to live with that.'

Mutti put down her tea. 'Fine. I'll leave the letter here for you to read. I think you should at least write to him before his mother poisons his mind against you. He was your friend, after all. I'll give him the letter when we get home.' She patted my hand as she stood. 'I'll go and find your father and see how he's doing with Greta.' She left the room with me standing there staring at the envelope she had placed on the table.

I had to read that letter. I couldn't help myself. I noticed it had been addressed to me and my hackles rose once again at the fact that my mother had opened and read the letter when she knew she was coming to see me.

Liebe Lotte,

I am finally free. I've been in Denmark since the last weeks of the war. I was able to escape from East Prussia and the Red Army along with a number of units. I ended up in one of the large refugee camps, one of very few doctors assigned to look after the refugees. That's where I stayed after the war ended, but as a prisoner of war, battling the rampant sickness and disease, made more acute by starvation and malnutrition. In some ways this was worse than what I had seen on the front line. Many of the deaths I witnessed were preventable.

Many were innocent children. Many who made it through the horrors of the war perished here. My blackest days were made bearable by thoughts of you and the conversations we might have.

Enough of the war and sadness. I am alive, safe and well enough. I am back in Germany now, in Hamburg. In a week or so, I'll be able to begin my journey home, back to München and back to you. I hope these last years have kept you and your family safe and well. I know in my heart that you are. I can't tell you how much I'm looking forward to seeing you again, to look on you with my own eyes, longing to kissing your soft lips, to touch you and hold you so I'll never let go.

Tell your mother to prepare our wedding.

Yours forever,

Heinrich.

I was a mess. This was my old life calling to me. A life of privilege and luxury, where my children and I would want for nothing. A life that could never be. The war had changed me and I was not the girl Heinrich had left in 1944. I could never go back. My greatest regret was how much I would hurt him. I wanted nothing more than to see him again, share stories of our years apart, but I knew he would never speak to me after what I had done. One of my oldest and dearest friends ripped away from me, as surely as if he were dead.

I ran from the cottage out into the meadow. I had to get away from the spectre of what I knew I had to do. I had to mourn my loss before I would be able to tell him goodbye. It was late summer and the last of the wildflowers, red, blue, yellow and white blazoned bright among the long, dry grass, reminding me that even when all seemed doomed and lost, hope was eternal. I had my memories of my time with Heinrich, of what we had shared. I had to remember them with fondness but my life with Erich and Greta was real and full of colour, like the flowers. Together we would tackle the difficulties we faced. I had immeasurable joy ahead of me, I reminded myself, my hand over the slope of my belly. This was my life now.

I turned back to the cottage, calm enough to write the letter Heinrich deserved to receive.

It became my habit to check the mail but when Heinrich's letter arrived several months later, I stood there, not believing it was possible. My legs were so weak I could barely walk back into the house. The letter sat on the dining table, making my head pound whenever I glanced at it. I couldn't concentrate on anything else and yet I waited until Greta was down for her afternoon sleep before I opened it. My hands shook so badly it took me some minutes to get the sheets of paper free from the envelope. A wave of nausea threatened to send me running outside, which was something I hadn't done since the early months of my pregnancy. Steeling myself, I took some deep breaths to calm my wildly beating heart.

Lotte,

I know you have been waiting for me to respond to your letter but I couldn't bring myself to do so until now. I was shocked by your news, angry and distraught. I didn't want to write to you in anger, with words I could never take back. My mother refuses to allow your name to be spoken in her presence and would not speak to me about what happened to you. Your mother has been good to me, confirming that you were forced into marriage with Erich, a result of the unusual and difficult circumstances you found yourself in.

The fact remains that while I thought of you every day, you were with this man, making babies with him, a family that should have been mine. I waited for you, to have you on our wedding night as you wanted, yet you wasted no time consummating your union with him, giving him a child.

All the same, I understand that you did what you had to. You had no assurance that I would return to you, that I was even alive. But here I am. I still love you. I don't want anyone else, just you. Your mother tells me to be patient if I truly feel this way about you. I would marry you tomorrow, if you would have me. The war is over now. Things we all did to survive that time are behind us. Leave Erich and come home. Live the life you were meant to lead, with me. I will cherish your children as my own. We can be a family together.

Only say that you will think about it.

You're in my heart always,

Heinrich.

I sat there staring at the familiar handwriting with conflicting emotions. He had forgiven me. How could he still love me after what I had done to him? I had been sure that he would hate me and had been prepared for that, muscles tensed, expecting an outpouring of vitriol. Instead, I was confronted with his declaration of love, horrified at his request, horrified that he had given me a choice and horrified that I was tempted. Here was the Heinrich I had craved during the war, a man willing to fight for me. Yet I would be the one to sacrifice my hard-won happiness, no matter my circumstances.

I couldn't help but imagine the large house with enough space to move, sparkling clean, with good quality furnishings, art and objects of beauty scattered tastefully around the rooms. I sighed wistfully at the thought of full indoor plumbing, hot, running water and electricity. The thought of fashionable clothes that actually fit, shoes – oh, the shoes – a nursemaid to help with the children, fine food and wide sweeping gardens with no mud and no stench of animal manure was enough to make my hand twitch with the desire to pick up a pen and reply before I could talk myself out of my fantasy.

True, Greta would have everything she desired, except her real father – a man who adored her, who adored me and who valued his family above everything else in the world. I didn't know if I could say that about Heinrich – words were one thing, actions were another – and I couldn't do that to Greta. I knew how important it was to be cherished and loved by both parents, to feel wanted, safe and secure in a family home. It was everything I didn't have growing up. Erich had taught me about love and family and it was his bed that I went to willingly every night.

Despite my longing for my old life and the dream of giving my children the very best, I couldn't do it. I regretted hurting him more than anything, but Heinrich would have to let me go.

*

It was a cold February day when I went into labour. I was home alone with Greta. I would never forget losing my first child and although Greta had been born with no trouble, I was on my own this time and I was desperately afraid of something going wrong. There was no midwife in Ickleheim and I doubted the midwife in Windsheim could arrive in time, even if I'd been able to call her.

I couldn't show my fear to Greta, who was tottering around now, chattering away in a language only she understood.

'The new baby is coming today,' I said to her. 'Come and help Mutti make the crib and get ready.'

She understood enough to help me for a while, preparing the crib with a blanket that she knew was for the new baby and making the bed with old towels and sheets. It was a novelty to her, something different to our usual routine. All the while I worried about how long I could last like this, hiding my discomfort and anxiety from her, bracing myself on the edge of the bed as ever-increasing waves of pain gripped me.

I sliced some bread and made sandwiches for us while I still could. Pouring Greta a cup of milk, I noticed a thin layer of ice had formed over the milk jug and a stab of concern jolted through me. The temperature was dropping quickly and it was only lunchtime. The wood fire keeping us warm through the night and fuelling our stove for a warm breakfast had long burnt out. I couldn't start another one yet, there wouldn't be enough wood to keep us warm through what would be a freezing night. With a new baby coming, we needed that warmth for when he or she arrived. I handed Greta her milk, thinking about my options.

'Let's get some wood for the stove,' I said to Greta. 'We'll surprise Vati and have it ready for him when he gets home.'

Stumbling out to the wood stack, icy wind blowing straight through us, I gazed at the lowering pewter sky and frowned. There was more snow on the way but how long until it would arrive I didn't know. At least it would be a little warmer then. I handed Greta a few sticks of kindling and collected an armful of smaller pieces of wood that I could manage to carry.

'Brrr, it's cold out here. Quickly, inside now,' I said, ushering her through the door as quickly as possible. I felt another pain coming on. I only hoped that Erich would be home before it got too cold. If not, I could start the fire, but I wasn't sure I could keep an eye on it long enough to last through to the evening.

My waters broke and my body moved into a new gear. Things moved along a lot quicker than they had with Greta. Breath ragged in my ears and heart pounding, I knew this baby was coming and soon. I dressed Greta in layers of warm clothes while I still had the presence of mind to do so, and put her down for a sleep in the playpen in the corner of the bedroom where I could still keep an eye on her. No matter what happened now, at least she was safe there. I guessed that she would cry when I limited her freedom, and she did. I sighed. I really needed to focus on the job ahead of me but I couldn't have expected anything else. I prepared string, scissors, spare towels and a bowl of water by the bed. After a while, I couldn't concentrate on anything else but the pains and I left Greta to cry herself to sleep in the corner, trying to muffle my groans as the pains came hard and fast.

I climbed up on the bed, thinking that this was happening too fast. 'Please let it be all right,' I whispered into the empty air. I couldn't entertain the thought that something was wrong. The pains were terrible, worse than they ever had been with Greta and my brow was beaded with sweat, despite the breaths I forced from my lungs forming clouds of mist in the frigid room. There was no respite and just when I wondered if I was going to die, I felt the urge to push. I reached down and felt the soft down on the baby's head before it retracted once again. I was nearly there. I steeled myself. I could do this. It only took a few pushes, barely time to think what I needed to do, before the baby arrived, solid, whole, wet and warm between my legs.

I didn't allow myself to slump in relief, the danger wasn't over yet. The baby took a big breath and began to cry, its little pink face turning red with rage. I couldn't help but smile. I'd be angry too, going from a warm, safe cocoon, into the freezing world. She was a girl, I realised, with ten fingers and toes, pink skinned under the waxy white substance that coated her skin, and perfectly formed. She was beautiful. Tying off the cord that bound us together, I waited a moment, staring at this miracle before me, flexing and stretching her little arms and legs in the air, before severing the link between us.

I wiped her dry and placed her to my breast, keeping us both warm, as she rooted around and finally began to suck. We waited, bound together in that precious moment of finally meeting, until it was time to deliver the afterbirth, and then I placed her into the crib.

Looking out the window to the gloom, I realised it was snowing. It was quiet now. Greta was finally in an exhausted sleep, her dark head resting on a teddy bear, oblivious to the new arrival. The baby, still bloodied, wrapped in a towel and blanket was in the crib. I had done it. I smiled with joy and contentment at the peaceful serenity of having both my children with me, children I had made and birthed. I felt strong and powerful.

It was then that Erich arrived home, tiptoeing through the house in case Greta was still asleep. He found us in the bedroom, a picture of domestic bliss, and he paled visibly when he realised what had happened.

'Shh,' I whispered, pointing to Greta in the corner.

Erich hurried across the room. 'Are you okay?' His brow was creased in concern and his eyes were wide with fear. 'The baby?'

'We're both fine,' I assured him. 'Here, meet your new daughter. I haven't cleaned her up yet. She was only born about half an hour ago.'

He scooped the baby up and gazed at her as if he was imprinting her face on his brain. 'She's beautiful,' he said, his eyes glistening. 'I'm so sorry I wasn't here for you.'

I shrugged. 'That's babies for you. They'll come when they want.' Erich stooped, the baby still in his arms, and kissed me long and deep.

'Congratulations, my *liebling*, my brave, strong, capable, wonderful wife. I'm the luckiest man alive. You did this all on your own and you're still smiling.'

'Look at our beautiful family,' I said, a wave of exhaustion washing over me. I shivered.

'It's cold,' said Erich, handing me the baby. 'Get some rest while you can. I'll start the fire and get you some hot water to clean up with.'

'The stove is ready for you to light. I prepared it in case it got too cold but I never got the chance to light it.'

He kissed me again. 'I love you more with each passing day, you know.'

'I love you too,' I said, wanting to hold on to this moment forever.

We called her Johanna, after my father. He was so pleased when we told him. Tears filled his eyes as he held his newest granddaughter, cradling her head with care. Greta didn't like this attention going to her new sister. She jumped up and down, her dark curls bouncing around her head, and pulled the new ribbon out of her hair in frustration. When that didn't work, she grabbed at Vati's trouser leg. Finally Mutti picked her up, whispering bribes of sugary delights to her.

I wrote to Tante Susie with the news of Johanna's birth but did not receive a reply. She and Onkel Werner had refused to make contact with us since we left, although I had tried. I wondered what had happened to make her so bitter. Mutti had no idea either. Tante Susie had also cut her off. It made me very sad. The war had taken so much away that I felt we should treasure the family we had. Tante Susie had been good to me and I missed her boys.

Towards the end of summer, just as I was beginning to surface from the haze of exhaustion, there was a knock at the door.

Erich answered, and when I joined him, I found a very attractive woman in her thirties standing on the porch, deep golden hair peeking out from under her headscarf. Erich stood limp with shock. He looked like he'd seen a ghost.

The woman was white faced and distraught, dark eyes flashing. She pointed an accusing finger at me. 'Is this the whore you married?' she screamed.

I jerked back as if I'd been slapped.

'Who is this?' I whispered to Erich, clutching at his arm. Fear churned my gut and raced through my body like wildfire, standing my hairs on end. Something was terribly wrong.

'This is Inga, my wife.'

'But she's dead.'

'I most certainly am not,' spat the woman. 'And neither are you,' she said, turning her wrath on Erich. 'Alive and well, I see. The rumours were true. I had to see for myself.'

'How can it be?' Erich, still clutching the door, had found his voice. 'I was told that you were dead.' His voice was rough as if he hadn't used it in a long time. 'The children?' I saw the desperation on his face. All I wanted to do was gather him up in my arms, protect him from this onslaught but I didn't dare get involved, not yet.

'They're alive,' she said flatly. 'No thanks to you.'

Erich stiffened. 'Are they here?'

Inga shook her head. 'I came on my own.'

'You'd better come inside. There's a lot to discuss.' I had to take control, determined to keep a cool, calm exterior for Erich's sake.

Inga hesitated, then nodded and walked inside, head held high, pausing to take in her surroundings, assessing how we were living and what we had. Erich followed her in a daze. I could hear Greta crying in her bedroom.

'Please sit down,' I said, gesturing to the tiny dining table. 'I'll make some tea.' I turned my attention to my shell-shocked husband. 'Erich, can you get Greta and put her in the playpen? I don't think she'll go back to sleep now.'

I went to the kitchen to prepare the tea but I couldn't help but glimpse back at Inga every so often, to make sure I wasn't dreaming, to embed on my startled mind that this was real. I watched her remove her scarf, revealing hair swept back in a fashionable up do. She was thin, as most of us still were, and hardship had taken its toll in the lines of worry etched into her pale face.

Inga's eyes narrowed as Erich brought Greta to the playpen, watching him enviously, greedily as he bounced our daughter in his arms, soothing her until he could put her down. He kept his back to Inga and didn't return to the table until I arrived with the tea, taking longer than he needed to pacify Greta. He sat and stared at Inga while I poured. The tension rose in the room as they each took the measure of the other, neither speaking a word until I sat next to him, steaming cups on saucers in front of each of us, a plate of plain biscuits in the middle of the table.

'Where have you been?' said Erich finally, his voice wobbling dangerously. 'I looked everywhere for you. Dear God, I searched a bombed bunker in Berlin full of dead people looking for you. Nobody had seen you in Sagan or Elend.'

'What are you talking about? I sent you postcards and telegrams telling you when and where we were going. Don't tell me you didn't receive them.'

'I received a postcard telling me you were going to Berlin and then on to Elend if Berlin wasn't safe.' He slammed his hands on the table in anger and frustration.

Inga didn't flinch, only stared at him belligerently.

'Then I received a phone call from the police in Berlin telling me they had found an envelope with my details on it in the public bunker at the Berlin train station. I went to find you and the children, to identify your bodies during the salvage operation, and I saw things that will never leave me. I expected to find your mutilated bodies, but I didn't. I thought you were all dead and I wished I was dead myself.'

I remembered too well how he had felt and slipped my hand under the table to squeeze his knee in silent support.

'I couldn't believe when I received a telegram a few weeks later telling me that you had left Berlin and were in Elend,' he continued. 'I was overjoyed and arranged for leave to come to you and bring you back to München with me. Then we discovered that the telegram had been originally sent from Berlin, not Elend, a month before. You must have left then.'

'No,' said Inga, leaning forward in her seat. 'Don't be ridiculous. You're just making this all up. I sent you that postcard towards the end of January. I never went to Berlin. We didn't leave until the second week of February because we waited until Gottlieb could take us all the way to Elend. He drove us there and we arrived in Elend three days after we left Sagan. I sent you the telegram then with our address. It was mid-February. I never heard anything from you.'

Greta began to cry again, upset by the loud, angry voices. I stood quietly and went to her wondering how this was going to end.

'I sent you and the children letters as soon as I received your telegram,' Erich countered, face flushed with anger. 'I never heard back from any of you. When I discovered the date, I thought maybe you didn't arrive in Elend at all.

341

I pulled all the strings I could to find you. I used military channels, investigators, the police and anyone who knew you but nobody had seen you anywhere.' I watched him count on his fingers to demonstrate the ways he had tried to find her. 'The military and police investigators we used both came to the same conclusion. They told me that you had perished while on the run from the Red Army – where, they couldn't say, maybe in the air-raid strike in Berlin, maybe somewhere between Sagan, Berlin and Elend. I did everything I could to find out what had happened to you.'

'You liar,' spat Inga. 'We were in Elend all along. Nobody came looking for us.' She glared at Erich with such venom and hatred, I was suddenly afraid for him. I put Greta back in the playpen and returned to his side.

Erich stood abruptly and leant across the table towards Inga, his face contorted in fury. 'How dare you call me a liar!' he roared.

Inga recoiled but stared at him with loathing.

'You have no idea what I went through to find you. If you'd left when I asked you to, none of this would have happened.'

The threat of violence loomed ominously over us, shimmering like the oppressive heat of the summer sun. I had never seen him so angry.

Greta was crying again, tears running down her little cheeks. My heart ached for her and I desperately wanted to pick her up but I didn't dare move. She would have to stay there a little longer.

'It's all about you, isn't it?' shouted Inga.

My heart leapt into my mouth, afraid that this could escalate to something physical. I had to do something, before one of them reached for the other. I laid my hand on Erich's arm but he didn't seem to notice. He was shaking.

'Erich, you're scaring Greta.' I pulled on his arm, trying to get him to sit down. That got through. He looked at me with the effort of keeping his temper under control and sat slowly.

He shook his head. 'Why Elend? Why not Berlin like we agreed?'

'Berlin wasn't safe with the air-raids and the Red Army advancing. If you care to remember, Gottlieb's family is from Elend, so we went there and waited for you. You never came. We couldn't find you after the war and we assumed you were dead.'

Erich looked startled, like he'd been punched in the stomach. I felt similarly stunned. We had never imagined that the tables could be reversed and Inga and his children had thought him dead. The wind went out of him, understanding how that knowledge might have cost his family, especially his two children.

Inga looked smug. 'It's not all about you,' she reminded him.

'Where are the children now? Where are you living?'

Inga picked up her cup of tea and sipped, as if she had all the time in the world and this was just a friendly chat. 'Still in Elend. Gottlieb's mother is looking after them.'

'You're in the Russian Zone,' I said, incredulous, unable to hold my tongue. 'How did you get out?'

Inga shrugged, her icy glare barely thrown in my direction. 'It's not too hard, especially when I had a very good reason to try.' She turned her attention back to Erich. 'I met someone who said you were still alive, living in Bad Windsheim.

I had to come and see for myself. It was worth the risk. When I arrived in Windsheim, I was told that you were living in Ickleheim with your wife.' She put down the teacup onto the saucer with a loud crash. 'I couldn't believe it was true, that you would abandon us. I had to know for sure.' She had tears in her eyes but they were tears of fury as well as pain.

Dread snaked its cold fingers over me and my skin rippled with goose bumps.

'I thought you and the children were dead,' said Erich, his voice catching. He was as fragile as glass and about to shatter.

'How long have you been married?' Inga's eyes glittered accusingly as she leant forward in her chair, watching us both.

I reached for Erich's hand, cold and stiff on the table. Together we were stronger.

'How long did you wait to start again?' She glanced at Greta, who was still crying, standing at the corner of her playpen looking out, her little face crumpled in distress. 'Not long from the looks of it. Have you once thought about your other children and what they're missing out on?'

The back of my neck prickled in warning. I had to trust my instincts. Deadly calm was deadly dangerous, like a snake ready to strike.

'I didn't know. I tried everything.'

Inga stood. Her face was impassive, deathly calm. 'You would have been better off dead. I've seen what I needed to see.'

Ice formed in my veins. I felt the crystals build up within me, numbing my body.

'When can I see the children?' Erich reached across the table in desperation and grasped her arm. 'We have to get you here to the American zone.'

Inga jerked away. 'Don't you touch me. So you think you can have it all, do you?' Her dark eyes flashed with anger. 'We'll see about that. But don't worry. You haven't heard the last of me.' She glanced at Greta one last time, whirled around and stormed through the room. Inga was seeking revenge, retribution for Erich leaving her and the children. The ice formed a solid lump in my chest.

'Please, Inga!' Erich dashed after her but before we knew it, she was out the front door, slamming it behind her.

Greta was screaming now and I hurried across to pick her up, holding her close, my emotions in total turmoil, in total shock. I didn't know what to think, I didn't know how to feel.

Erich's first wife and children had risen from the dead.

19

The meadow behind the cottage was the only place I felt I could breathe. I screamed across the fields in frustration until my throat was hoarse, pulling my hair. I had to let it out before I went back or I'd go crazy. I stared at the cottage. It looked peaceful, the scene of domestic bliss. I had left Erich inside the front door, his eyes hollow and blank with shock, after thrusting Greta unceremoniously into his arms. She was the only one who could bring him from his daze.

But now it was time to face reality and work out what we had to do. It didn't bear thinking about, in fact I couldn't for more than a second before fear flooded my chest and I found it difficult to breathe again. But this wasn't something we could sit on until a solution came to us. I had seen the way Inga looked at us before she left. There was more coming, and we had to be ready. I wiped the wetness from my cheeks, surprised to find I had been crying. I had to go back.

When I returned, peace had been restored. Greta was back in her playpen, absorbed in the chocolate Erich had given her, a piece of a Hershey bar one of the Americans had given him that he had put away for a rainy day. This was such a day I supposed. Somehow, Johanna was still sleeping.

Erich sat at the table, staring into space, his shoulders hunched in despair. I kissed his head and wrapped my arms around him.

'I'm sorry,' I whispered. 'I couldn't breathe. If I didn't go I was going to scream in front of the children.'

He patted my hand. 'I know. It was a shock but you're here now.'

I dropped into the chair next to him. 'What are we going to do?'

He shut his eyes and shook his head slowly. 'I don't understand how this happened. I did everything to find them.'

I kissed him lightly and held his hand. 'You did everything you could but remember how chaotic it was. Anything is possible.' I felt calm and logical now. One of us had to be.

'The envelope in Berlin? The telegram from Elend? None of it makes sense.'

'I think you're probably right when you thought that Inga's cousin had the envelope, maybe in a coat pocket. She must have died in that bombing. I agree that the telegram makes no sense. We know that the date was wrong. Who knows what happened to that telegram, whether it was sent to Berlin first by mistake?' I paused a moment, thinking through the conversation. 'Who's Gottlieb?'

'He's an old acquaintance of mine, a friend I used to work with in Sagan. He was the one I asked to help Inga and the children get away.'

I nodded and squeezed his hand. 'How wonderful to know that your children are alive.'

The smile on his face lit up the room. Then he crumpled to the floor, taking me with him as I tried to catch him. The wind was knocked out of me as I hit the floor, landing on top of him. As I pulled myself free from the tangle of arms and legs, Erich began to sob uncontrollably. I could do nothing for him but hold him. The pain he had carried deep within every day since learning about his family's demise erupted. I couldn't imagine what he was going through. We were both shocked, neither of us able to comprehend the enormity of what we had discovered, but I knew that only together would we get through this. I cried with him, tears of sadness, joy and despair. It was a bittersweet moment.

The demands of two tiny children soon overshadowed anything else. Numb as we both felt, soon I was changing Johanna's clothes, soiled by a leaking nappy, while Erich prepared the girls' bath. Greta was screaming in the playpen, trying to climb out.

A knock at the door took us by surprise.

'I'll get it,' said Erich, sighing. 'It's probably Inga again.'

'Herr Drescher? Erich Drescher?' asked a voice I didn't recognise. I had a bad feeling and scooped Johanna up, wrapping her in a towel and rushing from the bedroom.

'Yes,' said Erich obviously puzzled.

'You're under arrest. You have to come with us.'

Two police officers stood outside. It was déjà vu. I stopped in the middle of the room, Johanna squirming in my arms as I held her tightly, watching the scene unfold at the door.

'Whatever for?' he asked, an impatient edge to his voice.

'You've been accused of bigamy.' My heart sank and I wanted to be sick. Johanna began to wail in counterpoint to her sister's screaming. This couldn't be happening. Inga was getting her revenge.

'No! He's done nothing wrong,' I heard myself shout. 'It's all a mistake.'

The officer nodded sympathetically, seeing the baby in my arms. 'That might be so but Herr Drescher has to come with us until it gets sorted out.'

'But you can't take him,' I yelled hysterically, breaking into a sweat, the panic inside me rising.

'Lotte! There's no choice. We have to see this through now. Be strong. It will all be over before you know it.'

I threw myself into his arms, weeping, shaking with fear. 'It's not fair. You haven't done anything wrong.'

'I know, my *liebchen*.' He held me tight and I clung to him as if that would keep him from leaving.

'What will happen to you?'

'I'll be okay. It will be fine,' he whispered soothingly. He kissed me, a lingering, tender kiss, and then kissed Johanna, her face red with fury. 'I won't be long.'

One of the police officers pulled me off Erich while the other grasped his arm. I watched helplessly, sobbing, the soft weight of Johanna in my arms keeping me sane, while they marched him to the street and into the police car.

Erich spent the next few days in prison in Windsheim until he was formally charged. Released on bail, as a low flight risk with a young family and working for the Americans in Illesheim, he was allowed to return home until the court date, which had not yet been set.

Of course, we had no money to spare and it was with great trepidation that I telephoned my parents from the police station, to ask for their help. I had not wanted to tell them about our plight but I had to be a pragmatist and do anything to help my family get through this. I needed Erich home, to keep working so we could survive. Mutti would laugh at the irony of it all and at the first opportunity that she had, I knew she would harass me about my marriage yet again. The thought of it made me tired.

Thank God in Heaven, my father arrived to help.

'Thank you for coming, Vati,' I murmured, kissing his cheek and trembling with relief.

'It's all right now. We'll fix this. Don't worry.' Hugging him close was enough to make me feel that everything would be okay but his words also assured me that we could do this, we could fight this charge.

Erich and I were both so grateful.

We discussed the situation at length. Vati had trained in the law and believed that Erich's case had merit and was worth fighting. Of course, I could have told him that without a law degree. The penalty for a criminal conviction of bigamy was anything from eighteen months to five years in prison. We knew the court hearing would be in Nürnberg at the County Court and Vati suggested a solicitor who might take on Erich's case. I was never more thankful to have my father's support than at that moment.

I wasn't too surprised to hear from Heinrich shortly after. Despite my written assurances to him that there was no chance of us ever being together, Mutti had let me know that Heinrich would not let go of the faint hope he still held. His

letter expressed regret at my difficult situation and reminded
me that he was waiting for me and that it wasn't too late
to come to him, especially in light of this newest develop-
ment. I was furious that Mutti had said anything to him.
It wasn't her place to get involved. Heinrich had to understand that his was a fruitless hope.

The bigamy case loomed. Erich was back and forth to
Nürnberg to see his solicitor and sometimes I was required
to join him. The time had come to accept the reality of a
court hearing.

'There's a possibility of a prison sentence,' our solicitor
told us gently.

'How can that be?'

'We have to accept what might be,' said Erich, squeezing
my hand. 'We have to be prepared for every eventuality.'

'There's also a very real chance that your marriage will be
declared null and void.'

I gasped in horror. 'Our children would be illegitimate!
After everything we've been through.' I squeezed my eyes
shut, willing the tears away. I couldn't bear to think of it,
the shame to my beautiful daughters and the taint to their
names. 'How can the court make innocent children suffer for
something that has nothing to do with them?'

'I'll make it right,' Erich whispered to me.

The weight of a prison sentence now lay heavily on me.
My thoughts tumbled around and around as I tried to see
how I would manage with Erich in prison. How would I cope
if my marriage wasn't recognised?

Vati and Mutti offered to take Greta back to München with them to allow me to concentrate on the court case. My mother had been most kind and supportive, much to my surprise.

'Greta can come to live with us until Erich's court case is over or for as long as you need,' she wrote in a hastily penned note she had sent with Vati one day. We still had no telephone. 'It will be a pleasure to have her. Vati can't wait to spoil her rotten but I'll make sure she has her naps and eats properly. I know how difficult this is for you, my darling girl, but Vati and I are here for you. With one less to worry about, you can concentrate on Erich's case and the best possible outcome.' I let Greta go with my parents, knowing she would have a better time with them. I felt terribly guilty at the relief of only having to manage one child among the challenges Erich and I faced.

A few days before the court date in July, Erich and I were lying in bed, both restless, unable to sleep.

'It will be all right,' Erich whispered into the darkness.

'How could she do this?'

He wrapped his arms around me. 'It's done now. She can't hurt us any more.'

'We've done nothing wrong. We don't deserve this.'

'No, my *liebling*, we do not but you know the world isn't fair.' He kissed me on the back of my neck. 'We'll get through this, as we've got through everything else.'

I shifted restlessly in his arms, turning to face him. 'Everything will change after this.'

'The solicitor believes we will be okay. There's no evidence of wrongdoing on our part. If the worst happens, I doubt it will be a long prison sentence. You'll go home to your parents with the children until I'm released.'

'But—'

Erich kissed me, a kiss of promise. 'I love you. I will not abandon you. I will not leave you and the children, no matter what. You are my life. It will be all right, I promise.'

I nodded, shaking with fear. I couldn't help it. How could I live without him, even for a little while?

She was in the courtroom. Looking respectable in a tired, dark dress, she carried an air of martyrdom, like a fur stole worn with pride. She was smug and self-satisfied, just as I had imagined. Playing the victim. As if Erich and I weren't also victims of the circumstances we had found ourselves in. 'Marriage wrecker,' her expression seemed to say when she looked at me. I wanted to march across and slap her, wipe that smirk off her face. Instead, I stared ahead and ignored her.

Erich sat next to his lawyer. He was all alone. Although it made me proud to see him calm and composed, it made my blood boil to see him sitting there at all. He was the kindest, most gentle, generous man and did not deserve to be accused of anything. I should have been by his side as his wife. I wanted to climb onto the judge's bench and scream across the court room that this was ridiculous. Instead, I took a deep breath, twisted my fingers through the folds of my skirt and behaved as the decorous, upstanding young wife I needed to be.

The prosecutors, aldermen, the judge and chairman of the regional high judiciary sat before us with stony faces, giving nothing away.

The legal jargon used by the prosecutors, quoting articles of recent changes to the law, and test cases relating to this matter, not only bored me to tears, but made me furious at how this very human misfortune was reduced to a cold and calculating battle of words. It took all of my willpower to stay attentive, be the support Erich needed, strong and unruffled like he was, to never betray my emotions.

It was when Erich stood in front of the court that I nearly cracked. He began reliving his experiences, the helplessness and horror he had endured in 1945, when Inga and the children had fled before the Red Army, when he thought they were dead. His stormy green eyes, deep as the ocean, held my gaze as though I was his lifeline. I held my breath, my heart beating madly, wishing I could tell him to stop, pull him away, and put an end to his pain. A lesser man would have crumbled but he had done it, told his story, told the truth.

The faces of the aldermen and the judges remained impassive.

Every day I saw Inga's face and the way she looked at me, as if I was dirt. When I heard her testimony and the difficulties she had gone through, I felt sorry for her and the children. She had been a victim of circumstance as much as we had, I realised. We had all suffered.

Then it was my turn to testify. My stomach had been tying itself into knots all morning. I hadn't been able to eat a thing. The walk to the front of the room seemed the longest of my life, even longer than on my wedding day. I tried to keep a dignified and poised demeanour, while my head began to pound in time with my heart.

'Please state your name,' said the prosecutor. He was tall and thin with a face like a weasel. I knew he meant my maiden name as my married name was the one in question here, but the idea set my teeth on edge.

'Charlotte Elisabeth Katharina Augusta von Klein,' I said, clasping my hands tightly on my lap, unable to control my trembling.

And so it began. I described how I met Oberinspektor Drescher in 1943 when I began work as his secretary and continued to the events of early 1945, when Erich learnt of the death of his family. Although I was telling the truth, I found answering the prosecutor's questions more and more exasperating, the sneer on his face almost unbearable. Every time my gaze darted across the room, I met the accusing, aloof stares of the aldermen and judges.

'Did you intend to trap Herr Drescher into making promises of marriage, despite your knowledge that he had a wife and children already?' the prosecutor asked in an emotionless voice.

'No, I did not,' I responded calmly, desperate to rise from my hard chair and throttle him.

'Did you and Herr Drescher plan your escape from Riem airpark and your flight to Bad Windsheim as a means to prevent detection of a marriage you intended to enter into, knowing his wife and children lived in Elend?'

I couldn't look at Erich. I knew I'd see the outrage and pain I felt reflected on his face. Instead, I stared at the back wall, drew myself tall and focused on my family. I was above the prosecutor's pettiness.

'No, we did not.' I only wished I could explain the situation, how difficult those times were, how much we deliberated and agonised over the actions we took but Erich's lawyer advised us to answer the questions as simply as possible. He would do the rest.

'Why did you marry Herr Drescher? Did he induce you to do so?'

'We fell in love at Riem. We had both suffered terrible loss. When Erich took me home to my mother in Windsheim, something he had promised my father he would do, our love blossomed. I married him willingly. He never forced me to do so.' I stared, unflinching, at the prosecutor and he stared back unrelenting.

All this was true. Our love affair, if you could call it that, never happened until after Erich learnt that his family had perished. We had agreed not to mention my first pregnancy, much to my relief. It would only hurt Erich's case. Nobody knew about it except for my mother, aunt, uncle and the midwife. My family would never talk, besmirching the family name, and the midwife had since died. The burial plot of our boy was unmarked.

Part of me waited on tenterhooks for the prosecutor to ask about our son. I wasn't sure I could keep my composure if he did, but the question never came.

'I have no more questions,' said he finally, looking thoroughly frustrated.

I stepped down and returned to my seat, hoping everyone saw a young wife and mother, composed and wronged, innocent of any wrongdoing. I didn't dare look at Erich, in case I betrayed my relief and distress. I wanted to shrivel up and die, airing my personal life for the world to hear, especially *her*, devastated that she had made Erich live through his pain yet again. I prayed that it would be over soon.

As the prosecutor summarised the details of that fateful time from February to July 1945, he turned the events of that chaotic period into acts of suspicious behaviour, making out that Erich wilfully abandoned his wife and children so he could marry me. We were prepared for this line of attack, seasoned by the solicitor, but I noticed the slight slump in Erich's shoulders; he was a family man and I could only imagine what a blow this was. I found it difficult not to jump up and declare our innocence.

It was time for our case to be put forward. Erich's defence presented the results of his psychological assessment, aired to the court.

'He was suffering psychological shock,' testified the psychiatrist, an experienced and trusted voice in his profession. 'It was the result of the continued trauma he suffered, learning about his family's demise, the search through unrecognisable corpses in the bunker in Berlin and the consequent hopeful expectation that they lived, only to be re-traumatised by the news of their disappearance and probable deaths.'

'Would you agree that Herr Drescher's unconscious mind sought a way to put this experience and the crippling pain behind him?' asked the lawyer.

'Yes,' said the psychiatrist. 'By forming an attachment to Fräulein von Klein.'

'So, he was able to put his trauma to one side with the happy event of his subsequent marriage to Fräulein von Klein.'

I could see Erich's body tight as a coiled spring. 'That's right,' said the psychiatrist, leaning forward. 'However, his conscious mind was in no fit state to make rational decisions.'

Not exactly a glowing report on my character. I knew I was to be viewed as an opportunist taking advantage of a damaged man, or a mindless female who didn't consider the state of mind of the man she married. To hear it uttered in front of those who didn't know me, especially Inga, was another thing. Indignation and fury bubbled within me but I had to swallow my pride. I kept my head demurely bent. The price of ensuring we did everything we could to secure my husband's freedom.

The testimonies of the seemingly endless roll of witnesses frayed my nerves.

It was a month of agony. Erich and I were exhausted; revisiting the past and all its interpretations brought with it a measure of guilt. Had we done enough at the time, did we do the right thing, how would it affect our family? Cocooned in our own little bubble of pain and despair, we were unable to reach each other. Poor Johanna, everything I did was automatic. I was hardly present for her. If Erich went to prison, what would I do? I can't say that thoughts of Heinrich's offer didn't enter my mind.

Finally, the day of the verdict came. I was terrified, glad that I was sitting as my legs had turned to jelly. I don't know where Erich's strength came from as he stood in front of me, straight and tall next to his lawyer. I wiped my clammy hands on my skirt surreptitiously while I stared at the back of Erich's jacket, slightly crushed from sitting. The lawyer sent a reassuring nod my way after whispering in Erich's ear and I broke out into a cold sweat.

'In the criminal matter of . . .' the judge began. I could see his mouth moving but a loud roaring filled my ears, my vision doubled and I felt sure I was going to faint. The fateful words came to me as if from a long way away. 'It is this court's decision that Erich Drescher be acquitted of the charge of bigamy.

'This court has found that there was insufficient evidence to prove that he wilfully or intentionally entered into a double marriage.'

I reached forward to find Erich's hand. His grasp was solid and he squeezed my hand tightly. He turned to me briefly and smiled, the hard lines of his face softening. Reality began to set in. Elation flooded through me. We had done it!

Listening to the rest of the judge's ruling, my eyes widened in surprise to learn that our court costs were going to be paid by the exchequer, the government treasury. It was the best possible outcome although I would have preferred a proclamation of innocence and a public apology. I couldn't wait to embrace Erich and celebrate this joy with him.

I glanced across to Inga where she sat glaring furiously at the judge, and a small part of me went out to her. Despite her vindictiveness, she was alone, away from her children, and she had lost this battle.

'The marriage between Erich Drescher and Charlotte von Klein is therefore declared invalid,' the judge concluded.

I swayed where I stood, the blood draining from my face.

The shame of hearing that my marriage had effectively never existed threatened to suffocate me. My heart raced and I found it hard to take a breath. The fact that it had been announced publicly, and with Inga present, made me want to curl up in a ball and disappear one moment, and the next I wanted to rage against Inga and the world. We didn't deserve this, my children didn't deserve this. Everything I had been through, everything I had given up for Erich and my family had come to this. It threatened to split me in two.

I was still staring across at Inga, rigid with shock and despair, and I watched as a smile spread deliberately across her face, celebrating my misfortune. A rush of fury filled me. I regretted all the kind thoughts I had had for her. I had never been one to hate, but God in Heaven and damn me to hell, I wanted to wring her neck. I never wanted to see that woman again.

Our children were illegitimate. I couldn't get past that thought. I hugged Johanna with all my might when I returned home to her, as if I could protect her from our shame, to show her I loved her more than anything, despite the court's decision. I couldn't wait to see Greta.

20

'Why don't you come home and spend a few days with us?' pleaded Mutti over the phone. 'Vati will come and get you.'

'No, Mutti. Erich needs me now. He's been through so much. Can't you and Vati bring Greta home?' Erich had been ready for the worst – prison time – and although he had been exonerated, the court case had left him exhausted, empty and defeated. After everything, he couldn't save our marriage. I knew how much that destroyed him.

'Please, Lotte. Please come home and let Vati and me spoil you and Johanna for a couple of days.' I'd never heard Mutti like this. There was a hint of desperation in her voice.

'Don't worry about me,' Erich assured me when I discussed going to my parents'. 'You know I'll be working double shifts as much as I can. It will be good for me to be busy. I can't bear to think of what's happened to us.'

Tears pricked my eyes. Everything was a mess. I knew Erich blamed himself.

He pulled me into his arms and held me close. 'I promise I'll make this right.'

I squeezed my eyes tight, as a flood of emotion rushed through me – pride, anguish and relief. 'I don't want to leave you here like this. I'm worried about you,' I said.

'No, my darling.' He smoothed my hair. 'I will be fine. After these last few months, it'll be good for you to be with your parents for a break. I know how exhausted you are and you need help with the girls. Go. We'll work out what to do when you get back.'

He was right. We would work this out but I did need my parents, someone to help with the children, a good meal and some rest. The court case had taken so much out of me.

'All right,' I murmured. 'I'll go but not before I show you how much I'll miss you.'

I looked into the depths of his green eyes and saw the flame of desperate love and despair intertwined. I kissed him deeply; thankful he was still with me and not in prison. He was solid under my touch, immediate and real. I pulled him to the bedroom, desperate to feel his touch, longing to show him how happy I was to have him home with me.

It was wonderful to see Greta. I couldn't stop crying as I held her. She had grown taller, her dark hair long enough to stay in the pigtails Mutti gave her. She looked gorgeous – happy and healthy, dressed in a pretty dress and leather shoes.

Mutti couldn't wait to show me how Greta now sat nicely at the table. She could eat properly with a knife and fork and hold her spoon correctly.

'Clever girl! What lovely table manners,' I said, kissing her soundly on the cheek.

'Grossmama tells me I'm a big girl now that I'm three,' she said, her dark eyes alight with the praise, puffing her little chest out with importance.

'You are a big girl now that you're three,' I agreed, hugging her tightly, feeling guilty yet again for not being with her on her birthday, as we were in the midst of Erich's trial.

Greta was keen to see how Johanna had grown and was surprised that she was now walking. She would hold her sister's chubby little hand and walk with her, stopping when Johanna's steps became unsteady. Nothing was as precious as watching the two of them together, Greta's dark head leaning down to Johanna's blonde one, encouraging her, and Johanna staring up at her with adoring blue eyes. Everything we had been through paled into insignificance at the sight of my two girls playing together.

'I have something to show you,' said Mutti. 'I'll be back in a minute.'

When Mutti returned, she handed me her camera. 'Here, take some photographs of them before they get any bigger.'

The camera was heavy in my hand. I ran my fingers over the compact bulk, the feel of it as familiar as my own face. My own camera had only been used occasionally, as I tried to preserve the precious rolls of film Vati had given me. I stared at Mutti, incredulous.

'You have film?'

363

'Of course.' She couldn't help but smile at my excitement. 'Vati has been scouring the city for film and somewhere to develop it. He found a studio that's only recently been able to restock its supplies. We've been taking photographs of Greta whenever we can. When the film is finished, Vati will get it developed and give you the pictures. Give him any film you need developed and he will get it done and replaced for you.'

I hugged my mother, kissing her cheek in delight. Sometimes she could be so very thoughtful. 'Thank you, Mutti. I can't begin to tell you what this means to me.' Finally, I could keep my promise to my father and share with him the photos I had taken.

'I know, my *liebchen*. I've watched you with the girls, the wistfulness you get every now and then, especially on their birthdays when you can take only a few photographs.' She caressed my face. 'You can start taking photographs whenever you want again.'

My photography was an integral part of me, my passion and joy. To return to it was something I had dreamt of for years.

'Oh, Mutti,' I murmured, tears glistening in my eyes. 'You know me so well. How can I ever thank you?'

'Just take some beautiful pictures, like you used to. Vati and I only want to see you happy.' She squeezed my hand and turned her focus back to the girls. After everything, she had been paying attention. The thought warmed my heart.

It was wonderful to have the apartment to ourselves once again. The government had found housing for the wartime residents of our home and Mutti and Vati had spent a lot of time trying to restore the apartment to its original condition. The filthy walls had been stripped and repainted, and rugs covered marks on the floor that couldn't be erased.

'What will you do now?' asked Mutti lightly one evening as we sat in the parlour, Beethoven playing softly in the background. The room looked like it always had with the Rembrandt back on the wall in pride of place.

'What can I do?' I picked up a partially finished tapestry on its wooden frame, to hide the tears that sprang to my eyes, brushing my fingers over the neat stitches. The legal status of my marriage to Erich caused my chest to tighten with grief every time I thought about it. I couldn't get the look of disapproval those court officials had given me out of my head.

'You could stay here with us,' said Mutti tentatively. 'Greta is happy here. We could help you with the children.'

I glanced across to Vati, sitting near the gramophone. He nodded reassuringly. I put the tapestry down and gazed once again into my mother's face. I knew Mutti was unhappy about this state of affairs and I couldn't help but feel that I had let her and our family down. A scandal such as this was exactly what she had always tried to protect her family name from, and Vati's too.

'I can't,' I said, shaking my head. Erich needed me by his side and the children needed their father.

'Maybe you could get some work in photography and in time start your own studio,' she said. If only she had been so encouraging and supportive of my dreams during the war. I noticed that she was wearing her mother's cameo at her throat. She had passed away not long before Erich's trial and I was glad Mutti had seen her before she died, even if I had not.

It was tempting to stay here until Erich and I had a valid marriage once again. It was comfortable, easy, a breather from the difficult life we had been living. It wouldn't be for very long, I told myself. Then I remembered how it had been before I left and I knew I couldn't return. I wasn't the same person any more.

If I stayed, I knew Mutti would try to force Heinrich and I back together. Since learning of my marriage to Erich, Heinrich had refused to marry. Mutti still believed he was best for me, of my own class, wealthy and my oldest friend. Heinrich's father had died recently and he was now the sole beneficiary of the sizable Hoffmann family estate. Somehow their fortune hadn't been as decimated as Vati's after the war. In my mother's eyes, Heinrich could best provide for me, keep me safe and give me a good life. But I understood now why marrying Heinrich hadn't felt right. Erich was the one for me and I had made my choice. Erich was a man, proving he could care for me and our children during difficult years. Besides, I couldn't imagine life without him now. When I thought about Heinrich in Erich's shoes, I doubted he could have accomplished the same, been man enough to be flexible and do anything to look after his family.

'My home is with Erich and I love him,' I said. 'We have our children to think of and we are a family. I can't take their father away from them, like mine was taken from me.'

Mutti's eyes widened but she merely nodded. She picked up the tapestry, turning it over in her hands. 'When we divorced, your father demanded the boys stay with him. It nearly destroyed me. Your father drank and gambled away his fortune and my inheritance but nobody seemed to understand why I left him. The only way I could give you a decent education was to agree to send you to boarding school near your father. I'm sure it was just so I couldn't see you, to make my isolation and despair more complete. I came to München on my own, not only to get away from your father and his family but because I was determined to make a life for you here but I couldn't get a job. I had never worked before. I had no skills. If not for my grandmother's bequeath to me,' she gestured to the apartment, 'I would have been destitute.' She gazed at me, her blue eyes misty with memory. 'Just think about your future and the future of your children. You don't have to endure such hardship. I don't want your life to be difficult.'

'It's all right, Mutti.' My hand caressed her damp cheek. 'You did the only thing you could.'

'Yes.' Mutti nodded and took the handkerchief I handed her. 'But I don't want that for you. I want you to have a good life, a happy life.'

I grasped Mutti's hand. 'But I will. Erich and I will sort this out.'

Mutti sniffed and nodded but I could tell by the stubborn set of her jaw that she wasn't convinced.

'We have to let them be,' said Vati gently. 'It will take time to go through the legal channels to set this wrong right again. Lotte has made her choice and Erich is an honourable man who loves her and their children dearly. He will not abandon them and, if I know him at all, he would give his life to make this right and to provide Lotte and the children with a good life. It's time you gave him a chance.'

I smiled at Vati, the tightness in my chest easing. I could always rely on him to support me. 'Thank you, Vati, for having faith in him, in us. He's been through so much, I couldn't abandon him either.'

Vati rose from his chair and sat between Mutti and me, grasping both our hands. 'Mutti and I will support you in any way we can. Won't we, *liebchen*?' He looked at Mutti and she reluctantly met his gaze.

'Of course,' said Mutti, so softly I almost didn't hear her. 'She's my only child. Of course I will support her.'

I was preparing the girls for a walk to the park when I heard voices downstairs, not uncommon in this household; Mutti had an active social life and people were often coming and going from her parlour. Greta sped ahead to see who Grossmama had visiting her this day.

'Onkel Heinrich!' I heard her screech with delight. 'Are you coming on our walk? We're going to the park, you know?'

I felt the blood drain from my head and groped for the railing to steady myself, conscious of keeping a firm grip on Johanna.

'Look who's here, Mutti,' said Greta, dragging Heinrich by the hand to the stairs.

'Hello, Lotte,' said Heinrich, grinning sheepishly.

I stopped on the stairs, staring. Heinrich looked the same as always, smartly dressed and tall, blond, handsome, reminding me so strongly of my brothers. A warm rush of affection gushed through me and I smiled. I couldn't help it.

I was pleased to see him. He had been a big part of my life for so long, I realised how much I had missed him.

'Hello Heinrich.'

'Onkel Heinrich's coming to the park with us. Aren't you?' Greta's big brown eyes looked up at him, begging him to go along with her plan.

'I'm sure Onkel Heinrich has more important things to do than come walking with us,' I said lightly.

'Oh no,' replied Heinrich, smoothing Greta's dark hair. 'A walk with young Greta is just the thing to make my day.'

'Yippee,' shouted Greta, jumping up and down. 'Come on, Johanna, hurry up. Onkel Heinrich is coming for a walk with us.'

I realised that this was not the first time that Heinrich had visited. Greta seemed to know him quite well. Anger began to blossom deep in my belly. It was no accident that Heinrich was here now.

'Is this your youngest?' asked Heinrich politely, gesturing to Johanna, struggling to get down to her sister.

'Yes,' I said absently. 'This is Johanna.' Heinrich opened his arms to Johanna, gesturing to her to come. I was horrified when she let go of my hand, climbed down the next step and into Heinrich's waiting arms.

'Come then. It's a beautiful sunny day and the park is waiting,' said Heinrich. He strode out the door, Greta clutching one hand and Johanna in the other, leaving me dumbfounded.

'Are you coming, Mutti?' called Greta.

Heinrich was good with the girls – that surprised me. Greta rode on his shoulders and climbed up and tumbled off his legs countless times, while he spun Johanna around, urged on by her delighted screams.

'More!' they both pleaded, until Heinrich collapsed on the grass, panting.

'No more,' he groaned. 'I'm too old. I need a rest.'

'Come on, girls,' I said sternly, although I was bubbling with laughter and had to keep the grin from my face. 'Leave Onkel Heinrich alone now. Greta, here, take your refreshments under the tree and have them while I talk to Onkel Heinrich.' I passed her the bag I had packed earlier. 'Take your sister with you.'

'They're beautiful,' said Heinrich, while I spread out the rug for us to sit on. 'I can't believe what fun they are.'

'Yes, they are,' I said softly. Perhaps one day you might make a good father, I thought. I sat on a corner of the rug and gazed at my girls, picking up their grandmother's cake with delighted expressions. I remembered his father. 'I'm sorry about your father.'

'Thank you.' He nodded, his eyes clouding over briefly. Then he smiled. 'It's good to see you again, Lotte.'

'You too,' I whispered, my breath catching in my throat at my admission. It really was good to see him. His boyish good looks had turned into a rugged handsomeness and he seemed at ease with his large, powerful frame. I knew he had returned home after the war emaciated and worn down, but obviously life had been good to him since then. I hadn't known how Heinrich would be when we finally met once again, how he would feel, and I'd feared that the life and love we once shared would be overshadowed by the bitterness and hurt of what I had done. I was no longer the young girl he had known. The last years had been hard and pregnancy and childbirth had changed my body. I wrapped my arm over my belly self-consciously.

Heinrich took my hand. 'Don't do that,' he said. 'You're more beautiful than ever. Motherhood suits you.' He kissed my hand, a gentle, lingering kiss that made my heart race. When had Heinrich learnt what to say to a woman? I pulled my hand away.

'The children,' I said more harshly than I intended. My face flamed with embarrassment, remembering back to the days when we had fooled around in the meadows of the Englischer Garten. They were a lifetime ago but at this moment they felt like only yesterday. My breath quickened at the memory.

'They'll be fine,' Heinrich whispered. He grasped my hand again, drawing me towards him. Leaning forward, he kissed the sensitive skin above my collarbone, right at the base of my neck, making me shiver ever so slightly. 'Nothing's changed. I still want you,' he murmured, his breath tickling my ear.

I wrenched away and stood abruptly, glancing at the girls, who were oblivious to what had happened. I glared at Heinrich, mortified. 'Grow up,' I snapped, my heart pounding in my ears. I was furious with him and myself, wondering if he had seen my thoughts written on my face. 'You know this can't be. I have responsibilities now.'

Heinrich sighed, shaking his head. 'I'm sorry, I shouldn't have done that. It just felt like old times.'

I understood what he meant. It was hard to let go of the past, of what had been between us. It felt like the years had melted away and we were a young couple once more.

'Come and sit down. There are things I have to say to you. We must talk.' He patted the rug next to him. 'I promise I'll be good.'

The reality was that the past was behind us and neither of us could undo what had happened since. I tentatively sat back down on the rug, placing as much distance between us as possible.

'Come back to me.' Heinrich's face was alive with hope, tempering the wrinkles of pain around his eyes.

'You know I can't.'

'Why not?'

His closeness was causing me not to think straight, echoes of the last time I had seen him, before he went to war. When he had begged me to make love to him, I realised belatedly. Blushing furiously and irritated by my reaction to him, I savagely plucked blades of grass from the ground, disconcerted by layers of memories – the meadow in summertime many years earlier, a time before I had met Erich, when life was less complicated and Heinrich and I were happy.

'I told you, I have responsibilities now. I have the girls. You know how it was for me when my parents divorced. I shouldn't have to explain this to you.' I flung the grass away in exasperation, not daring to look at him.

Heinrich's large hand reached out and enfolded mine. It took all my willpower not to jerk away. 'I remember what you went through,' he said softly. 'I want you and I want your girls. Marry me and I will adopt your girls, like Johann adopted you. I will give you and your girls everything.'

I shook my head, not trusting myself to speak, pulling my hand away.

'There's no reason why you can't now,' he said desperately, leaning towards me. 'I know about the court case. You're free to do what you like.'

I stiffened, my breath tight in my chest. What he said was true. I shut my eyes, hating myself. How could I contemplate such a thing? The truth was I had chosen Erich and all that came with him. I couldn't imagine life without him. 'I can't abandon Erich. He's the girls' father.'

'I understand you married Erich because you were trapped.'

My eyebrows rose, wondering what my mother had told him but I didn't want to talk about it here. I cupped his cheek with my hand. 'You're a kind and wonderful man but I told you, I have responsibilities. I married Erich in a union we believed was legal. I have two children with him and we are a family. I'm bound to him now. It's too late.'

Heinrich placed his hand over mine and brought it to rest over his heart. It was beating wildly. 'Do you love him?'

'Oh, Heinrich,' I said wretchedly, pulling my hand free. I couldn't tell him of the uncontrollable fire between Erich and I, the unbridled passion that propelled me towards him all those years ago. I couldn't hurt him any more than I needed to. 'What is love? I thought I knew what it was once when I was young and naïve but in truth I had no idea. I've shared the most difficult and most joyful moments of my life with this man. We've formed a bond and only together can we carry the burden of what this war has cost the both of us. It's the only way we can heal.' I stopped, glancing away from his puzzled expression to the girls feeding each other apple slices. 'Erich is a good father and husband. The girls don't need another. He has proven he will do anything to provide for us. Is that love?' I turned back to look challengingly at him to find Heinrich staring thoughtfully at me.

'Do you still love me?' he whispered, wariness in his eyes for the first time.

How could I answer him? My feelings were so tangled. They weren't the electric feelings I had for Erich and the deep connection we shared, yet there was still something here. Perhaps it was just our history catching up with me. I stared at the grass, hearing the girls' chatter in the background. Searching for a non-committal response, I rearranged my legs beneath me, tucking my feet under my skirt.

'You're my oldest friend. You have shared so much of my life and you remind me so much of my brothers. How can I not love you?'

'You think of me like a brother,' he said coldly.

My head jerked to his ashen face. His eyes burned with anger.

'Have you always felt this way?'

'It's not like that,' I snapped. 'I'll admit I had doubts before our wedding but I wasn't sure if it was just nerves. You were all I knew about love. I had nothing to compare it to.'

'You weren't attracted to me?'

'How can you say that? Of course I was. Don't you remember how it was with us? How we were here in the garten?' My neck and face blushed hot with the memories. 'You were very handsome and strong . . .' My voice faltered. 'You still are, more than I remembered.'

He ran his hands through his cropped blond hair. 'Then what is it?'

'When I worked with Erich, he treated me with respect, valued my opinions like I was his equal, his partner. I had never experienced that before.' I dropped my gaze for a moment. I wasn't being entirely truthful. 'I never felt that with you. I always felt part of your plan, your possession, your prize. You never really listened to what I wanted to do with my life.' He opened his mouth to object, his brow furrowed in annoyance. 'No, not really,' I ploughed on. 'You would pacify me but I knew that you expected me to fall in with your plan once we were married. I sometimes wondered if you really loved me in that way at all. We were both naïve, I think. Maybe you didn't know any differently either.'

Heinrich looked at me, stunned. 'How could you doubt me? I've always loved you, even if you think I didn't say it often enough or in the way you wanted. What could be higher praise to you than wanting you to share my life? Of course I valued you. I was young and green I know, and I would do it entirely differently now but make no mistake, I love you. Come back to me.'

Tears welled in my eyes. I hadn't imagined meeting him again would be like this. 'You've been part of my life for so long that you are a part of me.' I looked at the girls digging in the dirt, blinking the tears away. 'You don't know what it was like when you went to war. I couldn't breathe some days, worrying about you, and then when we didn't hear from you and we didn't know if you were alive or dead . . . It was worse than torture. I couldn't bear to pack my wedding gown away until Mutti and I left München for the last time. I thought I had lost you.' I dashed away the errant tear that slid down my face in defiance of my desire to stay composed.

'I don't want to lose you again now that you've come back into my life but please don't ask this of me. I don't know if I can cope with losing you again.'

'So you do still love me,' he whispered.

I sighed in frustration. He didn't understand.

Then his face hardened. 'Yet you chose him.'

'I never meant to hurt you. I had an affair with Erich. I thought you were dead – I hadn't heard from you in months. I fell pregnant and had a choice to come home with Mutti or stay in Windsheim and marry him. I chose to marry him. Despite everything we've been through, I love him.'

'How can a man like him possibly give you what you need? He can't understand your background, he's a commoner. He has no profession that he can perform and he can't support you in the manner you're used to. You don't need to live like a peasant. I know you and I know what you need.'

Anger bubbled in my chest. I'd forgotten how arrogant he was, born with a silver spoon in his mouth, everything handed to him on a platter. He thought he could still make decisions for me. Maybe he hadn't changed at all. He truly believed the words he had spoken. My gut twisted with disgust. I had held those same beliefs once but now didn't know whether to feel indignant, enraged or saddened by his ignorance. Germany was a different place now. The war had swept all those grand illusions away. I was different too.

'I was wrong about you,' I spat, shaking with rage. 'How dare you presume to know what I need? How dare you speak about him that way? Erich's a good man – a better man that you'll ever be. How could I ever choose you when you're still such an arrogant boy?'

He stared at me, his face blanched of all colour, his brows raised in bafflement, then he closed his eyes and dropped his head, as if all the fight had gone out of him. 'I didn't mean to offend you. It's the last thing I wanted to do.' He lifted his head, his face resolute. 'Don't make a decision now. Go home and think about it. You're a free woman. Make the choices that are right for you.'

He sighed and then leant across to grasp my face in his hands and kiss me deeply. I was rooted to the spot in surprise. It was a possessive gesture that took me back to our passionate moments of young love, years earlier. His lips were as soft as I had remembered but the power behind the kiss now was not of the boy but that of a man. I placed my hands on his chest and pushed him away.

He stood. 'This is not goodbye.' Turning towards the girls, he called out to them. 'I have to go to work, girls. I hope to see you again soon.'

Greta ran to him and hugged him tightly. 'Goodbye, Onkel Heinrich. I'm going home with Mutti soon. Come and visit us there.'

I felt a stab in my chest at the closeness between them. Heinrich straightened as Greta ran back to her sister's side. He waved cheerily to them, turned once more to me, pain clouding his eyes, and strode down the path.

I was furious with Heinrich but I was also furious with my mother. She was out when I returned and I insisted that my father drive us home that afternoon. He didn't ask and I didn't tell him what had happened as I bundled the children into the car before my mother came home. I didn't want to confront her feeling like this. I needed time.

When we returned home, I found I could breathe a little easier. A warm glow enveloped me watching Erich with Greta. He was still long and lean despite being nearly forty. He exuded a grace and elegance that could not be learnt. His eyes were bright with excitement at his reunion with his daughters and I did not miss the look that was just for me, promising that he would welcome me home properly later. It made me weak at the knees. After all this time, Erich could still do that to me. The chemistry between us was strong and I could not resist him.

Greta sat on her father's knee while I attended to Johanna and dinner, chatting animatedly about her adventures at Grossmama's house, including our outing with Heinrich. She didn't fail to miss the kiss that he had given me and duly reported it to her father.

Later that evening, I returned hesitantly to the kitchen after tucking the girls into bed and reading them a story. I had seen Erich's thunderous expression when Greta had told him about Heinrich. I had a lot of explaining to do.

'What happened at your mother's?' he demanded.

'Look,' I said turning towards him, 'I was just as surprised as you are. I didn't know Heinrich was visiting Mutti often enough for Greta to know him. I didn't know he was coming until I saw him come out of Mutti's parlour.'

He nodded but continued to look sceptical, his brows knitted together. 'It's your meddling mother again,' he said bitterly.

'Yes.' I sighed. 'I'm furious with her.'

'Your family never ceases to amaze me.' He leant forward in his chair. 'So Heinrich's still pining after you and your mother's encouraging it.'

I nodded, blushing with embarrassment.

'He had a hide to kiss you.' Erich grabbed my arm, holding it tightly. 'He has no right, no claim to you any more.' The vein at his temple was protruding, a sure sign that he was livid. I was glad that I didn't mention Heinrich's other advance.

'It was a goodbye kiss.' I fiddled with the edge of the table-cloth. 'Heinrich knows there's no future for us. That's why I had to speak to him. I wouldn't have allowed him to join us otherwise.'

He let go of my arm and leant back in his chair, his eyes glittering. Not only was he angry, I realised, he was jealous.

'I don't understand why you felt you needed to say anything to him at all. Just ignore him. He'll soon get over you. For Christ's sake, you have two children!'

I had never seen Erich like this. I had never imagined him as the jealous type. But here he was, his face red with fury, his chest puffed out with indignation, losing the tight control of his emotions. All it did was stir my own anger, which had been smouldering in my belly all day.

'Don't be ridiculous! I was engaged to be married to him. After all these years, he deserved an explanation. He's a good man but he was encouraged by my mother. I had to make him understand how things stand.'

'How do things stand? It sounds to me that you enjoyed spending time with him.'

A burst of guilt flooded my body, making my fingers tingle with alarm. Heinrich was part of my old life and I had enjoyed seeing him but maybe it had been a mistake.

'Would you rather be married to him? Are you regretting being here with me?'

My face reddened as if I had been slapped and my breath caught in my chest. How could he say these things after everything we had been through, after everything I had told him?

I stood abruptly, the chair scraping against the floor. 'Have you forgotten that our marriage was declared invalid in front of a courtroom full of people? Have you thought about our daughters and how they are now illegitimate?' My voice caught. 'What are you going to do about that, Erich?'

He was standing too now and we were nose to nose. 'What do you want me to do? You're a free woman now, free to choose whatever you want. Don't let me stop you. I wouldn't want you to feel trapped by me.' He was shaking with rage.

I was mortified by his words. 'Go to hell.' I was tempted to go back to my parents with the girls. I didn't need any man. Then, as if a bucket of cold water had been tipped over my head, I realised what I was doing. We were teetering on the edge of an abyss that threatened to destroy everything we had. I dropped to my chair, face in my hands, feeling oddly detached from my body. I didn't want to fight.

'Stop this,' I sobbed. 'We are a family ... What are we going to do to make this right?'

He stared down at me, his chest heaving. Our eyes locked. I would not look away even with my tears, although my body was coiled with fear. Slowly the harshness faded from his eyes and the blue pulse at his temple slowed as he thought about what I had said. Clear reason returned, turning his eyes into luminous pools of liquid green. He sighed and looked out the window into the blackness.

'I have to divorce Inga. I'm sure she'll make it as difficult as possible. It might be some time before we can remarry—' his voice cracked '—if that's what you want to do.' The pressure of what he was asking of me, the sacrifice he would make for my happiness, was plain in the anguish on his face.

Frustration bubbled in my blood, frothing in my chest so it felt like I couldn't breathe. I glared at him. 'Of course that's what I want. I love you and I want us to be a family. I've already told you that.'

He dropped to his knees next to my chair. He seized my hand and brought it to his mouth with such fierceness that it startled me. 'I love you too. I have always loved you,' he said fervently and pressed his lips to my hand again. His touch was warm and solid, somehow rousing me, making me whole again.

'Oh, Erich!' I flung my arms around him. 'I don't want to go anywhere else. I can't imagine my life without you. You mean the world to me.'

He held me tightly, shuddering suddenly. 'I couldn't imagine my life without you either. I was so worried you wanted your old life back, that you wanted Heinrich and not me, that it made me crazy. I'm so sorry.'

'It's all right,' I whispered, squeezing him tighter. How could I be so blind that I hadn't seen his own fear and vulnerability?

Then he was on his feet and I was in his arms, oblivious to anything but the fire that raged between us. He carried me to bed, where furious, passionate lovemaking healed the hurt between us and tender words afterwards reminded us of what we meant to each other.

21

I looked around the tiny, rundown cottage listlessly, the smell of animal manure pervading the air. It wouldn't be enough. There were only two bedrooms, one for Erich and myself, one that the girls shared – and only one living space. Erich's mother, Karoline, was coming to live with us. Expelled from her home, like many Germans and like Erich, she was a displaced person and had nobody else. Her husband was still missing and the chances of him being alive grew slimmer by the day. When Erich had opened the letter telling him she was alive, we were both shocked.

'My mother's been found,' he whispered. I read the letter in his hand. It was from the Red Cross. They had found her in a Russian camp in Karpinsk in Western Siberia. I shivered in horror. She had survived for five years. I couldn't imagine what that had been like. She was on her way to a refugee camp in Hamburg. There was no word of Erich's father.

'I can't believe it.' I hugged Erich.

He nodded, his eyes blank. 'I never thought I'd see the day,' he whispered. Erich had recently started a new job at the Illesheim Ordinance Depot as a Safety Inspector and Engineer. He was delighted to be working in a field closer to his own profession and the work was easy for him. The pay was much better too and we had the option to move closer to the depot, into rental housing allotted to staff. It was something we definitely needed to investigate now that Erich's mother was part of our household.

The move happened quickly; we wanted to be in before Erich went to collect his mother from Hamburg. We found a lovely little house in Illesheim, with three bedrooms – one upstairs in the attic with a small adjoining space, perfect for Karoline. A tall beech tree stood like a guardian in the front yard, casting the front path and little wooden gate with dappled light. There was an enclosed garden for the girls out the back, where Erich envisioned a vegetable garden and I imagined brightening with some colourful flowers. A wonderful spot for family photos, I thought, candid shots of the girls with their father and grandparents. It was lovely to be in the village and away from the stinking farmyards and endless mud. We even had electricity and running water that flowed plentifully and easily from the taps. It was bliss.

Karoline hobbled into the house on Erich's arm. She was a tiny, wizened lady with hazel eyes, her grey hair braided and pinned to the top of her head. Erich looked very much like her. I could see the pain in her eyes each time she took a step but she bravely carried on, smiling sweetly as she came to greet me.

'My dear Lotte,' she said, holding my hands between hers, her skin dry and leathery with thick calluses across her palms. 'I've heard so much about you. It's a pleasure to meet you.'

'The pleasure is mine,' I said graciously. 'I'm so glad to finally meet you and for the girls to meet their grandmother.' The tears in her eyes sparkled in the light. I could only imagine how she was feeling. She had lived long enough to return to Germany, see her only son again and discover two new granddaughters.

Karoline didn't say too much in the early days, simply focusing her energies on her new surroundings. Readjusting to the noises of everyday life, particularly with two active little girls, she slowly regained her strength. Her body healed, her dreadful hacking cough disappeared and finally she moved without much pain. She loved spending time with the girls, walking around the village with them, pushing Johanna, who was now three, in the pram when she got tired. When she became stronger, they would walk past the village, into the farmland. Some days they would return with strange bulges under Johanna's blankets, all three looking innocent as lambs.

'Mutti,' Greta often shouted excitedly as they came through the door. 'Look what Omi found on our walk!' Johanna would pull back the blanket in her pram with a little screech of anticipation and displayed pumpkins, corn or cabbages, fruit or even on occasion, eggs.

I was always surprised, Karoline being a good Catholic and all. How could I explain to small children that this wasn't right when their grandmother continued to behave that way? Maybe the years in the work camp had honed her instinct for survival to such an extent as to override her morality.

'Put them in the kitchen, Greta,' I said countless times. 'Next time, make sure they don't belong to anyone else. If they do, we can't take them, it's stealing.' Greta nodded seriously but I wondered how much my words sank in when her grandmother continued to steal. Part of me felt like a hypocrite too, as Erich and I had done exactly the same thing when Greta was a baby.

Karoline insisted on prayers at the table before eating. Torn between amusement and dismay at her piety, I respectfully listened to her pray, amazed that Erich slipped back into the habit almost without thought. I couldn't help but wonder at the hypocrisy of thanking God for the food that Karoline had stolen but I let it go. Prayer had helped me before, maybe it was time to give a little back in thanks. Karoline began to teach the girls the words of the prayers and knelt by their beds with them at night, teaching them the bedtime prayer. It wasn't my way but it was obviously a tradition in Erich's family, so I allowed her.

Heinrich still wrote to me. Not love letters but letters telling me about his day, sharing his thoughts as we once used to. At first, I didn't reply, but he persisted. Finally, I replied with letters of my own, telling him about my life, about how the girls were growing and including the photographs I was now able to take of them. I didn't tell Erich. I didn't want him to become jealous again. I didn't want him upset.

Erich had finally begun divorce proceedings using the solicitor who had helped him in the bigamy case. I knew how much he wanted Eva and Walter closer to him and how he had looked into ways of getting them across to West Germany. He soon discovered that in order for the divorce to be finalised, it was best for Inga to be present in the West, perhaps even impossible if she was not at least in the country. I was not happy about Erich's hard-earned money going towards bringing Inga closer to us but it seemed I had no choice if I wanted this divorce to go ahead. I gritted my teeth and helped him investigate the best way to bring them across the border. This was not an easy thing to do with the tensions between Russia and the West escalating. It was a delicate endeavour that required the right connections and payments.

'They're coming,' Erich said one late autumn afternoon when he returned from work.

'What are you talking about?' I was folding washing at the dining table. The girls were upstairs with Karoline.

'Inga and the children. I've finally managed it. They're crossing the border in two weeks!' His face was alight with joy. He hadn't seen his children in over seven years.

'That's wonderful!' I smiled. 'Where will they go?'

'Here, of course.' Erich looked at me, dumbfounded. 'Where else did you expect them to go?'

I stared at him, the smile frozen on my face. 'What? You can't be serious. There's no room here.' Suddenly I felt light-headed. I put my arm out to steady myself and found the edge of the table.

Erich rushed across and pulled me to him, keeping me from falling. 'It's all right. This is the only way we can accomplish what we want. We'll manage somehow.' Erich wrapped his arms around me, kissing me soundly.

I pulled away. 'I won't have that woman here. She's the reason we're in this mess in the first place. If she hadn't reported you, everything would have been fine.'

'But, Lotte, the children.'

I turned away from the hurt in his eyes. 'The children can stay but she has to find somewhere else, preferably far away from here,' I said, sorting the washing absently. I knew I sounded bitter but I couldn't help it. The past two years of knowing our marriage wasn't recognised ate away at me.

'You can't separate them.' I could hear the note of exasperation in his voice. 'They've been through so much and the children don't know you.'

'I'm telling you, I won't have her here.' I shook my head in frustration, tears pricking my eyes. I couldn't do this. It was more than I could take.

'They're all coming, Lotte, that's the end of it,' said Erich irritably.

I swung around to him, face red with fury. 'If she comes here, don't expect me to stay. I'll take the girls and go home until she's gone.'

'It could take months until the divorce is done.'

'I don't care,' I said, 'I cannot live like that.' I stared him down, wanting him to know how serious I was, but my heart was racing, afraid of what he might do. He glared back at me, neither of us willing to give way to the other.

Finally, he jerked his eyes away, raking his fingers through his hair in frustration. 'Stop being so dramatic,' he snapped. 'It's not that bad. It won't be comfortable but we'll get through it.'

I couldn't believe it. I had seen the fear in his eyes – fear that I would leave, fear that he would lose his children – but I had been sure he would understand me. I stormed past him without saying a word. I couldn't speak. I grabbed my coat from the hook by the door, and left, slamming the front door quite satisfyingly behind me.

Inga and the children came to live with us. When it came down to it, I couldn't leave. I didn't trust Inga with my husband and I was determined to watch her like a hawk.

Much to my annoyance, Karoline was very fond of Inga, insisting that she stay in the attic with her. She did have a double bed after all, but her attitude to Inga irritated me further, leaving me tense and short tempered. Erich bought a little camp bed for Walter to sleep in next to his mother. Eva slept in Johanna's bed, while the girls shared Greta's. It was cramped and I was not happy.

'Thank you for putting us up,' said Inga stiffly to Erich when they arrived. She didn't even acknowledge me standing by Erich's side, falling immediately into Karoline's arms with a little cry of joy. 'Mutti!' she exclaimed, making me clench my teeth in aggravation. Of course she would call her Mutti.

'My dear Inga,' sobbed Karoline, her face wet with tears. 'It's been so long since I've seen you and the children. How I've missed you.'

'Hello, Eva, Walter,' said Erich softly to his children, who hung back shyly, near the front door. Walter, tall and gangly, almost in his teens, looked warily between Eva and his father, waiting to see what she would do. He was only a small boy when he had last seen his father. At sixteen, Eva was a young woman, and remembered her father more vividly. I stepped back to let them have their moment.

'Hello Vati,' she said, the edges of her mouth lifting in a small smile. Erich held out his arms and Eva launched herself into them.

'Come, Walter,' said Erich, holding his crying daughter, who now stood less than a head shorter than he. Walter came forward tentatively and Erich wrapped his arms around his children. 'It's so good to see you again,' he whispered. He kissed the tops of their heads, almost the same height, and I could see that he never wanted to let them go. I felt tears well in my own eyes. We had thought them gone. This was truly a miracle.

'Say hello to Lotte,' Erich said, gesturing to me, once they had dried their eyes. Eva and Walter dutifully and politely hugged me.

'It's so good to meet you both,' I said. 'There are two little girls who can't wait to meet you.'

I brought the girls over, who had surprisingly been doing what they were told and waiting in my bedroom, reading a book together.

'These are your sisters,' Erich said, pulling the girls to him. I could see Inga watching, her expression cautious, her shoulders hunched, but I could feel no sympathy for her.

We had explained to the girls about Eva and Walter being their sister and brother. They were confused at first and there were lots of questions but we needn't have worried. The girls took to their siblings with exuberance and joy, happy for new playmates to join in their games. Eva's and Walter's uncertainty and reluctance quickly slipped away with the welcome our little girls gave them.

Eva and Walter were very polite, but not sure how to take me. I don't know what Inga had told them but I was determined to show them that I was no ogre, that I loved their father and would love them too. I could only imagine how Inga felt about staying with us but I hoped that she harboured no thoughts of winning back Erich's affections. She was civil but cool to Erich and myself, spoke to me only when she had to, was kindly but distant to the girls. She insisted that her children help around the house and often called them away when they were playing with my children or talking to me. I felt sure that she kept a tight rein on how she was feeling. The only time I heard her in conversation was upstairs or outside with Karoline.

I didn't feel quite as able to keep my feelings in check. Not only was this woman, Erich's legal wife, sleeping under my roof, but Erich was providing for her too. I cooked, cleaned and washed, although Karoline insisted on doing Inga's and her children's things. Eva was a good help and Walter spent most of his spare time, when he wasn't at school, with the girls. I grew to love the children, as I knew I would. I had heard so much about them over the years. It was wonderful to watch all four of them together, a source of joy for all of us, except perhaps Inga.

'It's time to come to my tea party,' Greta called one day. It was warm and sunny, unusual for this time in autumn and the children were making the most of it before the cold really hit. I watched from the washing line, as Greta placed the last little leaf platter of berries and flower petals on a small patch of grass. She had set the 'table' beautifully with leaf plates, sticks as utensils, platters of 'food' and tiny flowers from the meadow. Four little acorn caps she had found sat by the plates as tiny cups of tea.

'Come on,' called Greta impatiently. Johanna appeared around the corner of the house holding Walter's hand.

'We're coming,' she said.

'Where's Eva?' said Greta crossly.

'Eva!' yelled Walter. 'Greta's tea party is ready.' Walter and Johanna arrived at the table. 'Where should we sit, madam?' Walter looked expectantly at Greta. Johanna giggled while Greta gestured to the place she wanted Walter to sit.

'If sir would like to sit here,' she said in a posh voice. 'And mademoiselle, here.' She pointed to where Johanna had to sit.

Eva closed the back door and walked towards the tea party. 'Such a beautiful spread,' she said. 'What an elegant table setting.' Her eyes widened in mock rapture and Johanna giggled even harder.

Greta nodded gravely but her eyes were dancing with joy. 'Would you like to sit here, madam?' she said to Eva. Greta served them food and Eva and Walter admired the dishes with 'oohs' and 'ahhs' from Johanna, while they all pretended to nibble and sip from their acorn cups.

Karoline and Inga joined me at the line with more washing, both standing, transfixed, next to me, watching the children.

'Aren't they beautiful?' whispered Karoline, a smile spreading across her face.

I nodded. 'They get on so well.'

'Eva and Walter are wonderful with the girls.'

'Yes, they are. The girls adore them,' I said. 'I wish Erich was here to see them like this together. I should go and get the camera – at least he can see the photographs. I want to get some portraits of him and the children all together sometime.'

Inga said nothing but made a huff of disgust before turning back to the house. I watched the back of her head as she disappeared into the house and I felt a sudden pang of sympathy for her. I had been jealous of the little tete-a-tetes between Inga and Karoline, ignoring me in my home as if I wasn't there. If I came into the room mid-conversation, Inga would stop what she was saying and just stare at me as if I was intruding. It made me wild. A couple of weeks earlier I had heard her talking to Karoline in the lounge room.

'I can't begin to tell you how hard it was on my own with the children,' Inga had said. 'I didn't know how we were going to get away before the Russians got to us. They were already in Oppeln. We thought we were still safe, but of course we weren't. They were in Brieg and then Grottkau by the time we left. I was worried about you and Vati and prayed you had left, that Erich had got you out.'

'I couldn't leave without my husband,' Karoline had replied, so softly I could barely hear her. 'He was still in Breslau with the Volkssturm. I looked after the furniture store as long as I could. Then it was too late. All I could do was lock myself indoors with all the others that chose to stay behind. It was my home.'

'I'm so sorry, Karoline.' Inga had paused as if wanting so say more but only sighed, continuing her story. 'Berlin wasn't an option for us. All the plans Erich had made were useless.

Gottlieb was good to us. He helped us while Erich was away and had been begging me to leave but Eva had been too ill to travel. He wouldn't leave us to fend for ourselves and decided that the only way was to drive us to his mother's in Elend. We had to wait until his unit was evacuated from the airpark. He should have left with his unit but he slipped away with us. We prayed that he wasn't discovered. God knows what would have happened to us then.'

'You poor girl.'

'I will never forget the sights on the road. People fled with whatever they could, on foot, horse and cart, bicycle, some with the retreating Wehrmacht vehicles. Everywhere there was desperation, fear and lawlessness. I made the children lie down in the back seat and shut their eyes, covered in their coats. It was so cold. When we finally made it to Elend and we couldn't contact Erich, I feared the worst but I couldn't tell the children I thought their father was dead.'

'He looked everywhere for you and the children,' Karoline had said softly. 'He would never have abandoned you. Now you are reunited, safe and well with your children.'

'What happened to you?' Inga had asked tentatively.

'We were taken by the Red Army. Women were raped in front of their children, girls too. Others were killed for sport, eyes gouged out, bodies left to freeze in the snow. There was so much anger and hatred for Germans. I wonder how any of us survived. Those of us strong enough were herded onto cattle trains with little food or water. We ended up in a Russian gulag and I worked as a labourer in a stone quarry. I never thought I would see any of you again, see Germany again.'

'Then the Red Cross found you, after Erich's letters to them. He found you,' Inga had said, her voice thick with emotion.

I cracked the door open. Their heads were bowed together, joined in their shared horror and pain, and their salvation.

Erich had saved us all, I thought. In one way or another. As much as it hurt me to see them bonded like this, I understood. I couldn't be cruel to Inga or think badly of Karoline's relationship with her. They had been through so much. I had had Erich by my side the entire time, there to protect me, keep me safe, to love me and care for our children. How could I begrudge Inga this small thing? I vowed to be kinder and more tolerant.

I took on some casual secretarial work at the American Army Garrison, partly to get away from Inga but also because of the extra load on our financial resources. Although I had vowed to be tolerant, Inga still grated on me and I felt the best thing was for the both of us to keep a wide berth. The work was simple enough, basic secretarial tasks but it was a good opportunity to brush up on my English. I enjoyed my days away from the house, interacting with other adults, discussing things other than children and housework. However, part of me became restless. Being employed reminded me of my photography – that was my calling. It was what I should have been doing.

We were still struggling to make ends meet. I worked like a dog from the time I got up until the time I went to bed, while Inga lounged about, chatting to Karoline. In the evening, she pandered to Erich, smiling sweetly, always looking her best for him. She was still a very attractive woman and she knew how to get a man's attention, that's for sure – even Erich's. He lapped up the praise and attention like a thirsty man in the desert. Anxiety grew within me, like a cold black mass in my belly. I felt the distance between Erich and I widening and I was helpless to do anything about it; I was asleep most nights as soon as my head hit the pillow. What if he really wanted her again? What if they had both changed enough to make it work?

I missed my parents so much. I wished I could go home, cry in their arms and tell them everything that had been happening but I couldn't. I remembered Onkel Werner's words: 'You've made your bed, now you have to lie in it'. This was my problem and I had to work it out.

Despite my vow and best intentions, the tension between Inga and I increased. She was my rival. All I could see now was a threat to my family. My initial feeling about her was right: she was a snake waiting to strike. Erich was either oblivious to my misery or unwilling to do anything to change our situation. I felt alone, cornered and vulnerable.

'Inga, could you pass me the potatoes?' I asked one mealtime. She pretended not to hear, keeping her eyes fixed on her plate. I sighed with irritation. How childish.

Erich glanced at me, a frown of worry flitting across his features, and reached across the table to pass me the potatoes in silence. I scooped up the potato and placed a portion on Greta's and Johanna's plates before my own, banging the spoon on the side of my plate harder than I needed to. Erich's gaze flicked across to me for a second but he said nothing. Inga looked up and glared at me and I stared back until her eyes returned to her plate.

'Greta, tell Tante Inga about the letters you learnt to write at school today,' said Karoline, trying to break the tension but aggravating me more than ever. Greta began to ramble excitedly about her letter writing.

Inga looked up, her eyes glazed over. 'That's nice, dear. Soon you'll be reading. Won't that be good? Now you'd better finish your meal.' My blood boiled.

Erich laid a hand on my thigh, squeezing gently. 'Could someone pass the sauerkraut please?' he asked, keen to divert my attention. 'I just have to have a little bit more. It's my favourite.'

Much to my disgust, Inga immediately reached across the table to where the sauerkraut sat in front of Walter. She handed it to Erich, smiling sweetly, making sure their hands touched. I'd noticed that she took any opportunity to show me up, to prove she was better for Erich than me and to be close to him whenever she could.

'It's my favourite too, especially the way your mother makes it.' Karoline beamed at the compliment.

It was as if I wasn't even there. If I got up and left the table, I wouldn't be missed. The way everyone behaved, they could almost be a family without me. I wanted to reach across the table and strangle Inga on the spot.

Six months after Inga and the children had arrived, the divorce still hadn't been finalised. I was at the end of my tether.

'The girls and I are going home to visit my parents.'

Erich and I were ready for bed, both exhausted. I expected little resistance from him at this hour but a piece of me

396

hoped he would fight me. I needed him to show me that he wanted me.

'When?' he said, turning down the bed.

'Tomorrow.' I noticed that he barely even looked at my naked body as I slipped on my nightgown. The blackness within me threatened to well up and overcome me. We had hardly touched each other since Inga's arrival. I swallowed hard and willed away my tears. Tears weren't going to solve anything. Not any more.

'Why?'

'It's Vati's birthday in a couple of days. I've told my parents I'm coming for a week but I don't know if I'm coming back.' My voice caught. I wasn't sure I could do this. If I went down this path, it very well could be the beginning of the end for us. I took a deep breath and steadied my nerves. 'That depends on you, really. I can't live like this any more. I don't feel comfortable in my own home. I do everything around here and I'm tired of it.'

'They've got nowhere to go, Lotte. They won't be here forever, just until Inga gets on her feet.'

'When will that be?'

'I don't know.' He sighed, exasperated, and climbed into bed. 'We've been through this so many times. I don't have a crystal ball.'

'Well, it doesn't look like she's trying very hard to me.' My voice rose. 'She's happy enough to live off us. Why would she try?'

'Have you thought about Eva and Walter?' Eric's voice was cold and I shuddered at his tone. He was right. Those poor children were the ones who sat in the middle of this mess, the ones who suffered the most. 'I haven't seen those children for seven years. Have you thought about me or about anyone but yourself?'

I turned to him then, ready to slap his face. 'How dare you' I whispered, shaking with the effort to keep my self-control. I was so angry that I was worried I would scream and wake the whole house. 'I've given up so much for you. I've stayed by your side through everything and this is where I've ended up, living with your first and legal wife, who wants you back, and your mother, who I'm sure wants the same, cramped in a tiny house, working like a dog with two small children to contend with and the only time I see you alone is in bed when we're both so exhausted we can't even speak, let alone touch each other.'

'Lotte,' said Erich, reaching out to me, his expression stuck between anger and remorse.

'Don't. I don't want to speak to you.' I rolled onto my side and huddled into a ball, willing myself not to cry. I waited for him to come to me but he stayed on his side of the bed, as if we were separated by an ocean. I waited a long time, silent tears slipping from my eyes. I knew he was awake and yet he didn't budge. I had my answer. He didn't want to fight for me. I felt my heart break, like an unrelenting ache in my chest. I felt like I was drowning in emptiness. I forced myself to breathe, thinking about my girls. I had to be strong for them. Finally, in the small hours of the morning, sleep came to me.

I stayed with my parents for a couple of weeks. I moped about the apartment through the day and at night cried myself to sleep. I couldn't believe that Erich of all people could treat me this way, that he couldn't understand my discontent, my misery. He was always my champion and my rock.

Mutti could see I was on edge and for once declined to hound me about Erich. She never mentioned Heinrich either. Vati entertained the girls, who were delighted to explore München with him.

My thoughts went around and around unable to find a solution to my situation. If only Inga were gone, I was sure we could work our problems out. As far as I was concerned, she was the problem. The solicitor couldn't tell me how much longer the divorce would take and part of me wondered if Erich found the delay quite acceptable. He had everything he wanted. All his children were together, his mother was with us and he had two women who both wanted him. Inga simpered and stroked his ego, playing up to his sense of responsibility, while I cooked and cleaned. Why would he change any of it?

Unless he did change our situation and prove his commitment to me and the girls, I couldn't take much more.

I became more depressed as my desperation grew. Mutti's worried glances and whispered conversations with Vati irritated me and finally, I lashed out at her, telling her I wanted to be left alone.

The very next day Mutti and Vati took the girls to visit some friends for the day, leaving me blissfully alone, to wallow further in my misery. All I could do was imagine Inga playing up to Erich, cooking for him, looking after him, offering comforting words about my absence, showing him she was better for him than me. I couldn't be sure Karoline wouldn't be complicit.

It was then that Heinrich chose to show up. Foolishly, I answered the door. Still in my dressing gown, my eyes red rimmed from crying and my nose raw from blowing, I was a mess. Heinrich looked immaculate as always.

'What do you want?' I snapped, highly embarrassed at him seeing me like this.

'My mother asked me to drop these books off to your mother,' he said, taken aback.

'Still doing whatever your mother tells you, are you?' I knew I was being unkind and unfair but between my misery and embarrassment, I didn't know how to act.

'Lotte, what's wrong?'

'Nothing.' I dashed away the tears that came unbidden to my eyes. 'Nothing that you need to worry about.'

'Can I come in?'

I stared at him like he was talking another language.

'Come on, talk to me like you used to. Maybe I can help.'

I shrugged listlessly, past the point of arguing, then stepped aside and let him pass, closing the door behind us.

We sat side by side on the settee in the parlour. I was too distressed to change my attire. I didn't care how I looked. I was numb and stared into the distance while Heinrich made us tea. It gave us both something to do while he listened quietly as I told him what had been happening. I spoke haltingly at first, unsure that I wanted to expose my pain. The sympathy in Heinrich's face was almost too much to bear. After talking to him for a time, I realised that all I wanted was someone to listen without judgement, a sympathetic ear, and I knew he would understand.

Once I began, the floodgates opened. The tears came then, along with the anger, despair and desolation. Heinrich offered me his handkerchief and that was enough to make me sob, unleashing the pent-up sorrow and loss I had buried within me. I was brokenhearted; unsure I could ever mend things with Erich.

It was only natural that Heinrich put his arms around me to comfort me and that I leant against his firm, broad chest for support. We were old friends after all. He was familiar and had consoled me like this many times before. It was habit and instinct that prevented me from pulling away immediately when he pressed his lips against mine.

'Oh Lotte,' he murmured.

Heinrich pulled me towards him. It felt good to be wanted, of course, but I had to resist. All I wanted was Erich here with me. His hands slid lower down to settle on my behind, drawing me closer even as I struggled, so there was little space between us.

Heinrich pushed my dressing gown impatiently aside, ripping open my nightgown. His hands were warm and smooth on my bare breasts. I didn't want this – I only wanted Erich. My beloved husband, his green eyes brimming with love.

'Stop!' I slapped Heinrich's hands away.

'Come now, Lotte.' He held me tightly to him, attempting to kiss me again.

I turned my face away. 'No. This is wrong. I can't.'

'After what you've told me, you have every reason to do this,' he said gruffly, barely controlling himself.

I pulled my robe around me and we stared at each other, breathing heavily.

'You're worried I'll abandon you once I've had you?' he asked softly. 'I would never do that to you. You mean everything to me.'

I shook my head and sighed, sliding away from him.

He brought my hand to his lips, then, kissing it fervently. 'Marry me, Lotte. I promise you I will love the girls like my own.'

I remained silent.

'Marry me and I will worship you as you deserve, treat you like a goddess. You have my heart and soul.'

In that moment I knew what I had to do. It came to me crystal clear like the sun shining down on a pristine stream. I wondered how I could have been so blind. Joy rushed through me, to fill all the dark places that inhabited my being, making me shiver deliciously. I was living my life, a life I was born to live. A life of passion, of love, strengthened by hardship and trouble along the way and that's what made it even more precious and meaningful.

'I can't. I love Erich and I have to work this out for myself,' I said. 'I don't know what's ahead for us but regardless of the outcome, I won't marry you.'

'This can't be goodbye.' He clutched at my arm in desperation.

The heavy thud of regret and sorrow lay across my heart. I knew what he was feeling and was immeasurably sorry for the suffering I had caused him but it had to be said. I removed his hand from my arm and placed it between us.

'You have to let me go. I don't belong to this life any more. I've changed.' The pain that clouded his eyes was almost more than I could bear. I took a breath. 'I would suffocate here,

402

living a life that wasn't truly mine. I won't be told how to live, how to make my choices any more, as we did under Hitler's rule. We lived a lie for so many years and I will not live that way ever again. Germany's changed and we have to change with it or get left behind. The old ways will soon be gone. I can't return to a life of mindless opulence and lavish waste when I've seen how people survive on next to nothing and yet remain proud and full of dignity, when I know how much people have suffered. My life might be hard but at least I'm alive. I'm making my own choices, forging my own path and truly living.' The blood sang in my veins. For the first time, I felt free – free as a bird coasting the breeze. I could choose whatever path I wanted.

'I don't want to live being told what to do either and I want to make my difference through medicine, improving the lives of others through my work but I dòn't understand how that makes us different, why you can't be here with me?' His brow was creased in confusion.

Heinrich was a good and compassionate man. It's what made him a good doctor, but he hadn't yet made the connection that I had, thanks to Erich. Living the way he did, as a wealthy man from an influential family, perhaps Heinrich never would. The supreme effort he was making to try to understand touched me and made my heart ache for him.

'We're friends from another time, another life. Let's leave it at that. Let me go, and live your life, Heinrich. I love you enough to want you to be happy. Find someone who adores you like you deserve, someone you can love in return. I'm so sorry.'

He hung his head in despair. 'Are you sure?'

'I am.' I held my breath, rigid but no longer as fragile as glass.

'Then I had better leave,' he said quietly. He stood, smoothing his shirt and jacket. 'Goodbye, Lotte.' His eyes were so blue, even filled with tears.

'Goodbye, Heinrich.'

22

I couldn't wait to call Erich at work. I had been so stupid. I had nearly thrown away the best thing that had ever happened to me. No matter what, I couldn't live without him. The distance between us was killing me. I had to find a way for us to reconnect again, to find that uncontrollable fire. I knew it was smouldering away, ready to be reignited.

'I'm coming home,' I said. 'I'm sorry I ran away but I didn't know what else to do.'

'Shh, it's all right. I should never have let you leave. I've been miserable without you.'

My heart leapt. 'You have?'

'Of course. You know I can't do without you.'

'I've been so miserable without you too. I'm coming home today.' My heart felt light again. The blackness within had disappeared and I felt joyful, like I had been reborn.

'Lotte?'

'What is it?'

'Inga is leaving with the children. I asked her to go.'

All the weight I had been carrying, which had been smothering me, dissipated like a cloud of smoke. He had fought for me.

'Really? What will she do? What about the children? I know you want them with you.'

'It's okay. They won't be far. Inga has a job in Stuttgart and we can have the children during their holidays. I'll tell you more when you get home.'

I nodded although he couldn't see me. Maybe this would work out.

'I'll be home soon. I love you.'

'I love you too.'

I packed our bags and was waiting to leave when my parents and the girls returned.

'I'm going home,' I said. Mutti and Vati looked at each other and smiled.

'Vati had better drive you, then,' said my mother. 'Come on, girls, toilet and hands.' She led the girls to the bathroom while Vati picked up the bags ready to pack in the car.

'You look happier,' said Vati.

'I am,' I said. 'I'm going home.'

I arrived in Illesheim not long before Erich was to drive Inga and the children to Stuttgart.

He hugged me tightly the minute I walked through the door, as if he would never let me go. He reluctantly released me to the sound of little girls calling his name, pulling at his trousers. Picking the girls up, he kissed their chubby little cheeks, hugging them so they squirmed and begged to be let down to see Eva and Walter.

Erich grasped my wrist and pulled me towards him. 'Welcome home,' he whispered in my ear. Then he kissed me deeply. 'I promise I'll make it up to you. Wait for me until I get home.' The glint was back in his eye. I felt weak at the knees, my heart beating rapidly like a silly schoolgirl.

'I'm not going anywhere,' I said, meaning it. If we could weather this storm, I knew we could get through anything.

It was hard to see the children go but I knew they would be back. Erich had looked into helping Inga find a job through the American Army. A vacancy in Domestic Services was available in the Helenen Garrison in Stuttgart, a few hours away. Erich was able to arrange accommodation for them too. Now they had bonded with the girls, their father and grandmother, I knew they considered this their home too, just as it should be. It was very emotional and I tried my hardest to be kind to Inga.

'I wish you all the best in your new home and with your new job,' I said, hugging her goodbye.

'I'm sure you do,' she said bitterly. 'Anything to get me away from Erich. You only hurt him and our children by what you've done.'

'Don't be like that,' I said, gritting my teeth. 'I'm sorry we couldn't have been friends but let's try to be civil for the sake of the children.'

Inga laughed, holding me at arm's length. 'Of course. You know I'll always be a part of Erich's life, whether you like it or not. Our children will continue to bring us together. We have a long history and share many things that you and he never will. You're not the right woman for him.' She went to Karoline, hugging her and turning on the tears.

I stopped myself just in time from rolling my eyes. Erich was watching.

Karoline said nothing while Erich was away. I knew how sad she was not to have Eva and Walter with us. I didn't know if she blamed me for that or whether she would rather have had Inga stay and me go. I couldn't deal with her approval or disapproval, I was only relieved that she turned her attention to the girls.

I stayed up until Erich arrived, long after the children were asleep and Karoline had gone to bed.

Erich slumped at the table, exhausted, sipping on his tea until I came to join him. 'I'm sorry I hurt you,' he said softly. 'You were right. Inga had to leave. The way we were living was no good for any of us. I knew it but I couldn't bring myself to force the issue.' He hung his head – in sadness or in shame, I couldn't tell. I caressed his cheek.

'I know it was hard for you. The children . . . you couldn't let them go after thinking they were dead and not seeing them for all those years.'

'I don't love Inga, you must know that.' He held my hand, kissing my palm. 'It's you and only you.'

'I know,' I said, my face crumpling into both relief and dismay. I regretted the way I had handled the situation. Although at the time it had felt unbearable, I was sure I could have been more patient, more considerate and more resilient. He hesitated, glancing warily at me, but I wasn't going to cry. I had cried enough in the last week. I nodded for him to continue.

'But I felt like I owed her something. After all the years we'd been together, the years she and the children were on their own during the war, the hardships she's had to endure . . . this was the least I could do . . . and the children and Mutti were so happy.' He shook his head. 'I knew it couldn't last.'

'I could've tried harder,' I whispered, squeezing his hand, close to tears again, feeling guilty.

Erich pulled his hand away and grasped my face with both of his hands. 'No, you did more than what was reasonable, more than most would have. I pushed you too far. Can you forgive me?' His tone was despairing, his expression beseeching, his eyes daring to hope that we could breach the gap between us.

'We both could have done things differently. Of course I forgive you but we have to work together. I never want anything to come between us again.'

Erich kissed me, long and deep. 'I don't want to lose you.' Gently, he wiped the tears from my cheeks, gazing into my eyes. The fire between us was alive. I felt slightly breathless.

'I don't want to lose you either.' I threw my arms around him and hugged him tight. 'I love you. You mean everything to me.'

Shortly after Inga left, Erich lost his job. The American army unit he worked for at the Ordnance Depot was being deactivated.

'As part of the reduction in force, due to a phase-out of installation,' I read from the paperwork Erich gave me. 'Where does that leave us?'

'They've promised to find me another job.' He raked his fingers through his salt and pepper hair. Erich was forty now, and still couldn't find work in the aeronautic industry. The German air force was defunct and jobs in the commercial sector were hard to come by. He had tried to find a job as an aeronautical engineer but he was up against younger men, those who had recently trained through the universities.

It made me so frustrated and angry because I knew how good he was at his job and how passionate he was about aircraft. He had taken to flying gliders again at the airfield and that helped but he needed more.

'How long will that take? What do we do in the meantime?' I couldn't help it. This was just added stress we didn't need. We were happy together but the divorce still loomed over us like a dark cloud. We didn't need to add further money worries to our problems. I had continued my casual secretarial work for the Americans but it too had dwindled to almost nothing. The ground beneath us was shifting and changing yet again. I was unsettled and, if I was honest with myself, frightened for the future.

Erich shook his head. 'I don't know. I have some annual leave pay that I've accrued. That will help, but we'll have to pull in the belt a little until I have another job.'

'If only I could get work as a photographer. Maybe we have to move back to München.' Erich frowned. 'Or some other city,' I said quickly. He wasn't keen to move anywhere near my mother or Heinrich. 'Surely you could get work at one of the big airfields? I could work my way up to managing a studio and maybe even one day own one.' I held my breath, watching for his reaction. This was my dream. Maybe it was time to make it real.

'It doesn't matter where we go. It's like this all over Germany. I can't see it improving any time soon. If I can't get a job, photography won't be enough to keep food on the table.' He grasped my hand and squeezed gently. 'I know how much you want to get back to it. Be patient a little longer. I know you will do it soon and I'll be so proud of you.'

'It's all right,' I said, knowing he was right, but feeling disappointed anyway. 'Let's find you a job first.'

'Yes, but I've been wondering if the only other way is to leave Germany, to emigrate to a country that's crying out for engineers like myself.' He watched me warily. I was dumbfounded. I couldn't have spoken if I wanted to. 'Gerd from work told me that his son was making enquiries into going to Australia. You remember Barry Thompson? The Australian that's been working at the depot with us?'

I nodded. Barry had been to our house for dinner once and I had seen him at the depot. I remembered his fantastic stories of jumping kangaroos and tree bears, sweeping, rugged coastlines and golden beaches, of red desert and thick bushland. It sounded magnificent but was essentially a wilderness. I dismissed his stories as delightful flights of fancy.

'He's been telling us all about Australia, how it's crying out for skilled workers. It's experiencing an economic boom. I could find work there and once we're on our feet, we could buy a house and you could open up a photography studio.' He brought my hand to his lips, kissing it gently, his eyes shining with the fantasy he was dreaming up. 'We could even have another child. The boy we've always wanted, although another girl would be wonderful too.'

411

The breath caught in my throat and tears stung my eyes. After all these years I still felt grief at the loss of our son.

'The girls could have a carefree, healthy life, in the wide open spaces and sunshine. Can you see it? It could be right for us.'

'Don't be ridiculous,' I said, huffing in irritation that he could make such a wild and impractical suggestion. 'The idea of uprooting our family and taking them far from everything they know is crazy. We're not that desperate.' But times were uncertain and Germany wasn't what it used to be. It was a crippled nation, still down on its knees and we, its citizens, were suffering. Life was difficult and it would be for quite some time before things changed and life began to improve for the average person. 'Besides, you couldn't be parted from Eva and Walter now that you've found them again.'

Erich nodded. 'It was just a thought. I'll just have to take whatever work I can get with the Americans. It's our best bet.'

A month later, the divorce papers arrived, the proceedings finalised over a year after they had begun. Karoline had gone to visit a friend and then collect the girls from school and Erich and I had the house to ourselves. Opening the divorce papers was the most exciting moment since the birth of Johanna. I stared at the words that allowed Erich to become a free man, finally.

'At last.'

'At last,' he agreed. 'Let's toast to the future.' Erich opened a bottle of champagne. I laughed as the cork popped, hitting the ceiling, the froth spilling over the mouth of the bottle. It was cheap champagne, not at all what I was used to, but he had brought it home for the occasion. It was a lovely gesture.

'To the future,' I said, after Erich had filled our glasses.

'To us,' Erich replied softly, clinking glasses with me. He held my gaze with those green eyes and I knew he was serious.

'To us,' I repeated.

The bubbles went straight to my head. I wasn't used to drinking champagne any more.

'I never thought this day would come,' I told him, my feet on his lap as we sat on the lounge.

'I was beginning to wonder myself.'

'What are you going to do with yourself, now that you're a free man?' I teased, a little breathless, wondering if this was the time to discuss our plans.

'Hmm . . . ' Erich pretended to think. 'I could have my way with the gorgeous woman next to me without being branded an adulterer.' He ran his hands up my leg.

'Really? Now?' My eyebrows rose in mock surprise. Life had returned to normal for us after Inga's departure but an underlying tension had remained and our spontaneity had all but disappeared.

'We have the house to ourselves and we have a very special celebration.' His hand rose higher and I closed my eyes, feeling the passion welling inside of me, like a river that had been dammed for too long.

Afterwards I lay in a haze of pleasure, limp and languid, happy and satisfied. What an afternoon it had been. Erich, lying on his side, his head resting in his hand, reached out to touch me, as if to make sure I was really there. I understood that feeling, rolling onto my side to look at him. He was

413

staring at me with such intensity, like he was imprinting this moment in his memory. I slid my hand over his ribcage to his back, his skin warm and damp. We would need to get up and attend to the girls soon.

His forehead against mine, we stared into each other's eyes and straight into each other's soul. 'Will you marry me?' he murmured.

A thrill rushed up my spine, exploding into millions of tiny bubbles that fizzed through my blood. His eyes were sure and still, peaceful and calm. Waiting.

'Yes,' I said, grinning from ear to ear. 'I will marry you.'

Erich's face broke into a dazzling smile that took my breath away. His lips reached for mine, kissing me deeply.

Epilogue

October 1956

Clutching Greta's and Johanna's hands, I stood at the railing of the *Skaubryn*, jostled by the many other emigrants vying for a position to say goodbye to their loved ones. Already the noise was deafening. Amongst the continuous shouting back and forth, wails of despair and tears of grief surrounded us. It was overwhelming. Erich was behind me, holding me steady, keeping us safe. I could feel the weight of him against me as he was pushed forward by the surging crowd.

Even in the frigid North Sea breeze, a fine sweat broke out on my brow. My skin was clammy and hot and I felt faint. Maybe it was the frantic activity around me and the push and shove of the crowd but I thought not. This was the point of no return. My anxiety began to soar – had we really been so desperate to consider this?

'Look, Mutti,' shouted Greta, pulling on my arm. 'See the crane? It's lifting the bridge away from the ship.'

My heart started to race. In a few moments, any chance I had to stand once again on Germany's soil would be behind me.

'I can't see,' whined Johanna, trying to balance on tip-toes, craning her neck to see over the rail. She wasn't as tall as her sister.

'Here,' said Erich, his voice almost in my ear. 'Come on. Climb up on the bottom rail, so you can see.'

'She'll fall,' I snapped, more crossly than I intended, my nerves stretched to breaking.

'No, she won't.' Erich's hand was on my shoulder in reassurance. A surge of strength flowed into me, grounding me, calming me just a little. He pushed past to stand behind Johanna. 'I'll hold her.'

The harbour was filled with the stirring strains of 'Must I Say Goodbye?' and tears welled in my eyes. Brightly coloured flags and handkerchiefs were waving on the pier. Final words of farewell were shouted. We had said goodbye to our families a few days earlier. It was hard leaving them for the last time, not knowing when or if we would ever see them again.

The ship jolted and juddered. The girls jerked against the railing and out of the corner of my eye, I saw Erich tighten his grip instinctively around Johanna, just as I did with Greta.

'Can you see the tugs?' Greta yelled excitedly above the noise. This was such an adventure to her. She squirmed in my grip and I loosened my hold enough for her to climb onto the railing.

The ship began to move away from the pier. I leant my head against Greta's back, squeezing my eyes shut for just a moment, a little breathless, to get my crushing anxiety under control.

Erich wrapped his arm around me, dipping his mouth to my ear. 'Are you all right?'

I nodded, clasping his hand for a moment.

'It will be okay.' He pulled me close. 'I know it. This is our fresh start, our new beginning.' He was so optimistic, confident that this was the right thing for us, but I felt like my heart was tearing in two. After everything we had been through, and in the end we had to leave the country we had given up so much for, the country we loved with all our hearts.

The expanse of water widened, the wharf receding further and further away.

'Say goodbye to Germany,' Erich said to the girls. He held the three of us tight, as if he could keep us safe from the unknown that loomed in front of us. I dashed the tears from my cheeks.

I watched the shore silently with my family. At least we were all together. I could do this only with them by my side.

Erich kissed me deeply. 'Australia is our future now,' he said softly.

'Yes.' Maybe we could finally leave behind the darkness and sorrow of our homeland. Maybe now we could look with hope to a future filled with light, to a place where our family could grow and prosper, in a land where opportunities beckoned, hard work was rewarded and anything was possible. As long as we were together, the future was bright.

'Australia will be our home,' I said and kissed him again.

Acknowledgements

When I first sat down to write *The Girl from Munich*, the stories my German grandmother had told me since I was a child were foremost in my mind and the main inspiration for my writing. I remember being fascinated by them, by the things that she witnessed as a young woman in Hitler's Germany, during World War II and then in post-war Germany. She was a strong, vibrant woman who had a profound effect on my life. I thank her first of all; for her stories and for her encouragement to follow my dreams and passions. I hope I've done her proud.

My eternal gratitude to the team at Simon and Schuster Australia, especially Dan Ruffino, CEO; Fiona Henderson, Publishing Director, and Roberta Ivers, Managing Editor, and Larissa Edwards for taking a chance on an unknown author's manuscript and turning it into a debut novel. My special thanks go to the amazing Roberta for taking me under her wing and also to Kylie Mason, Vanessa Pellatt and Michelle

Swainson for helping me to shape my manuscript into the story it is today. I couldn't have done it without you and I've learnt so much along the way. I also take my hat off to Kirsty Noffke and the incredible sales and marketing teams. Thank you for all your hard work behind the scenes. You add that special lustre and shine to this exciting process of publishing.

Heartfelt thanks to Fiona McIntosh for encouraging me to write my grandmother's story and for helping me to realise that this was the right time to tell it. Your continued support and guidance is much appreciated and gratefully received.

To my agent, Selwa Anthony, thank you for believing in me and for your wealth of knowledge, expertise and inspired ideas.

I couldn't write this book without the support of friends and family. My deepest thanks goes to my dear friend Jane Kurta, first and last reader, for her unwavering support in me, the seemingly endless drafts she's read and the deep conversations we've had on how to improve my manuscript. I wouldn't be here without you.

To my mother, Giselle Brame, thank you for your support and the many hours of sifting through papers, translating documents and reading my manuscript. I loved every minute of this journey with you.

Thank you to my readers Sharron Stokes, Kath Brannan and Roswitha Pisch, for your feedback and encouragement and to Manfred Schueler for advice on the use of German idioms. Your generosity and kindness has touched me. To my father, Domenic Martino, my in-laws, Christine and Terry Blanchard and to Trish Casey, thank you for your support and love.

Finally to my wonderful family. I started writing again when my children were small, stories of wizards and fairies, princes and princesses. My family have been with me every step of the way and my children were the first ones to tell their friends and teachers that Mum was a writer! I wanted nothing more than to prove to them that with hard work, determination and perseverance, dreams can come true. My family's total belief in me during my writing journey and support even when I felt I would never get this book done has buoyed me up, kept me sane and spurred me forward. To my husband Chris, my anchor, who is always by my side through life's ups and downs, I could never have done it without you. Hollie, Nathan, Benjamin and Chris, you make it all worthwhile.

About the author

Tania Blanchard was inspired to write *The Girl from Munich* by the fascinating stories her German grandmother told her as a child. Coming from a family with rich cultural heritage with a German mother and Italian father, stories have always been in Tania's blood. Following a career in physiotherapy, it was only when she had her family that she decided to return to her passion of writing. Discovered through Australian bestseller Fiona McIntosh's Commercial Fiction Masterclass, *The Girl from Munich* is Tania's debut novel – the story she always wanted to write – to be followed by the sequel, *Suitcase of Dreams*, set in Australia in the 1950s. She lives in Sydney with her husband and three children.

If you enjoyed *The Girl from Munich*, you'll love *Suitcase of Dreams*, the eagerly anticipated story of Lotte Drescher and her family as they settle in postwar Australia, available from November 2018.

Read on for a sneak peek at the first chapter.

1

11 November, 1956

Clusters of tiny light were scattered across the darkened land before us. As we drew closer in the predawn, I was loath to relinquish the peace I felt, even amid the excitement and apprehension that swirled around me. Clutching the cold railing, I breathed deeply, taking in the sea air – Australian air – and held on to that moment of calm.

The rising sun lifted above the horizon, dusting the port of Fremantle and the ocean in a soft golden glow. Sandy beaches and small dwellings appeared out of the inky blackness, dotting the coastline and harbour. Australia, the golden land, was welcoming me and my family to our new life with open arms. I knew I would never forget this sight.

Erich was by my side and I could feel the thrum of excitement course through his body. At that moment, I felt that we were the only two people who existed, waiting on the edge of the world, relishing these moments of quiet and united in our desire for a better life.

'We made it, Lotte. We made it,' he whispered into my ear.

'Yes, we made it.' Relief flooded me. Our old life was gone – Nazi Germany, the war and a country changed forever – and our new life beckoned. Finally I would be able to cast off the pull of the rigid traditions and expectations I had grown up with and escape the poverty that had come with choosing a life with Erich. This was a new start and we could be anything we wanted to be. Australia was a young country, with opportunities for all people, we'd been told, opportunities that would never have been possible for us in Germany, our ruined homeland. Here we would have the freedom to choose the life we wanted.

'Look, isn't it beautiful?' He pointed to the shore.

'All shiny and new.'

'Perfect for our family ... Perfect for our new life.' His anticipation and hope were plain to see under the deck lights and I felt sure that my face mirrored his.

'It has to be.' We'd left everything we knew behind us in search of a better life for ourselves and our girls.

Erich placed his hand over my chilled fingers, sharing his strength, warmth and comfort. 'It will be.'

He gathered me into his arms and kissed me deeply.

Chaos erupted as we docked. Most of the passengers on the *Skaubryn* were German, as were those welcoming the ship to Australia, and bursts of our mother tongue drifted across to us, the shouts and screams of family, friends and acquaintances waiting on the pier for those who were disembarking. There was frantic waving of banners and handkerchiefs. The atmosphere was reassuring. It would be the last time we would hear the sound of our homeland on Australian soil, I thought, before the inevitable tide of English was upon us. For a moment, I pretended we were still home and not halfway across the world. I wished we had someone greeting us, smoothing our transition into this strange country, but we knew nobody here.

Erich held my hand, his green eyes meeting mine. The girls were jumping out of their skins with excitement that we had finally arrived, fidgeting restlessly, keen to leave the ship for the day and explore, and my conflicted emotions were pushed to one side as we surged towards the designated areas for passport and health control.

'Don't leave Mutti's side,' whispered Greta to Johanna, her dark head against her sister's blonde one. 'I've heard that kangaroos jump down the streets here and take little children and stuff them in their pouches.'

'They do not,' said Johanna indignantly.

Greta nodded knowingly, her hands on her hips as if daring Johanna to prove her wrong.

'Do they?' My younger daughter shot a worried look to me. Her eyes were blue today. They often shifted between blue, like my own eyes, and green, like her father's, and sometimes it was hard to say what shade they were at all.

'Of course not,' I said, exasperated, but quietly, not wanting to make a scene. 'Don't tease your sister,' I said to Greta, giving her my sternest expression.

Greta just grinned at me, her brown eyes sparkling, her nose peeling from hours in the sun. She was ten years old and a month at sea had exhausted all the adventurous opportunities available as far as she was concerned; now she wanted to discover what excitement Australia had in store. Johanna, with her sun-bleached blonde hair, like my own, was two years younger and adored her sister. She was more sensible, wary of new experiences and fond of reminding Greta of the dangers of her latest endeavour. They were a good team, balancing influences, and fiercely protective of each other, despite the usual sibling rivalries. Whatever was ahead of us, I knew that they would be fine.

I spotted Erich returning with our paperwork. He cut an impressive figure – tall, athletic and broad shouldered – and he carried himself with a natural elegance that many admired. Despite the humidity that embraced us and the throngs of anxious and impatient people, his crisp white jacket remained uncrushed. The matching wide-brimmed hat sat jauntily on his head, covering the luxuriant dark hair, now threaded with silver, that was swept back from his forehead.

'All finished,' he said. 'We can take the bus to Perth.'

'Where's Perth?' Greta pulled on his jacket sleeve. 'Is it far?'

'Not too far. I've been told there's plenty to see. Come on, let's not waste another minute.' We were all excited to get our first glimpse of Australia before boarding the boat once again for the final leg of our journey to Melbourne.

The girls grabbed his hands, and Erich laughed and set off. The vice around my heart eased a little to see the joy on their faces. Erich had the energy of a man half his age but I still sometimes marvelled that he had decided to uproot his entire life and begin again in a new country so late in life. I had struggled with the idea much longer than he had, even though I was only thirty-one. The girls' dark and blonde plaits swayed gently across their backs as they tried to match their father's footsteps. They were why we were here.

It was a beautiful day and our decision was made, so as I first stepped onto Australian soil, I was determined to stop worrying about the uncertainty ahead.

It wasn't until we were standing on top of the hill in Perth's famous Kings Park that I truly got a sense of Australia. The girls were eating ice cream and Erich and I drinking Coca-Cola as we surveyed the city, the beaches and the ocean beyond. Trees unlike any I had seen before were plentiful – the eucalyptus trees we'd been told about on the boat, their leaves fresh and pungent. The dry and dusty paths and the succulents that bordered them reminded me that we had left the verdant green of Germany behind. It was springtime but already evidence of the hot, dry climate was easy to find. I took photographs with the camera Erich and I had bought for the journey, beginning to grasp the vastness of the wild, tough landscape.

We arrived in Melbourne's bustling port five days later, thousands of lights and neon signs illuminating the pier. The screaming and shouting was deafening. Banners, flags and balloons jostled for prime position on the pier as names were called between land and the ship. Everyone wanted to be first to find their loved ones but it was nearly midnight before passengers could step ashore and into waiting arms. That was when the hysterics really started: tears of joy were shed by all at the happy reunions but there were more than a few who cried tears of sadness, those who had no family or friends here. Those who missed their homes desperately.

We could go ashore for the evening too but it was late, and while those who disembarked made the most of their reunions, many of us would stay on board for one final night. A train would take us to the Bonegilla migrant camp the next morning where we would be processed, given job placements and sent to our new homes.

'It'll be all right,' said Erich, drawing me into his arms as the emotions began to affect me too. 'We'll get through this together.'

I clung to him. He was my anchor and I knew he was right. Despite the difficulties of moving to a strange new country, we had every reason to believe that better times were ahead for us.

'Let's go to bed. We have an early start in the morning and the girls won't give us a moment's peace once they're up.'

The following day was a blur as we made our way off the ship and through the crowd still clustered around the gangways. Pamphlets were thrust in our faces by faceless figures, promoting what, I didn't know. The girls stayed close to us, overwhelmed by the cacophony of voices calling out in different languages.

A group of dock workers stood a little apart from the fray and offered them ice cream and lollies. 'Welcome to Australia,' they said.

The men didn't look like they could afford to give out treats, so I felt obliged to accept, and the girls were very excited to have sweets to sustain them through the hours of the train ride ahead.

The workers didn't force their pamphlet on us but Erich took one willingly and thanked them for their kindness. The pamphlet was promoting trade union membership to new migrant workers. Erich wouldn't need to be part of a union in his profession and new job, but it surprised me that Australians were proactive in the labour movement; we had been led to believe that they were a very relaxed people. Under the Third Reich in Germany, trade unionism was banned as a manifestation of communism and workers had no voice. But I was pleased that migrants were being welcomed so readily into the Australian way of life and, through the unions, would be guided and looked after by those who knew and understood Australian ways. It looked like freedom of choice and the freedom to speak your beliefs was a reality in this country and our hope for this was part of the reason we had come.

Then we were through customs with our luggage and onto a train bound for Bonegilla, six hours away. It was hard to believe that we were finally in Australia. At one point on our passage across the world I wondered whether we would arrive at all – the *Skaubryn* was one of the last ships to make it through the Suez Canal before it was closed by the crisis. It was still closed and nobody knew when it would open again.

'When will we get there?' moaned Greta and Johanna on more than one occasion. Each time, I threw them a frown. We were not alone in the carriage, sharing it with a doctor and his two sisters. Erich chatted amiably with them while I tried to keep the girls under control. My nerves were already frayed, worried about what would greet us at the end of this journey, and their restlessness didn't help my state of mind. The supply of lollies had dried up long ago.

'Look out the window for the kangaroos,' said Erich to the girls when it was clear that I would soon lose my patience with them.

'I've seen three already,' said one of the doctor's sisters, winking surreptitiously to me.

I smiled in thanks as the girls' attention was drawn to the rolling countryside once again.

'It goes on forever,' I said to Erich. 'I can count the number of small towns we've passed on one hand.'

'Australia's so much bigger than Germany.'

'Yes, I know, but I never imagined how vast it would be and how few people live in such a big place. It's so different from home.'

'Not really. It's mainly hilly farmland like at home and the cattle and sheep look much the same.'

'Erich, you can see the farms are much bigger here and the countryside's nowhere as green.' Erich was only trying to soothe my anxiety but he was irritating me. 'Besides, the never-ending sight of eucalyptus trees is a constant reminder that we're not in Germany anymore.' I took a deep breath to calm down, gazing out at the blue-shaded mountains in the distance and wondered what mysterious things might be found upon their slopes and rugged peaks.

Erich squeezed my hand. 'I know. It all seems so strange at the moment. We'll get used to it, I'm sure.'

I nodded and stared out the window once more. Although it was certainly going to take a while to adjust to all the changes we would find here, we had each other. And after what we'd been through during the war, and afterwards, we were well used to supporting each other through the toughest of times. Erich was my rock – and I was his. It would all be okay.

We reached our destination mid-afternoon, our nervous energy swirling around us as we alighted from the train to board the bus to camp.

'Look, Mutti and Vati!' said Johanna, pointing out the window to some figures lining the camp driveway.

'Aborigines!' said Greta with excitement. The three young men wore nothing but shorts, their tanned bodies and faces streaked with white paint. We'd heard about the Aborigines and their ancient culture while still in Germany and after experiencing exotic Colombo, Greta had hoped to see Aborigines everywhere.

The bus driver laughed. 'No, love. They're Swedes. They've been in the sun too long and burnt to a crisp.'

Although I didn't quite understand exactly what he said, I understood his meaning and translated for Greta. Her face fell and I had to hide my smile with my hand.

'But what about the paint?' Erich asked.

'That's calamine lotion for the sunburn. Don't you have that where you come from?'

'No.'

'Oh well, you'll soon get to know it. It's useful for all sorts of things, from sunburn to stinging nettle rash.'

Erich shot a perplexed look at me. I shrugged. I didn't know what he was talking about. Erich's English was now even better than mine but I somehow felt that we were not prepared for the variety spoken in Australia. It would take some time to understand all the strange things Australians said.

Bonegilla migrant camp lay close to the town of Albury. It was a beautiful spot, hilly and leafy with a large water reservoir nearby. We could see mountains beyond the camp, which we were told were only a fifteen-minute walk away. Behind them lay the Australian Alps, still snow covered this late in spring. The girls were excited by the thought of swimming in the reservoir and although Erich's eyes twinkled when he learnt that motor boating was popular, I knew that, just like me, he couldn't wait to go hiking in those mountains.

The camp was enormous, with all the facilities we could want – hospital, school, kindergarten, canteen, cinema, theatre and churches. Each block was a small village of twenty corrugated-iron barracks and each barrack had ten small rooms, partitioned with plywood and sparsely furnished. There was a communal kitchen, dining room, laundry, shower room and toilets. It wasn't a palace but it was much better than the dilapidated farm cottage we'd lived in after the war. Erich and I had lived with my mother and aunt and her four boys with no electricity, no running water, only a little fuel to cook once a day and no heating. We'd managed then and we'd manage now.

'Look at the geraniums,' I said to Erich as we walked to our barracks. We'd been given two rooms: one for the girls and one for Erich and me. 'They're enormous compared to the ones at home.' The colours around us were vibrant, with flowering plants and bushes lining the paths and buildings of the camp.

'Everything seems bigger and brighter here,' said Erich in awe as we stepped inside our room. 'Even the sky is bluer. We'll make it feel like home for however long we're here,' he said as we looked around the room. 'Once you put your touches on the rooms, they'll be cosy and welcoming. Just you wait and see.'

'I know,' I answered. 'How long do you think we'll be here?'

'I've been told that it's only for a couple of weeks. I see the employment office in a couple of days. Hopefully they have a job already for me. I'm excited to be working in engineering again. It's been too long.' He sighed, kissing my neck. 'We'll stay only as long as we have to. We'll have a place of our own soon.'

A few days after we arrived, Erich came home, face drained of colour. Thank God the girls were outside with some of the other children in our block, looking at where the fireworks display would be held to celebrate the beginning of the Olympics in Melbourne.

'What happened?'

'There's no job,' he muttered, almost to himself.

My heart began to pound in my ears. I wasn't sure I'd heard him right. 'What did you say?'

Erich looked at me then, and his face crumpled. 'There's no job waiting for me. I've let you down.'

I grasped his arm, not sure if it was to give him strength or to make sure I wasn't in some horrible nightmare. I led him to a chair and sank down beside him. 'What do you mean?'

'I presented all my documentation. Everything was in order, but it didn't matter. Foreign qualifications for professions like medicine, law and engineering – professions like mine – are not recognised in Australia. I can't work in my field unless I go to university here and retrain.'

Erich knew everything about planes and how they worked. He had been unable to find work in his field in Germany after the war and had struggled to find continuous work to sustain our family. But the Australian Consulate in Frankfurt had promised him engineering work in Australia and that information had helped us make the decision to migrate.

'How can this be?'

'They lied to us to get us to come here. We've been lured here under false pretences.' Erich's voice was hard and flat.

'That is ridiculous! How can they get away with it? It's not right . . .' I raked a trembling hand through my hair. 'What are we going to do?'

'We have no choice. I was reminded of the fact quite clearly today.' He looked me in the eyes. 'We're committed to staying here for two years. I have to take any job I'm given, regardless of what I was promised. Besides, even if we wanted to go back now, we could never repay our passage to the Australian government.'

I stared at Erich. His words were like a slap in the face. All the planning, the heartache and the difficult decisions . . . We'd been through so much. But he was right – false hope and indignation weren't going to get us anywhere. We had no choice.

'I'm so sorry, my *schatz*,' he said. 'You don't deserve this.'

I wrapped my arms around him but I wanted nothing more than to scream and shout – to throw something at any Australian official who crossed my path. But none of that would do us any good. Bureaucracy could not be swayed by the act of a single person, righteous or not. I sat back, steeling myself against what was coming.

'So what happens now?' My voice sounded small, although I was trying to put on a brave face.

'The best they can offer is to find me work in some related field, probably as a mechanic.' He shrugged. 'We're no better off than we were at home.'

'It's not your fault.' I squeezed Erich's hand, summoning my strength. 'We've done it before, we can do it again.'

He straightened in his chair, pulling himself together. 'Maybe it's a start. I can save some money and get us settled and then perhaps I can study to get my qualification.'

The vein at his temple was throbbing and I could see the supreme effort it took him to remain calm and logical. As much as this blow devastated him, he had his family to provide for. We had to come first.

I kissed him and held him tight but a little voice inside me wondered how long it would take for us to find our feet.